ROOT

~⊙~ SPIRIT ERA ~⊙~

ROOT

What if we could change the world . . .

AURÉLIE BENATTAR

Translated by Heather Hulick Allen

Aurélie Benattar

Published by Aurélie Benattar, Petah Tikva, Israel
aureliebenattar.com

Edited and designed by Girl Friday Productions
www.girlfridayproductions.com

Translated to English by Heather Hulick Allen
Cover Design: O'lee Graphiste
Character Illustration/Art Credit: Anava Maman
Book Graphics/Art Credit: O'lee Graphiste
Project Management: Emilie Sandoz-Voyer
Editorial Management: Bethany Fred

ISBN (paperback): 978-965-93051-0-0
ISBN (ebook): 978-965-93051-1-7

*To Moshe, who pulled me out of the water
and brought me back to earth.*

PART ONE

INTO THE UNKNOWN

#THEKEEPER #SAVETHEWORLD

POST 1–THE FIRST KEY

JUNE 18, 2035

WHAT LIES IN STORE FOR FUTURE GENERATIONS?

For centuries, prophets and visionaries have made baseless dooms-day prophecies about the extinction of life on Earth. But today, in the year 2035, the human species as we know it may well cease to exist in the near or not so near future.

The latest Intergovernmental Panel on Climate Change (IPCC) report is clear: our efforts to reduce greenhouse gas emissions have failed. Every year, the dire effects of global warming claim more lives and destroy more ecosystems. Human plundering of the natural environment has put the planet at risk, as have our political, economic, and cultural conflicts. Our materialistic worldviews tend to accentuate what sets us apart. From each other and from our true selves . . .

To bring to light what we have in common, I, the Keeper, have designed a powerful artificial intelligence, an AI program unlike any other, capable of leading us to greater spiritual awareness, that source of all individual and collective harmony. I have named the program:

Spirit Era.

With access to worldwide data streams and integrated ethical reasoning capacities, Spirit Era can accurately predict the future. To quiet the disbelievers, as conditioning and convictions will no doubt cause many of you to have serious misgivings, I have decided to share a few terribly real predictions of natural catastrophes:

1. This coming June 25, an F5 tornado on the Fujita scale will hit the state of Alabama, in the southeastern United States, between 7:30 a.m. and 11:00 a.m. local time.

2. On July 31, torrential rains will cause the Gard River in southern France to jump its banks, provoking historic flooding throughout the region. Rainfall exceeding one hundred milliliters per hour, for a period of forty-three hours, will cause severe damage to the city of Nîmes and ninety surrounding municipalities.

3. On September 4, an earthquake of 7.2 on the Richter scale will hit Sendai, the capital of Miyagi Prefecture in Japan.

And this is only the beginning.

According to the program's calculations, a cataclysmic disaster will destroy the Earth on July 27, 2037, unless a spiritual awakening and the creation of a new value system enable humanity to radically alter its individualistic ways. Yes, the verdict is in. We have roughly two years left before . . .

THE END OF THE WORLD!

At the age of fifteen, I have chosen silence.

Contrary to the post by the Keeper that is causing such a stir . . .

Today is June 25, 2035. Footage of the damage from the tornado that hit Alabama earlier this morning is getting non-stop coverage. Journalists are having a field day. A clear connection to the program's prediction can be made, but many of them are calling it a coincidence, citing facts and scientific data.

"Extreme weather events like these are common in the United States. Statistically, there are more tornadoes in the US than any other country in the world . . . The location of what is referred to as Tornado Alley accounts for their frequency in the region . . . According to the National Climatic Data Center, Alabama has the ninth highest number of tornado occurrences in the country."

They want to keep a lid on things, I think to myself as I lend an absent-minded ear to the news. An estimated thirty-eight dead, sixty missing, hundreds injured, and countless buildings destroyed. But what's just as disturbing is the timing. The prediction is spot-on!

At the age of fifteen, I like reading and writing. Words on paper give you time to think. They can be properly digested. With other kinds of words—the ones you hear—you need to be quick, make yourself clear, have a ready answer. Words fade away for the most part. They are flimsy, often pointless. But others take root. And sometimes cause pain.

At the age of fifteen, I have read the Keeper's post on social media. It was published last week and immediately went viral. A deluge of comments followed, some expressing excitement, others outrage, the most unscrupulous of them venting hatred. People were fired up not so much by the content of the message but by the guy's anonymity, by his so-called audacity. But what they really wanted . . . was to create their own buzz.

At the age of fifteen, I'm a teenage girl like any other. Outwardly, at least. On the inside, I'm a mess. My father just died.

"Are you daydreaming again?"

The deceptively soft tone of her voice—still hoarse from the funeral almost three weeks before—brings me around. My eyes open. My hands are ensconced in rubber gloves, the sink is full of soapy water, and my forehead is covered in beads of sweat. I wonder how long I've been standing in front of the pile of dishes, lost in thoughts of the past. When it was just the two of us. Before Laureen.

Every day, without fail, my father would tell me a story. Even when his work as a publisher kept him late at the office. If I was already asleep, he would wake me after the babysitter had left. Old Mrs. Rivera from next door. He'd tickle me, we'd laugh, and I'd pick out a book—any book I wanted. My father's stories are still there, inside me. They always will be.

Behind me in the kitchen, the familiar voices of my half sisters are set off by the news stream. Mia is quiet, Joyce is loud. Mia takes life as it comes, like a long, lazy river. Joyce jumps in with a great big splash. Mia is seven. Joyce is five. The same age I was when my father took me to the local pizza place with a ridiculous look on his face and a white rose in his lapel. His forehead was damp, and his dark-chocolate hair, the same color as mine, clung to his brow. Like me, he always got sweaty when his emotions ran high.

When Laureen entered the pizzeria, I knew right away. She was eight years younger than him and wore a white rose in her soft brown locks with subtle caramel highlights. The rest of the evening was a mere formality. He pretended the decision was mine, but the die was cast. My father had fallen for her, hook, line, and sinker. The woman with all her fairy loveliness was my stepmother-to-be.

Laureen never attempted to stand in for my mother. She just wanted to be my good friend. Until becoming a mother herself, that is. I never knew my real mother. She died giving birth to me. I can't remember my father ever talking about it, but I know how my mother died.

"Hellooo . . ." Laureen's voice cuts in again. "The dishes aren't going to just wash themselves, you know."

I wipe my brow with the back of my sleeve and plunge my hands into the water. The sponge squeaks its way around the rim of a glass, the girls squabble over the last piece of cake, and I imagine what Laureen really thinks about me—her aversion is so strong at times, I can almost feel it.

My silence of three weeks remains unbroken.

If everything froze right then and there, it would have looked like a "stepmother working a stepdaughter to the bone" moment. The cliché of the jealous stepmother. Pretty flattering for me, but a far cry from the truth. I rarely did the dishes, my closet was bursting with clothes, and Laureen, at the age of thirty-five, was drop-dead gorgeous.

She could hardly be jealous of me, the little late bloomer, with my gangly prepubescent build, a pinched face and ordinary brown hair, and a wide nose my friends like to say is "strong, just like you are." Not much to write home about, really, except perhaps my fierce dark eyes. Like little bits of coal, my father used to say, burning with curiosity and intelligence.

"This whole business is really unbelievable," my stepmother comments.

She is watching the news.

"This mysterious Keeper and his predictions. His next forecasts concern the lives of hundreds of thousands of people in France and Japan. No wonder people are worried. I would be, too, logical explanation or no."

Joyce gives her plate a few final scrapes—she got her way in the end—finishing off the last morsel of cake before a new squabble breaks out. This time, it's about her sister's stuffed pony, whose formerly white mane has been given a fluorescent-pink makeover.

"I wonder what I'd have done if he posted something, no matter how far-fetched, about where we live," Laureen goes on. "I'd probably have bought four one-way tickets to Vancouver."

Laureen adores the sophisticated Canadian city just a two-and-a-half-hour flight from San Francisco. She's taken us there several times to see the galleries, museums, theaters, and concert halls. She has quite a few friends there, too.

"What do you think about all this, Rachel?"

Personally, I have other things on my mind. It all seems pretty far away. Light-years away, really.

"Listen, Rachel, how much longer are you going to keep it up, this little silence game of yours?"

She knows I hate it when she calls me Rachel.

"You haven't been to school for nearly a month now. Don't you think that's long enough?"

I reach for the scouring pad.

"I'm not questioning Dr. Clark's abilities. He's a very reputable child psychiatrist. But 'post-traumatic aphasia' sounds a bit like a copout to me. Besides, I'm sure your friends miss you."

"Oh, dang it," Joyce interrupts, "I forgot!"

"Joyce . . ."

"'Dang' isn't a swear word, Mommy."

Joyce comes running over to me, her blond locks wrapped in plastic hair rollers swiped from one of her sister's dolls.

"I forgot to tell you! Kim called again. She wants to know if you're going to the school party. She's called three times today."

My five-year-old sibling clutches my leg excitedly—with the voltage of a stingray! My rubber glove slips, and a spattering of soapsuds flies into the air.

"Mia, look! Rae's got white poop on her head!" Joyce giggles with delight.

Reaching for her napkin, Mia pushes back her chair and walks over to the sink.

"Here," she says, handing me the napkin with the straight face of a librarian.

I pull off a rubber glove, take the napkin, and wipe my hair. Mia stands there expectantly, her slender fingers laced against the front of her skirt.

"Aren't you going to say thank you?" Joyce jumps in, also hoping she can get me to talk.

I give my little sisters a smile, Joyce lets go of my leg, and Mia unclasps her hands.

"So, anyway," Mia says, "are you going to go to the party or not? I think you should."

"Yeah, you should!" Joyce repeats. "Right, Mommy?"

"Right, what?"

I sneak a glance in Laureen's direction. She is staring through the kitchen window at the garden, her expression filled with regret, her weapon of choice in recent years for punishing her husband.

Regret that he had a daughter from a previous marriage—who would take care of Rachel if anything were to happen to him? Regret that she moved from New York to San Francisco—Haight-Ashbury couldn't hold a candle to Manhattan, where she went to shows on Broadway and was invited to art openings and gala events.

Regret that she didn't find the perfect catch—sure, publishing is a prestigious line of work, but books didn't bring in all that much money, and for Laureen, all that much isn't enough. And that she believed she could make a marriage work with a husband neither present enough to give her the security she needed nor absent enough to grant her complete freedom.

"That way," Mia continues, "if you go to the party, you'll have no choice. You'll be forced to talk."

Without taking my eyes off them, I shake my head in a disappointing albeit expected "no," then kneel down and give them a great big hug. For a few seconds, possibly longer.

Laureen, the whole time, hasn't moved a muscle. It must be when she decides to send me to boarding school—when she finally realizes my silence isn't going to go away. That it will weigh on her and reopen old wounds. There is nothing anyone can do about it. I am his physical embodiment, a constant reminder of past regrets.

My silence will weigh on the girls—on *her* girls.

And it will weigh on me.

At first, I ignored my little voice.

It was last year, or a short time before. It seemed easier to put it down to my imagination, to a slight fever or the radio left on somewhere in the house. Or maybe the TV. After all, it was only a little voice. Just a voice, though the tone was always the same, calm and muted, both familiar and strange. In any event, it wasn't mine. I heard the voice every so often but had no idea why. It spoke to me, murmuring and singing in tones so soft and fleeting I wondered if it wasn't the wind, or if I had dreamed it. Like all girls my age, my head was full of dreams. So, the little voice inside my head was no big deal.

Then I started hearing it more often. Its murmuring tones grew sharper and clearer, and increasingly difficult to ignore. One day, the voice prompted me to go to the library—I had inherited my father's passion for reading—where the most recent volume of a highly in-demand series was available for checkout! Another day, it encouraged me to play opposite Miss Davis in our class reading of *Romeo and Juliet*. I'd wanted to volunteer for ages but had never dared. Another time still, the voice saved me from totally bombing my math test by whispering the answers to me. Useful but disconcerting.

I tried plugging my ears, hiding under a pile of pillows, sticking my head under the showerhead—but it was no use. Without being invited, the voice had forced its way, little by little, into my daily life, like a family pet that is first forbidden from climbing onto the sofa but ultimately stretches out on the bed.

I had to face the facts: The voice was there. It existed. *Inside me.*

As time went by, I thought I was going crazy. I'd seen stories on TV of schizophrenic kids hearing voices. I was convinced I'd end up like them one day, a social outcast zonked out on meds in a padded cell, with the sound of keys and empty corridors as my only company. I was convinced of it. So, I buried it deep down inside. I swore I'd never tell anyone about it, about the voice. Ever.

*

Just before my father died, the voice fell silent.

For once, it was quiet. And I, in turn, out of mimicry and probably to listen more closely, kept quiet, too. That's when I felt the lump in my throat. And I knew something was terribly wrong.

Yet it was an ordinary day like any other. I was in the cafeteria lunch line with my two best friends. Chris was complaining about all the homework the English teacher was giving us, and Kim was ogling the captain of the JV hockey team.

"Miss Davis has got to be out of her mind . . ."

"There he is! Right ahead of us, just five trays away!"

". . . hand in our Shakespeare assignment by Friday!"

"Don't both look at him at once! Don't look!"

"Does she think we're a bunch of bookworms, or what?"

The plates on Chris's tray were piled high with food: mounds of potato salad, chili con carne, corn, and chicken nuggets. Kim's was just the opposite, the dictates of fashion already determining what food she would allow into her precociously curvy body. And she liked to keep each type of food separate on the plate.

"I mean, really, no one except you, Rae, could cram in four hundred pages in just two days."

"Oh my God! He just looked at me! Did you see that? He was looking at me."

"I know. We've been working on the damn book for a month now," Chris went on. "Twice as long, actually, in my case—I wedged it under the leg of my wobbly desk!"

We exchanged smiles as Kim babbled on about her crush.

"Act like you didn't notice anything!"

"You are going to give us an outline of the play like you did last time, aren't you, Rae?"

The outline was ready, of course, but I refrained from mentioning I had started reading another Shakespeare play the night before. Or that something had been keeping me awake at night lately, though I had no idea what.

Suddenly, the lump came back, like it had before in class. But, this time, it didn't just catch in my throat. It practically strangled me.

"Hello, Rae? Anybody home?"

My smile had vanished of its own accord. Try as I might, I couldn't answer Chris. I was petrified. I had no idea why . . .

"Yeah, your tray is empty, Rae," Kim chimed in. "What are you waiting for?"

I knew I had to leave before it was too late and I would have to explain. Explanations are for the lucky, for people who understand things, who take the ball and run with it. Something I'm no good at. So, I waved my hand to indicate I wasn't hungry, and with a faint smile—the best I could muster—I rushed out of the cafeteria, leaving my friends and my lunch tray in the lurch. I wasn't worried. I knew I'd find them again, not necessarily in the same place in line, but they'd still be there for me. That's what friendship is all about.

Besides, my two best friends were used to my sudden disappearing acts. They know me well. We know each other inside out. We're solid, we have each other's backs. We tell each other everything—or almost—and we're not ashamed of outbursts of laughter, anger, or tears. We never hide our faces or look away.

"Say no to Christal, Kimberley, and Rachel!" we'd chanted.

Ever since that day in grade school when we'd made a petition to shorten our first names, we've understood each other perfectly. Most of the time, that is—things can be pretty complicated when you are only fifteen. But when we don't, we forgive each other, no matter what.

How the high school principal, a woman I barely knew, wearing an impeccably cut suit, found me on the bench behind the gym, I couldn't say. Maybe when she was my age, she was partial to the secluded spot hidden behind a row of bushes maintained by the groundskeeper. A place to shut out the noise, to press "pause," if only for a minute.

"Rachel?"

The sound of her voice—cautious, unusually gentle—immediately alerted me. I knew right away. My inner voice hadn't been silent all morning for nothing. Something had happened.

"Nooo . . . It can't be!" I wailed.

"But I . . . I haven't even told you what . . ."

Except I already knew. In seconds, the voice had told me.

"Daddy! Daddy!"

I heard myself screaming.

"H-how . . . how did you know what . . ."

I kept screaming. Why did that lousy trucker have to drive

all night without making the mandatory stops? Why didn't he bring along a thermos of coffee? Why did my father have to cross his path? Why?

"I'm so sorry, Miss Telford," said the principal.

Next came the blur of empty words, of hazy figures moving about, of Chris and Kim trying to put their arms around me, their eyes brimming with tears. And the nausea rising in my throat, the sound of my scream . . .

Then, in the car on the way home, complete silence. Not a single tear, either. Just the passing streets, frozen and utterly lifeless—familiar and strange in the haze of a waking dream. A nightmare. One thing was certain: I no longer wanted anything to do with the world. I'd let nothing else in, nothing else out. No words, no anger, no life.

That was when everything froze.

It all went very quickly after that. The car ride home. Mia and Joyce—half sisters on paper, whole sisters in my heart—huddled in my arms, two tiny lost lambs. Laureen, locked away in her bedroom. The funeral.

And my new life.

#THEKEEPER #SAVETHEWORLD

POST 2—THE FIRST KEY

SEPTEMBER 5, 2035

WHAT IF WE COULD CHANGE THE WORLD?

Human activity is massively responsible for the global disaster predicted to take place in less than two years' time. The good news is, we have the power to prevent it. Yes, we are the masters of our fate—even if it's easier to play the blame game.

Surplus, lust, anger, greed, envy, pride, and boredom. Alas, a cure is yet to be found for those seven great afflictions, each a potential source of annihilation. For humanity has forgotten a vital truth: like the life energy of the chakras, our life spring is within.

Based on this observation, the program has created seven mantras—seven immersive VR microcosms reconstructing what scientists consider the seven most probable apocalyptic disasters.

Mantra 1: Barren Mother EARTH
Mantra 2: WATERS Unleashed

Mantra 3: Deadly HEAT
Mantra 4: Robotized LIFE
Mantra 5: Rampant EPIDEMICS
Mantra 6: Global Nuclear WAR
Mantra 7: Catastrophic METEOR

One of these will trigger the 07/27/2037 apocalypse. Which one? Spirit Era alone knows the shape of the impending disaster, and to avert it, we are being given one last chance: a key of life bearing a message of spiritual renewal has been hidden within each of the seven mantras. For we, as individuals, have to change from within before lasting action can become a reality. So, I, the Keeper, am issuing A CALL FOR:

Seven teenagers, symbols of change, ready to embrace life and the awakening of a new mindset—an age when anything is possible, when life forces are not restrained by prejudices.

Seven teenagers emboldened with the courage to enter the program livestreamed on the internet.

Seven teenagers ready to set forth on a quest for meaning, to save humanity by uncovering the seven lost keys of the chakras.

If you are between the ages of thirteen and eighteen, you are eligible to apply.

Will you be one of the seven? And . . .

WHAT ARE THE SEVEN KEYS?

While the first post sent shock waves through the media world, the second message was off the Richter scale.

The enigmatic Keeper had people everywhere distraught, amazed, outraged, and terrified. Especially since his message was published the day after the program's last prediction had come true, and both the floods in France and the earthquake in Japan had caused large amounts of dead and injured. A small number of people, concerned by the predictions, had temporarily taken shelter elsewhere—and most likely saved their own lives.

Rescue teams from around the world were traveling to Sendai, and the Health Division of the Western Pacific Regional Office had declared a state of emergency. Had the predicted disasters involved a wildfire or a breached dam, authorities might have suspected foul play. But a tornado, torrential rains, and an earthquake . . . There was no way such events could be pinned on the creator of the Spirit Era.

The president of the Conference of the Parties (COP40)— yearly intergovernmental conferences to assess progress in dealing with global climate change—had described the latest

IPCC report as more than a warning. It was a wake-up call. The goal of the last fifteen years to keep the increase in global average temperature below two degrees Celsius had failed, and the ensuing damage and devastation would spare no one. The whole world was in an uproar. A flood of articles inundated the media in a convergence of headlines:

7 TEENAGERS ~ 7 CHAKRAS ~ 7 KEYS
THE RACE TO SAVE THE EARTH IS ON

The Web was equally ablaze. Wild rumors ran rampant. It was all anyone talked about. And public opinion was divided.

"De malheureuses coïncidences, aucune menace tangible."

"Unfortunate coincidences, no tangible threat." (French)

"Tā bìrán shì xiānzhī."

"The Keeper is a prophet." (Chinese)

"Un ecologista loco, y eso es todo!"

"A nutty environmentalist—nothing more!" (Spanish)

"Eto blef, utopiya bez vsyakoy sily."

"It's all a bluff. The guy is powerless, a Utopian dreamer." (Russian)

"Uyafutheka! Isihlubuki sobuphekula!"

"A fanatic in cahoots with terrorists!" (Zulu)

"My teens and their friends are all worked up about it. This has to stop!"

Yet even the world's best police forces and cybersecurity experts were unable to unmask the sender. His IP address was untraceable, and not only because he was using intermediary servers. "I've never seen a firewall like it!" wrote one tech specialist.

Stranger still was the vague application procedure: no form to fill out, no personal statement—just enter a smartphone number and click a link when it magically appears on your screen. Then, fill in your name and date of birth. Some made themselves younger, and others, older, to fall within the thirteen-to-eighteen age requirement.

And so, around the globe, the mystery deepened.

*

When the second post was published, it'd been three months since I had lost my father. Three months of total silence that, this time, Chris and Kim couldn't forgive.

My friends could have accepted my not speaking to them—I never was much of a talker anyhow. When my turn to treat them to ice cream came, Chris would have simply ordered three scoops with hot fudge and sprinkles, and said something like "So long as you're only stingy with words"—sometimes I envy her spontaneity and sense of humor—and Kim would have given Chris one of her reproachful looks. They could have accepted my not being around, too. Officially, I wasn't the one who decided I'd go off to boarding school.

However, my absolute silence, my refusal to write to them or to even reply to their messages, that was too much for them. Because not writing was a choice, though, perhaps unconsciously, not speaking was, as well.

So, I got fewer and fewer audio and text messages, especially from Chris. For a while, only Kim was writing. But in the end, she adopted the same attitude as Chris, and perhaps also her anger. Radio silence.

At my boarding school in Pennsylvania, on the outskirts of Pittsburgh, I try my best not to think about them. Not to think about my sisters, either, or about my life before. The school is known for its demanding English lit program, and this was the excuse I gave for choosing a school so far from San Francisco: a seven-hour flight, counting the layover. Laureen didn't try to change my mind. Not all schools accept students with my kind of "disability."

At night, I read. During the day, I make myself scarce. I am happiest in the small hours of morning, when the words still warm from books feel almost like my own, when the other girls in the dorm room are still asleep. They are no more my friends than they are my tormentors. When I first arrived, a few attempted to get to know me, but seeing my lack of interest in communicating—not even with the mini-pencil attached to the notepad the teachers require me to use during class discussions—they rapidly lost interest.

It's September 18, I've been in boarding school for three weeks. The bathroom is cloaked in silence, as dreary as ever. Through the window, the day is dawning with difficulty as a light rain runs over the antique glass panes. I do a few stretches to try to get warm: arms overhead, arms to my sides, squat jumps, running in place. Then, whoosh! Sock-skating over the tiled floors, an activity that brings back memories of Mia and Joyce, of old Mrs. Rivera, too.

And the mirror. It always feels strange to find my reflection looking out at me.

I'm constantly surprised it's really me, as if I expect to see someone else. Yesterday, armed with scissors, I lopped off my hair the way you would a rosebush. I didn't think it would turn out so well: a bob, a few inches below the chin line, and practically straight. I also did my bangs, but they are far from horizontal: I angled them on purpose. They remind me of the slate roof on our Victorian house in Haight-Ashbury. They'll be an additional barrier between me and the other students. Luckily, I am practically invisible to them, and the teachers couldn't care less about my hair so long as I write in my little notebook when asked. An additional protection between the world, which is definitely out of whack, and Rachel.

Later, I've been going over my history notes for about an hour when the voices of two girls talking at a table next to mine pull me from the trenches of World War I.

"Phew! That's enough for me. Should we take a break?"

"Okay, but just five minutes. We still have a ton of stuff to do for tomorrow."

"The nerve of that teacher, a test at the beginning of the year!"

"It's to assess what we learned last year."

In the study hall, students divide themselves into age groups.

"Have you finished the math homework yet?"

"Are you kidding? I haven't even started it. When is it due?"

"Tomorrow . . ."

One of the girls flashes the same acerbic grin that Kim did, with her notorious lemon face, the time Chris swiped a minia-ture bottle of tequila from the family minibar.

"And to think the seven lucky ones chosen by the Keeper won't have to bother studying anymore."

"What do you mean?"

"You can't be expected to take part in his program and go to school, can you? That's what everyone's saying."

"Pfff, that's just a lot of talk."

"No, I'm serious! The Seven are going to go to school at the

Keeper's place. And since they'll be famous all over the world, they'll graduate without taking any exams."

"Seriously?"

"The Keeper's got to be mega rich. He'll fly the Seven to his secret island by private jet, and they'll live with him in a mansion. They'll each be given a luxury suite, a personal servant, and a dressing room. And anything else they ask for."

"Do you really think so?"

"Definitely. Gotta have a few perks if you're about to save the world!"

"The program's predictions are just a bluff. The planet isn't really in danger."

"Well, personally, I believe him. And so do a lot of influencers. Remember what GreenAss always says."

"Green who?"

"GreenAss. That super-hot eco-activist YouTuber. All his videos start with a shot of his ass painted green. Every morning, he sounds the alarm: 'If we don't get off our asses, the shit's going to hit the fan!' He didn't wait around for the Keeper to announce the end of the world. Apparently, every twenty minutes, a plant or animal species disappears forever."

"Don't you think your hot little GreenAss is a bit much?"

The girl gives a snort of laughter, then continues.

"But really, do you think we have a chance at making it into the Seven?"

"No way! There must be zillions of participants."

"Now who's exaggerating?"

"Maybe, but I'd be super psyched if I got selected!"

"Me, too!"

"Imagine we both get chosen. Wouldn't that be *amazing*?"

Two boys at the desk in front of them wave in annoyance for them to be quiet. I read the rest of the girls' conversation on whispering lips.

"It's been almost two weeks since the Keeper's announcement. When are the winners' names going to be announced?"

"The winners? It's not a lottery!"

"Yeah, whatever. So, I guess you don't know."

"Nobody does. And we don't know anything about how they'll be selected, either."

"Yeah, it's a total mystery. We'll just have to wait for the next post to find out more."

But to everyone's surprise, there is no next message.

Some say the Keeper hasn't found any suitable candidates, others that he is trying to generate even more buzz. Others think it is all a bad joke and that eventually there will be a logical explanation about how his software accurately predicted the recent natural disasters. A few days pass, and still no news.

One night, I receive a strange e-mail. Strange because it didn't arrive in my e-mail inbox or via the usual online messaging apps. A new app icon just showed up on my smartphone's home screen from out of nowhere. An icon only visible when I am alone, I later realize incredulously. It is a blue logo composed of a triangle in a circle bordered by petals with a spiral in the middle that reads "FOR RAE" when I click on it.

That in itself seems odd. Only the people I'm closest to know my nickname, and none of them are geeky enough to pull off a computer stunt like this.

Later that evening, I lock myself in the bathroom and open the app, my heartbeat racing in spite of myself.

All those who aspire to receive everything have nothing to give.

Only those who take chances are ready to receive.

Are you ready to seize yours?

The one person in your school who did not apply is the one person I have chosen.

WILL YOU HEED THE CALL?

Yes? Or no? A little bird tells me . . .
But what does your own little voice say?
Signed: The Keeper

4

He knows everything about me.

There's no point wondering how. Besides, the shock is too great for me to even think. But I guess if you are capable of fooling the world's best computer experts, hacking into a teenager's smartphone is child's play.

The Keeper knows what I look like. He doesn't care about my crooked bangs. He knows I miss Mia and Joyce so much I could scream, and that I haven't sent a single text since I've been at boarding school, to either my sisters or to Chris and Kim. He knows I don't speak and that my inner voice, the only one I trust, has been silent since my father died. That it's the only thing that could get me to come out of the shell I've retreated into. He must have suspected it, anyhow. The second I got his message, the voice resurfaced. Strong, gentle, and beautiful. In my head and from the depths of my being. Telling me to—*go for it!*

The Keeper knows everything about me. So, he exfiltrates me from boarding school without a hitch in the late hours of the morning on September 20, 2035, two weeks after his call on social media. He gets Laureen to believe that I've been selected to join a program for high-potential students on account of my outstanding academic achievements. The contact information of the program coordinator, a certain Kassandra something, is sent to my stepmother, who buys the whole story, lock, stock, and barrel.

The school principal received an official letter from "Laureen" requesting my return home, with proof of my being enrolled at a school in our hometown, explaining she was sending her "sister," my purported aunt, to pick me up. A woman carrying an oversized tote, the "auntie" I do my best to hug, exchanges no more than a few words with the principal, and then, we leave.

It's only when we get to the deserted bus stop, a long way from the Pittsburgh secondary school, the principal, and the students, that it suddenly hits me—I'm doing something crazy. Only then, still dressed in the school's mandatory skirt and navy-blue blazer, do I dare look more closely at my chaperone.

"You surely must have a lot of questions," she says. "For one, why did the Keeper contact you when you didn't even reply to the call? When you didn't ask anybody for anything? Why you? What makes you so special? Or different?"

She is reserved but doesn't beat around the bush. Her long auburn hair spills over a pale-colored dress that is somehow timeless. She cannot be much over thirty.

"Well, the truth is, I have no idea. The program, not the Keeper, selected the Seven. But the program *is* the Keeper, you may rightly say. And yet, not exactly. The student has become the master, the creature has surpassed its creator."

The young woman's enigmatic words and hushed tones give her an aura of otherness.

"You do understand that the identities of the Seven have to remain secret?"

I nod. After sending my reply to the Keeper, I was in-
structed to sign a nondisclosure agreement by pressing my
right thumb against the bottom half of my phone's screen.

A few minutes later, we climb aboard an ordinary
Greyhound bus heading to Harrisburg, according to the sign
above the windshield. I take a seat in the first row, and, suddenly, I feel completely disoriented. I had imagined we'd be
traveling by car, a more discreet means of transportation and
one more conducive to conversation. The situation is becoming increasingly bizarre.

Now, my eyes look about for something that makes sense
to focus on, something familiar. Inside the bus or outside. On
my seat by the window, my legs tremble lightly, as does the
tomato-and-cheese sandwich with lettuce and mayonnaise—
my favorite—placed on my lap. Kassandra handed it to me
without a word as the bus pulled out. Honestly, I don't know
what I'm doing here. My stomach is churning. Then, I notice
her hands—delicate, practically diaphanous, with the fingers
of a pianist. Hands that tempt you to draw closer, or to at least
try, moving calmly, slowly, as if dancing to the sound of a silent
melody.

The driver's movements, the passengers getting on and
off the bus, Kassandra is keeping tabs on everything, though
you'd hardly know it. After a while, she notices my untouched
sandwich.

"Eat," she says, her lips unsmiling and stern. "It's going to
be a long trip."

Her mouth hardly moves when she speaks, and her fixed
hazel eyes seem somehow vacant. Kassandra reaches for a paperback in her tote.

"*Of Mice and Men* by Steinbeck. Have you read it?"

I shake my head no.

"Take it. You must have had to return yours to the library."

Is this another message from the Keeper? Has Kassandra

been given a full report on me? I take the book and open it. It's dog-eared and worn. On the title page, words scribbled in pencil read, "Who are the mice and who are the men?"

She remains silent for the rest of the journey. Beyond the window, the monotony of the wooded landscapes of Pennsylvania makes it impossible for me to keep my bearings. Kassandra's proximity makes me uncomfortable. I try not to move, to breathe as quietly as possible. I turn the pages but have no idea what I'm reading.

It's going to be okay . . . It's okay . . . Everything is fine . . .

My inner voice is what got me on this bus, for better or for worse—I'm not quite sure which—with an aunt who isn't an aunt, heading to some unknown destination. To an uncertain future. For now, the voice is the only thing keeping me from running away.

"We get off here," Kassandra informs me with her usual aloofness, her voice dispelling my thoughts.

Kassandra gets up before the bus comes to a stop, grabs her bag and hands me mine. In the distance, a filling station bordered by a row of houses stands out against the setting sun. The gold-tinged swirls of dust raised by the wind seem to scrape away at the gas dispensers' flaking red paint.

"I imagine you could use the restrooms and a cup of hot chocolate by now?"

Kassandra imagines right. I've been crossing and recrossing my legs for a good half hour. As we exit the bus—we are the only passengers getting off at this stop—I need to pee so badly I am practically waddling like a duck.

The place is deserted. At the gas pumps, there is neither vehicle nor employee in sight. Through windows in need of a good washing, I make out an elderly station attendant at the register. The bus pulls out just as we're about to enter the convenience store. I notice the passenger in the back seat. He seems to be staring at us. His insistent gaze makes me squirm.

All the more so when Kassandra hustles me into the dilapidated building with unnecessary haste, a tense look on her face.

"Good evening, ladies," the man at the register says in a thick accent.

"Good evening, sir."

"Rotten weather, eh? Wasn't so windy yesterday. This kinda wind is bad for business. It kicks up the dust."

The old man seems happy to have company. The tiny convenience area smells musty. One of the lights in the ceiling is flickering. Two low shelving units, a beverage vending machine, and a cooler display the store's meager offerings. And indeed, the dust has spared nothing.

"Do you have a restroom, sir?"

"Of course we do! What kind of question is that! Over there, behind them shelves."

He gestures indignantly toward the back of the store.

"Go ahead," Kassandra intervenes—and she doesn't need to tell me twice—before turning back to the cashier.

"We'd like to stock up on groceries. Do you have any sandwiches?"

"Sure. Tuna or cheese?" he asks.

The voices become inaudible as I move away. Contrary to what I was expecting, the narrow windowless restroom—ventilation grate in the ceiling, no mirror over the sink—is quite clean. I wash my hands with a discarded bit of soap next to the faucet. By the time I come back, Kassandra's ready to leave.

It's nighttime when we exit the building. A car with an elongated hood has pulled into the station. As the elderly attendant places the pump nozzle into the tank, again, I feel like we're being watched. This time, by the man behind the wheel.

You're imagining things, my little voice tells me.

Kassandra hands me a paper cup. It smells like hot chocolate. From time to time, the headlights of passing vehicles illuminate the poorly paved road. Within five minutes, we're boarding another bus, this one three-quarters empty. Oddly enough, Kassandra makes her way straight to the back row, where one of the seats is already occupied by a hulking young guy.

The passenger stands up.

"Hi, Ka!"

I guess they know each other.

"Good evening," Kassandra greets him briefly, settling into a seat near the window.

"Where do you want me to put the bag of grub you asked for?"

She nods toward an empty seat. I stand there awkwardly, still in my school uniform, not exactly sure what to do.

"Hi. My name's Chayton."

He's loud, with sleek dark hair down the middle of his back, a strong jaw, and a thick neck. He holds out his hand, smiling. At an utter loss, I give it a quick shake. An awkward silence ensues, on my part, at least. As for Chayton, he appears completely at ease.

"Right . . . So, you are . . ."

I cast an anxious glance at Kassandra. Her forehead is pressed against the window. She's already fast asleep!

"What's your name?"

I point to my mouth, shaking my head, eyes averted.

"Oh, so you're mute?" Chayton bellows.

A passenger a few rows ahead of us turns around. I nod, then take the seat next to Kassandra, my bag placed squarely between my new acquaintance and myself. After that, I dive back into my book, still clueless as to what it's about.

"Gosh," he continues, settling down, "I can't believe it. You're mute!"

Not that he appears overly concerned about it. More like he just says the first thing that pops into his head.

"No disrespect meant, right? I mean, we have been chosen among millions, haven't we? Possibly billions."

He leans his broad chest closer to me and lowers his voice.

"You know. We're part of the Seven, although I have to admit, I thought there'd be . . ."

Chayton seems to hesitate before speaking.

"I mean . . ."

You thought there'd be six other nitwits like yourself?

My inner voice brings a smile to my face from behind my book.

"Mind you, I don't really care whether you can talk or not."

How big of you . . .

First, Chayton exerts himself to come up with a name for me.

"Let's see . . . raven hair . . . Tiny, like a little bird, like a . . . That's it! Like a sparrow."

Then, book or no book, he gives me his whole life story.

He turned sixteen just last week. He's a Quechua and grew up in Peru. His American buddies gave him a huge going-away party. He left his native Sierra two years back to seek his fortune in the United States. His size made it easy for him to fake his age and get a job at a hotel in Los Angeles.

He is from a family of farmers, the youngest of five brothers; his father named him after his grandfather. A Native American of Dakota Sioux descent, a great healer and traveler who made the same journey as Chayton, but in reverse, in search of new plants. "Chayton," in Lakota, means hawk. Chayton always felt different, always dreamed of another life—of fancy cars, designer clothes, and girls. He had been there, done that, and is going places.

After what seems like an eternity, Kassandra opens her eyes at last. With a catlike stretch, she grabs her bag and stands up. A minute later, we are off the bus. We change buses three times, take a cab, then a train, then another bus and another train—a cattle car this time, without the cattle but with the overpowering bovine scent permeating the straw nonetheless. I don't sleep for twenty-four hours. That and the stress of heading to an unknown place have just about pushed me over the limit.

"You can never be too careful, you know," Kassandra remarks casually. "We have to make sure we are not being followed."

"Who do you think is following us?" Chayton asks. "When we talked in LA, you said Spirit Era had enemies."

"Did I say that? I shouldn't have."

"Yeah. I mean, it's pretty much a no-brainer. If the program is able to predict the future, it must be worth a shitload of money. I bet every country in the world would like to get their hands on that neat little gadget. Even if most don't take the end-of-the-world prophecy seriously, Spirit Era did prove it can raise the alarm. Knowing in advance where the world's next natural disaster is going to strike is one hell of a superpower!"

Chayton, seated on a bale of straw, pulls a couple of packets of nuts out of the grocery bag, pours some in his palm, and gulps down a handful. Practically without chewing.

"Want some, Ka?"

"No, thank you. I'm not hungry."

Cool air comes in through the half-open door, and her legs dangle over the passing rails. Kassandra's mind seems elsewhere.

"Are we almost there yet?"

"Chayton . . ."

"I know, I know! No questions."

He pulls out an apple and takes a bite.

"How 'bout you, Sparrow? You want anything?"

I shake my head no.

"I guess you eat like a bird, too. Come on, just a little piece of bread!"

I shake my head again.

"You're going to have to keep up your strength, you know, to accomplish our mission. Here. Just a few crumbs!"

And the nitwit sticks a piece of bread in my face. With the back of my hand, I send it flying to the other side of the boxcar.

"Hey! Look what you did. It landed in cow dung. That's disgusting."

At that moment, I lose my cool. I leap to my feet, breathing hard, fully determined to shove the entire apple down his throat!

Chayton's eyes widen in mock amazement.

"Well, what do you know! Hey, Ka, look at Sparrow. She's all worked up."

"Her name is Rae, Chayton," Kassandra replies, unflappable. She gestures for me to sit back down.

"Yeah, whatever. But still, no reason for little Birdie to get all worked up."

"Her name is Rae, I told you. Not Birdie, not Sparrow, but Rae. Got it?"

"Yeah, sure, I get it. I'm not an idiot, you know."

"Yes, I do know. You, on the other hand, don't seem to realize it. Otherwise, why would you insist on behaving like one?"

Bam! I'm starting to like this makeshift auntie of mine.

"Birdie, Girly, Sparrow. You are the only one who those diminutives diminish, Chayton."

Chayton sticks out his lip like a little boy caught red-handed in the cookie jar.

Her concluding remark has cut him to the quick. He gathers up his things, puts the food into the grocery bag, shoves it aside, and walks away muttering. He flops down in a corner of the boxcar and throws back his head, a loud whack filling the air when it bumps the wall. His eyes close, easing the tense look on his face. Seconds later, he's snoring.

Kassandra smiles at me. A genuine smile with no trace of pride or mockery in it. A dialogue between us ensues—in silence.

5

I sure would love to get that girl into bed!

Chayton's voice wakes me up with a start. My eyes open. He's standing at the opposite end of the boxcar, a wild look in his eyes. The train is at a standstill and Kassandra isn't around. Hair tied back in a low ponytail that somehow emphasizes his manliness, Chayton stands there squarely, fists on hips.

Right here, right now . . .

Hey, what's going on! Is he trying to . . . ? Uh-oh, he's moving closer!

. . . in the straw. Even better that way . . .

I jump to my feet with a single prodigious leap. Practically three feet off the ground.

. . . undo the buttons of her shirt . . . and her jeans . . .

What is he thinking? What jeans? I've still got my uniform on!

"What's up with you, Spar . . . uh, I mean, Rae? Something wrong?"

I back away toward the door of the boxcar.

"You're right, Chayton," a voice behind me rings out.

I turn around in disbelief. A girl!

"You sure have a way with the ladies!"

A girl is standing there on the tracks. She lets out a laugh.

"This one looks more like she just saw Dracula."

She laughs again, tosses her bag into the train, and hoists herself effortlessly into the boxcar. She's tall and slender with tousled, short sandy locks. She is overflowing with energy and life and is wearing a button-down shirt . . . and *jeans*!

"G'day, I'm Ali."

Chayton was going on about her! She was the one he wanted to . . .

"Nice to meet you."

Same here!

"You guessed right, I'm one of the Seven. Though, that doesn't mean much for the time being, does it!"

She extends her hand confidently, the way Chayton had one day before, flashing a smile as bright as the midday sun—not unlike the gold sun stud she's wearing in her nose. Despite the incongruity of the situation, I can't help but return her smile. Her energetic handshake radiates so much heat it practically burns my hand.

"You've been snoozing for quite some time. Chayton and I have had time for a good long chat. Your name is Rae, and you're not much of a conversationalist, am I right?"

The new girl can't stand still, a real live wire.

"So," Ali goes on, "no point wondering if Kassandra has answered your questions any more than she has mine! But I guess we'll get some answers once we arrive. Wherever that is. That's a mystery, too."

"The program has to be kept secret. You agreed to it, didn't you?" Chayton asks Ali. "Just like we did?"

"Yeah, kept secret from the eyes of the world. To protect it. But when we're alone, we can talk about it. Seems strange to me."

"The mystery makes it even more exciting, if you ask me,"

Chayton responds. "Besides, we're free to leave anytime we want."

"Yeah, I know. Except if you're here, then you believe the end-of-the-world prediction, just like me. So, leave, but to go where? Incidentally, Rae, how old are you?" Ali asks, turning to me.

I hold up ten fingers and then five.

"Fifteen? You look younger. I would have guessed thirteen, like my brother."

She runs her hand through her sandy locks, mussing them even more. Her light-colored shirt, sleeves rolled up and half tucked in, reveals slender, muscular arms. She's an athlete. You can tell right away.

"Do you have any brothers or sisters?"

I nod, then launch into a series of gestures: "Two—little—half—five—seven—and you?"

"I'm almost seventeen."

It's amazing how I manage to communicate with her without speaking or knowing sign language. Even more amazing is the fact that I even want to.

"Ka's gone out for food. With everything that hulk over there ingested while you were sleeping, we're completely out."

"Yeah, and you know what the hulk says . . ."

"Oh, come off it, Chayton. I was joking. Don't be a crybaby!"

Oddly enough, he smiles.

Hmm, she's a feisty one! Just how I like 'em.

It's starting up again!

It's super sexy.

What the heck is going on?

Look at that body of hers.

Why can I hear Chayton's voice when he isn't talking?

"By the way, I forgot to ask you earlier. What's Ali a nickname for?"

"Alyssa. But don't even think about calling me that—or

else! I was hardly old enough to talk when I decided it'd be Ali."

So, just like Chris, Kim, and me, she took issue with her first name and renamed herself.

"And where are you from?"

"You wouldn't know it from my accent, but I'm an Aussie. I grew up in Perth, on the west coast of Australia."

"Is that where your family is from?"

"Three generations back on my father's side."

"What do they do there?"

"Diamonds."

"Whoa, they must be super rich!"

"Loaded."

Ali's smile turns bitter.

"Except money, you know, isn't all there is in life."

"That's because you've never been without it."

"Maybe so. My oldies may well have millions in the bank, but that doesn't mean they're happy."

"Yeah, but it helps."

"Not even. If you only knew how pessimistic they are. Dead inside. Never satisfied. They've never been interested in anything except themselves. Although, as far as school goes— or *schools*, I should say, I've been to quite a few—it's fine by me. My grades were a disaster, except in gym. The teachers couldn't get me to sit still for two hours straight."

Ali's bright-gray eyes seem to darken suddenly.

"My kid brother hasn't gotten over it yet. He's always trying to make them happy on the rare occasions they're home. They barely looked at the registration papers for my new sports-study program in Florida."

"So, that's what your cover is? What sport?"

"Baseball."

"Do you play?"

"Of course I play. It had to be a credible lie."

So, as far as our families are concerned, Ali is in Florida playing baseball, Chayton is raking in a fortune in Los Angeles, and I'm taking an advanced course in literature in Pittsburgh. There is a definite geographical thread to it all, at any rate—every place is in the US so far.

"Do you think they bought it?"

"I couldn't care less. What I do mind is having to leave my brother, Remy, behind. And my board."

She's a surfer. That's why she has that hot body.

Oh no! Not again!

I've never bagged a surfer before.

The guy sure thinks he's the cat's meow!

"You a surfer?"

"No, I was talking about my ironing board, of course!"

Speaking of ironing boards, too bad her tits are so small . . .

The voice again.

. . . they remind me of that English tourist, the chick . . .

Be quiet!

. . . the beach in LA. The sand all over the place . . .

It's a nightmare. Chayton's voice is in *my head*!

"Rae!"

Outside the wagon, I hear Kassandra calling my name. Her timing is perfect. I jump down onto the tracks and hurry over to her. The urge to tell her what's going on has my stomach in knots.

"Would you mind giving me a hand?"

Her arms are loaded with bags of groceries. People are unloading cattle and goods in the distance. A tank car hides us from view.

"Our train departs in ten minutes. We'll have real seats this time."

We divide the bags up and start walking. Cloud cover hides the sun, but it's warm out. Snatches of conversation come from the boxcar. Ali and Chayton seem to be arguing. I hope he didn't say out loud what I heard him thinking . . .

"Our trip will be over soon."

Ka's slow, easy steps tells me she's not in a hurry. That's when it hits me. Chayton's voice is no longer occupying my head!

"Silence can be a land of refuge," Kassandra remarks casually.

Her words seem to echo what just happened! But that's impossible. How could she know?

"It's not just a place devoid of words. Remember that."

Her words are like the ones in books. Gentle and comforting. For once, I let them sink in.

Her eyes fixed steadily on the boxcar, Kassandra continues.

"And beware of prowlers seeking refuge, too. Your silence may provide them with a temporary shelter, but it can also be taken over and settled for good . . ."

I think back to what happened earlier when Chayton's thoughts were in my head.

"Destroying you in the process."

That is the last thing Ka says to me before we get to the Keeper's destination.

It's pitch-dark out as we exit the station.

The air is cold for mid-September. The single-side platform of the Amtrak terminus borders a plain redbrick building. I can make out the word "Rutland" on a nearby sign—but I have no clue as to where it is.

A four-door pickup is waiting for us at the station. An old-fashioned bottle-green snub nose with a flatbed that could easily load ten times our gear. The interior smells of stale tobacco. We roll and bounce along for two hours straight. The driver, a sixty-year-old, ill-shaven farmer sporting a baseball cap the wrong way around, doesn't make a sound—other than a slight rasping cough that sounds like he peppered his food with a heavy hand—and neither does Kassandra, sitting next to him.

Some stretches of asphalt are in sore need of repair. The ride is bumpy. I feel a little sick to my stomach. There are no road signs, not a living soul in sight. All we know is that we are making our way up the side of a mountain. From time to time, Ali looks over at me before turning her head back to the window, hat and hood pulled over her ears. She hasn't said a word to Chayton since we left the train. Her luminous smile has turned cloudy. I can tell she's on edge. Chayton pretends not to notice, but inside, I can tell he's seething. Stuck between the two of them in the back seat, I'd say the tension is palpable.

The truck slows down as it enters a village.

"Are we almost there?" Chayton is losing patience.

A few poorly lit houses on either side of the road are practically hidden by the thick vegetation. We pass a church—white walls, steeple, and slate roof.

"Boy, am I starving! I hope the food is good at the Keeper's," he complains.

At present, we are surrounded by overgrown nature, and the pickup is winding its way over a densely wooded mountain. Ali, to my left, is becoming increasingly restless. Every time Chayton opens his mouth, she tenses up, seeming ready to lash out.

I place my hand on her arm. She doesn't seem to mind. Her muscles relax a little.

"We're there," Kassandra says at length.

The pickup lurches to a stop in a dirt-and-gravel yard flanked by an imposing clapboard farmhouse and a pair of outbuildings. The main building's high-pitched roof is punctuated with a row of dormer windows and twin brick chimneys.

"Where, exactly, are we?" Ali asks.

"Near Brownsville, a village in a remote corner of Vermont."

"So that means we're near the Canadian border!"

"Yes, about a hundred miles from here."

"Gosh, then we certainly took a roundabout route."

"And you know why."

"Yeah, right. It all has to be kept secret. I think we got that."

The driver climbs into the back of the pickup and tosses our bags onto the ground. When he stands up, we can see his stocky build, broad shoulders, legs on the short side.

"Hey, easy with our stuff!" says Chayton.

"Oh, you poor dear! Your bag got scuffed up!" Ali's voice drips with sarcasm. "What's the matter, Chayton? You had a Ming in there?"

"A what?"

"A Ming. A priceless porcelain vase from China. It's a figure of speech."

"Yeah, whatever. But don't get all high and mighty with me. You didn't have to slave away for the stuff in your bag. But at a hundred dollars a pop, I don't want my bottles of cologne smashed to smithereens."

Chayton follows Kassandra, scowling at Ali, who gives me a triumphant smile.

The doorway to the building opens into a rustic open-plan kitchen and living room: oak cabinets, old workbench converted into a central island unit, impressive dark table flanked by high-backed chairs straight from the Middle Ages, and two commanding freestone fireplaces on either side of the living room. Running the whole length of the high, exposed log-beam ceiling is a balcony with a row of impressive doors. The place looks like it used to be an inn.

Preceded by Ka, who hasn't opened her mouth again except to tell us to be ready for supper in an hour, we go straight upstairs. The dining room looks enormous from the balcony. Chayton is shown to a room on the right. My room, next to Ali's, is at the other end. It is plainly furnished with a bed with a white comforter, a desk in front of a half-open dormer window, a wooden chair with a straw seat, and an old-fashioned wardrobe. A low, recessed area leads to a small but practical and much-welcome bathroom. Before going in, I empty the things in my blazer pockets onto the bedside table: a couple of Kleenex tissues; a tiny pencil and notebook; and my smartphone, on silent mode since I left home. I only use it to check the time.

In the shower, I clear my mind for a good long while under

a stream of hot water. It's just what I need. Then, as I lather up, I remember the girls in the study hall at the boarding school. If only they could see me now! In any case, they got it all wrong about the private jet, luxury villa, dressing room, and razzle-dazzle.

I wrap myself up in a towel and lie flat on the bed. The thought of Chayton's voice in my head earlier in the day has an unsettling effect on me. Fortunately, it hasn't happened again, but Kassandra's advice didn't come with a user manual, either. What if it happens again? I'm used to my own inner voice: it's my own, it's part of me. Hearing Chayton's voice, on the other hand, made me feel like a thief stealing someone else's thoughts!

Random images—Mia and Joyce, old friends, new faces— flash through my mind. They start to blur, then eventually make way for my father's smile. It comforts me.

I realize I've nodded off when there's a knock at the door.

"Rae?" Ali's voice calls out.

I get up and let her in.

"You're not ready?"

No, I guess not! I'm still wrapped in my towel. Ali has changed into snug-fitting army fatigues and a tank top, both the same attractive shade of yellow. A girl with a head of gorgeous ginger hair accompanies her.

"This is Helen. She's in the room next to mine."

"Hello, nice to meet you!" the redhead says with a pronounced accent.

"Do you two have reception?" Ali asks. "I can't send a message to my brother. He thinks I'm at my sports-study program in Florida, but he's used to me writing every day."

I check my smartphone and shake my head.

"Me neither," Helen says, pulling hers out of her pocket.

From the sound of her quick rolled r's, I can tell now she's from Scotland. Helen is wearing the same close-fitting outfit as Ali, but all in orange. She gives me what I guess is her best sugar-sweet smile, and I smile back, but I'm not falling for her little show: everything may look perfect on the outside, but it's always best to have a look under the hood.

Ali does a swift backward plunge onto my bed.

"Guess what? Helen is seventeen just like me! Well, I'm almost seventeen," she says, turning to Helen.

"Pretty much the same, isn't it? Anyhow, Rae, hurry up and get dressed. Ka's called us twice already."

Catching the look of uncertainty on my face, Helen walks over to my wardrobe and throws it open with an incredibly feminine gesture. The wardrobe is empty.

"Wait, that's not all."

She feels around, pressing a spot in the left bottom corner. The back of the closet slides open.

"Presto! Kassandra showed me the trick: a safety measure to keep our outfits hidden. I didn't say anything to her, but I was a little disappointed. I'm an artist by nature. I design and create my own clothes, so the uniform, obviously . . ."

To my surprise, several outfits like the ones worn by Helen and Ali are arranged on hangers in the secret compartment. And a faded-blue leatherette biker jacket.

"So, what did I tell you?" Ali asks Helen as she sits up on the edge of the bed.

"Well, that doesn't mean blue is her favorite color."

"Well, Rae," Helen asks, "is it?"

It is. My mother started collecting children's books before I was born. Each had the word "blue" in the title—*Bluebeard*, *The Blue Bird*, *The Blue Tales of the Perched Cat*. And my father continued the tradition. Yes, blue is my favorite color.

"You see," boasts Ali, "I was right! And I bet it's not just a passing thing."

Right again. Blue, in memory of my mother, who died just after I was born. I knew because my inner voice, the guardian of my earliest memories, told me. When my father was unable to find the words, it told me about the happy first instants of my life and—my mother: the joy she felt holding me in her arms, the tears in my father's eyes, the calm baby and the wondrous silence, my gaze fierce and present, full of awe.

"Burning with curiosity," my father said.

"Rachel," my mother named me.

And then: the commotion in the delivery room, my mother's hands growing limp, letting go of my small, slippery body, the other hands taking hold of me, taking me away from her. The urgency of it all, the hemorrhaging and the shouting, my father and I being rushed out of the delivery room, both of us crying. And after, the two of us alone, my father and I, my mother gone. Forever.

"See. All our clothes are our favorite color," Ali insists, shifting her legs restlessly on top of the comforter.

"No, they are not!" Helen snaps.

I slip away to get dressed in the bathroom, sneaking a quick look at the new girl through the cracked door. Her wavy hair cascades down her back, almost to her waist. Her seagreen eyes, rimmed with eyeliner, betray a torrent of emotions. She may think she's hidden behind her dramatic makeup, but her expression gives her away, and at present, it reveals her distress.

"There has to be some other explanation. The color assigned to us is neither a matter of preference nor chance. The icon of the smartphone app that the Keeper contacted me with is orange, too," Helen says.

"That's true," Ali agrees. "Mine is yellow. Let me see."

But Helen isn't alone so the icon doesn't appear.

"And besides, I hate orange!" Helen exclaims just as I am exiting the bathroom. The irony of it makes my eyes dwell on her hair longer than intended, and naturally, she notices.

"That's exactly why. I've had it up to here with 'carrot-top'!"

Beneath a spattering of delicate freckles, Helen's pale skin turns pink. A brief lull follows.

"Helen, be careful around Chayton. The bloke's a total phony. He pretends he can get any girl he wants into bed. I don't know about the others, but Chayton's one to keep an eye on." Ali walks to the middle of the room and stretches, arms outspread like rays of sunlight taking possession of the room— and us. "Helen, watch out! There's a bee on your shoulder."

Before she can move, Ali blows on the insect. It flies into the air, then disappears through the half-open dormer window.

"Thanks," Helen says. "You just reminded me of my mother. She loved honey and bees. I lived with just my mum."

"Your parents are divorced?" Ali asks.

"It was my dad's decision. Found himself a younger woman. Classic."

"What about your mother? Didn't she meet anyone?"

"No. Thirty years of cooking, laundry, and housework, that was all she knew. After the divorce, she shut herself away."

Helen's emotion is tangible.

"When my two older brothers left home, it was just the two of us," she continues. "Gradually, the apartment got messier, the washing machine stopped spinning, and the fridge was only filled up when she managed to get out of bed. I convinced myself it wouldn't last. And I started going out, to erase the image she gave me of women. Going out a lot."

Her voice falters. Suddenly, she's crying unrestrainedly.

"I didn't see it coming. She started drinking in secret, then it was antidepressants. It happened on a Saturday night, six weeks ago."

The sound of her sobbing subsides, followed by a lengthy silence. A terrible silence.

"I'd just gotten back from a party. There'd been lots of drinking. Jamie brought me home in his father's van. We stopped in a secluded spot. With us, it was just for fun. It was four in the morning when I walked through the door of our apartment."

Helen is wringing her hands, trendy rings on every finger. With a quick motion, Ali reaches for them and holds them tight—as if to ward off what's coming.

I shudder. I know what's next.

"I found her in the living room. She had hanged herself."

The rims of her eyes are a vibrant red, and tears silently streak down her cheeks.

"I didn't see it coming."

7

The air is fragrant with the scents of pumpkin, potato, and spices.

From the balcony overlooking the kitchen area, I see pots and pans on the stovetop. Kassandra is seated at the head of the table, presiding over the gathering as mistress of the house.

Opposite her, an empty high-backed chair—it must be the Keeper's. I wonder what he's like. At times, I imagine he's young—handsome, dark, and elusive. At others, I imagine he's a wizened patriarch, a great sage and protector.

"Hey, girls!" Chayton calls out as we come downstairs.

On his right, a boy who seems no older than ten with straight jet-black hair and delicate Asian features lowers his eyes self-consciously. The color of his jacket is green. On his left, an androgynous-looking teen—small dark-blue eyes, lanky frame, and a peach-fuzz mustache on an impassive upper lip—sits perfectly still. He is there but not altogether present. His clothes are purple.

"We could hardly wait!" Chayton laughs.

The brick-red hue of his clothes suits his dark complexion.

As soon as he sees Helen, Chayton rears up like a Quechua stallion.

"Whoa!" Hair untied and tank top hugging his powerful torso, he lets out a low whistle.

"Easy there, Chayton," Kassandra admonishes perfunctorily.

Chest stuck out and strutting like a peacock, he walks over to Helen, who, puffy-eyed or no, immediately turns on the charm. Fluttering eyelashes, seductive smile, nonchalantly swaying hips—she's on display.

"Shit! When did you show up? Redheads aren't usually my thing, but you . . ."

"Chayton . . ."

"What now, Ka? I'm just telling the truth! You're the one who told me to stop lying."

Kassandra raises her eyes heavenward.

"Some truths are better left unsaid," Ali remarks sarcastically, pushing Chayton aside to let Helen past. "Didn't your daddy ever tell you that?"

"My father," Chayton mimics Ali in a mocking tone, "is a real man, not a sissy like yours! No farting in fancy silk sheets for him!"

"I believe you. Mine, however, doesn't treat women like cattle."

"You don't know a thing about my father. He was eighteen when he married my mother. They survived it all together: years of toiling in the damn quinoa fields, the unpredictable weather in the Sierra mountains, and nine mouths to feed—five kids and two grandmothers. Family is sacred to the Quechua. And that tongue I tried to slip you back in the train isn't going to change a thing!"

Ali is clenching her fists, beside herself with anger.

"Okay, I messed up," Chayton admits. "But after the right hook you gave me, we're even."

Tsk-tsk, Chayton . . . Good thing she couldn't hear his thoughts, my own inner voice interrupts. Not the best timing, but at least it was mine, not his.

"Come on. Let's just put it behind us and move on," he says, apparently meaning move on to Helen, only adding fuel to the fire, though she seems to like the attention.

I sit down on the chair across from the Asian boy who, despite his downcast eyes, seems to be listening carefully. The moody towhead, on the other hand, still hasn't shown any sign of interest whatsoever.

Helen, in the meantime, slips into her chair with the fluidity of water taking the shape of a container. Her long legs somehow don't get in the way. A perfect fit. Chayton walks over to the blond kid and gives him a "friendly" tap on the back that practically sends him reeling.

"Hey, buddy, you wouldn't mind switching places with me, would you?"

As if he has any choice in the matter!

"Thanks, I owe you one, uh—it's Stephan, right?"

"Stepan," Kassandra corrects him. "And he doesn't speak our language very well. Neither does Keiji. They're going to be taking an accelerated course."

Chayton sits down opposite Helen, his eyes devouring her like a buttercream rose on a birthday cake.

"Well, Chayton, are you done with your little show?" Kassandra asks.

"Can I at least ask the fair lady her name?"

"Helen," the fair lady replies, with all the guile of a sorceress.

Chayton sits there gawking.

"Miss Kassandra?" Keiji asks, timidly raising his hand like a schoolboy.

"I told you, you can call me Ka."

"Uh, yes, Miss Ka. I ask a question?"

His Asian accent is very strong.

"Of course, go ahead."

"I travel very long time. When to see master?"

All eyes turn to the vacant chair at the end of the table.

"Not tonight. We have a lot to go over, and it's getting late. You'll see him tomorrow."

That's when it occurs to me. There's another empty seat next to Stepan's. Stepan, Chayton, and Keiji, Ali, Helen, and me. That makes six. The seventh chair is empty.

"What does the Keeper look like?" Helen inquires.

"Ha!" Chayton laughs. "Ka isn't going to tell you anything. Are you worried you won't be able to draw him into your web?"

"My web, luv? You've got it all wrong. Girls like me, we use ultrasonic whistles."

"Woof, woof!"

Helen dissolves into laughter with Chayton like she's known him for ages.

She's a slippery customer, that girl is, my inner voice comments.

Under the table, I can hear Ali's foot irritably keeping time, while my own attention is focused on the seventh empty chair.

"How are you doing, Stepan?" Kassandra asks. "Can you understand what they're saying?"

"Nyet." That's the only answer she gets, though it seems to imply he understood the question, at least . . .

"So, uh, tell me, what's next on the 'program'? No pun intended," Ali asks.

"You'll have to be patient a little longer, Ali. Not everyone has arrived."

Well, then, I guess the last of the Seven has been delayed. I wonder who it is. As if on cue, the guy who drove the pickup comes in through a service entrance, diverting my attention.

"You've already met Mr. Mann. He runs the farm and does the cooking."

As ill-shaven as ever, he has traded his baseball cap for the worn leather apron of a farrier. He plunks down pots and pans on trivets scattered across the large table.

"Thank you, Mr. Mann. Bon appétit, everyone!" Ka says.

Eyes riveted to the ceiling, Stepan seems to be searching for a spider. Chayton immediately lifts the pot lids. "Where is the meat?"

"On my farm," the cook answers, the sound of his voice as hoarse as his cough, "we don't feed on the suffering or death of other creatures."

"Oh shit!"

"Food is our energy, and not just in terms of calories and nutrients. You wouldn't think of putting diesel into a car that runs on gas, would you?"

"Yeah, but I didn't sign on to being a vegetarian!"

"Neither did I," Helen adds.

"Me neither," Ali chimes in.

"And we're not asking you to convert for good," Kassandra intervenes. "Only here, at the farm. And I'd like to encourage you to learn about other culinary traditions, too. Keiji, for example, was raised in a monastery in Japan. He eats according to the Buddhist tradition that forbids taking the life of any living being."

"*Shojin-ryori*," Keiji adds, reaching for a paper bag under the table. He places five bundles on his plate.

"Or, food for spiritual elevation," Ka translates. "In addition to not eating meat, one must avoid eating five overwhelmingly pungent vegetables. And the pattern of five—five tastes, five colors, and five ways to prepare—must be respected. More than a set of rules, *shojin* is associated with inner transformation, the aim of which is to attain enlightenment. To quench the fire, that is, of the three poisons: greed, hatred, and ignorance."

The bundles are made of food I've never seen before. I run through the colors in my head: green, red, yellow, white, and black. Keiji removes a pair of chopsticks from his jacket pocket and starts eating.

"Here, you will learn to see beyond what's on your plate."

A lengthy silence ensues as we all watch Keiji eat and we try the contents of the pots and pans. But from the tone of our mentor's voice, we know Ka isn't simply referring to food.

"And now, everybody, hand over your phones!" Mr. Mann breaks in.

He picks up a basket full of peeled onions and holds it out. "In here, please."

Without arguing, Keiji takes a burner phone from his pocket and tosses it into the basket. Chayton, scowling at his plate, follows suit. Stepan digs into his food, simply stating with a Russian accent, "I don't have."

"What!" Keiji wonders out loud. "How master you contact?"

Stepan lets out a sigh instead of answering as if to say, "Not interested."

"I don't agree!" Ali protests. "I signed the confidentiality deal, and I won't break it. I'll leave my phone off and only use it to text Remy at night. He's counting on me."

"We'll see to it he gets messages from you," Kassandra attempts to reassure her.

"No way!"

"Your little brother will be fine, I promise. You don't want to put the program at risk, do you? We can't have your phones tracked here."

"Why not? We're not being monitored, as far as I know! I've had enough of all this. We're stumbling around in the dark!"

"Ali is right," Helen concurs.

"Look, I understand it's upsetting," Ka says. "But I'm asking you for a little more time, a rare commodity these days in our increasingly rapid world of instant everything. And yet, remember, like the bud that develops, from blossom to flower, and then turns into an apple, time is a precious ally."

"But . . ."

"If you've been chosen, Ali, it's for a good reason. I might not know what that reason is, but I have faith in the program. It has brought together the seven keys that humanity has lost— or perhaps never had. And only the Seven have the power to find them."

Her words are greeted with silence.

"But to bring about change, you need the courage to question everything, starting with yourself."

Mr. Mann holds the basket in front of me as Helen drops her phone into it. I gesture that mine is in my room, that I'll go get it after dinner.

"Courage," Ali repeats, as if in a trance.

Without further ado, her phone flies through the air in a graceful arc and lands in the basket.

"Would you mind telling me something," Helen asks. "Why onions? They're going to make our phones smell awful."

"Why do you think?" Mr. Mann replies, clearly impervious to her charms. "The onion riddle ought to be small potatoes for the Chosen. I'll give you five minutes."

"Smartphones," Chayton begins, always ready to take up a challenge. "They're bad for your health because of radio waves and all that."

"Yes . . ."

"Smartphones are bad for you, and onions smell bad."

"I see, but no." The man's grin speaks for itself. Kassandra doesn't seem to find it very funny, but she doesn't say anything. As for me, I'm more interested in the riddle of the empty chair than that of the onion.

"When peel onion," Keiji attempts, "layers like us. In smartphones, too, some of humans."

I can't quite get his meaning. Ali, who is having trouble sitting still again, takes advantage of the enigma to jump to her feet. She looks from Helen to Chayton and back.

"Opposites attract. Onions are strong tasting. Smartphones are the opposite, no flavor or smell at all."

"Well, not bad! But nobody has found the answer, and time is up. Ding!"

Keiji, opposite me, makes a startled movement. I notice a slight scar on his left cheekbone. The farmer takes his voice down a notch.

"In 1919, when the Spanish flu claimed the lives of most of the farmers in the village and of millions of people worldwide, my great-grandmother, a young girl at the time, is said to have saved her life by cutting an onion in half and placing it in her room. The onion was believed to have absorbed the virus."

With that, Mr. Mann instructs us to clear the table and do the washing up, then slips away with his basket hooked over an arm.

"Totally unverifiable," Helen says.

"And potentially dangerous—to believe an onion is a miracle remedy! What does that story have to do with smartphones, anyway?" Ali exclaims, exasperated.

"They're full of viruses," says Chayton.

"They *are* the virus," Stepan corrects him, uttering an entire sentence for the first time.

His voice is monotonous, but he's not so bad at our language after all.

"Yes, well, virus or no virus, it's only a machine," says Helen.

"So, what if it is? If an onion can act like a blotter on germs, maybe it can absorb the energy released by smartphones," Chayton ventures.

Ali, increasingly agitated, asks Kassandra to explain. But Ka is about to take her leave.

"The onion riddle got you to think about things from a different perspective. That's what matters . . ."

For a moment, Stepan doesn't appear to be totally bored, Keiji's eyes meet Kassandra's gaze, Chayton lets down his guard, Ali stops incessantly moving, and Helen isn't on display.

"To think outside of the box, to open new doors . . ."

As usual, her words float in the air and make a lasting impression, like words printed on paper.

In the meantime, one door will stay shut tonight—the door to the farmhouse. And the seventh chair remains empty.

PART TWO

FIRST CONNECTIONS

I wake up and the sun is already shining.

Through the slightly raised dormer, the soft caress of daylight spills into the room, its gentle and calming presence reminding me of where I am and why.

I take a moment to reacquaint myself with the lavender scent of the linen, the firmness of my pillow, with my bed and my surroundings. The night before, fatigue got the better of me. Now, I am taking it all in. No, it is not a dream; all of this is real. Surprisingly, for the first time in three months, I slept through the night.

I pause to listen, the way I always do when I open my eyes. When you stop formulating words for other people, the ones you keep inside take on more weight. Other senses become more acute. In my case, my senses of hearing and observation.

I listen to the morning air. There is not a noise in the house, except the far-off hum of a machine, perhaps a water heater or ventilation system. The sky through the dormer, blue-gray wisps of clouds on an orange-shaded backdrop, calls to me. I put one foot on the floor, then the other. The wood boards feel warm; they creak under my weight. I climb onto the chair and open the window.

A blast of cool air rushes into the room. I breathe it in and, with it, my new world. The sounds of chirping birds, of a creaking shutter, of bleating goats—I hear it all without even looking. A crowing rooster, too.

I stand on tiptoe. In the morning light, the courtyard seems narrower than the night before. The bottle-green pickup is parked in a different spot. Clumps of grass fleck the dirt-and-gravel yard. In the middle, a small flower garden sets off an old-fashioned well. A wooden bucket attached to a rope is wound around the crossbeam of its small pitched roof.

From my window, I can see two single-story structures adjoining our building and a chicken coop near the entrance of the yard: to my left, a façade with three solid wood doors and three six-pane farmhouse windows, and to my right, what looks like a stable.

It's still early. I'll have time for a quiet look around. After a quick shower, I slip on the regulation attire: blue pants and matching tank top. Ali's right, I do love that color. The fabric is soft and formfitting, and the honeycomb pattern of the waffle knit gives it lots of stretch. And a pair of comfortable earth-tone combat boots. The boots are sturdy. Why were we each given two pairs? As usual, the Keeper got everything just right. My clothes and shoes fit me to a tee. I grab my jacket from the chair where I'd left it the night before and exit the room.

As I make my way quietly downstairs, I realize I'm not the first one up. In the kitchen, the oven is on, and a basic but modern-looking coffee maker has been placed on the work-bench countertop. The air is filled with the fragrant scents of coffee and hot chocolate. Breakfast is set out on the long farmhouse table: jars of fruit preserves, artisanal cheeses on wood-bark trays, an enormous loaf of farmhouse bread cut into slices, and baskets piled high with other baked goods and fruit.

"Hello, Rae!" a strange voice says from out of nowhere. "I was expecting you sooner."

Confused, I look left and right. There's no one there.

"I was counting on you to boost the number of early risers in this place."

What! How does the voice know that I . . . ?

That's when I notice an elbow sticking out from an armrest.

"The early bird catches the worm, right?"

Someone is there, hidden by the high backrest of the old-fashioned chair—the chair that was empty last night!

"Well, don't look so surprised, Rae!"

Huh? How does he know I'm here? His back is turned. I walk closer, heart pounding, to stand in front of the chair . . . and in front of the last of the Seven.

"I'm here!"

He says it like I've been waiting for him my whole life. He appears to be about seventeen, and though I don't know a thing about him, I'm immediately intrigued.

"It's me. Alpha!"

He's wearing a blue outfit like mine, but in a deeper, darker hue. He has on his jacket, as well.

"I know you don't talk . . ."

Silence.

"And I respect your choice."

He is the first person not to have used the word "mute."

"Old Mr. Mann and I, we got here at five in the morning. He immediately set to work getting breakfast ready. I didn't wait for you. I was starving."

Though not exactly handsome, Alpha is one of those guys who has a certain allure.

"There's coffee over there. Help yourself!"

His magnetism is unsettling. I nearly spill my latte—less babyish than hot chocolate—when I set it down on the table.

"Hold on. This isn't a barn dance, you know. Girls on one side, boys on the other. Come sit over here instead."

It's impossible for me to say no to him already. As I sit down, I can detect the faint scent of aftershave.

"I'm from Abidjan. Do you know where the Ivory Coast is?" I nod. It's in West Africa.

"That said, even if you didn't, it'd be hard to guess wrong. With my skin color, I hardly pass for a Swede!"

Alpha reaches for the fruit basket and grabs a bunch of black grapes.

"See this? It's the real thing. One hundred percent Afro!" With a mischievous smile, he rubs his hair, tosses a grape in the air, and swallows it midflight. I look away, a little intimidated. I like his hair: shaved short on the sides with twists on top.

"Hey, don't take me too seriously, all right, sister?"

With his blend of good-natured cynicism and razor-edged lucidity, Alpha's quick on his toes. I can tell dancing with him is going to be tricky—even with a caller announcing the steps!

"Come on, have something to eat. We'll get along fine, you'll see. And if you're wondering why my English is so good, it's because I went to the international high school in Abidjan."

He smiles at me. This time, it's genuine—no trace of sarcasm. The guy may be complicated, but he's right, we probably will get along just fine.

Keiji joins us, quiet and polite as usual, followed by Stepan, who acts as if Alpha isn't there.

"You can sit over there, Stepan, the place you were sitting before Chayton asked you to move."

How did Alpha know about that, and how does he know our names?

"At the far end of the table, right?" Alpha asks.

"*Da*. Not part of the herd."

"How old are you?"

"Fourteen."

It's the first time he's answered a question. Up until now, no one was able to get more than a few words out of him. Stepan moves his chair away from Keiji and takes a piece of bread. He hollows it out with a finger and disposes small balls of dough on his plate.

"What about you? Where are you from?" Alpha continues.

"Japan," Keiji answers without lowering his gaze.

"Japan's a pretty big place."

"Village, far from urban Tokyo center: Omiya."

Miniature bowls of soup, rice, and pickled vegetables are laid out on the table in front of Keiji. Using a pair of chopsticks, he snaps up a vegetable and pops it into his mouth.

"Mann-san I polite to, but me permission keep ramen bowls."

"Is all of that from back home?"

"Yes, and provisions bought Mann-san."

Chopsticks are obviously second nature to Keiji. They fly over his plate, deftly plucking up morsels of food.

"Hey, you bunch of greedy guts!" bawls Chayton from the top of the stairs. "Leave anything for us?" Right behind him, Ali and Helen have just come out of Helen's bedroom.

Alpha's behavior changes straightaway. He leans back in his chair to prepare his response.

"Hey there, slacker," he says with exaggerated nonchalance.

In a few quick steps, Chayton plants himself squarely in front of Alpha.

"So, you're the new guy?"

Alpha's reaction is visceral. Face, neck, arms, and shoulders—everything is braced for battle.

"If arriving a few hours after you makes me a new guy, then yes."

He stands up, eyes hardening, his demeanor arrogant. He has a medium build and barely reaches Chayton's chin.

"In the chicken coop," Alpha articulates tersely, "there is a Brahma rooster and ten Rhode Island reds. The inn has twenty-three windows and twenty-four doors—ten to the outside and fourteen between rooms. There are five varieties of shrubs and seven perennials in the garden by the well. If anyone's interested in the names, shoot."

But nobody wants a lesson in botany.

"There are more important things in life than when you arrived. For example, Chayton, you didn't take a shower last night. You thought you'd do it in the morning, but you got up too late. You doused yourself in fragrance instead. Aventus by Creed. You put your hair in a ponytail so you wouldn't have to brush it. You hate that. And your right shoe pinches. The instep is too narrow."

"How . . . how does he know all that?" Chayton looks at me.

I gesture that I haven't the slightest idea. Alpha turns away from us and walks over to the girls to administer the final blow.

"You see, buddy, the important thing isn't *when* but *how* you make your entrance. Hi, Ali, nice to meet you!"

"Hi," Ali answers, shaking his extended hand. She smiles broadly, visibly pleased with his little number.

"Nice to meet you, too, Helen," Alpha says, keeping his distance. "I'm Alpha."

"Greetings, O mighty Alpha!" Helen replies.

"Well, I don't know about you, but I'm starving," Chayton announces.

With a defiant stare, he takes the middle chair opposite the newcomer—there are no seats left on Alpha's side of the table—hooking his muscular arms over the adjacent chair backs to mark his territory.

"Well, then, enjoy your breakfast, everyone!" Helen says cheerfully.

Her attempts to pacify the troops work. Ali fixes herself a coffee, then sits down across from Alpha and me, first pushing Chayton's arm away. Proud to have beautiful Helen in his camp, Chayton pops a bite-size muffin into his mouth while rapidly heaping a little of everything onto his plate. With Helen, it's just the opposite: she carefully arranges the food on her plate in separate areas. It reminds me of Chris and Kim in the high school cafeteria.

"How come you weren't here last night?" Ali asks.

"A minor setback," Alpha says in a dry, laconic manner.

"How old are you?"

"The same age as Helen, and you, too, soon."

Alpha, the juggler, is in command, expertly catching balls in midair, calculating the toss and trajectory, then returning them to the senders.

"Does anybody have any idea what the Keeper wants us to do, exactly?"

"Find seven keys lost chakras," Keiji answers. "They hidden in program."

"That much," Ali says, "I understood. Thanks. But what else?"

"The entire universe is made up of energy," Alpha replies, "and so are our bodies, even if we can't see it. It's scientific. And inside each of us, there are seven invisible energy wheels, the seven centers of our life-force energy."

"I don't really buy into that stuff," Helen says. "None of it's been proven."

"What about intuition? Haven't you ever had a hunch? Like when you can't stand someone—a girl, for example—when you've only just met her?"

I don't know whether Helen picked up on it, but it sounds like Alpha means her.

"Of course I have. And my intuition is often right."

"Well, then, there you have it. None of that is proven, but it does exist. The sixth chakra, located in the space between the eyebrows, is the center of our intuition. It is one of the three upper chakras and . . ."

"Sure, of course," Ali interrupts, "but no lectures, okay? We all read about that on the internet."

"Not me," Chayton counters, his mouth full. "Too busy with work in LA. Didn't have the time."

"Or the intellectual curiosity," Alpha scoffs. "But what else can you expect when you set the bar low?"

"I'll show you what you can do with that low bar of yours!"

He leaps to his feet, knocking his chair over. Alpha sips his coffee deliberately, as composed as Chayton is impulsive.

"Alcohol, weed, sex . . . I imagine you've dabbled in all of them. Even all three at once, huh?"

"What if I have! Why the hell do you care? And what does any of that have to do with the chakras?"

"Well, pal, let's just say that you must have used the internet for at least one of those activities! The fact that you didn't bother to do a little online research before coming here shows the degree of your involvement, that's all."

It shuts Chayton up.

"Well, internet or no," Ali intervenes, "I didn't find anything about the lost chakra keys."

"She's right," Helen concurs. "What exactly are these so-called missing keys?"

"They open doors," Chayton grumbles, righting his chair. "Ka said so last night. Like the keys in video games."

"So, you think the program the Keeper mentioned in his posts is some kind of VR simulator?" Ali asks.

"Yeah, with headsets or 3D glasses, or some state-of-the-art technology."

"I don't think it's that simple," Helen contradicts him, laying a hand on his forearm with a seductive smile to lessen the sting.

Chayton falls for her little number, much to Ali's annoyance.

"What about you, Alpha? What do you think?" Helen asks, unapologetically redirecting her feminine wiles. "You seem like you're more than just another pretty face . . ."

Helen is attracted to the newcomer, and she's not ashamed to show it. If that girl were a dessert, she'd be a molten lava cake—she oozes sex appeal.

"For the time being, nothing. Nothing at all," Alpha answers, dropping her like a hot potato to go get another coffee.

Tensions ease as we reach for seconds, get up for refills, and chat about this and that. Kassandra is greeted by a cheerful commotion when she enters from the yard.

"*She's* certainly not going to help matters," Alpha whispers to me, casting a furtive glance at Helen. "I wasn't expecting it. That girl is too much. Too much everything."

Visibly upset, he downs his espresso in a single gulp.

"I mean, it is all very well to take an aspirin when something hurts, but the pill conceals the source of the pain. You know what I mean?"

Not exactly, but I nod.

"You and I, we understand each other. You'll make sure I don't slip up, right?"

I nod again. After all, every alpha needs its beta. And yes, I do want to make sure Alpha's slipup isn't called Helen.

"You'll be my secret guardian angel, won't you?"

Yes.

LOGBOOK
INSTRUCTOR: KA
SEASON I

SEPTEMBER 22, 2035

Everything so far is going according to plan. Alpha's arrival has disrupted the fragile group dynamic created the day before. Knowing him, it's bound to happen again.

The road to self-discovery also emerges from the relationships we form with others. Some things we know at a glance, though we don't always realize it. We tend to lack confidence in our intuition and powers of deduction.

Awareness and confidence are key.

The Seven are here to explore the pathways of their instincts, ideas, and intuitions. At times, they will be led in the right direction; at other times, they won't. But in those cases, they will come out even stronger. That's why Head Instructor Shepherd and I need to keep out of their way. The less we tell them, the freer they will be—to shape their minds on their own and to forge stronger bonds.

Ali seems to have found her feet with Helen and Rae. A trio of girls is often dangerous. But that is not a bad thing. Especially for Rae.

As for the group of boys, what divides them is commensurate with their chemistry.

Earth, water, fire, air: the four elements are united.

Now, we just have to hope the program isn't too wide of the mark.

"Come on, Chosen Ones."

Kassandra's hazel eyes seem to have softened into shades of honey. Her smooth coppery locks reflect the same steady energy that beats in her veins, ready to burst into action and come to our rescue in the event of an emergency. She is wearing another of her timeless pale-colored dresses.

"It's time we got started."

We've already cleared the table and done the dishes under the watchful eye of our she-wolf mentor. Apart from Stepan, in a world of his own, as seems to be usual, we all did our part: Helen and Keiji redoubling their efforts to be polite; Ali making jokes about the minimalist configuration of the fridge; and me trying my hardest to place the containers of milk, butter, and jam in their designated areas. Alpha and Chayton even went so far as to wash the dishes together, although their show of cooperation didn't fool anyone—especially not Kassandra, who kept a close or distant eye on them the whole time.

We all gather outside in the farmyard, except for Stepan, who remains behind, his purple jacket buttoned up to his chin. Kassandra approaches him. We have no idea where he is from.

He refused to tell us. His slicked-back blond hair reminds me of a 1950s KGB agent. My father adored Cold War espionage stories and occasionally took me to see old movies at the film institute.

"Come on, Stepan, you come outside, too. Just like everyone else."

"Nyet, not like everyone else," he objects, reluctantly exiting the building.

Our group now complete, Kassandra throws open the stable shutters and door. Light and air pour in, and the stench of goat pours out.

"Oh," Helen exclaims, hurrying forward. "It's a goat shed!"

All eyes are on her, except Alpha's. He is intentionally ignoring her.

"They're absolutely adorable!"

Inside, we find a row of pens divided by wooden fences. Each contains roughly a half dozen goats that draw near us, inquiringly, tossing backward-curving horns. Some are light brown, others dark brown with a black line down the center of their backs, and others white.

"I love animals!" Helen exclaims.

A long hay-filled trough runs the entire width of the shed. A layer of straw covers the ground. Each pen contains a billy goat, distinguishable by its longer beard and wider horn span.

"My mother never let us have a dog or a cat. 'Our apartment's too small,' she'd say, or 'I don't want all that cat hair everywhere.' She hated it when—" Helen breaks off, swallowing hard. She kneels and strokes the head of a white goat that gladly accepts the attention.

"Hey, look!" Ali says.

At the far end of the shed, there is a pen reserved for baby goats and their mothers. With Helen and Ali in the lead, we all walk over to take a closer look. Even Stepan appears mildly interested.

"Look how tiny they are!"

The little creatures bleat and leap about as we lean over the fence to pet them. The more timorous stick close to the mother goats' sides; the others come up to us, intrigued.

"Hey, look!" Chayton bursts out laughing. "The big golden-brown one over there in the corner. The one that isn't moving. It looks just like Stepan!"

Quite unexpectedly, Stepan joins in with an oddly re-sounding, riotous laugh.

"And the big dark-haired one over there," Alpha shoots back, "is Chayton!"

This time, we all burst out laughing.

"And this one is called Keiji!" A deep baritone emerges out of nowhere. The goats scatter, revealing a broad-shouldered man in his early fifties stretched out on the ground.

"He's the newest addition to the family." The man is lying in the straw with his fingers laced behind his head and his ankles crossed as if sunbathing. A tiny goat is nibbling at his salt-and-pepper hair.

"Say hello to our friends, Keiji," he says to the delicate creature. A linen shirt conceals the man's broad shoulders, a black cloth sash tied around his waist. There is an aura of quiet strength about him that immediately commands respect.

"You see the white one over there? The one that is nursing? That one's Helen." He stands up, the baby goat under one arm. His serious expression, strong jawline, and finely lined brow sharply contrast his disheveled hair.

"And that one over there running about everywhere," Ali joins in, "I bet it's named after me!"

"You guessed right!"

The man comes over to greet us. The skin beneath his stubbly beard is deeply tanned, his lips are dry and cracked, and a slight scarring under the nose, perhaps a childhood cleft palate repair? I've read about those.

"That's so sweet to have named them after us," Helen says in a lilting voice. "How old are they?"

"Six weeks."

"Six . . ." With a sharp intake of breath, her delicate features stiffen—even her freckles seem to freeze—and the translucent skin around her eyebrows takes on a fleeting tinge of pink. Ali and I give each other a knowing look. Six weeks ago, her mother hanged herself.

"So, who else is left?" Ali asks with a forced note of cheerfulness. "Right, Rae and Alpha . . ." Her diversion is successful. All eyes turn to the two of us. "Between that black one in the middle and the skinny little thing over there, it's a no-brainer!"

Behind us, Kassandra breaks into a round of enthusiastic applause as the stern-eyed goat keeper plants himself directly in front of Keiji, compelling him to meet his eye.

"Take good care of him. Take good care of Keiji-goat," he says, thrusting the little goat into the timid boy's arms. They really do look alike!

"Are you master?" Keiji asks point-blank.

Silence follows. Naturally, we were all wondering the same thing.

"Well," Chayton adds, with his usual heavy-handedness, "are you the Keeper or aren't you?" By way of reply, the man opens the pen gate and motions for us to enter. Our goats come running over.

"You will each take care of your namesake," he says. I pick up my scraggly little creature. I can feel Rae-goat's protruding ribs as I gently stroke her. The other goats all bleat noisily, but mine remains silent. Our eyes meet, and we look at each other intently.

"Food, water, exercise. Goats need a lot of fresh grass. Our goat milk produces the best cheese in town."

I look over at Alpha. He is sitting in the straw scratching the head of his namesake kid—all black, aside from a spot of white on one shoulder. He is smiling like a little boy, though like he said himself, he isn't a child anymore. You can sense it. Something inside is broken. But his angelic features, mysteriously stamped by impenetrable suffering, are undeniably appealing to me.

"Nyet," Stepan protests weakly. "Not here to milk goats."

"Well, Ka, then you tell me," Chayton blurts out, his patience obviously wearing thin, "is he the Keeper or isn't he?"

"This is Head Instructor Shepherd," Kassandra says at last.

"So, he not the master . . ."

"He is and he isn't, Keiji. He is a judo master, a fifth dan black belt. He will be your instructor."

"Instructor of what?" Stepan grumbles, relentlessly negative. "Me, I say nyet judo, nyet physical labor, nyet milking goats."

"Who said it had anything to do with that?" Kassandra replies. "There are as many kinds of instruction as there are types of people."

And with that, she slips away.

"Personally, I don't get it," Chayton says with his usual plainspokenness. "Are we going to train or aren't we?"

"It's really not so hard to understand," Alpha quips. But before another quarrel can break out, Instructor Shepherd holds up a hand. We all fall silent at once. The baby goats return to their mothers.

"This way, please." He closes the gate to the pen and walks to the back of the shed. Suddenly—how, I don't know, it all happened so quickly—the wall vanishes.

"Oh!" Helen exclaims.

Chayton, unruffled, gives a low catcall as if he's seen a pretty girl.

"A sliding wall. Not a bad trick," Alpha acknowledges.

I can't see anything beyond the opening. It's too dark.

"Come with me. The Keeper is waiting for you."

10

The goat shed is a front.

Behind the sliding wall, there is an enormous circular room with white paneled walls. There are no windows or doors, and not a living soul inside. We follow Instructor Shepherd into the room. In the middle, there is a large round mat bordered with colored cushions. I half expect Chayton or Alpha to make a crack, or Keiji to shoot off a round of questions. Instead, we all stand there expectantly . . . waiting to meet the Keeper.

The head instructor removes his shoes and socks, walks to the middle of the mat, and, hands at his sides, performs a judoka bow.

"Welcome to Flyfold, your training room."

He invites us to sit down on the cushions. Alpha, with what seems to be his usual ease, is already barefoot. He returns the judoka greeting. Ali's socks are mismatched, one blue, the other green. Unsurprisingly, she left the black ones that came with her outfit behind. The ones she is wearing give her outfit a personal touch.

"Why waste time rolling them into pairs!" she whispers, mussing up the angled slant of my bangs with a warm and cheerful puff of air. Then she pats Alpha on the back—he flashes a grin in return—helps Helen take off her second boot, and sits on the yellow cushion that matches her outfit.

Stepan, as a matter of course, withdraws to the opposite side of the mat, and Keiji sits down next to me. For some reason, he's been seeking out my silent presence all morning. Helen, in the meantime, nonchalantly sets out for Alpha's side of the circle but redirects her trajectory under his withering stare, settling lithely alongside Ali on her cushion, instead.

Leaning her head of braided ginger locks against the radiant Ali's shoulder—a study in orange on yellow—Helen is unable to hide the intensity of her emotions. Like a thwarted child in a woman's body, she puts a thumb to her mouth and quickly removes it.

"It's time to get started," Instructor Shepherd announces.

He sits back on his heels with a solemn expression; a projector and screen drop from the ceiling, and unsettling music fills the air—violin, xylophone, harp—mixed with weird and wonderful silences.

Welcome!

The distorted metallic-sounding voice is devoid of human warmth. An image appears on the screen six feet above the ground.

Welcome, the Seven Chosen Ones!

A shadow . . . We can only see a silhouette . . .

For your own safety, and for the safety of the program, I am unable to reveal my identity, but that, I assure you, does not matter. What matters from now on is you.

Our disappointment is palpable. The Keeper will remain faceless.

The young people of today will be an inspiration to future generations. You are all at a pivotal age, an age of limitless possibilities when minds and doors can be opened. I have been working on Spirit Era for years. Not only does

the forecast have a ninety-nine percent degree of reliability, but thanks to the autonomy it has developed from the Three Laws of Robotics, it is able to provide solutions. The program is the only way to prevent the end-of-the-world prediction from coming true.

The message is recorded. I am completely absorbed when—*I am ready for my mission*—someone else's voice pops into my head!

Shisho has been preparing me for years, I won't let him down.

No, not that! Not now!

If the Keeper is the master, then why doesn't he address the Seven Chosen Ones directly?

This time, I have Keiji's thoughts in my head. It's crazy! Plus, his English is perfect, with no accent whatsoever!

Insanity, according to Albert Einstein, is doing the same thing over and over and expecting different results. Drawing on data from the entire pool of human knowledge, Spirit Era has concluded that history is an eternal and exponential cycle of repetition. For centuries, men have made the same mistakes over and over, massively destroying their fellow human beings and, today, the environment. In light of this, the program cannot hand us the solution on a silver platter.

In the monastery, too, Keiji's thoughts continue, *nothing is served on a silver platter.*

On one hand, there is the material world—the physical components of everyday life that are entirely accessible, tangible, and, for the most part, functional. This aspect of life, I call Materia. On the other, is the spiritual dimension— the expression of the soul, abstract, mysterious, and at times even frowned on before being investigated. This element I call Spiritua. These two different dimensions are

complementary—not opposed. But today, they have become unbalanced.

I am going to have to be careful.

The program holds the key to reestablishing balance. It has generated virtual immersive microcosms, seven mantras re-creating the seven most probable forms of apocalypse, drawing on scientific research and the seven great afflictions of humanity: surplus, lust, anger, greed, envy, pride, and sloth. Each scenario contains a life-force key capable of averting the catastrophe. With the end of life on Earth predicted for July 27, 2037, that leaves you exactly twenty-two months and five days. You have seven seasons, one key per season, to find the seven keys.

They probably aren't telling us everything...

Find the seven lost keys of the chakras, my Chosen Ones, and the world, like you, will enter a new age of maturity. It will evolve. Real change starts from within. The sensors I've integrated into your uniforms will allow your quest for the first key to be broadcast around the world, live, two hours a day, for an entire week. In terms of safety, there is nothing to worry about. Spirit Era continuously modifies its internal security system, so it is impossible to hack.

Who among us have true hearts? Are there any false brothers?

Your mentor, Kassandra, and your head instructor, the Shepherd, will teach you the fundamental laws for exploring the first of the seven worlds. As I said before, the program is unlike anything you have ever experienced. Becoming a part of it is difficult, and leaving it, even harder...

The weird and unsettling music comes on again.

I could reveal everything now, but you will each have

to experience it for yourselves. **Your training period will last two months, followed by seven days in the program's immersive VR microcosm. Seven days, two hours a day, to find the key to the first chakra.**

And the voice concludes:

Good luck to you all!

The projector and screen retract into the ceiling as Instructor Shepherd performs a seated bow.

"The term 'mantra' is derived from Sanskrit," our teacher explains. "It is a sacred utterance, an invocation according to Buddhist and Hindu tradition believed to have spiritual powers. The mantra 'aum' is the sacred symbol of unity. The sound is chanted in yoga to stimulate the body's vital energy and to create a sense of unity with other yogis. In mantra therapy, physical vibrations generated in a diseased organ make it possible for the healing process to begin. Drawing on these lessons, the program has developed seven mantras to heal our diseased world."

An insidious shiver runs down my spine, especially since I now know for sure—a new voice has taken up residence inside my head!

"We are going to begin the training course right away," our instructor announces.

He asks us to stand up and form a large circle. I put a little space between Keiji and myself, hoping his voice will leave me alone.

Why is she going over there? Is she uncomfortable around me, too? I like Rae.

Well, other than offending him, I don't seem to have accomplished much.

Shisho was right. Don't become attached to them. Think of them only as teammates.

No, Keiji, you're wrong! Not getting close to people doesn't help. And believe me, I tried. I tried distancing myself from

Mia and Joyce, from Chris and Kim, and it doesn't work. So, I return to his side, a faint smile on my lips. He returns my smile.

"Any volunteers?"

Alpha springs eagerly to his feet and enters the circle, determined to beat Chayton to the punch.

I like Alpha, too . . . Um, I mean, he could be a useful partner, at any rate, sounds Keiji's voice inside my head. I have a headache. I put my hand to my forehead. It's overheating like a connected unit. The Shepherd gives me an inquisitive look as Alpha turns to talk to him.

"I do Kwaloklaï karate. Have you heard of it?"

"Yes, it's a martial art from the Ivory Coast."

If only my brother . . .

Enough! I'm tired. And Ka said I should not let prowlers lay claim to my silence.

. . . had been a little like Alpha . . .

Listen, Keiji, I'm telling you nicely. The shelter is closed!

"I'm the national junior champion," Alpha boasts.

"Hmm . . . Right . . ." Stepan isn't interested in the least. He sits there, staring into space.

"Are you going to divide us into groups, since I'm already an expert?" asks Alpha. "Will I be getting private lessons?" Rather than answering, the instructor turns to Keiji.

"Would you please come into the circle with Alpha?"

The boy bashfully complies.

"Rei!"

"What . . . ," Alpha stammers. "What's that?"

"It's Japanese. Bow, please." The Shepherd is the kind of person whose authority is best left unchallenged. We look on in amazement as our two comrades greet each other.

"Hajime! Begin!" I can't believe it. The two are going to compete.

All at once, their hands and feet fly through the air.

Forward and backward. They jump, throw, punch, and kick. We all stare in silence, dumbfounded. Against all expectations, they are equally matched.

"Yihaaa!" Keiji bellows, his leg sweeping Alpha's out from underneath him. In spite of his size, the small Japanese boy throws his opponent off-balance. Alpha springs to his feet like a jack-in-the-box, stunned. The opponents exchange bows, then bow to the instructor. Keiji returns discreetly to the circle without further ado, respectful of the loser.

"Lesson number one, strength and humility are inseparable."

Alpha lowers his head sheepishly.

"I recognize the value of competition, but one must not attach too much importance to it. It is a comparison at a given time and place. It answers the question 'What am I worth?' But it does not teach us much about ourselves. 'Who am I?' is the first question we must ask ourselves."

The instructor walks over to one of Flyfold's paneled wall sections and slides it open. He removes a satchel from a concealed set of shelves, slides the panel shut again, and distributes the contents: we each receive a mirror the size of a sheet of standard letter paper.

"To begin, you must plumb the depths of your consciousness. In this exercise, which I call the Psyche Maneuver, you will stare into your own eyes until you see your true self."

"Uh, that's today's exercise?"

"It is, Chayton. For the next two months, besides basic combat techniques, you will be learning about how to best defend yourself. But not just on the mat—in life."

As usual, it is strange to see my reflection in a mirror. And even stranger to stare into my own eyes. I have never done anything like this before.

"Discovering your true self—that is the first step."

11

"What about you guys? Did you see a lot of weird stuff, too?" Alpha asks in a hushed tone, looking at each of us in turn, his silhouette sketched in charcoal.

Earlier, in the middle of the night while I was fast asleep, he rapped lightly on my door. Still half asleep, I stumbled to the hallway, where Ali, Keiji, and Alpha were waiting for me, giggling nervously.

"Secret meeting!" Alpha whispered.

It didn't take much more convincing for me to tiptoe downstairs with them, pajamas still warm and my blue jacket thrown over my shoulders. Getting a shutter open was easy—less creaky than the barn door. Climbing into the goat shed silently and without laughing was harder. And slipping into the pen without the baby goats and mothers bleating, almost miraculous.

"Did you see anything bizarre when we did that Psyche Maneuver?" Alpha asks, his kid pressed up against him. "I saw some stuff I wasn't expecting."

We were sitting near the trough. Each of our baby goats

had joined us. The other three didn't stir. I was sitting cross-legged with Skinny nestled in my lap.

"What kind of stuff?" Ali asks.

From the sound of her voice, I can tell his comment struck a chord.

"At first, I just kind of focused on my irises. They may well be brown, but there are tons of colors in them, streaks like tiny shards of glass."

"Iris like DNA," Keiji says. "One special per person. In monastery, Shisho read iris for health."

"What else?" Ali asks Alpha.

"Then, I could see my face reflected in my eyes."

"I saw flames in mine," Ali says. "They flickered, then formed indistinct shapes. And then I saw my own silhouette. What does it mean? That I'm going to die in a fire?"

"Come off it, Ali! Anyhow, we all end up dying of something."

"Yeah, except being burned alive would be a horrible way to die."

"Fire not horrible," Keiji interrupts. "In Buddhism, fire inside. Heart is hearth, and flame, mastered self."

Light streams in from the courtyard through the partly opened shutter, revealing a tribal tattoo on Alpha's arm. It's the first time I've seen him without his jacket on. From shoulder to forearm, the white ink of the tattoo contrasts his dark skin. It's on the same side as his goat's spot.

"And the Keeper," Ali bursts out. "What is he the master of? We don't know a thing about him. Maybe he's some kind of a creep who has hidden cameras in our bedrooms. Or a serial killer, or a human trafficker who deals in children!" Her she-goat gives a start.

"Anger, bad counselor," Keiji whispers, stroking his baby goat, who is as calm as he is.

"Knock it off! Your words of wisdom are starting to get on my nerves!"

"Not wrath guide your choice, Shisho said. Because choice is guide."

Ali's eyes flash fire. I half expect her to lunge at him.

"He's only thirteen," Alpha says to calm her.

"Exactly. So why did you ask him to come?"

Alpha was clearly taken with Keiji the minute he set eyes on him. No telling why. And since their encounter on the tatami, I could see he both liked him and respected him.

"Age has nothing to do with it, we proved that earlier." Alpha is referring to Keiji's victory. I know he considers the two of them to be on equal footing.

"Speaking of which, what kind of karate do you do, Keiji? It's not *Shōtōkan-ryū*," asked Alpha.

"*Wadō-ryū*: 'school path of peace.' Better avoid than block," Keiji says.

"Yeah, right. But shoto-whatever or wado-thingy, he's still just a little kid!" said Ali.

Then, for once, Keiji raises his voice.

"You are my age, brother. But not better than me, you!"

"What's that got to do with it?" Ali asked.

"Shisho say age like envelope, empty. It's stamp that tell direction to take. And letter inside, deep truth."

"Who the heck is this Shisho of yours?" asked Ali.

"Master of Keiji. I live with monks since six years old. Learn everything at monastery."

"You didn't live with your family?" Alpha asks.

"No. One child only in Japan official circle. If first child is boy especially." He lowers his voice with a bitter note. "Honorable mother was old. I am child of shame."

"Well, our parents are responsible, not us," Ali concedes. "You didn't ask anyone for anything."

"My brother . . . ," Keiji goes on, absently running a finger over the thin scar on his left cheekbone. "Brother inherit nursery, the bonsais. Family tradition. Shisho register Keiji with program. Good for evolution of world. My honorable parents not informed."

Outside, a muffled creaking startles us. We remain silent, hearts racing, listening carefully for the slightest sound.

"Okay," Ali whispers at last. "We'll have to ask the others what they think about this whole Keeper business."

"Not a good idea. I don't trust Helen and Chayton," Alpha says.

"It wasn't a question. I say we need to stick together."

"And I say you're a little pigheaded!"

Like every alpha, he hates not being in charge. Something dark and hidden, like a snake in winter, crawls out of its lair and flashes in the depths of his eyes.

"We already have a moron, a nymphomaniac, and a mental case, not to mention a garden gnome and a mute girl. The only thing missing is a donkey!"

A blast of cold air sends a shiver down my spine. I hold Skinny tight. The rush of air has apparently roused Alpha, too, who jumps up, jostling his kid a little. The creature begins to bleat.

"You're not going to start, too, are you!" he says, stepping over the fence in a rage. "Talk about a team of misfits!"

A few seconds later, he vanishes in the night. Alpha's goat goes back to its mother, its ears drooping.

"Who the hell does he think he is?" Ali is furious. "He's not the boss!"

"For first secret meeting, I not expect that," Keiji concurs.

My goat is suddenly restless. Some of the other baby goats begin to bleat, and, in a pen toward the back, a billy goat starts pacing nervously. It is time to leave.

As I hurry across the chilly farmyard behind Ali and Keiji, I can still feel the sting of Alpha's words. He called me a mute. Even worse, he called me a mute *girl*.

I didn't expect that, either. Not from him.

I am afraid.

This morning at breakfast, the ill feelings of the night before have vanished. The secret goat shed gang acts like everything's normal, Helen and Chayton share private jokes, and even Stepan loosens up a little.

We talk about anything and everything, pour each other orange juice, and offer to make more coffee and tea. The atmosphere is deceptively laid-back as if we are at summer camp. Bursts of laughter fill the air, and free smiles are distributed all around, especially by Alpha, who grins so brightly he could be in a toothpaste ad.

"Take it easy with the coffeepot!" Mr. Mann grumbles. "I'm the one who has to clean up after you."

What he calls "coffeepot" is actually a coffee machine. Mr. Mann, in his worn leather apron, is busy doing ten things at once: peeling vegetables, wiping surfaces, watching a saucepan on the stovetop, preparing a casserole in a Dutch oven, making mint lemonade . . .

"You're right," says Helen as she heats milk for her coffee.

With her sweetest smile, she puts down her cup and wipes up the spilled milk.

"Do you have any children, Mr. Mann?"

"Yup."

"So, you're married?"

"I was," he answers reluctantly, brow furrowed.

Helen doesn't press the point.

"Do your children live on the farm with you?"

"My daughter, Anais, does."

"She does? Why haven't we seen her yet? How old is she?"

He snorts gruffly, slamming the oven door and turning on the tap. Usually sparing with words, he seems vexed.

"Have you been working here for a long time?" Alpha asks, angling for information, in turn.

"I've been working here my whole life. The farm belonged to my parents."

"So, this is your house we're staying in?"

"Yes and no." His short answers are infuriating.

"In any event, Instructors Shepherd and Ka aren't from here. How long have you known them?" But you can't put one over on guys like Mr. Mann. Visibly annoyed, he shuts the faucet and turns off the oven and stovetop.

"Listen up, all of you. When you're done with breakfast, I want this place spick-and-span." He abruptly turns on his heels and heads to the exit, the scent of stale tobacco trailing after him. "If everything isn't shipshape, I'm going to call it a day, and you'll have to make do with undercooked half rations."

"Good job!" Chayton explodes after the farmer has left.

Alpha lets it go—it's apparently no time for a fight—and begins clearing the table instead. The rest of us promptly pitch in, wielding brooms, mops, sponges, and towels. Stepan alone stands idly by, back in his own world as usual. Is he really that disconnected from reality? Or is he the most calculating of us all, like Alpha thinks he is?

"Damsel Helen!" Chayton exclaims, pretending to sheathe an imaginary broomstick-sword. "Your beauty today is irresistible."

"Kind thanks, Sir Knight!" the damsel replies with a studied wipe of the dish towel.

Knee bent, our hero kisses the lady's proffered hand. The pair bursts into laughter. Ali is clearly irritated by their sudden display of complicity, and even Stepan casts a sidelong glance. Everyone is wondering what's up with them. Not me—I know.

After our late-night escapade, I couldn't sleep a wink. Gazing at the stars through my dormer window, I lay in bed brooding over the showdown with Alpha, trying not to think. I wanted to empty my head, to forget Chayton's voice and Keiji's. To send Alpha's spiteful words flying to the back of the barnyard with a good kick.

At daybreak, I heard a noise in the corridor. Opening the door, I saw Helen tiptoeing back to her room—my inner voice had warned me she was a slippery one—in a skimpy nightgown, slippers in hand. She had just left Chayton's room. Smiling, she put a finger to her lips. No need to say more: we both knew her secret was safe with me.

So, nothing from last night's confrontation remained. Helen and Chayton's one-night stand, or perhaps more if the two hit it off, and Alpha's false debonair attitude—everything was back on track. On the surface, that is, because I could clearly hear the time bomb ticking away.

It's crazy what you can see if you take the time to look. I mean, really look. You can see things about people they haven't even figured out themselves. And it's the small details that lead to the greatest discoveries. That's why I am afraid. Ever since I caught sight of that dark and disquieting something lurking in Alpha's eyes, I can't help it. I'm afraid it is going to resurface.

"Are you all right?" Keiji asks as the others chatter away.

I nod. He stands there, staring at my bangs—or so it seems. I finally realize he's not looking at my bangs. He's looking at me.

"My neighbor in Omiya. You remind me of her. Not see Aiko since I leave, seven years ago."

A faraway look comes into his eyes. His stance—even straighter than usual—and choked voice tell me Keiji cares about her. I'd gladly ask a few questions, but seeing as I don't speak . . .

"Not return to honorable parents. When I will be fourteen, my choice—stay with Shisho, be monk and never marry, or leave and have new life from zero."

I am sorry for him.

"Aiko give me two good-luck bamboo. She say, 'When bamboo stay together, we stay together.' They in my room, always."

"Look!" Ali says. "There's a note on the fridge."

"You're right," Helen concurs, "there is."

"It's from Ka. 'Meet me in the barn for your first class,'" Ali reads, then adds incredulously, "She's going to give us our lesson in the barn!"

"What else were you expecting?" Chayton answers. "Our mentor is incapable of doing anything like everyone else!"

Outside, the air is warm. There is not a cloud in the sky. A barn made of vertical weathered boards sits behind the farmhouse at the far end of the yard. Its sheet metal roof and the narrow ladder running the length of the façade are stained with rust.

"It's a beautiful day!" Kassandra greets us.

Standing in the middle of the barn, she is radiant in her long camel-colored dress. The floor is almost three-quarters covered with stacked bales of straw. Tools and farm equipment are piled in one corner.

"I know, I know. This isn't exactly what you were expecting." She cuts to the chase. We all know she's referring to the Keeper.

"If it makes you feel any better, no one knows who he is. Not even us. So, don't waste your time with wild theories."

Could Ka possibly have found out about our secret meeting? Maybe, maybe not, but four of the Seven Chosen studiously avoid meeting her eye.

"Head Instructor Shepherd and I were each contacted a year ago to work on the program. We quickly understood its potential and believed its predictions. I am an AI engineer and a computer scientist with a PhD in philosophy. I have published a number of papers in scientific journals. Instructor Shepherd is a former US intelligence operative who decided to leave everything behind a dozen or so years ago to live completely off the grid. I don't know anything else about him. Other than the fact that he is as determined as I am to do everything in his power to ensure our project's success in the limited amount of time we've been given. And the protection of its founder. The two go hand in hand."

Looking up, I see multiple tiers of lofts connected by rickety ladders. Some contain animal feed and burlap bags. Others are full of junk or are completely empty.

"Can you imagine what would happen if Spirit Era fell into the wrong hands? The ability to predict when and where future natural disasters will occur is tantamount to knowing the economic and political futures of the nations of the world. Individuals who refute the 7/27/37 apocalypse would consider it to be a source of unprecedented power."

"Exactly," Ali counters. "Whether you believe the end-of-the-world prophecy or not, it seems pretty strange to entrust such an important mission to seven teenagers!"

"Yeah, especially since we have nothing in common," Alpha adds. "We don't know each other; we haven't been trained for this. So, why us?"

"And why didn't we get to choose the color of our uniforms?" Helen complains, on a more personal note. "Can I change mine?"

"No," Ka answers.

"It's not fair! The others all got the colors they like. But I'm dressed like a carrot."

"The colors they need, not like," Ka clarifies.

"But it must be a mistake. I hate orange!"

"The time has come to put certain wrongs right. You guessed correctly. The colors were not assigned by chance."

Kassandra knows about that, too? We didn't tell anyone about the conversation in my room the night we arrived. What's going on? Could there be hidden microphones everywhere?

At the sight of Helen's crestfallen face, Ka attempts to reassure her: Helen is not the only one who needs to reconnect with a greater truth.

She invites us to sit down wherever we want. Stepan climbs the ladder to the first hayloft and perches on the edge, legs dangling over empty space. Alpha hoists himself onto an old, partially dismantled tractor. Chayton takes two pieces of strawberry-flavored gum from his pocket, unwraps the first piece, pops it into his mouth, then offers Helen the second. She turns it down. Slipping the gum into the fair damsel's jacket pocket, he goes and lies down on the top bale of a haystack, using it like a recliner. Helen and Ali take up residence nearby, on bales placed directly on the ground. Keiji and I do the same, but on perches behind them, a little higher up.

"Let's start with the heart of the matter—the chakras." You could have heard a pin drop. "A mystery dating back to the early traditions of Hinduism. To this day, little is known about them and, in most cultures, nothing at all."

"Not mine."

"True, Keiji. The East has a greater understanding of the life force represented by the seven chakras—the wheels of energy that radiate inside us like suns."

"How do we know they exist?" Chayton asks.

"From a purely logical point of view, we don't, nor has anything proven the contrary. Science, it is true, enables us to understand, to explain the physical world and the interactions of various processes. But science, with its detached objectivity, does not indicate the path to follow. Ethical values, such as justice, freedom, responsibility, honesty, and respect, are defined by the laws of morality and philosophy."

Ali can't sit still. She jumps to her feet on her bale of hay.

"From a historical point of view, ideas and practices involving our radiant inner energy, or the so-called subtle body, have existed for centuries, both in the East and the West, in India, with the study of prana, and in China with qi. Scientists and mathematicians, such as Helmont in the seventeenth century, have evoked the existence of vital energy, an immaterial, gaseous element found in the natural world. A pure vital spirit that permeates all living bodies. Studies over the centuries, the world over, all point to the same thing: energy, the very essence of the chakras, is the source of universal life."

"I don't know. For me, seeing is believing!"

"Material things, Chayton, including money, are neither a hunger to alleviate nor an end in themselves."

"Maybe so, but in the meantime, you can't deny it—money and sex make the world go 'round!"

"Yes, their necessity is undeniable. The program only intends to change the place we attribute to them, and the use we make of them. I'd like to tell you a story."

Ali sits down again, all ears, lightly swaying like a metronome.

"Many years ago in a faraway land, three earthenware jars representing the world—material, emotional, and spiritual—were entrusted to a village chief. Day after day, the village elder carefully filled the enormous clay jars, ensuring happiness and prosperity for the village: in the first, he placed coins, small gifts, and fruit from the harvest; in the second, love, joy, sadness, and anger, along with the other raw emotions; lastly, in the third, he placed the unexplainable. The jars representing the world were properly balanced. But one night, the village was attacked, and the jars were stolen. The leader of the gang of thieves knew the value of the earthenware jars and began to fill the first with the money, food, and goods he had amassed. He poured all his repressed emotions into the second jar—his feigned joy, his possessive love of women, his obsession with himself. But the third jar—the spiritual one—he neglected to fill. Why bother with the unexplainable? After several weeks, the three earthenware vessels had completely changed. The first jar was never satisfied, emptying itself like a bottomless pit as soon as it was filled until the robber had poured into it all his riches. A crack appeared in the second jar, and the best craftsmen in the land were powerless to prevent it from growing. Under the weight of insincerity, it eventually shattered. The thief grew increasingly bad-tempered and self-obsessed, eventually cutting himself off from the rest of the world, including his wives, children, and friends. As for the third jar, deprived of all spiritual nourishment, it dried up and crumbled, and blew away in the wind. The robber died soon after, and his bones, like the clay of the broken jar, turned to dust and were dispersed by the wind—along with the robber's soul."

The end of Ka's story is greeted by silence.

"Now, I'd like each of you to close your eyes."

Soft music, the sounds of bells and panpipes, fills the immensity of the barn. More hidden speakers? I don't know about the others, but I'm dying to know what's coming next.

"Relax, let your mind fall quiet, let your thoughts fall silent and wander. Everything can be seen through the prism of your chakras. I would like you to visualize them."

I instinctively picture a staircase descending within my body.

"The chakras are part of our forgotten inner landscapes. The first one, at the base of the spine, is the root of our tree of life. It is red in color. The symbol of the root chakra is a lotus with four petals. It is the energetic center of survival and physical well-being. It allows us to feel grounded in ourselves and in the world. Its element is the earth."

Chayton gives a nervous giggle that quickly fades.

"The second chakra is located below the navel. Orange in color, it is the sacral or creative chakra. It is a source of creative expression, the center of sexual energy and reproduction, of relationships with ourselves and with others. Like a six-petal lotus, it is the door to our emotions. It is associated with the element of water."

I hear Helen, sitting right in front of me, breathe in sharply.

"The third chakra, the solar plexus chakra, is the chakra of fulfillment, symbolized by a ten-petal lotus. Its color is yellow, its element fire. Through it, we radiate strength and ambition."

"Like an inner sun," Ali comments with enthusiasm.

For the time being, I keep my eyes closed, happy to soak up the sounds.

"The fourth chakra, or heart chakra, is situated in the heart region. It is a green lotus with twelve petals and is characterized by generosity, compassion, and love. It is the seat of balance and acts as a mediator between the three lower chakras, which regulate our instinctive physical abilities, and the three upper chakras, which govern our intellectual and spiritual abilities. Its element is air."

Around me, I notice our slow, deep breathing has become synchronized. I am in a trancelike state.

"The fifth chakra is the throat chakra, a lotus with sixteen petals. Its color is blue. It embodies the cycle of giving and receiving and is linked with self-expression. It is our center of verbal, physical, and mental communication. Its element is ether."

As I listen to Kassandra's voice, I picture the oblong petals of a sapphire-blue daisy dancing in my windpipe, massaging my vocal cords like a warm caress. I am overcome with the urge to sing.

"The sixth chakra, the third eye, is indigo blue. Symbolized by a lotus with two petals subdivided into forty-eight parts, it is located between the eyebrows, slightly above. It can be likened to the two hemispheres of the brain: on the right, intuition, and on the left, intelligence. It is linked to intellect and the seat of intuition. The third eye is the door to our sixth sense."

I haven't heard a sound near the dismantled tractor since Kassandra began talking. I glance over at Alpha. He's in the exact same position, sitting cross-legged on the rusty hood. His eyes are closed, his expression calm. His face looks perfectly smooth as if he is smiling within. I want to keep looking at him, but Ka will notice.

"The seventh chakra is the crown chakra. It is purple, a lotus with a thousand petals, and it is located at the crown of the head. It is the center of spirituality, enlightenment, and cosmic consciousness. It facilitates the inward and outward flow of energy on the top branch of the tree of life."

On his perch, Stepan makes a little birdcall.

"I invite each of you, when you are ready, to open your eyes. For now, keep your impressions to yourself. Keep them inside. Let them resonate and grow like ripples on the water."

Learning with Kassandra is like riding a shape-shifting carousel. Its course seems unpredictable, and yet nothing is left to chance. Everything is connected.

"As I'm sure you now realize, the colors of your outfits are the incarnations of your chakras. But besides your being more mature than your peers, you have each been chosen for a specific reason . . ."

Her words hang suspended in the air and send my mind reeling. All of this is crazy. Everything here is crazy.

"A reason that gives each of you, as individuals, the chance to discover the seven keys. For while each of us has a dominant chakra, according to the program's data, with you seven, it's different."

I have no idea how this applies to the others, or to me, but one thing is certain: nothing will ever be the same. I can hear Ka's words before she drops the bomb, smashing the merry-go-round to smithereens.

"Each of you *is* a chakra."

The horses of the carousel have broken free.

And leaped into the unknown.

13

Each of us is a chakra? Then which one am I?

I don't understand. It's all so confusing. Ka left as soon as the lesson was over, and our circle broke up. Moreover, she had announced without warning that we would connect to the program for the first time this afternoon. It would merely be a technical run, but it would be decisive for the future.

One after the other, my companions left the barn, each in a different direction. Except for Stepan, who remained perched on his ladder. We all needed a break—it was so intense. We needed some time alone, some time to think. Myself included.

"Each of you is a chakra," Stepan echoes Ka's words.

Without warning, he asks me to come join him. Intrigued, I start climbing the ladder. He moves to let me past, and the two of us sit cross-legged on the floor. The loft is half filled with gunnysacks and tools. The scents of straw and dust tickle my nose.

"It reminds me of the signs of the Zodiac," Stepan continues, looking me straight in the eyes.

His eyes are not dark blue, after all. They are calm and

luminous, transparent blue. Am I only just noticing them because of the Psyche Maneuver?

"I used to have a passion for astronomy. I learned to speak English reading science magazines."

His sentences are short but correct. It's the first time I've heard him string so many words together.

"Later, I discovered astrology, the way celestial configurations influence human activity. I didn't sleep for days."

My confusion must have shown on my face.

"Okay, I confess. I pretended not to understand at first. The best way to understand people is to go unnoticed, to examine all the parameters."

It's odd. Stepan is talking to me like a close friend, and yet, it is the first time he has ever spoken to me, or to anybody else here, for that matter. He asks for the notebook he saw me slip into my pocket earlier in the morning, then sketches the shape of a body.

He adds seven bubbles, from the top of the head to the base of the spine.

"The most spiritual to the most basic chakra. Heaven to Earth."

Next he writes:

Seventh Chakra-Crown-Purple-Enlightenment, Cosmic Awareness-Stepan. KNOW.

Sixth Chakra-Third Eye-Indigo-Intuition, Discernment-Alpha. SEE.

Fifth Chakra-Throat-Blue-Communication, Expression-Rae. SPEAK.

Fourth Chakra-Heart-Green-Love, Compassion-Keiji. LOVE.

Third Chakra-Solar Plexus-Yellow-Heat, Action, Strength-Ali. ACCOMPLISH.

Second Chakra-Creativity-Orange-Inspiration, Emotion-Helen. FEEL.

First Chakra-Root-Red-Instinct, Determination-Chayton. BE.

Seeing it written there in black and white emphasizes how absurd it is. Either there has been a mistake or it is all a big joke. Meaning, my place on the list, of course. How could someone like me, who is mute, embody the communication chakra?

Stepan looks disappointed. Upset, even.

"The Seven are going to enter the program today. Just like that, without any preparation. We haven't even chosen our avatars. That little guy, Keiji, I can picture him as a giant troll, and Ali, an Amazon hunter with a bow and arrows. I could see you with a Kalashnikov rattling off words. And me . . ."

His eyes roll heavenward; he blinks hard to realign them.

"I have so many ideas . . . to keep our followers online interested, something with no connection to reality . . ."

Suddenly, his face contorts into a grimace of pain. His hands fly to his temples, his fingers latching on to the sides of his head like octopus tentacles.

"Aah, my head! It hurts!" He lets out an excruciating scream.

I move in closer to help, then change my mind. I have no idea what to do.

He is writhing in pain. I am about to go for assistance when I catch sight of the figure he sketched. At the very top, there is a crown and, inside the crown, a circle. Stepan's name is written next to it. The Crown. Stepan's chakra.

"Aaah, aaaahh . . ."

I remember my father cupping my throat with the palm of his hand. It was warm and comforting. I often got sore throats when I was little. My father would say my pipes had got the pip. So, slipping into the role of my father, I do the same, but on the top of Stepan's head. The contact of my hand on his blond hair, slick with brilliantine, feels strange. His initial look of astonishment immediately fades. He closes his eyes. We sit there in silence as he gently massages his temples, my hand over his head like an impromptu miniature roof.

"Thank you," he says, at last.

After a moment of awkwardness, we both get up.

"I don't know how you did it, but it's over. It usually lasts much longer."

Stepan's reed-thin silhouette nears the edge of the hayloft, much too close for my liking.

"The headaches are a side effect of the medical drops they used to make me take. My mother left Russia with her boyfriend when I was six. My father started to drink. He brought me up as best he could. We were always dirt-poor. He used all his money for his addictions: research and alcohol. I didn't fit in at school. My teachers referred me to specialists. I was placed in a psych ward twice so I would stop seeing things other people didn't see."

He had never said a word about his personal life before. Now he was pouring his heart out. He places a hand on his forehead again.

"My father was a famous scientist. He used to take me on expeditions. The last one was at a Russian research station in Antarctica. He almost died there."

Without a sound, I move closer to Stepan—we sit side by side. The carpet of hay spread below our feet is like a soft, warm pillow for sharing secrets.

"Of cirrhosis. He was in a coma for days. Alcohol had destroyed his brain and liver. The negative-fifty-degree Celsius temperatures at Bellingshausen Station hadn't helped. We lived there for several years along with thirty other scientists." It is like he's reciting a geography lesson. "Officially, there were no children at the station. In reality, there were two of us—two children sacrificed in the name of science. My father was a glaciologist."

I cast him a sidelong glance. He's staring into space, his eyes reflecting memories of vacant polar regions.

"The other kid was thirteen when we arrived. I was ten. He was sort of on the spectrum, so people wrongly assumed that he couldn't do anything. It seemed like a good deal to me. No more homeschooling or homework, no set schedule, and unlimited access to the observatory telescopes. The stars were the only friends I had. So, I decided to become a little autistic, too."

Stepan made it sound like you developed autism the way you would a new skill.

"We were eventually repatriated using my father's disability pension. Luckily, my father didn't remember a thing, even that he had a son. I kept on doing whatever I wanted. Sometimes, he would mistake me for the building super or a delivery boy. Coming here was easy. I didn't need an alibi."

A distant look washes over his face.

"Becoming autistic was easy, too . . ."

His voice fades to a whisper as if I'm no longer there.

"But I didn't realize it would be so hard *not* to be."

14

We are the Chosen Ones, the Seven about to enter the program.

To see it, hear it, and experience it firsthand. As with every first, it will be a moment of truth. To think we were chosen among millions and that we, alone, have the power to unravel the mystery of the keys created by Spirit Era—I still can't wrap my head around that!

Flyfold was given a makeover for the occasion. The giant screen was already lowered, hovering in the center of the room about six feet above the floor. The lights had been dimmed, and Instructor Shepherd is there to welcome us.

"This way, please," he beckons, more like a theater usher than a leader.

He shows us to our respective places one by one. Enormous baskets made of thick wool-like strands the same colors as our uniforms had been placed in a circle around the mat. They resemble giant nests.

"You'll need your boots when you enter the program," the instructor reminds Stepan, who is sitting on the edge of the mat undoing his laces.

Stepan's headache no longer bothers him. By lunchtime, he

had even shown a certain willingness to participate, making eye contact a few times and helping with the cleaning up.

We all walk closer to our respective nests while Stepan re-ties his laces. A transparent wall panel at the back of the room reveals holograms of mathematical formulas, equations, and graphs with strange patterns and signs. Kassandra reorganizes the images with her long, diaphanous fingers, then walks over to us quietly. She is barefoot.

"You've already signed the confidentiality agreement, so your fingerprints are in our database. Everything is ready to go for the first connection."

"But, Ka, we haven't begun training yet!" Ali bursts out.

"Spirit Era can only evaluate your progress if it makes an assessment of your capacities prior to any preparation what-soever. It will provide the program a calibration value, so to speak. If it doesn't get an exact measure, all future calculations will be thrown off."

"But what are we supposed to do when we get there? The Keeper said you were going to teach us the fundamental laws for exploring the first world," Ali adds.

"The virtual world you will be entering today is only a trial run. We need to verify a few things in the system. It does not involve the mantras and the keys created by the program. The immersion today will not be broadcast."

"Where are the 3D glasses or the connected headsets?" Chayton asks. "Don't you have the latest equipment?"

"The program isn't a video game, and it's not a simulator, either. You will not have multiple identities, magic powers, or more than one life. You won't even have an avatar."

"Won't even have an avatar," Stepan repeats, baffled like the rest of us. He brings a hand to his face. His complexion is pale.

"In video games, players interact in virtual environments. In our case, it is just the opposite."

"But isn't our identity supposed to be kept secret?" Alpha

asks. "Without avatars, the viewers will recognize us. The sensors in our uniforms transmit images as well as sound."

"And if Spirit Era isn't a simulator, then what is it?" Helen adds. "I just don't get it!"

"Not even an avatar . . . ," Stepan says again. I hope he isn't about to have another fit.

"It is time to tell them a little more about the program," Instructor Shepherd interrupts.

"You are right," Ka replies. "But before proceeding, I want each of you to enter your quantum pod."

The head instructor places a hand on Stepan's shoulder. It seems to have a grounding effect on him. His eyes widen as if he is waking from a bad dream. Guided by the Shepherd, he climbs into the purple nest.

We each follow suit. My feet dig into the basket's coarse mesh. The moment I sit down, its blue strands of yarn bristle with a burst of static electricity. The ends branch out in all directions and connect to the honeycombed pattern of my waffle-knit uniform. The color of the yarn blends perfectly with my outfit. We form a single block.

"Now, all of you. I want you to listen carefully."

Standing in the middle of the tatami, our mysterious mentor holds our attention as Instructor Shepherd squats discreetly in the background.

"Senior scientists from the Artificial Intelligence Department of Massachusetts Institute of Technology and their colleagues in the robotic studies department are developing a brain capable of creating a virtual world, a simulated environment it can inhabit. This is real. This is not fiction. Other researchers are also experimenting with creating an avatar developed from our collective personal data. Why would they want to do this? Because the real world is too dark and difficult a place to bend to their designs? At any rate, scientists are inventing a simulated version of the world, a double that satisfies the needs and expectations of humankind. A world behind a screen, that is. Meanwhile, the Earth is slowly dying and, along with it, our future." The blue threads hooked to my uniform start to quiver, their soft vibrations producing a pleasant rubbing sensation on my skin.

"Spirit Era uses groundbreaking capabilities to create virtual worlds from which entire cosmoses can emerge, each bearing a spiritual message of its own. For the first time ever, virtual reality technologies are not being used to create worlds we can escape into but rather to create worlds we can emerge out of—improved. And with the skills to improve life in the real world."

The vibrations stop.

"Quantum physics has taught us that everything tangible is comprised of energy. But can this energy be made visible in the real world? How can the chakras be made visible to the naked eye?"

"Exactly. How can they be?" Ali asks.

"Through practice. The same way you train to run in a marathon. The same holds true in our case. Inside the program, instead of having multiple identities, you will have only your own, the one you need to develop. Instead of magic powers, you will develop your natural gifts. And instead of fantasizing about immortality, you will learn to take advantage of the time allotted to you. So, there is no need for avatars. Quite the opposite, in fact."

"But the viewers will recognize us!"

"Not if they can only see what is inside you, Ali. Only your silhouette will be visible, lit from behind with a halo of light."

"The energy fields of our respective chakras . . ."

"That's right, Alpha. Your uniforms will envelop you in an aura of color. The public will gradually become accustomed to perceiving things differently. And Spirit Era has designed item-clues to steer you in the direction of the hidden keys."

"Bonuses, like in video games!" Chayton exclaims.

"Except the objects are not power-ups, Chayton. They won't give you special abilities. And if you manage to bring them back, you can use them in real life, just like the seven keys."

"Bring them back!" Helen exclaims incredulously. "The program may be more than a simulator, that part I get. But we are talking about a virtual world here! How do you expect us to bring something back?"

"Using a sophisticated system involving the additive manufacturing technique of three-dimensional printing. Your quantum pods are all equipped with new-generation 3D printers. But you will only be able to use them once each per season, in either direction—either going into the program or coming out of it."

"It's time," Head Instructor Shepherd says, standing up.

Kassandra's intense gaze meets my own for an instant—like an unspoken message of encouragement. Then, she approaches the transparent wall panel in the back of the room, and more holograms appear.

"She is Spirit Era's guardian," the head instructor says. "The computer cluster is hidden in a secret cellar directly beneath Flyfold. It was built in World War II."

"What is called a 'render farm' in computer science," Ka adds. "So, it all adds up, doesn't it?"

"My job," the Shepherd goes on, "is to look after the flock."

"Look after?" Keiji inquires.

"In case the Big Bad Wolf shows up!" Chayton laughs. But no one is in the mood for joking.

"While you're connected to the program, your body will remain present, but your mind will be elsewhere. Disconnecting from the program too abruptly could leave you in a state of shock, like a sleepwalker awakened without proper warning."

"So, how then come back from program?" Keiji asks.

"By pronouncing the name of the place you want to return to, either out loud or in your mind."

"Flyfold?" Keiji has trouble pronouncing the word.

"That's right. Be sure you're all together when you say it! You will have a week to discover the first key. Two hours of connection time a day. But time in the program goes by at a different rate. You will all have to wear these."

The instructor reaches into a pocket and pulls out seven digital wristbands that are the same colors as our uniforms. As he hands them out, he continues:

"These waterproof smart watches will help you keep track of time. Their timers are set to go off when the two-hour countdown is up."

Mine has the same blue logo that appeared on my smartphone when the Keeper recruited me: a triangle in a circle bordered by petals with a spiral in the center. Now I know it is the symbol of the fifth chakra.

"The instructions today are simple: stay together and come back here the instant the alarm goes off. Are you ready?"

No answer in the room, other than dead silence.

"Good luck!"

Transparent hoses drop from the ceiling like oxygen masks on an airplane. Head Instructor Shepherd takes hold of the purple one and walks toward Stepan. For once, he seems totally present.

"You connect to the program through your navel. You will just feel a slight prick, nothing too unpleasant. After that, it's up to you."

Stepan unbuttons his jacket and reaches for the tube. Lifting up his shirt, he connects the hose to his belly button without a moment's hesitation, his face utterly devoid of emotion—as if the whole thing is perfectly normal! The operation doesn't take long. Five more times, each of the Chosen connects to their color without batting an eye—until it's my turn. They all must be crazy, I think for a moment, the Shepherd included.

"Rae?"

I hesitate. Ali winks at me reassuringly, and Keiji smiles sweetly. Alpha is concentrating too deeply to notice.

What are you waiting for? my inner voice asks.

I don't know . . . I'm not so sure anymore . . .

Well, what is it? Are you telling me you miss boarding school?

Boarding school? No way. That place seems like a foreign planet to me now.

Can you imagine going back there?

Never. Not on your life.

So, I take the hose from Instructor Shepherd's outstretched hand and, stiffening slightly, connect it to my navel. At first, the sensation is unpleasant: a slight tingling, like getting your ears pierced. Then, some kind of fluid, thick and blue and very unsettling, begins to slide through the transparent tube, flowing out of the ceiling and toward me, slowly but surely.

Gently, the azure-blue substance reaches my navel. The tingling becomes a soothing warmth that spreads to my abdomen as the umbilical cord—or whatever it is—continues to diffuse its sustaining fluid. My eyes close.

Suddenly, Ali's words pop into my head: "Maybe he's some kind of a creep who has hidden cameras in our bedrooms. Or a serial killer, or a human trafficker who deals in children!" But it's too late. We have reached the point of no return. We have leaped off a ledge without looking down and offered ourselves up—to a wolf in sheep's clothing, perhaps?

Only time will tell.

#THEKEEPER #SAVETHEWORLD

POST 3—THE FIRST KEY

SEPTEMBER 24, 2035

THE SEVEN CHOSEN HAVE ARRIVED.

In the first days of autumn, they are learning, training, and finding their feet—and not without difficulty.

They want to develop a greater understanding—we all do—of the world around them. They want to gain a greater understanding of themselves. But today's understanding is not the same as yesterday's or tomorrow's.

In the past, people found inspiration in ideals of love, courage, and beauty. Then our hearts and minds were won over by the figure of the antihero. Today, exposing weaknesses and flaws is thought to be a sign of courage. Admitting we are vulnerable is considered a strength.

The names and faces of the Seven Chosen will remain anonymous. Their private lives will not be exposed, not according to the accepted practices of the contemporary world, in any case. Fame is not a celebration in itself. The quest for the key to the first chakra will be livestreamed on

November 22, 2035 . . . Thus, their quest can become yours, and their personal transformation may lead to universal change . . .

I would like to thank all who answered the call. The rest will now be the work of time.

Time for breathing, listening, and preparing.

Time for change.

NOW IS THE TIME.

PART THREE

TRAINING

15

The city is dark.

It is hard to say whether it is night or day. There is no sun or moon, just a neon-ultraviolet sky. The scattering perhaps of the countless artificial light sources illuminating the streets, buildings, and storefronts? Or perhaps the glow of something else, of some larger light source in the sky.

Craning our necks, we see the tops of lofty skyscrapers against the deep-purple sky. Five minutes earlier, we opened our eyes simultaneously to find ourselves standing on a crowded city sidewalk, a sea of unreadable faces pressing around us. Most had fresh-from-the-salon hairstyles and were hidden behind futuristic glasses. It was impossible to catch anyone's eye. The whole thing was very bewildering; we were as insignificant as little ants.

"Hey, look!" Helen bursts out suddenly. "Our jackets!" Her voice pulls me out of my reverie. She is smiling from ear to ear. Our outfits are covered in fluorescent symbols and squiggles, the same color as our uniforms but in a range of tints and shades. No doubt the work of the ambient UV glow.

"They look amazing!" said Helen.

Helen has something to be happy about, all right. Her carrot-orange uniform is livened up with an array of apricot, honey, and rusty tints. Ali's is practically aglow with yellows, whereas Keiji's, Chayton's, and Stepan's are dappled in greens, earthy reds, and Day-Glo purple.

"I feel kind of groggy. What about you guys?" Ali asks.

"Yes, groggy," Keiji pronounces carefully.

I'm feeling sort of fuzzy and numb myself.

"I can barely move. I'm a total leadbutt!" Chayton frowns.

"Argh, me, too," says Stepan, attempting to lift a matchstick leg, his jacket buttoned up to his chin as usual.

"It won't last," Alpha declares with authority. "You'll see."

"Sure it won't, Mr. Know-It-All. Whatever you say!" Chayton concedes facetiously.

"He's got a point there, Alpha," Ali remarks. "How would you know?"

"I know because I'm one step ahead of you," Alpha replies, unwilling to give an inch. "I'm feeling fine now, apart from the heat. Phew, it sure is hot here!"

Alpha takes off his jacket and ties it around his waist, baring his shoulders and biceps and revealing a royal-blue tank top. The strange tribal patterns of his white tattoo contrast brightly with the dark tone of his skin. The tone, too, appears ready for a mission.

"It sure is," Helen concurs, slipping off her jacket.

I feel the heat, too. My forehead is perspiring—like my father's used to, I think with a pang.

We all remove our jackets, apart from Stepan, who doesn't even unbutton his. Slowly, my brain fog subsides, and my arms and legs loosen up. Alpha was right.

"Beware of this place," Stepan mutters to himself. "There's more here than meets the eye . . ."

The road is empty between our sidewalk and the one opposite. There are no traffic lights or crosswalks, just rails laid directly on the asphalt. And not a single tree or even the slightest bit of greenery in sight. No smells, either—apparently the program cannot reproduce them, at least not now.

We follow the stream of passing people. Streaks of light crisscross the skyscrapers' mirrored façades. A train with tinted windows rushes past at full speed, its body streamlined like a silver bullet.

"Look!" Keiji exclaims, pointing upward. The name of the city is scrolling vertically over one façade: "Welcome to TOPTOWN. TOPTOWN. TOPTOWN. TOPTOWN."

"And look at those shop windows!" Chayton blurts out. "They don't mess around here."

The window displays are incredibly lavish: giant fragrance dispensers, futuristic outfits embossed with golden skyscraper logos, multipurpose satchels that can convert from fanny pack to shoulder bag and backpack to suitcase, a volcano made of plastic candy spewing lava into an artificial lake.

"It's like Aladdin's cave!" Helen exclaims.

"More like Hansel and Gretel in Dubai," Alpha observes. "The bling is almost obscene."

Suddenly, a group of small children breaks away from the throng and besieges us.

"Swap something, please? A swap, a swap, a swap!"

The mass of heads—all dirt-streaked prominent cheekbones and disheveled hair—forms a block.

"Roses, roses! Get your pretty roses!"

"Hey, lady! Hey, mister! How about a pretty rose?" one girl calls out, waving a bunch of plastic flowers like a cluster of little pink artichokes. She turns to Chayton.

"A pretty rose for the pretty lady?" she asks, pointing to Helen.

"For the *lady*?" Helen repeats affectedly. "Do I look *that* old?"

But no one takes any notice. Our eyes are all riveted to the girl with the plastic bouquet. She is wearing used boys' clothes a few sizes too large and a pair of beat-up sneakers. Her long tangle of golden hair partially conceals a large mole on one side of her forehead. And her eyes—how can I put it?—are like pools of liquid honey flecked with sorrow.

"Why not," Chayton answers, reaching for his pocket. "Ah shit! I forgot. We don't have any money."

He gives the flower girl a smile. She is clearly surprised, but wary, too.

"Don't you have anything you can swap for it?" another kid asks.

He is the youngest of the gang, probably seven or eight, with a tuft of blond hair sticking straight up that gives him a comical look. In one hand, he is holding a strange musical instrument, in the other, a tattered bit of cloth like a blankie.

"No, he doesn't," Alpha intervenes. "I think we'd better go."

"So do I," Ali agrees. "It must be time to go back soon. I feel like we've been here for hours."

"Really? It only seems like a few minutes to me," Helen says. "How long has it actually been?"

"Nearly two hours," Alpha answers, glancing at his watch. "Only a minute to go."

"I've got it! The gum!" Chayton exclaims. "Helen, is that piece I gave you still in your pocket?"

"Huh?"

"The piece of strawberry gum I gave you."

He reaches for her jacket pocket before she has time to answer.

"Hey!"

"I have it!" Ali cuts in. "Helen gave the chewie to me."

She pulls it out of her pocket and waves it in the air. Two dark-haired kids with olive complexions stare at her in wide-eyed amazement. One is a tall and skinny kid, the other a little younger; they are probably brothers.

"Wow! What's that?" they ask, imitating Ali's gesture like a couple of Bobbsey Twins. "It's flat and narrow. And look at the funny wrapper!"

Their enthusiasm is contagious. Ali hands the stick of gum to the flower vendor.

"What the heck are you doing?" Alpha bursts out. "We can't give them anything. It's just a trial run today."

"Says who?" Chayton roars, grabbing the piece of gum.

He hands it to the girl with the mole, who immediately gives one of the artichoke roses to Helen.

"Thank you, but no. Keep your flowers. It's a present."

The girl can't believe it.

"Come on, give me back the gum, please," Alpha insists, making a grab for it.

The girl recoils, throwing her hands to her face as if afraid of being hit. Chayton is furious. He rams headlong into Alpha, who, thrown off-balance, topples backward onto the pavement. When he gets up, his left palm is bleeding a little. He broke the fall with his hands.

"Aaahhh!"

The children break into a chorus of mice-like squeals and scatter. The flower seller jostles Helen as she leaves. Not five seconds later, the group of panhandlers is swallowed up by the tightly packed throng.

"Good show, Chayton!" Helen snaps.

"What? I, uh, didn't want to . . ."

"We are all aware of that, but you act too impulsively. The least you could do is to say you're sorry."

"Yeah, well, sorry."

"Don't worry about it," says Alpha. "It's nothing."

Beep-beep! Beep-beep! Beep-beep! All seven watches go off at once.

"Phew. I've had more than enough for a trial run," Ali declares.

"Flyfold!" six voices ring out in unison. Plus mine, in my head.

We open our eyes simultaneously. We are each in our respective nests. The wool-like strands automatically detach from our uniforms and retract, and the cables unhook from our navels and disappear into the ceiling. Standing in the middle of the room, the Shepherd carefully observes the scene. He appears satisfied.

"I'm hungry," Stepan says.

"Me, too," Helen agrees. "I'm starving."

"Let's just hope Mr. Mann thought we did a good job cleaning the kitchen," says Ali, getting to her feet. "Otherwise, don't forget—it'll be half-cooked half portions for everyone!"

My stomach is gurgling, too. The two hours we spent in the program seemed twice as long, and apparently we've burned a lot of energy. A joyful commotion fills the air as we head toward the farm. We're all eager to tell Ka about our experience. With Flyfold behind us, there's no trace whatsoever that we ever entered the program.

No trace? Not exactly. I am the only one who seems to have noticed one little detail, confirming my belief that the details are what lead to important—and in this case, alarming—discoveries. A detail that, if proven true, could radically alter the stakes of the game.

Alpha's left hand has not left his pocket . . .

16

"Each of you has a gift."

The next morning, Kassandra asks us to meet her in the living room adjoining the kitchen area. The far wall is flanked by a pair of massive brick chimneys that command attention, even without roaring fires.

"We all do, actually. And I don't mean rare abilities or fantastic powers, but what I call 'natural' gifts."

She has already told us we will spend the next two months training with her in the mornings and with Head Instructor Shepherd in the afternoons.

"Natural gifts . . . ," Stepan says pensively.

We are seated on a couple of shabby brown couches covered in wide-wale corduroy. On mine, there's not a lot of room—no surprise there, seeing as I am squeezed in between Chayton and Stepan. Ali, Keiji, and Helen are sitting on the other one—with Helen clutching the handbag she brought down from her room as if she is about to take off at any minute. And Alpha is in an armchair at a bit of a distance from the rest of us—with his left hand still hidden away in his pocket.

"These gifts are still little known today, and most people,"

Ka continues, standing before us, "have no idea they even exist. To encounter them, you first need to determine the source from which they originate, the physical paths, that is, through which all energy travels: the chakras."

"Our natural gifts . . ."

"Yes, Stepan, and you are not the only one here for whom those words resonate. Some of you have already experienced your gift with varying degrees of intensity and disappointment. Without necessarily understanding it or even wanting it. I know how frightening it is to be different. It isolates you. But now, you are no longer alone."

Kassandra seems to be staring at me, throwing my little voice into a panic: *Nobody can ever know about it. We swore it would remain a secret!*

"The first step is to identify your dominant chakra. For the Seven, that part is easy—each of you was chosen because of your dominant chakra. But, for most people, it's not that obvious. They are governed by several roughly equivalent chakras."

I am the fifth chakra, the throat chakra. There is no doubt about it. My gift is connected to my inner voice. It's all starting to add up: I don't need to use my vocal cords to communicate. With myself, especially, but also with others, judging by what happened with Chayton and Keiji.

"Secondly, you need to pay attention to the signs, to take them in and let them develop. It's a process that requires practice, discipline, and consistency. In other words, motivation. You need to *want* to develop your gift."

"What do you mean by 'signs'?" Helen asks nervously.

At dinner the night before, she hardly said a word as the rest of us chatted away and devoured the feast on the table before us. Rather than making good on his threats, Mr. Mann had gone all out in the kitchen to celebrate our first connection. Chayton had chalked Helen's silence up to fatigue, but earlier, at breakfast, it was the same thing all over again. Clearly, something was bothering her.

"I'm referring to signs from the world around us. They come in all shapes and sizes, but most of the time, they go unnoticed. They can be messages from the natural world or our dreams, or little things you notice in everyday life. We need to ask ourselves whether they resonate with us or are simply passing by."

"Passing by what?"

"By us, Helen. Do we enjoy putting our hands in the earth or taking a swim in the sea, which is not the same thing as a pool, a river, or a waterfall? Our preferences make us who we are, and they hone our natural gifts. Do you crave the adrenaline rush of a parachute jump, or a ride through the clouds comfortably ensconced in the seat of a plane? Anything can be a sign, of course, and with no hierarchy whatsoever. But such cases are rare. The two examples I gave you are connected to the four elements—earth, water, fire, and air—and can therefore be seen as clues to help discover the dominant chakra from which each gift originates. This holds true in all areas of life. The way we eat, walk, and dress."

"Natural gifts . . ." Stepan, the broken record, is back.

I give him a little nudge with my elbow.

"Helen, you hate it when the food on your plate is mixed together. You like it when everything is kept in the right place."

"What! How do you know that?"

"Because the second chakra, the chakra that governs creativity, is connected to the element of water. The water element is all about flow and flexibility; water can adapt to fill any space. But it needs structure. Water and oil don't mix, for that matter . . ."

I think about Kim, who also hates mixing food on her plate. Does this mean she has the same dominant chakra as

Helen? They certainly don't look alike. What about Chris? She heaps food onto her plate just like Chayton does. Maybe she's a root chakra, too?

As usual, Ka seems to be reading my mind.

"This is a generalization, of course. But in your case, owing to your strong alignment with your chakras, it applies. Not to say that people can be neatly placed into one of seven categories—that viewpoint would limit us to the materialist perspective of Materia. We all have a unique inner landscape, a specific chakra map that guides our choices and makes us who we are. The more confident I am in who I am, the less vulnerable I am to outside forces. By gaining greater self-awareness through the prism of Spiritua, we can inform a prospective employer, for example, that we are strongly aligned with our heart chakra, whose element—air—makes us best suited for work where we can go unnoticed. As transparent as air."

"The opposite of someone with a strongly aligned sun chakra," Ali breaks in, clearly referring to herself, "who would do better at a job where they can shine."

"That's more or less the idea. So, to take up the example of . . . let's call him Mr. Air. Had his parents known about his governing element, they would never have forced him to perform in the school show. Likewise, his teachers could have promoted his strengths rather than his weaknesses. No one chakra combination is better than another. There are only differences to be understood."

An ideal world, a far cry from reality . . .

"How did you sleep, by the way?" Ka continues. "How are you all feeling after the trial connection?"

"I didn't sleep a wink," Helen answers. "I've got a problem."

"What is it?"

"I don't know what to do with this."

She pulls a plastic artichoke rose out of her bag. Ka's eyes widen.

"The quantic printer, it works! That's fantastic!"

"I found it when I took off my jacket to shower last night," Helen continues. "The flower seller must have put it in my pocket when she jostled me and ran off."

"Well," Chayton says with a whistle, "isn't she a clever one!"

"It's all your fault! You never should have given her that piece of gum."

"I thought it was only a trial run. Anyhow, it's not like it's the end of the world or anything. No pun intended."

"You're right, it was a trial run, Chayton," says Ka. "But it means Helen won't be able to bring another item-clue out of the program. And Ali won't, either. The gum was in her pocket."

"There's something I don't quite understand," Alpha says. "Ali didn't bring the gum with her on purpose. Would it have counted if she hadn't taken it out?"

"No. The printer is only triggered when something switches from one world to the other."

"Going from there to here, I get it," Alpha continues. "The artichoke flower was duplicated with a 3D printer. But what about the other way around? Is the gum still in Ali's pocket?"

"There should be a small pile of synthetic sand there instead. To reflect as closely as possible whatever happens in the mantras, anything you leave behind in immersion is disintegrated by the quantic strands connected to your suits. Spirit Era was designed for such exchanges—to allow you to recover the seven keys for raising awareness and changing the catastrophic course of humanity. Its aim is to preserve life on our planet. It uses VR technologies to alter the real world."

"If I had known, I would have brought the gum there myself," Chayton responds.

"Oh well. At least the kid will be able to enjoy it," Ali says. "It's only in the simulation, granted, but that's better than nothing."

"And you and Helen will be able to exchange items again next season, after Christmas break."

"Aren't we supposed to stay at the farm the whole time, Ka?"

"No, Chayton. We need to be careful not to raise your families' suspicions. It's hard to come up with a good excuse for not returning home over the holidays."

"Well, nobody in Peru expects to see me anytime soon."

"Maybe so, but the search for the keys has been organized this way. Assuming you find the first key in time—during the week of November 22, that is—you will return to the farm after Christmas vacation to start looking for the second. One key per season, remember? If you fail, Spirit Era will close its doors for good, and humanity will have to face its destiny on its own."

"The program accurately predicted the natural disasters that struck over the summer," Alpha interjects, "so, surely, it knows what will happen on 7/27/2037. Why not publicize the threat and make the danger more tangible? It would certainly help persuade the skeptics. We've seen it again and again with the alerts issued by COP40 in the past few years: people don't take the threat of danger seriously until it affects them directly."

"Hmm," Stepan mumbles, thinking out loud. "The predictions are ninety-nine percent accurate. That leaves only a one percent chance of being wrong. Before coming to the farm, I read a survey in the newspaper. It said that less than five percent of the world's population believes the end-of-the-world prediction. And they told *me* I was crazy!"

Ka puts a hand on his shoulder in a show of solidarity.

"The scenarios of the seven mantras coincide with what scientists believe to be the most probable cataclysmic disasters. One of them reveals the cause of the apocalypse the program has predicted will take place two years from now. Which one? That must remain a secret, as it is directly tied to the keys to life that humanity needs to discover on its own."

"What about summer holidays?" Ali asks. "We have a two-month break. That leaves us more or less a month for the fourth key."

"It shouldn't be a problem with a lot of method and a little imagination," Ka replies. "I'm sure you will have no shortage of ideas. But we'll cross that bridge when we come to it."

"Yeah, great," Helen cuts in. "But thanks to Chayton, I won't have an item-clue for season one."

"If the program selected that item for you, it's no accident."

"You've got to be kidding! A plastic flower!"

"It must have a hidden meaning."

"What meaning is that?"

"You need to give yourself time to mature, like an apple. In today's worlds, perfection and performance are valued over knowing who we really are. But the greater our self-knowledge, the easier it is to determine the path we must follow. Everyone has their own."

"A great idea for a new start-up company—a customized GPS for finding your way!"

"You have a point, Chayton. We each have an inner GPS. We call it our conscience. But we cannot find it by using an external device. Honing a new mindset takes practice and discipline, just like learning of any kind does. Contrary to today's modern standards of instant everything, lasting change does not happen overnight. Over the next two months, you will learn to develop your energy centers and to recognize cues from the root chakra."

"What kind of cues?" Ali asks, stretching her legs.

"In the past, our lives were much more closely linked to nature. We looked to the earth to find answers to our questions, and we honored all creatures big and small, from the majestic elephant to the tiny ant. Today more than ever, they have much to teach us. They bear secret messages."

"Secret messages," Stepan repeats. He has switched records at last.

"We all have our own, an animal totem."

"I've always loved pumas. Their speed . . . ," Ali says.

"No, I'm talking about an animal that will be your guide, an animal that will choose *you*."

"Well, how will I know which one it is?"

"By paying close attention to the world around you. It can reveal itself in nature and in your daily life. It may appear repeatedly, either as a physical or a spiritual manifestation."

"What do you mean?"

"As an image, an object, a dream . . ." Kassandra's voice trails off. "Once you have identified it, your messenger-animal will show you the way."

17

"Keiji! Stepan!"

Ali gestures with a free hand, holding a picnic basket in the other.

"Keiji-goat, Stepan-goat, that's enough! You're dawdling again!"

"Uh, don't think that's going to help much!" Chayton laughs. "Try whistling instead."

He places his thumb and index finger in his mouth and gives a shrill whistle. Barefoot, his long dark hair flapping in the wind, he certainly looks like a Dakota Sioux.

"Right, as if that'll work! They're goats, not dogs."

With his usual mulishness, Chayton whistles again. Ali lets it go for a change, joining Helen, Alpha, and me, instead, under the tall, shady tree we had chosen for our picnic.

"Can you help me, Rae?" Helen asks, unfolding a large coral-colored tablecloth.

I grab one side, and we spread it on the ground, the fabric's lumpy surface betraying the tufts of grass and clumps of earth hidden underneath as if we've stumbled upon a kingdom of moles.

"It was nice of Ka to give us the afternoon off," Ali says, putting her basket down.

Alpha has already set down the one he was carrying at the foot of the tree. He is still keeping his left hand hidden from sight.

"Yes, we needed it," Helen agrees. "And it feels good to be out of our uniforms for once."

She is wearing a handmade dress with a turquoise cherry pattern and blue sneakers, the perfect look for a picnic. Earlier that morning, we found baskets prepared by Mr. Mann waiting for us in the kitchen. They were bursting with food. In one, there was a map with instructions for taking the kids and mother goats to a mountain pasture.

"Keiji! Stepan!" Ali calls out again, restless as usual.

Skinny and her four companions are grazing nearby. So are all the mothers. The goats followed us happily—as if we had been shepherds our whole lives! In the distance, Keiji-goat and Stepan-goat appear at last. The latter makes a beeline for his namesake as the other joins the herd. Chayton stretches out on the tablecloth, his mane of hair spread like seaweed around his face and his bronze skin blending with the coral tones of the fabric.

"Any room for me there?" Helen asks in a mellifluous tone.

"Watch out, a wasp!" Chayton exclaims, clenching a fist as if to squash it.

"No, Chayton, don't!" Ali shouts. "It's a bee. Leave it alone."

Not knowing its life has been spared, the insect makes its way slowly across the tablecloth. Helen watches it with a funny expression on her face.

"Another bee . . . Strange . . ."

"You're right. Another bee!" Ali exclaims. "The bee must be your messenger-animal. You're so lucky!"

"Do you think so? But why the bee? What message does it have for me?"

"I'm not quite sure. But I do know a lot about pollinators. Bees are essential to life on Earth, you know. Our neighbor in Perth has a homemade hive in his yard. It's a large piece of wood with holes bored into it, hanging in a tree."

"I didn't know you could make them."

"Sure you can, or you can buy them in garden supply stores."

"Why worried, Chayton?" Keiji asks, noticing the look on his face.

"Why did I react that way?" Chayton murmurs. "My first instinct was to squash it. I wasn't brought up that way. My father's grandfather, the one I was named after, was a healer. On the last page of his medicinal plant herbarium, he wrote: 'the fifth child of my fifth grandson shall follow in my footsteps.'"

"What you say interesting," Keiji says.

"I read his notes over and over again when I was little. I still have them here in my bag. But when I grew up, I realized treating people for free wasn't my thing. Anyhow, there's a lot about bees in my great-grandfather's notes: 'Honey is delicious but also has unique healing properties. Global crop yields depend on pollinators: we need to protect them to survive.'"

"Yes, today more than ever!" Ali chimes in. "Pesticides are decimating bee populations. It's unbelievable when you think about it. Not only do pollinators enable plant and crop reproduction, but they are also critical to maintaining biodiversity. I have always loved those tiny gals with their little striped jackets."

"Tiny gals, tiny women . . . ," Helen says to herself as the bee continues its procession across the tablecloth. It flies into the air, staying close to Helen, who starts humming a cheerful tune.

"You have a nice voice," Chayton tells her, digging his toes into the grass. "You should take off your shoes. It feels amazing."

As Keiji starts taking out the food specially prepared for him, and Ali lays out the other picnic fixings on the tablecloth, Alpha motions for me to join him. We move away from the group. Helen watches us, her gaze cold and hard—a far cry from her usual ingratiating smile. She leans her head on Chayton's shoulder and brings a thumb to her mouth—the only indication her shell may be cracking—then quickly withdraws it.

"Come on, let's go for a walk," Alpha says to me.

As we set off, our baby goats come frolicking after us, Alpha's leaping and bleating, and my skinny one trotting proudly behind. A fitting replay of Alpha and Rae.

"I know you know."

My eyes settle on Alpha's left palm. He isn't trying to hide it anymore. The cut is still raw, but it doesn't look serious.

"You have a way of observing things. When you lose one sense, it heightens the others."

Alpha seems to know what he's talking about.

"It will have to remain our little secret," he whispers, indicating the cut on his hand.

I shake my head no. "What if there's a bug in the program? What if there is something wrong with it? It is impossible for virtual environments to physically alter reality . . ."

"You're right. If we can hurt ourselves for real when we are in immersion, then we can die, too. On the other hand, one of the Seven dying is nothing compared to the annihilation of the entire human race. I am convinced that the end-of-the-world prediction is right. It is not just a story meant to scare us. Even so, I think it's best not to mention it to the others for the time being. It might keep them from giving it their all, and each of us has to be fully present to uncover the first key."

Very true. I hadn't thought of it that way.

"I saw a program about hypnosis once. Apparently, it can be used for certain kinds of operations instead of anesthesia.

If our brain can control pain, it can do just the opposite, too, don't you think? I mean, it could inflict illness or injury."

"Yoo-hoo!" Helen shouts at us.

"Come eat! We're starving," Ali adds, jumping to her feet. Bounding effortlessly across the high grass, her goat close behind, she grabs me by the hand and drags me toward the shady tree, her laughter bubbling up. The wind has picked up, blowing my bangs sideways, and large, dark clouds are gathering. I take a deep breath to chase away my gloomy thoughts.

We sit down, and Helen passes around a basket of mixed vegetable sticks. Stepan grabs a couple of carrots and offers one to Stepan-goat. His kid hasn't left his side since we arrived.

"He's not a rabbit." Chayton bursts out laughing, but no one pays any attention to him.

"What's up with you, Alpha?" Ali asks. "You're pretty quiet today."

"I'm eating, that's all."

"That looks good," she continues, eyeballing the skewer of colorful dumplings on Keiji's plate. "What is it?"

"*Dango,*" he answers, popping one into his mouth.

"What are they?"

"Sweet rice balls, made with sticky rice. Too bad, no green tea."

"Can I try one?"

"No."

And he promptly stuffs the last two dumplings into his mouth. Keiji, normally so kind and thoughtful, tends to be stingy when it comes to food.

"Olives?" Helen asks, playing hostess.

"All these veggies are going to turn me into a rabbit, too! Make me a sandwich instead. Okay, sweetheart?"

Helen freezes, dropping the basket like a hot potato.

"'Sweetheart'? Save it for your brood of chicks. I'm not your skivvy!"

Her outburst seems disproportionate. An awkward silence follows.

"And I'm not any man's maid, for that matter! Got that, you four?"

"All right, already, no sandwich!" Chayton grumbles. "Evil spirit, be gone, and return our Helen to us!"

Helen lets out a furious belly roar just as—*Boom!*—a clap of thunder rends the air. The baby goats bleat skittishly, and Ali's bounds across the tablecloth, toppling glasses in the process. Helen bursts into tears, jumps up, and takes off through the field.

"Wait!" Ali shouts.

She leaps to her feet to run after her. Chayton watches them, dumbfounded, as they dash down the hill. He had no way of knowing he'd struck a nerve—Helen was reliving her mother's pain.

"Helloo!"

In the distance, on a side path leading to the farm, a young girl appears to be calling to us. She is wearing a light-colored dress, and her long flaxen hair is covered by a brightly patterned headscarf. Surrounded by a sea of goats, she is holding a shepherd's staff in one hand and is gesturing to us with the other.

"You'd better finish up!" she yells, pointing skyward. "It's going to rain!"

No sooner have her snatches of words reached us than it starts to pour. Against the dark clouds massed on the horizon, the shepherdess rushes after her flock—already scrambling down the hill—and vanishes into the distance.

"Quick!" Keiji exclaims, first putting his uneaten food in one of the baskets.

The wind is blowing even harder now. As Chayton attempts to round up the goats, or, at any rate, to prevent them from taking off without us, Alpha and I toss the rest of the food higgledy-piggledy into the other baskets. There is nothing left on the tablecloth by the time Stepan snaps out of it and offers to help. He folds it carefully as if we have all the time in the world, oblivious to the fat raindrops that have started to fall.

"Come on, let's go!" shouts Chayton, unable to contain the mother goats any longer.

Keiji, Stepan, and Alpha each grab a basket, and we hurry down the hill. It's pouring rain by the time we reach the path where the girl appeared. A flash of lightning followed by a second, even louder clap of thunder rips through the air. The frightened goats pick up speed, making a beeline for the goat farm. They know the way by heart.

The goat farm is their shelter ... And, in a way, it's mine, too.

The fact is, I feel more at home there than I did in San Francisco. It's Laureen's house now. As I rush down the hill behind my companions, I feel a weight has lifted off my shoulders. I feel free. It's a new feeling for me—almost tangible.

Almost like flying.

LOGBOOK
INSTRUCTOR: KA
SEASON I

The human brain is a strange beast.

Part kid, part wolf, it can bring out both the best and the worst in us. As I am writing these words, research on the subject is still in the flat-Earth stage. Even so, scientists do tend to agree on one thing: we only fully utilize a tiny percentage of our brain's capacity.

The human mind can create disease, cause pain, and cure illnesses. I suspected the border between the program's virtual world and the real world would be somewhat permeable. Alpha's injury has confirmed this. The wound on his left hand may be superficial, but it is extremely significant: the Seven Chosen Ones can be physically injured when they are connected to the program.

So long as Spirit Era follows the Three Laws of Robotics, however, it will create safety measures to ensure their protection; the brains of the Seven may reproduce injuries suffered in the program, but their lives will not be in danger. For the time being, they know nothing about the modifications made to their uniforms following yesterday's test connection: I gave them the afternoon off so I could improve the field of their waterproof microsensors; the uniforms' cameras need to be able to capture high-resolution images, regardless of whether the jacket is being worn. It is better for Rae and Alpha to think we know nothing about the cut, as well. They need to figure things out on their own, to make mistakes and fall, to get hurt, even. Their growth as individuals depends on it.

Meanwhile, the Keeper's third post announcing the selection of the Seven Chosen has sent shock waves through the social media world. Millions of participants worldwide were torn between disappointment and curiosity, and when the release date for the first livestreamed event was announced, subscriptions to Spirit Era Channel skyrocketed, despite being entirely devoid of real content. (There's no response to any of the comments; its sole purpose is to post messages and to broadcast the livestream.) The channel currently counts over 400 million followers.

For now, the Seven are entirely cut off from the outside world. They are unaware of the numbers. The mounting excitement must not jeopardize their preparation. They will have time enough for the media storm when they return home for vacation. How will they deal with the pressure then? They'll be the most-talked-about people on Earth, but they will be completely incognito.

Anyhow, no need to worry about that for now . . .

18

It has been two weeks since our training sessions began.

With Ka's classes in the morning and the Shepherd's training sessions in the afternoon, we have reached cruising speed. The latter always begins with one of three types of warm-ups: running, to stay physically fit; stretching, to increase flexibility; and endurance training, to improve our mental strength. During our free time, we often take the baby goats out for exercise, and I even managed to find time to read. I've finished the book Kassandra lent me, *Of Mice and Men* by Steinbeck.

She must have chosen the novel on purpose. Two fellow travelers—Lennie, the simple giant, and the small but quick-witted George—dream of a better future, of settling down on their own piece of land. George tries to protect his friend, but Lennie's rash behavior constantly puts him in danger. The story raises questions about the nature of the oppressors. And while the parallel between the animal and human worlds is obvious, I sense the words in pencil on the title page of the book have a hidden meaning: "Who are the mice and who are the men?" That's why I haven't returned it to Ka yet. Maybe the novel contains a coded message of some sort. Maybe it is connected to my messenger-animal? Maybe it's a mouse?

"Hajime!" the Shepherd exclaims.

We are training outside today. He has set up gym mats under the large, shady trees bordering the farm. We are barefoot, practicing the judo techniques we have already learned: eight throwing techniques, five pinning holds, and how to get out of certain situations on the ground. We are now familiar with the Japanese terms *hajime, mate,* and *rei*—start, stop, bow.

Instead of getting private lessons, Alpha was put in charge of our interminable practice sessions. He has made no secret of his boredom and frustration, and gradually, the little patience he had has given way to irritation, especially toward Helen, who is a slow learner, and Stepan, who is equally lacking in coordination and motivation. As for me, with the help of my inner voice constantly whispering advice in my ear, I am making good progress and have even managed to successfully complete some *ō-soto-gari*—a throwing technique in which one opponent pulls the other forward to destabilize them and then sweeps their leg out, knocking them down. I have to admit I enjoy seamlessly linking the moves together, like dancing.

"Mate!"

We aren't just learning basic techniques with the Shepherd. We are also studying the history and origins of different martial arts practices. Humans have been developing systems and traditions of combat for millennia, the world over, primarily for reasons of self-defense but also to unlock the mysteries of the body. In India and China, Qigong, therapeutic exercises combining breathing and the activation of energy points, was developed to better recover from strenuous effort and to manage one's energy during combat. Building on traditional

Chinese medicine, which provides knowledge of the human body's vital energy meridians, Qigong can interrupt the circulation of the opponents' qi, or "life energy," so they no longer pose a threat.

Every day, we finish with the Psyche Maneuver: connecting with our inner energy is the first step in developing our gift. We can now stare into our own eyes for increasingly longer periods of time. We have all seen images reflected in our gaze. It's a bit like in a dream, but we remember everything. This self-confrontation is enjoyable at times, bewildering at others, and sometimes downright unpleasant. After the exercise, we can volunteer to share our experiences with Kassandra and the group in order to improve our self-understanding and the alignment of our chakras.

"I'm not afraid of fire anymore," Ali said, not long ago. "You were right, Keiji, I am a hearth. The third chakra's element is fire. It's part of me. I will learn to master it. When I stare into the mirror, I often see myself playing hide-and-seek with the sun—without getting burned! But I also see a little animal flying around me. Only, I can't tell what it is yet. It moves too fast, like a trail of light."

"It must be your messenger-animal," Helen chimed in. "Was it a bird?"

"More like an insect," Ali clarified.

"A fly?" Chayton suggested with a snarky look on his face.

"Nice, thanks. And what's the connection you see there? Maybe you think I like to hang around shit?" Ali replied, glaring at Chayton so we'd all know she meant him.

"And what about you, big smartass," Ali went on, "have you identified your messenger-animal yet?"

"Uh, no. Not yet."

"My guess is—hippopotamus!"

Chayton glowered, no longer amused with their little game.

"Insect," Keiji interceded, providing a diversion. "You maybe see detail? There is one fast, like you. Fly at seventy kilometers an hour, in the six directions, even backward. For samurai, it is symbol of agility and spontaneity. It is dragonfly."

Ali liked that. I knew she would keep his suggestion in mind.

The only one who hadn't opened up was Alpha. When the two of us were alone, which wasn't often, he said much less than before. I knew almost nothing about his life. He'd been sleeping poorly since we began training and was having nightmares. I knew the lack of sleep was starting to get to him. He'd retreated into himself.

"Today," the Shepherd continues, "we are going to practice the Oak Exercise. First, you need to step off the mats."

We all do so and form a circle around him.

"Now that you have identified your dominant chakra, it is time to move on to the second step: the relationship, that is, that we all have with the earth. Simply plant your feet, close your eyes, and imagine you are an oak tree. Once you are firmly rooted, raise your arms skyward. Your arms are the branches, and your breath, the wind that bends them."

It is easy for me to imagine my body as a trunk—not very wide around but covered with thick bark—and my outspread arms as branches covered with greenish-blue leaves and acorns. I picture my roots, thin and twisted, reaching downward into the earth, but on one side only: the right side. On the left side, there is nothing. The void, I sense, caused by my mother's absence.

"The oak tree is sacred in Celtic mythology. It is the symbol of courage and strength, of the union between sky and earth. It is the doorway from one world to another. Turn your attention to the life force flowing through your veins like sap. Is it vigorous and fluid, or slow and thick? Are your branches soaring to the sky or stretching outward? Are they leafy or bare? And are your roots anchored securely in the earth?"

We hold the oak tree position for a good fifteen minutes, and then the Shepherd divides us into pairs: Alpha and Ali, Helen and Keiji, and Chayton and me.

"Stepan, you stay with me. Your roots are practically non-existent, and the other six need your feet to be planted firmly on the ground. You are going to continue practicing the Oak Exercise with me."

Stepan stoically takes up the position again.

"The rest of you will finish the session with the Psyche Maneuver. But, this time, instead of looking into a mirror, you will look into your partner's eyes. You will be mirrors for each other. Being interested in others—genuinely interested and free of bias—is a difficult challenge. But it is something you can practice, just like sports or mathematics."

The Shepherd instructs us to find a secluded spot. Chayton and I choose a majestic tree at the entrance of the small wood behind the farm, where we are completely hidden from sight.

"How you doin', Sparrow?"

We are sitting face to face, cross-legged at the foot of the trunk. I feel a little self-conscious, though I would have been all the more so sitting opposite Alpha. Chayton tries to put me at ease. Take a deep breath, he tells me, and focus on the tree, on the sounds of the earth. I can feel the damp through the fabric of my pants. I'm a little cold.

"You seem distracted. Is something bothering you?"

Alpha's cut, I think to myself. It has healed over, but he is adamant about not telling the others.

"Stressed about taking a little peep at my underbelly? Or perhaps at letting me have a look at yours?" His smile is contagious. "Don't worry. It'll stay just between the two of us."

Despite his reckless nature, Chayton can be rock solid at times. Reassuring. And surprisingly, he has a better head on his shoulders than Alpha does. This makes sense, actually, since one is the custodian of the chakra that is the most closely aligned to the earth, and the other, of the sixth chakra, the third eye, that belongs to the realm of the skies. You can never tell what Alpha is thinking. Chayton's calming presence makes me want to tell him everything. My hand grasps the notebook in my jacket pocket, and I consider taking it out.

"Hey, what's with the scary look on your face? You're not going to find out I'm Frankenstein or anything. Cross my heart! Sure, I've done a few stupid things in my life, but nothing super bad."

The notebook will stay put . . .

"Getting by in LA without a green card wasn't easy at first. I didn't find work right away. This British guy spotted my potential and introduced me to the underground street-fighting scene. Street fighting—that's how I managed to eat in the early days."

Our eyes eventually meet. We'd done the Psyche Maneuver so often by then, we were well beyond the stage of laughter and impatience. You have to take your time, to be mindful of discovering who you really are—or who someone else really is. Yes, that, too, is reflected in their eyes.

After a minute or two, I sink into Chayton's gaze like warm sand on a beach. Once past the outer superficial layer, I find myself in hidden, more intimate depths. But I don't see his life simply flashing before my eyes. It is more sensorial: the warmth of being part of a clan, the sounds of singing, the heat of the campfire, the smell of roasted corn and potatoes.

Then I see myself, my own face reflected in Chayton's eyes. How bizarre! Images flash by without my having any say in the matter: a wreath of stinging brambles coiling around my neck, choking me; a flock of fluttering birds surrounding me—blue parakeets—pulling at the wreath with their beaks, unwinding it; blue stains on my neck from the bird feathers . . . Clear blue skies and bottomless oceans . . . Then I see myself running, leaping and flying, wings sprouting from my back and the parakeets escorting me, twittering joyously, into the azure vault.

"Rae . . ."

Chayton's voice disperses my vision.

"Rae, it's going to get dark soon."

Already?

"We have to go back."

Chayton stands up. He's been calling me for a while, apparently. He extends his hand, and I take it and stand up, a bit shaky, then fall into step with him as we walk toward the farm. He is pensive, too. I wonder what he saw in my eyes.

Suddenly, he turns around.

"When we were doing that exercise, I stared into your eyes so hard, I went over to the other side. Do you want to know what I saw there?"

I nod.

"You were sitting on a bench. There were flowers everywhere. Not just at your feet but literally all around you, filling every inch of space. Your chakra's element might be ether, so maybe that's why. Yeah, I know, it may not seem like it, but I listen to what Ka is saying during class."

He hesitates to go on.

"There was this big hole in the middle of your stomach, Rae. I could even see the bench through it. The weird thing is, associations somehow started coming to me, instinctively, of their own accord. Sorry if it's just my imagination, but that hole, it made me think of an irrevocable loss, like after a pregnancy . . . And your mother's death. Did she die when you were born?"

Silence.

"I'm sorry, Sparrow. Ka told us you lost your father in a car accident a few months ago. You . . . I've gone to such great lengths to get away from my family and everything it represents, but you . . ."

He chokes up. I've never seen Chayton overcome by emotion before.

"After, I saw this flock of predatory birds. They burst out of the sky, screeching and squawking in different languages—it sounded like gibberish—and swooping down at you. You covered your ears, then tried to chase them away. But it was no use. I hope you don't mind my digging so deep."

Why would I mind? I've already heard Chayton's thoughts echoing inside my head!

"And then, I saw myself. I was a white rhinoceros . . ."

What with my parakeets and Chayton's birds of prey, there is definitely a common thread to our messenger-animals: they were all birds.

"Ka says our gift will reveal itself as we learn more about ourselves and are able to better connect to our chakra. In my case, I have to say, it's still pretty fuzzy. Have you figured out yours yet?"

I think I have. Mine is my inner voice, and the voices of other people occasionally ringing in my head.

"It's pretty frustrating, you know, how you refuse to use that little notebook of yours! It sure would make things a lot easier for us."

And a lot harder for you and me, my little voice comments.

"How could your gift possibly be related to the communication chakra, I wonder?"

Keep pretending not to know. Can you imagine if someone found out about me? They'd think you were crazy. Or a liar.

So, I'll keep on hiding it. My voice. My gift.

19

School with Kassandra is a unique experience.

It is unlike anything we've ever attended.

In the first place, learning is not confined to the walls of a classroom. We are not squeezed into seats behind desks, which to me, at best, are meant to separate the students from the teachers and, at worst, to make them feel inferior. Ka regularly holds class outside. Seeing as we're in the middle of nowhere, it's easy for her to choose secluded spots where we won't run into any locals.

Secondly, her classes are interactive. Ka believes she can learn as much from us as we can from each other. She believes knowledge is all about sharing. It is not a one-way street with a set destination. Rather, it is a dynamic process of mutual growth. So, in Ka's class, no one uses notebooks or pencils—except me.

"Our brains only register what we are willing to believe," Ka said one day. "Acquiring knowledge requires trust. Reading and writing for the sole purpose of recording information or note keeping is tantamount to disregarding our brains' limitless capacities. It makes us little more than parrots."

She believes in freedom of speech and fundamental rights. She often moves about, and dances even, while discussing botany or a book she loves. For Ka, knowledge and movement are inextricably tied.

"We can benefit every day from learning to listen better and being listened to. Sometimes, even, from being heard."

So, Ali, who can never sit still for long, moves about as she pleases. It is her way of expressing herself and absorbing knowledge. Ka tells us there are as many ways to learn as there are human beings. We acquire knowledge from books, of course, and from many different types of school, but nature, manual activities, the arts, our bodies, and life in general can all be drivers of learning. Since Ali is free to get up and move around in class, she is able to concentrate for hours on end.

"We need to look beyond appearances, to hear what's hidden behind all the talk and lies. This is critical to the evolution of humanity. Only then will we be able to see behind the smoke and mirrors, to widen our vision and see past the end of our nose. Change is painful because it begins at home."

The farmyard is bathed in morning sunlight. We are seated on the bench-like boulders bordering the central flower bed. Alpha has been keeping to himself, pensive again. He told me he's been having a recurring nightmare. It woke him up at four in the morning.

"I was shut up in this cage high above a city. I'd been left there to rot," he let out in one fell swoop before retreating into his shell again.

"Consumer society extols fame, wealth, beauty, and physical strength. These attributes are held up as the ultimate model to live by. This excessive, and often exclusive, devotion to appearances numbs our ability to look inside."

Kassandra's long auburn tresses, untied, as usual, spill freely down the back of a dress made of undyed hemp. She is leaning against the old-fashioned water well, radiant in the shade of the small pitched roof sheltering the wooden bucket, rope, and central crossbeam.

"The world is comprised of two parallel planes: Materia is the physical plane where we go about our daily lives; Spiritua is the immaterial realm where the language of the soul is expressed. By focusing on the exterior alone, we have become blind to everything inside."

Over the past few days, Ali has become convinced that the dragonfly is her messenger-animal. Whenever she goes outside, a new dragonfly—with a blue, red, or multicolored body, and wings either transparent or colorful—hovers nearby. One has just landed on her shoulder.

"Take the dragonfly, for example. On the Materia plane, it is merely an insect that can be reduced to its physical attributes: elegant design, role in nature, Wikipedia page, and so on. For Spiritua, however, the dragonfly is not just a wonder of aerodynamic design. It is a messenger that reflects something about ourselves, that shows us the path to follow."

"I know what it is trying to tell me."

"What is that, Ali?"

"To accept who I really am. I am energetic and spontaneous, just like my messenger-animal."

The dragonfly flits away, and Ali stands up on her rock bench.

"I've never been able to sit still. My parents and teachers were always criticizing me. Rather than encouraging me to make the most of my strengths, they did everything they could to make me change."

"Too, wings change color," Keiji adds.

"And?"

"Dragonfly, messenger of light. You, sun chakra."

Keiji has hit the nail on the head again. Ali's attitude toward him has started to change. She is less and less inclined to treat him like a baby.

"Just think," she says, indicating her sun-shaped nose stud. "I got this when I was fourteen. My father went ballistic, of course, but there was no way I was taking it out. Just goes to show. We know without knowing . . ."

"If I understand you right," Helen cuts in, "on the Materia level, Ali's parents saw the nose stud as a provocation, as an act of rebellion pushing her away from them. Whereas, on a deeper level, it was the exact opposite. From the Spiritua perspective, she was only telling them she wanted to be accepted for who she is, to let her inner light shine through at last."

"That's right," Ka answers. "But there's no need to oppose the material and the spiritual, so long as each is given its rightful place."

"What about me?" Helen asks. "The bee is definitely my messenger-animal. Those little gals in striped jumpers—to use Ali's words—are just as inspiring to me as women are. I remember seeing this documentary once. Over the course of a single month, every bee in the hive has a number of different jobs: nurse, housekeeper, architect, builder, organizer, guard, forager, and explorer. That reminds me of my mother, of course. But what about the plastic rose? I still can't make any sense of it."

"The rose is the queen of flowers," Chayton chimes in, "and the symbol of perfect beauty."

"How do you happen to know that?"

"My great-grandfather knew a lot about the symbolism of flowers. It's all in his notebook."

"And rose, symbol of love, too," Keiji adds.

"You're not the heart chakra for nothing, Keiji!" Chayton says with a laugh.

"The Virgin Mary is referred to as the 'mystical rose' in sacred texts," Stepan remarks. "The Queen of Heaven and Earth."

"Whoa!" Chayton exclaims. "That's your cosmic chakra talking there! Am I right?"

"That's all well and fine," Helen cuts in impatiently, "but this rose is made of plastic. If it is my item-clue, what is that supposed to mean? That I'm a fake?"

The Queen of Fakes! my inner voice quips, and I have to admit, the remark strikes a chord with me.

"Is that how you see it?" Ka inquires.

"Yes, Ka, it is."

"And the interpretation doesn't suit you?"

"Of course it doesn't suit me!"

"In that case, get rid of it."

"How?" Helen asks.

"I want each of you to think of a negative influence," Kassandra replies, her eyes composedly scanning our little circle. "Something you no longer want to be part of your life. Then, one after the other, you will each pick up a stone and throw it into the well."

"Do you mean physically?" Chayton asks.

"Yes, I do. But symbolically, you are throwing off a weight holding you down, as well. We will start with you, the first chakra. What do you want to rid yourself of?"

Chayton grabs a stone and stands up, walks resolutely toward the well, then tosses it in without a second thought.

"Lies!" he bellows, turning around and facing us straight on. "I want to stop telling lies to try to make myself look good. There was no going-away party for me. My pals in LA couldn't care less that I was leaving. And I didn't make all that much money, either. I blew it all on partying and gambling."

"Your honesty is commendable," Ka encourages him. "Your true nature is to stand tall, firmly rooted in the earth. Earth is your chakra element. The material excesses you mentioned simply mean your root chakra was out of balance."

"Is it balanced now?" Ali asks.

"Finding harmony is a lifetime quest. But trying to find it is the first step."

Helen's turn is next. She leans on the well's railing for a moment, then drops in her stone with a whisper. "I'm getting rid of everything that seems fake about me. It's not true; I'm not a fake!"

Kassandra says nothing, and Ali tosses her stone into the well from where she is standing. "Basket!" she hollers. "I'm freeing myself of my parents' disapproval."

Next, Keiji walks over to the well and casts his stone, simply pronouncing the words "my brother." I do the same after writing the word "self-doubt" in my notebook.

"As for me," Stepan bursts out, not waiting his turn, "I am going to throw my entire body into the well!"

"Easy there," Kassandra says softly. "Your spirit inhabits abstract realms that are far beyond traditional understanding. We've already been through that. Being the guardian of the last chakra, the one closest to the heavens, is a difficult role. You must be careful to keep your chakra balanced: if it becomes overdeveloped, your migraines will increase, and you know what that means."

So, Stepan's attacks are related to his dominant chakra.

"Try again but, this time, formulate it differently. It sounded like you wanted to kill yourself."

"To kill myself? It's just the opposite, Ka! I want to bury my old self and be completely reborn."

"I understand, Stepan. Now, throw the stone into the well to symbolize your decision."

"At least I will make the Shepherd happy," Stepan adds. "It's my whole body I want to put in the earth, not just my feet on the ground!"

Stepan's convoluted logic is touching. I realize how

misunderstood he must have felt his entire life, and why his only friends were the stars.

Lastly, Alpha stands up. He walks toward the well in total silence, then freezes, pronouncing a few words in a flat, colorless voice: "The demons of the past."

Mr. Mann is a complete mystery.

At times a purveyor of rural knowledge. At times a buttoned-up introvert—a grump.

The week before, we helped him in the vegetable garden. The enormous plot is located behind one of the two buildings adjoining the farmhouse, in which he apparently lives; Alpha saw him come out of it once. He placed a wooden crate on the ground and introduced each of the vegetables in the garden to us, one after the other, as if they were his children.

"Picking is a delicate business. You need to handle the plants with care and use both hands. But first, you need to take a minute to commune with them, to tune in to their energy and fully experience the present moment."

Mr. Mann closed his eyes and briefly extended his powerful arms. Then, quickly removing a penknife from his pocket, he squatted with ease next to a row of lettuce, made a clean cut through one of the stems, and tossed a head of lettuce into the crate.

"Leave about one inch of the stem in the soil. If you pull up the roots, no new shoots will grow. There is a proper way to harvest every fruit and vegetable. It just takes a little observation. Ali, you are standing next to the tomato plants. Do you notice anything particular about the stalks?"

"Hmm . . . There's a joint of sorts where the stem branches off."

"That's right! It's the detachable part. It gets softer as the tomatoes ripen to encourage picking. Certain plant species grow fruit that is appealing to hungry animals, and they gulp down the fruit and disperse the seeds in their feces. It's the plant's way of exploring the world in search of the ideal place to grow."

Alpha joined Ali to help pick the tomatoes.

"Only pick what we are going to eat today. Vegetables keep better on their stalks than they do in the fridge!" said the cook and gardener as he continued the tour of the property. "Who can identify the vegetable to which this leaf belongs?"

"Carrots," Helen answered, smiling. "Eating carrots, now, that's something I do like!"

"And that's just the way it should be! To harvest them, you need to pull the entire plant up. So, you see, vegetables are just like people. There's not just one instruction manual."

Following his orders, we set about fetching tools, weeding, hoeing, and pruning. Chayton and Ali took off their shoes, Helen watered the plants, and I stuck my hands in the soil—with great enthusiasm, I have to admit.

"I'm going to tell you a secret," Mr. Mann said, at last. "In the physical sphere of Materia, each vegetable has its own nutritional value: calories, vitamins, minerals—the biological aspect of reality. But the body isn't the only thing that needs nutrients. We need to train ourselves to look beyond the world's physical aspects. Alpha, you are the custodian of the chakra of the third eye. Maybe this means something to you?"

"Uh, no . . . I . . . I'm not really sure yet . . ."

"Yes, right. Of course. It's still too soon. You need more

time. Miss Kassandra has told me that often enough. I just can't wait for you all to know, I guess."

"To know what?" Ali asked.

"That we all come with our own instruction manual—the same way vegetables do, by golly! I just told you that."

Then, with an expletive-laced rant, he began gathering up the tools.

"In the immaterial realm of Spiritua, the food you eat has an altogether different significance. For example, avoid eating red food when you are feeling angry or annoyed, and steer clear of sauces and heavy food when you are burdened by worries. If you're feeling listless and world-weary, on the other hand, treat yourself to a plateful—of beans!"

With this, Mr. Mann picked up the crate and headed to the kitchen. We didn't quite get it, but as soon as he left, the mood lightened. I guess we all needed to unwind.

Ali started dashing about the garden. Vaulting over a low bush, she picked up a half-rotten tomato and threw it at Chayton. He sidestepped it, laughing, and started chasing her, jostling Helen in the process, who, hose still in hand, inadvertently sprayed Keiji. Next, Alpha joined the fray, dousing Helen with water from a nearby bucket, and Stepan, too. Chayton, in the meantime, had stopped running after Ali—she was too fast for him—and turned his attention to me, instead. Picking me up, he gave a nod to Ali, who readily grabbed the garden hose and sprayed the two of us.

A full-blown water fight and a fit of general laughter ensued. The plants got watered, too.

*

We haven't seen much of Mr. Mann in the last few days, only brief appearances at mealtimes or as he goes about his work in the farmyard. It turns out the blond-haired shepherdess we saw the day of the storm is his daughter. We were able to worm the information out of Ka, but no one has seen the girl since. You'd think she didn't live on the farm.

After tossing and turning all night, I'm up at the crack of dawn. I've routinely woken up later than usual since training began, but not today. I creep softly along the quiet, dark balcony. From my vantage point, I can see Mr. Mann in the dimly lit kitchen. He is already busy at the stove.

As I make my way down the stairs, his voice, like boiling water, sputters, "Good morning, Rae!"

How did he know it was me? His back is turned to me, and I didn't make a sound.

"Bring me ten eggs from the chicken coop, please."

Without so much as a glance, he nods in the direction of a basket near the entrance. He already has his hands full with his usual assortment of baking trays, saucepans, dishes, and cutting boards.

I pick up the basket and exit the kitchen, leaving Mr. Mann to his cooking marathon. A glowing light beyond the horizon tints the sky with streaks of orange, announcing the new day; the small copse of trees on the far side of the farmyard stirs with life. I push open the gate of a chicken-wire enclosure surrounding a wooden shed. Through an opening in the middle, I can make out the hens sleeping inside.

"Oh, it's you!"

I wasn't expecting to see anyone, especially not Chayton the Late Riser.

"I've been mulling over my messenger-animal all night. I didn't sleep a wink," he greets me.

His massive body is stretched out in a patch of flattened grass. His head is propped on the hand of one bent arm, a hen nestled in the crook of the other.

"And don't you go thinking she's the one! I'd rather have the rhinoceros, though I can already hear Alpha making fun of me: 'Of course it's the rhino, that hulking, horned pachyderm that knocks down everything in its path!'"

His brusque tone gives the hen a start.

"Sorry, chickie. Everything's fine."

Apparently reassured, the hen nestles back into the crook of his arm.

"Well, at least there's one chick who doesn't get all worked up about my calling her that!" he says, stifling a muted laugh so as not to upset his feathered friend.

I can't help but smile.

"She's injured. Her wing was bleeding. She must have caught it in the wire mesh."

In the safety of his warm embrace, the hen seems alert but perfectly calm, happy to stay put, her breath keeping time with Chayton's. Everything about her—round eyes, red comb . . . even her beak—seems surprisingly relaxed.

"I noticed a *sábila* in the garden by the well. That's what my people call aloe vera, a succulent plant species with healing properties. It's described in my grandfather's notebook."

He has slathered a gel-like paste on the chicken's wing.

"I have to tell you something, Sparrow. Where I come from in Peru, we all have animal nicknames. It's the way of the Quechua. So, that makes you part of the clan, I guess."

He lets out a sigh, ruffling the feathers on the hen's neck.

"I messed up with Helen, you know . . . I shouldn't have . . . Well, anyhow, it sort of complicates things. Do you think she'll stay pissed for long?"

Suddenly, a blond head appears in the opening of the henhouse.

"It's better to feel remorse than regret!"

We immediately recognize the magnificent locks poking out from under a vintage headscarf. Her hair is silky and looks freshly brushed.

"Like my dad always says, we learn from our mistakes."

"Anais, right?" Chayton asks.

"Yes," Mr. Mann's daughter whispers, almost an animal whistle, bewitching.

She climbs out and stretches and lets out a good yawn just as the rooster begins to crow.

"I am so happy to talk to you two, at last," she says, fixing her large and expressive dark eyes on me. She is very petite and has an unsettlingly deep gaze.

"That's right. I mean both of you, Rae. Just because you don't say anything, that doesn't mean there are no words inside of you."

"Hey, you sound like a book. Is that a quote?"

"You could say that."

"How old are you?"

"Thirteen."

Without warning, Anais opens her arms wide with a mischievous smile and throws them around Chayton and the hen. She's certainly not like most girls her age.

"Uh . . . What the . . ."

Anais is simply giving them a hug.

"Thanks for helping Daisy. I know, it sounds more like a cow name, but the hens here all have flower names."

She then walks over to me and wraps her slight arms around my neck. I can feel her cool cheek against mine as she gives me an affectionate squeeze. The tenderness of her gesture overwhelms me, reminding me of my sisters. It hits me all at once how much I miss them.

"Don't you go to school?" Chayton asks.

"Not for the time being," the girl replies.

"Why not? Is Ka afraid you'll spill the beans?"

Anais sidesteps the question. "You know, I've been hoping to talk to you for days now. I'm bored here. Do you like my scarf? I have a collection of headscarves to match my outfits. It's a family tradition passed down from my grandmother.

Besides, when I sleep with it on, I don't have to brush my hair in the morning. I hate it when my hair gets all ratty."

"I'm with you on that!"

In the distance, a hoarse cough cuts through the crisp morning air.

"Darn! It's my father," Anais stammers with a start. "Please don't tell him about any of this. I'm not supposed to talk to you."

"Why not?" Chayton asks.

"He's trying to protect me, that's all," Anais answers.

There is a flicker of fear in her eye, a vague, inexpressible dread that I can't quite put my finger on. She runs to hide in the henhouse as Mr. Mann's gravelly voice rumbles across the yard.

"How about those eggs? We don't have all day, you know!"

"We're coming," Chayton replies, obviously grasping the urgency of the situation.

The door to the kitchen shuts with a bang, followed by the familiar sounds of Mr. Mann's grumbling.

"Okay, little chick. Time to go home," Chayton tells Daisy, who, like an obedient dog, returns to the brood of hens.

From the opening in the henhouse, we catch sight of Anais's hands, and eggs begin appearing, two at a time. A few minutes later, Chayton places the basketful of eggs on the kitchen table.

"Sorry, Mr. Mann. Rae was late because of me."

The chef carries on with his work without a word of thanks. The farrier apron tied around his waist emphasizes his stocky build. Chayton and I sit down on the stairs. From the noise in the bedrooms overhead, we can tell our companions are getting up.

We are both a little shaken. First, there was the hen. Not only did Chayton heal her, but he seemed to possess some mysterious power that also soothed her. Then, there was the meeting with Anais Mann. It left us both with a funny taste in our mouth. Why was she hiding from her father, and what could he be trying to protect her from? It didn't make sense. The girl was clearly afraid, but of what? Or of whom?

What if Mr. Mann is more than an endearing albeit surly farmer? What if, beyond the program, other unmentionable secrets are hidden at the farm?

21

Over the weeks, the Shepherd's salt-and-pepper stubble has grown thicker.

Bushy facial hair now conceals the slight scarring of the head instructor's repaired cleft lip. He's been teaching us for almost two months now, and we know practically nothing about him.

He never talks about himself. He only answers questions that have to do with our training and the program. He's like those sports addicts who eat, sleep, and breathe sports. On the rare occasions he sits down with us at mealtimes—he usually prefers tramping about outside or tending to the animals—he sits in silence. Our eyes often meet.

"I have no interest whatsoever in the work I did for the US intelligence department," he often tells us. "The United States and other major powers have lost sight of what really matters. A global disaster is looming on the horizon, and the world's decision-makers are not even questioning their actions. True courage demands rethinking our entire value system. What I did as a government operative is no longer relevant. That part of my life is a closed chapter."

Closed or no, we would have loved to hear more about it.

"As you know, I have never seen the Keeper. That doesn't matter at all. What does matter is Spirit Era. I believe the program's predictions. I spent fifteen years in a cabin in the woods, and it was enough time for me to understand the extent of the damage we are inflicting on the planet. Mankind has destroyed so much of nature that our own destruction would be a fitting end."

Unsurprisingly, he doesn't live on the farm like Ka. It's hard to imagine him shut up within four walls. The location of the Shepherd's campsite is a complete mystery, however. Alpha says sometimes, when it rains, he sleeps in one of the haylofts in the barn.

"During the second month of training, you will be exploring other rudimentary combat techniques to widen your range of possibilities and help you choose your own style."

These last few weeks, Keiji, Ali, and Chayton have introduced other forms of martial arts in Flyfold. Not Alpha, though. He's served only as Shepherd's assistant, no doubt as a further lesson in humility.

We began with the basics of *Wadō-ryū* after first being subjected to a brief lecture from Keiji. The accelerated language course he is taking with Kassandra has helped him improve his English, and he is proud to display his proficiency daily. Stepan, on the other hand, only attends the class intermittently. His English is actually quite good already.

"*Wadō-ryū* is school of karate and jiujitsu started by Hironori Ōtsuka. It be made popular in the 1960s. The founder say: 'Violent actions can be understood as path to martial arts, but true meaning is to seek path of peace and harmony.'"

In *Wadō-ryū*, the emphasis is placed on evading rather than blocking attacks. We practiced using *atemi* techniques—blows or strikes delivered by any part of the body to any part of the opponent's body in Japanese martial arts—using our fists and our feet. The strongest among us succeed in throwing their opponent off-balance. I was only able to topple Keiji. I caught him off guard during one of his demonstrations. Everyone else is taller than me, although Keiji says size doesn't matter.

With Ali, it was a different story. She has always been extremely athletic and has tried a lot of different sports. Baseball and surfing are her favorites. Her teaching philosophy was based on freestyle fighting techniques, a mix of Western boxing, Israeli Krav Maga, and Bruce Lee's school of Jeet Kune Do. She had ended up by chance in an Australian club where her best friend and her friend's family used to train together. At first, she considered getting her parents to join, too, but she quickly gave up on the idea. They weren't interested in self-defense any more than they were in their daughter.

Confidence, tolerance, and self-control are the keys to freestyle fighting. Stick fighting was the first technique we tried, and I have to confess, I was pretty good at it.

Until then, Alpha had been making no effort to hide his bad mood. But when the Shepherd asked Chayton to come forward, he left the circle altogether. His rival's promotion was too much for him. Especially since Chayton learned to fight in the streets, a sharp contrast to the years Alpha spent participating in official karate competitions.

"When someone is attacking you and it is not for sport, you need to eliminate the danger before it eliminates you. It's a question of survival," the Shepherd told us.

The self-defense techniques he then showed us were not meant to be part of a rigorous martial arts training program, he explained. We would learn them mainly to develop greater body awareness. They were only to be used in the program's mantras as a last resort. He and Chayton gave us a demonstration combining boxing, wrestling, and jiujitsu techniques. I could see that Chayton's center of gravity was very low. He kept his legs bent most of the time, staying close to the ground and leaning his weight into his movements. In other words, he was aligned with his root chakra.

Of course, both sides delivered blows sparingly. At one point, however, I thought the fight was about to get out of hand. Chayton had just delivered a rapid, carefully aimed kick to the instructor's calf, momentarily bringing him to his knees. The Shepherd jumped back up and toppled his opponent, however. Then, using the weight of his body to pin him to the ground, he pressed his knee into Chayton's chest and his fist into his throat. Chayton's red face and contorted features spoke volumes.

"Hey, take it easy there, Instructor!"

It was Alpha, oddly enough, who spoke out. The Shepherd immediately released his hold and held out a hand to help Chayton to his feet. Chayton was gagging.

"*Rei!*"

The opponents bowed to each other as if nothing had happened. Nevertheless, for a split second there, it had looked as though our instructor was about to lose it, or rather, that his old fighting reflexes had returned. The past may be a closed chapter, but I guess it is never that far behind.

"Nowadays," the head instructor went on composedly, "there is an international hand-to-hand combat federation dedicated to self-defense practices. In certain situations, hand-to-hand combat is ethical. When you are in mortal danger, it is a legitimate self-defense technique." With deliberate steps, the Shepherd went over to Alpha. He was still on the sidelines. "It all depends on what you are fighting for," the instructor added.

"I get it, Instructor!" Chayton chimed in from behind. "We don't break bones for money. My street fighting days are over!"

"What about you, Alpha? What did you learn from the demonstration?"

"What's it got to do with me?"

"Wouldn't you say anger is generally not directed at others but primarily at ourselves?" the head instructor inquired.

"Humph . . . I'd say that's irrelevant," Alpha countered.

"On the contrary. It's the crux of the problem."

"What problem is that?" Alpha snapped.

"The medals . . ."

"What are you talking about?"

"From the perspective of Materia, the hand-to-hand combat techniques Chayton used are identical to those he fought with in Los Angeles. It's the intention that has changed. Through the prism of Spiritua, he now has a choice. The question is no longer about how to fight but what for."

Alpha got to his feet slowly, his gaze riveted on the Shepherd's.

"What about you?" the older man went on. "Do you know what your deeper motivations are, what you have been fighting for up until now?"

That was the last straw. What, exactly, was the Shepherd driving at, anyway? Alpha stormed out of Flyfold in a rage. We didn't see him again until the following morning.

#THEKEEPER #SAVETHEWORLD

POST 4—THE FIRST KEY

NOVEMBER 21, 2035

THEY ARE READY.

    Ready to set off.

    Ready to face their destiny.

    Ready to sweep you up on their journey.

    Two hours a day for one week, livestreamed around the world. That is the time they have been given to find the first key. The root chakra key. Tomorrow at 20:00 CUT time, you will be able to watch their first connection to the program—CUT: Coordinated Universal Time, primary time standard by which the world regulates clocks and time.

    In Mantra 1, homes are nothing like the ones we know. A tiny minority has a monopoly on wealth, and the masses are poor. So poor, the earth has literally swallowed them up. It is a world of criminal overabundance and deadly famine.

    The Seven Chosen have decided to go the route of courage. Soon, in the face of the dangers threatening the world, you, too, will be forced to decide.

    TO MAKE A CHOICE.

PART FOUR

THE START

22

"Tomorrow is the first day of immersion."

Kassandra has on a long white dress today. A cross-body canvas satchel hangs on one side. As usual, the timeless quality of her outfits suits her perfectly.

"The program has chosen you among countless applicants. Your high potential makes you the emissaries of humanity. You will have to do everything within your power to find the seven keys."

We are sitting in a half circle opposite our mentor in a small, secluded clearing at the edge of the woods. She is seated under an enormous gnarled tree with exposed roots. Sunlight is streaming through its leafless branches. We walked more than usual to get here. Generally, we stay near the farm for Ka's classes.

"We have gathered here for the Spirit Era oath-giving ceremony. I hereby declare the ceremony open."

Kassandra stands and asks Chayton to follow her. They walk to the other side of the tree together and vanish. A few minutes later, Chayton reappears, beaming. He is holding a small branch in one hand.

"Helen," he says simply before stretching out in the grass next to me.

Then, each of my companions is called one after the other, in the order of the chakras. None of us speaks as the ceremony unfolds. When Keiji returns and pronounces my name, my forehead starts to perspire.

I stand up and walk over to the tree and make my way around its knotted, moss-speckled trunk. It is so large, I count ten steps before I get to a good-sized opening in the back of the tree. It is about waist high, but I have no trouble slipping through. Kassandra, as I predicted, is waiting for me inside—the tree is hollow!

"Welcome to the Chakra Tree Ceremony!"

Ka is wearing a shawl. It must have been in her satchel. Dry leaves cling to her clothes and make it hard to distinguish her from the earth-colored background. The carpet of dead leaves crunches under my feet as I walk over and sit cross-legged opposite her. Overcome by emotion, a lump rises in my throat.

"Give me your hands." Her own are reassuringly warm.

"Rae, do you swear to faithfully serve the program?"

I nod, my eyes returning her deep, penetrating gaze.

"Each and every one of us is a tree of life, Rae. We all have roots, a trunk, bark, limbs, and branches. Your dominant chakra is the fifth chakra, the chakra of communication, but that doesn't mean the others do not exist inside of you. It is my honor today to present you with your Chakra Tree. It will help you to achieve a greater understanding of yourself. Look, Rae!"

I lift my eyes. A beam of sunlight penetrates the hollow trunk. The bark inside is aglow with a rainbow of colors. Above my head, the crown is illuminated with a hint of violet gradually changing into a blend of deep indigo and sky blue. Where the branches and trunk meet, there is a mix of lovely hues of green and, at the bottom, a hint of yellow, a touch of orange, and a good deal more red.

Kassandra lets go of my hands. With a sweeping gesture, she scoops up an armful of dry leaves, then tosses them into the air. They come raining down on us.

"The Chakra Tree has spoken."

She pulls a set of markers out of her bag, picks up a small tree-shaped branch, and begins to color it.

"A touch of violet . . . You do not have a strong connection to the realm of the abstract . . . A great deal of deep indigo blue. Your spiritual world is highly developed . . . Indigo is associated with the third eye chakra, our source of intuition, and sky blue, with your dominant chakra. The throat chakra, of course. The powerful connection between your fifth and sixth chakras is what makes it possible for you to hear your inner voice. But above all . . ."

Okay, I guess if the Keeper knew about my voice—not that I understand how—then Ka must know, too. I suspected as much.

"Above all, the connection between the two enables you to communicate with other people telepathically."

So, she knows about that as well!

"The gift of communication generally goes hand in hand with the sixth chakra. In your case, this is certainly heightened by your highly developed intuition chakra and your silence. You have the power of telepathy, Rae."

My mentor isn't telling me anything new, of course. But hearing her put it into words, and understanding how much she knows about me, gives me a jolt. She pays no attention to me and continues coloring.

"The shades of green are harmonious. Your heart chakra is balanced. The lower three chakras related to the physical world are weak, however. The first, the root chakra, is sufficient. You have enough red, even if it is spotty. The creative chakra and the sun chakra, however . . ."

The ray of sunlight vanishes the moment she finishes

coloring my Chakra Tree Map. The bark inside the tree takes on its former dark, earthy shades.

"This is for you," Ka pronounces solemnly, handing me my Chakra Tree.

I teeter out of the trunk in a bit of a daze, my chakra map in hand. I vaguely remember walking past Alpha before dropping to the ground in the clearing. In front of me, I see one thing only: the azure-blue sky, unbroken and soothing. Blue, my color, whose timeless presence softens the words that have been whirling in my head ever since Kassandra pronounced them.

I have the gift of telepathy. I can read minds.

23

To be heard without speaking . . .

So that's what it means to be the custodian of the throat chakra, although my own throat—be it deliberately, unconsciously, or from post-traumatic stress—is drier than the Sahara. I don't even know if I will ever speak again. My gift: a voice without words in the realm of Materia, albeit loud and clear in that of Spiritua. A contradiction that is there, inside of me, of its own accord. As are the silent voices of other people, deeper than words. Though I still have much to understand and learn, I have discovered one thing, something I could not have imagined before coming to the farm: my voice and my path are one and the same.

It turns out we won't be hearing from the Keeper before we enter the program. Well, not exactly. Ten minutes earlier, we heard that familiar, unsettling music—violin, xylophone, harp, and silence—and the darkened silhouette of the Keeper once again appeared on the lowered giant screen. As promised, he came back for the end of our training period. For some strange reason, the minutes that followed seemed like a hazy, compressed dream to me. I have only a brief recollection of the Keeper's words:

Greetings to the Seven Chosen. Tomorrow the program will be aired for the first time. At which point, you will be an integral part of it . . .

The Mantras generated by the program reflect the seven great afflictions that plague humanity. If a better awareness is unable to alter our individualistic course, one of these microcosms will trigger an apocalyptic disaster. The program's seven scenarios were designed in relation to each of the seven chakras, its element, and its symbolic manifestations.

The metallic-sounding voice of the Keeper was as unreal as ever.

Mantra 1: Barren Mother EARTH—Chakra 1: Root.
Mantra 2: WATERS Unleashed—Chakra 2: Creation.
Mantra 3: Deadly HEAT—Chakra 3: Sun.
Mantra 4: Robotized LIFE—Chakra 4: Heart.
Mantra 5: Rampant EPIDEMICS—Chakra 5: Expression.
Mantra 6: Global Nuclear WAR—Chakra 6: Third Eye.
Mantra 7: Catastrophic METEOR Collision—Chakra 7: Crown.

And lastly, sounding more distant:

In the first mantra, excess spells doom for humanity. We will meet again after week one of immersion. Good luck to you all!

The haze disperses as the Shepherd begins outlining the rules in solemn tones.

"Tomorrow you will have a full day of rest before the live broadcast, which begins at eight p.m. The immersion will last two hours. In total, you will have seven chances, one per day, to bring back the first key."

This time, it's for real.

"The viewers will see your actual silhouettes through the prism of Materia," Kassandra continues, "but they will also see your aura, your energy field in the color of your chakra, through the prism of Spiritua. Furthermore, your voices will be modified, and your names changed."

"Changed to what?" Ali asks.

"You will each be named after your chakra in Sanskrit, the sacred language of ancient India."

Without warning, the Keeper's solemn voice rings out.

The audience will hear:

With hymnlike solemnity, our new names resonate within the walls of Flyfold.

Stepan: Sahasrara.
Alpha: Ajna.
Rae: Vishuddha.
Keiji: Anahata.
Ali: Manipura.
Helen: Svadhisthana.
Chayton: Muladhara.

"Remember," Ka continues, standing ramrod straight, "the hidden objects in the program will help put you on the path to the key. You will not discover them through the prism of Spiritua. Apart from Helen, who already has hers, and Ali, who gave her the piece of gum, you are each allowed only one material transfer between worlds, voluntarily or not. The quantum pod activates the 3D printing system the minute an object is exchanged in either direction."

The more she explains, the more on edge she appears.

"Another thing. You don't have to stay together the whole time you are connected. But you must be together at all costs when you say the name of the place where you want to return. As you already know, time unfolds at a different rate inside the program: the first mantra may trigger a state of stupor. It may feel unsettling, unlikely, and even dangerous."

Kassandra takes a deep breath as if she's lacking oxygen herself.

"If one of the Seven misses the call when the alarm on your wristbands go off, there is another way to bring you out of immersion: Head Instructor Shepherd can simply unplug you from the program. But when your mind is immersed in the depths of Spirit Era, it is no longer directly connected to your body, and an abrupt unplugging could cause neurological damage."

That's not the only risk; I can't help but think of the cut on Alpha's palm. If there is any real danger, the others have the right to know about it before our immersion.

"Life in the program will continue during your absence. As the Keeper told you, he designed it for real autonomy."

"Real autonomy?" Stepan is a total geek, and even he doesn't seem to get it.

"The starting point of AI research in the 1950s was to see if a machine could learn, right?"

"Yes," Stepan concurs.

"Um, like AI for dummies?" Chayton asks.

"No, what I mean is artificial intelligence," Ka clarifies. "The machine-learning algorithms that make it possible to build intelligent machines. The Keeper has dedicated his life to endowing Spirit Era with both autonomous decision-making capabilities, rooted in the reality of Materia, and capacities for processing immaterial, abstract information, from the perspective of Spiritua."

"In other words," Stepan recaps with a dreamy look in his

eyes, "the program provides solutions through allegories, the same way algorithms provide solutions to computer problems. The seven keys . . ."

"That's right," Ka says. "But nobody knows what is in store for you, or what the first key looks like."

"Do you trust yourselves?" the Shepherd cuts in abruptly. "Do you inspire trust, and are you ready to trust others?"

"What do you mean?" Ali asks.

"Those are the three questions you have to ask yourselves."

"Pardon, Shepherd-sensei," Keiji responds hesitantly. "I don't understand."

"Neither do I," Chayton admits.

"Solidarity," the Shepherd replies tersely.

"How so?"

"Solidarity is the prerequisite to finding the seven keys, Chayton. And it starts at home, as do the three types of trust. Over the course of our practice sessions, you have shown you are capable of trusting yourself and of inspiring trust in others. But the question remains—are you able to trust them?"

"Uh . . ."

"The first chakra represents our connection to the earth," the Shepherd continues. "Warm and nurturing, it embodies our sense of security and grounding, our connection to the physical world. How are we connected to the earth? Do our feet move lightly over its surface or absently, without thinking? Are they firmly rooted in the ground or, on the contrary, trudging through heavy mud?"

My father gave me a sense of security and grounding. Now that he's gone, I don't really know.

"It is time."

Kassandra nods, then utters one final sentence, her voice shaky.

"And once they are there, they will be on their own."

LOGBOOK
INSTRUCTOR: KA
SEASON I

NOVEMBER 22, 2035

Immersion is just a few hours away.

They are ready, I try to convince myself, to banish all thoughts of the dangers that await them. The cybernetic experts at the C7 Unit created by Interpol are already hard at work trying to hack into the program, and their efforts to locate us will no doubt redouble during the live broadcast. I know the IT security is strong, but how things are going to play out inside the program is an entirely different story.

For one thing, we don't know how the brains of the Seven Chosen will respond to immersion in terms of either the Materia or the Spiritua—how it will affect their bodies and souls. For another, the limits of the security shield designed by Spirit Era to protect the Seven haven't been tested. If the technology is only enough to keep them alive, then the danger is far too great.

"They are ready," I tell myself again. The Seven have strengthened their connection with nature thanks to Head Instructor Shepherd's root chakra training sessions. A few have already encountered their messenger-animal—it will be an invaluable source of inspiration and strength—and the Chakra Tree Ceremony has revealed the chakra maps to each of them, and I have revealed their gifts.

Chayton has the gift of animal magnetism; he suspected as much. His power to heal springs from the invisible natural fluid present in the world and absorbed in greater or lesser quantities by all living things. His exceptionally strong connection to the earth allows him to attract great quantities of it. So, the tough-skinned, bellicose-looking white rhinoceros—actually a sociable herbivore—gives him the self-confidence and balance he lacks. For his gift to fully flourish, however, Chayton will need to look to the might and solidity of his native Sierra mountains.

Helen has the gift of heightened chromatic perception. Though she has only used it to design clothes for the time being, her enhanced sense of sight allows her to see much more, to see the colors and the shapes of auras. Her messenger honeybee, the symbol of creativity, will encourage her to explore, harvest, and share her creative talent.

As for Ali, the dragonfly's external balance and impressive agility are still well out of reach. She will only be able to develop her gift of telekinesis—influencing physical objects with her mind—once the fire inside her has subsided.

For the others, it is still too early, especially since the spiritual attraction of the upper chakras pulls them away from the earth. Each of the Seven will evolve in conjunction with the search for the keys of the seven mantras. For now, they are heeding the call of the first, the root chakra, personified by Chayton, though the others will have the opportunity to grow, as well. Whether they will take it remains to be seen . . .

They are ready.

24

I feel a burning sensation in my belly button.

The strands of my quantum pod were connected once again to my uniform's honeycomb waffle knit, and I was overcome with the same sense of soothing warmth. I welcomed the transparent hose that dropped from Flyfold's ceiling like an old friend and eagerly awaited the azure-blue fluid as it started its slow descent through the giant umbilical cord. I felt confident.

Eyes closed, I tried to imagine what lay ahead, what our immersion into the first world would be like, what fate the program had in store for us. Images from the last few weeks flashed through my head. Everything blurred together: the training sessions and the mysterious encounter with Anais Mann, my companions and Alpha, Helen's bewitching beauty and her siren song luring Alpha into her net. I envied her. I wanted to wake up one day and find myself in her body. I felt dizzy . . . couldn't breathe.

But right now, my belly button is on fire as if a hot poker is being pressed into it. The burning is almost unbearable. I am on the verge of crying out in pain when it suddenly ceases. My mind goes blank. I open my eyes.

Mind the gap between the train and the platform as you leave the High Express. The suave tones of a recorded announcement echo through the compartment.

Stand clear of the closing doors.

"The subway," Ali says. "We're in a subway car!"

The doors close, and the train pulls out. It is an articulated open-corridor vehicle. At the front end, a few yards from where we are seated, is a crimson-red door with a round opaque window that leads to the driver's compartment, or so I assume.

"Yes, a train," stammers Keiji, who is seated opposite me. "We are in belly of giant snake."

Flexible tubular rolls connect the wagons so they can move independently of each other. When the articulated high-speed vehicle rounds a curve, it feels more like a spinning teacup ride than it does a subway.

"Ugh, the rocking! I don't feel so well," Keiji adds. He is, indeed, looking rather green around the gills.

Not far from him, Ali is all eyes and ears. On my left, without having to look at her, I can make out Helen's silhouette. Stepan has a booth seat all to himself, whereas Alpha and Chayton are seated nearby with their backs to each other.

"I think . . . ," Keiji stammers, clutching his head. "I think I'm going to be sick."

"Don't look down," Ali advises him. "Look straight ahead and concentrate on your breathing." There's nobody on the train but us. It feels a bit strange to be alone in this never-ending corridor. The train's minimalist design is even stranger—sleek but excessively cold.

"Rae, would you mind giving Keiji your seat? Riding backward makes me feel sick, too."

I move aside, agreeing without words.

"Thanks," Keiji says.

The block of leather seats has a unique undulating shape. There are little built-in tables, oval shaped like the windows, that remind me of miniature mushroom clouds. Apart from a narrow strip of tinted mirror running the length of the ceiling, the coach's interior fittings, from the plush, impeccably clean carpet to the frosted-glass windows, all have a matte-black finish. The opaque windows completely block the view outside. We have no idea where we are.

The train eventually slows down.

Mind the gap between the train and the platform as you leave the High Express.

The doors open. From where we are seated, we have a hard time making out the station. Two men dressed to a tee, with slick hair and futuristic glasses, board the train.

Stand clear of the closing doors.

With an odd, jerky step, the Adonises make a beeline for a couple of seats a good distance away. They don't look alike but somehow still seem like twins. Their gestures and strangely elegant gray suits are perfectly synchronized.

As the train pulls out, an odorless mist descends with a faint hiss from the overhead strip of mirrors and rapidly dissolves. Nobody says a word as the subway snakes its way silently along. I wonder where we are going and how we can even hope to begin looking for a key in a world we know nothing about. We don't even know where to start. We might as well be looking for a needle in a haystack.

Across from me, the empty seat seems to be breathing. As I stare at it intently, I can practically make out the shape of a woman. I blink hard, but the slender, athletic shape in matte-black leather is only more distinct: I am looking at a creature, part female, part seat. A bench-woman!

At the next stop, another well-groomed young man boards

the train. He is wearing a dark-gray turtleneck and a pair of matching pants and has a book with a red and black cover in one hand. I dub him Stendhal, like the nineteenth-century French writer my father introduced me to. Right behind him comes an elderly woman with frizzy white hair and an impeccably cut suit. She is carrying a loosely knit, sock-shaped bag. I will call her Lady Fluff.

Again, the doors close, and the same inexplicable veil of mist descends from the ceiling. In the meantime, the seat opposite me has gone back to its initial form and function. *A pity,* I think.

The journey continues in absolute silence. The atmosphere is increasingly oppressive. My companions and I exchange inquisitive glances—we have no idea where any of this is leading. What should we do? Get up, start a conversation with one of the passengers, get off at the next station?

Mind the gap between the train and the platform as you leave the High Express.

This time, when the doors open, a small crowd rushes in. By tacit agreement, Alpha comes over to sit by me, and Chayton moves to sit next to Stepan. We'd better stick close together.

Stand clear of the closing doors.

The tone of the announcement is unctuous and slightly patronizing. It sounds fake.

Pscht, pscht. The veil of mist descends on us again.

"Please, sir, please, ma'am, a pretty rose for you?" a voice rings out.

Its lively, lilting tone is like music to my ears in this atmosphere of overly polished anonymity. I recognize the girl at once.

"Roses! Get your pretty roses!"

It's the flower seller from Toptown, the girl with the long

tangle of golden hair. She is still swimming in oversized boys' clothes, and she has the same prominent cheekbones and large mole on one temple. Yes, it's definitely that girl.

Funny, there was supposed to be no connection between the trial run and Mantra 1.

"A rose, kind sir? A rose, ma'am?"

She isn't with the gang of children anymore, and the artificial flowers she is holding up look like leeks, but she has the same wary look in her eye.

"A pretty rose for the kind gentleman?"

Neither of the Adonises deigns to answer. They simply pretend she isn't there. The small girl must be about the same age as Anais Mann. Her dirt-streaked cheeks make it hard to tell. She continues on her way, moving from one passenger to the next.

She heads toward Stendhal, who is sitting near the rubber connector at the end of the coach. It expands and shrinks, expands and shrinks again. It reminds me of a giant accordion. My companions are all staring at that part of the wagon, too. Even Stepan.

"Roses! Get your pretty roses!"

Stendhal ignores her as well. But that's not what fazes me. It's something else. Something crazy, extraordinary, and— utterly horrifying. Neither Stendhal nor any of the other passengers seem to notice, but the flexible gangway connector starts to balloon outward into a weird, distorted shape. The bulging black rubber form expands its accordion-like pleats, grows larger and larger until its enormous head reaches the ceiling.

Before us, like a hulking colossus, stands a figure like none I'd ever encountered before, not even in books. Its skull is like an oil drum, its neck, a tractor tire . . .

It's an . . . *accordion-monster*!

25

An accordion-monster has come to life . . .

I keep repeating the words to myself, in utter disbelief. An accordion-monster has emerged from the subway, begot of the floor and the flexible rolls connecting the wagons. It is towering before us, only a few yards away, in all its dreadful grandeur. I pinch myself—I must be dreaming!

"A rose, ma'am?" the flower seller asks Lady Fluff.

The giant's shape is growing sharper. It flexes its articulated rubber pleats like it's doing warm-ups. Amazingly, the two Adonises, Stendhal, and the other passengers seem unperturbed. Apparently, we are the only ones who can see it.

"A pretty rose, pretty lady?" the young girl tries again.

Without a word, Lady Fluff plunges an arm into her sock-shaped bag and begins rummaging through it. Just then, the monster's accordion legs swing into action, and it struggles to move forward on its crumpled spatula feet. The colossus makes its way over to Lady Fluff, who continues rifling through her bag without batting an eye.

"Aha!" Lady Fluff cries out victoriously, extracting an article from her carryall. The proffered item leaves me speechless—figuratively, that is to say. In exchange for a leek flower, the old woman is offering a bit of soap, about the size of a walnut. From the flower seller's smile, you'd think it was a precious gemstone!

But what comes next is even more shocking. While the sock-bag woman and the flower seller are busy with the transaction, the monster stations itself behind Lady Fluff; plunges a massive paw, quick as lightning, into her bag; and pulls out a bunch of red paper packets—like the ones for dry yeast.

"Hey, you!" Chayton calls out, jumping to his feet. The girl startles and looks over to the accordion-monster. With fierce, bulging eyes, he stares back at her, seeming eager to squash her like a pesty insect.

"What's the matter with you?" the woman asks Chayton, blind to the monstrous pickpocket towering over her.

"There, behind you!"

"Behind me! What do you mean?" Lady Fluff shrieks, instantly thrown into a panic. "What is it?"

Alarmed by her screams, the passengers all fix their gazes on her.

"There's nobody there at all," says Lady Fluff.

She stands up, visibly shaken.

"Aahhhh!"

Now it's the flower seller's turn to shriek—she recognizes Chayton. Pointing a finger, she backs slowly away from us, deathly pale, like she's seen a ghost.

"No, don't go," Chayton calls out. "There's nothing to be afraid of! I won't hurt . . ."

Mind the gap between the train and the platform as you leave the High Express.

The girl darts out of the wagon in a panic as soon as the sliding doors open, dropping her bouquet in the process.

"If that's your idea of a joke, young man," Lady Fluff reprimands Chayton, "it's in very bad taste."

"We should report the incident to the Brigade," says one of the Adonises as they exit the train.

"Indeed," the second Adonis chimes in. "Behavior like that is insufferable."

"Madam," Chayton stammers disconcertedly, "I can assure you there was . . ."

But the accordion-monster has vanished as if into thin air.

"You were robbed . . ."

"Please, excuse him, ma'am," Alpha cuts in, his voice drowning out Chayton's. "It was an unfortunate mistake. Anyhow, this is our stop."

His loud, insistent tone prompts us to jump to our feet and rush through the doors just as they are closing. Except for Chayton, whom Alpha literally yanks onto the platform by the collar.

"Nice job!" Chayton grumbles as the train pulls out. "You made me look like a royal fool."

"Quick, follow me!"

"What's up with you, Alpha?" Chayton snaps.

"No time to explain," he answers, indicating a handful of passengers rushing toward the station exit. "Come on!"

"No way!" Chayton balks. "We don't have to take orders from you."

It's dark on the platform, and the air is warm. The pencil-thin towers of Toptown slice through the ultraviolet night sky on the other side of the open-air subway station walls. Unlike the trial connection, our outfits are no longer glow in the dark. Rather, they have taken on shades that blend with the ambient gloom.

"Yeah," Ali chimes in, "if it's not too much to ask, try to remember that we're a team!"

"The Great Alpha, as usual, would rather go it alone!" Chayton persists. Alpha turns his gaze uneasily toward the passengers at the far end of the platform, his lips curled.

"The way I see it, I don't really have a choice," he says at last.

Oh yes, Alpha, I think to myself. You do! You can choose to banish that dark something hidden in the depths of your eyes. You can choose to look at me the way I look at you. You can choose to see all of us as partners, as a team you can draw strength from. Or better yet, as friends.

"Anyhow, the girl selling flowers . . . Do you realize what her being here means?"

"That we're in the same world as last time," Ali answers. "So what?"

"It means that our first connection wasn't a trial run," Alpha goes on. "It means they lied to us. What happened here the first time we connected did count. The flower seller recognized Chayton!"

"I say we ought to leave the station," Chayton declares. "That way, we could ask around about the key."

"I don't think it's a good idea," Alpha counters. "We must have landed in the subway, and not in the city like we did last time, for a reason. The flower vendor must be the connection between the two, and thanks to you, Chayton, we've lost her!"

"Fine, we get it," Ali chimes in. "I say, if we are going to follow a trail, let's look for the subway monster. I've never seen anything like it."

"That's the whole point. Remember how the kid reacted when Chayton had another one of those light-bulb moments of his? When he called out to the creature?" Alpha's voice is dripping with irony.

"She flinched when she saw the monster," Keiji answers, relying as usual on his keen sense of observation. "But that impossible, because—the monster was invisible to everyone else. Unless, the whole time, she . . ."

"*Could see the accordion-monster, too!*" Ali and Keiji cry out in chorus.

26

Empty.

The Toptown subway stations are utterly empty: not a single sign or billboard in sight. Everything is sparkling and sanitized. There are no trash cans—though the floor looks so clean you could eat off it—and not a single living soul, apart from the occasional commuter with impeccably styled hair and futuristic glasses. Not a voice to be heard, not a smile to be seen. No tunnels, escalators, or corridors, just a string of identical platforms with the same undulating black leather seats that were in the cars and a single exit leading, presumably, to the streets of Toptown.

I say "presumably" because we don't dare leave the transit system. We are afraid we won't be able to reenter. We haven't encountered any kind of turnstile or checkpoint, only strange tinted-glass flat-screen units set into the platform walls, but we don't know whether the entrance is free. What we do know, however, is that the landscape outside is the same at every stop: skyscrapers with mirrored façades and the name of the city invariably scrolling upward. Almost like a Hollywood movie set. An illusion.

"Welcome to TOPTOWN."

We ride a couple of lines in quick succession, hoping to discover the whereabouts of the flower seller.

"I've had enough of our little search," Helen complains at length.

"Maybe she is in the city, like last time," Keiji intervenes.

"Then this is all a waste of time," Helen replies.

Mind the gap between the train and the platform as you leave the High Express.

"Let's keep looking a little longer," Alpha says.

"How about taking a vote?" Helen suggests, instead. "Who is for and who is against staying in the subway?"

Stand clear of the closing doors.

Again, a spray of odorless mist descends from the ceiling.

"Against," Chayton is quick to reply. "I still say we go look for clues in the city."

"I need air," Stepan gasps. "I'm suffocating down here. I vote for fresh air!"

"The accordion-monster is on the train, not in Toptown," Ali says. "So, this time, I'm with Alpha."

"Rae, too," she adds as I wave in her direction in a show of agreement. "That's three against three. Keiji, you'll have to tip the scales."

"Uh . . . me . . . ?"

He hunkers down in his seat as the train picks up speed.

"I . . . not really know . . ."

Keiji doesn't like rocking the boat. Choosing sides for him must be torture. In the end, he chooses the city—perhaps because Alpha is less inclined to hold a grudge.

"The majority wins!" Chayton exclaims triumphantly. "We get off at the next station."

Suddenly, an alarm sounds in the wagon. It's so high-pitched we have to cover our ears. Stepan grimaces in pain as if his eardrums are splitting.

"Brace positions, everyone!" a passenger shouts, bending over and placing his hands on his head.

The brakes slam, sending my head hard into the seat in front of me. Keiji is propelled forward and lands on the floor.

"What's going on?" Helen cries out.

"I bet it's another SA!" a nearby passenger answers. "Another sick person who decided to get it over with instead of rotting away in the Center for the Infected."

"I hope not." The woman next to him sighs. "Last time, we were stuck here for two whole hours."

"An SA?" Helen asks.

"A suicide attempt, obviously! What planet are you from, anyway?"

"Of course, how stupid of me," Helen says carelessly. "I forgot."

All passengers are requested to evacuate the train. Mind the gap as you exit the train.

The car empties the minute the doors open. We blend into the crowd.

Stand clear of the closing doors.

It is dark outside. An unpleasant smell hangs in the hot, dry air. The program can apparently reproduce smells now, contrary to what we experienced during the trial connection.

"What the hell is going on?" Chayton mutters. We are standing on a narrow, screened-in platform. The passengers are making their way toward the front of the train in small groups.

Attention! Sanitization . . . Attention! Sanitization . . .

A stream of mist pours out of the ceiling into the empty compartment. This time, it is cloudy green. It slowly drifts downward and fills the entire space. The windows quickly fog over, coated in droplets of moisture.

"L-look . . . Did you see that?" Alpha stammers, putting on a show for the woman next to him. "It's the di-disinfection f-for . . ."

"For Bulbosis. Right you are, my boy. It's the least the Council can do to protect us from that horrific disease, though I doubt that Repulsecure really works. How can it, if we still don't know where the contagion is coming from?" With that, the woman joins a group of onlookers toward the front of the train.

"What are they waiting for? Why aren't they clearing the way?" we hear voices asking, utterly devoid of feeling.

"Apparently, the SA is in a piteous state. But she is still breathing. The suicide prevention pit apparently did the job."

"Damn that pit! Who wants to end up a vegetable in a nuthouse! If I had Bulbosis, I'd kill myself, too."

The gawkers are huddled together discussing the scene with their best news-anchor voices. Preceded by Alpha, Chayton, and Ali, we reach the front of the train. Our eyes turn toward the rails, but the onlookers, in a collective surge, move to block our passage. By the looks on their faces, there is no point challenging them. Two men in black uniforms emerge from the rails below, pulling their ski masks to the tops of their heads. On one shoulder of their uniforms, there is a logo in the shape of a golden building like the one we saw in Toptown's designer boutiques. They march past with soldierly gaits.

"Where is the cleanup crew? What are they doing?" the first agent asks.

"They should be here in five minutes," the other answers.

"Is that her shoe over there?"

"Sure looks like it."

The guy stands there, stock-still, and gives a low whistle.

"That was one hell of a tumble she took."

"We're seeing more and more SAs every day. Why the Council allows those filthy beggars up here is beyond me!"

"Has it even been proven the infection is coming from the World Below? I've heard that the *crats* . . ."

"It's the same thing, either way. They're all vermin. I say we eliminate them like we did the crats!"

"That's pretty extreme, isn't it? There are other ways of eradicating an epidemic."

"Not with Bulbosis. That stuff is nasty. It spreads like wildfire."

"It's all over. She's dead." A woman's voice from the tracks below covers the ambient chatter.

"Evacuate the body, immediately!" another voice rings out. "Call in the Brigade!"

The two men in uniform pull down their ski masks. It's back to the daily grind.

"Make it snappy!" another voice calls out. "Let's get the power back on and the traffic moving. I've got a train to run!"

Two minutes later, the passengers all pile back onto the train. We do the same, zombielike. The smell of mothballs hangs in the air.

Stand clear of the closing doors.

None of us sit down; we're all clearly troubled. As we clutch absently at the vertical pole and grab rails, I'm sure each of us wonders how we got into this mess. Frankly, it's not what we were expecting: a decontaminated transit system, a contagious disease, a suicide attempt . . .

Beep-beep! Beep-beep! Beep-beep! Our seven watches go off at once.

We weren't expecting that, either, not that soon.

27

"Already?"

"I can't believe how fast it went!"

"But it seemed a lot longer than two hours, too."

Ali's and Helen's voices reverberate around the immensity of Flyfold. The Shepherd looks on in silence. Kassandra, standing slightly behind him, begins: "So, how are you feeling after your first day of immersion?"

"Exhausted!" says Helen.

"I'm okay," Ali replies, "but starving, like I just had a good workout."

Alpha, Chayton, Keiji, and Stepan agree, and so do I. Though our bodies were at rest in our pods during immersion, I can tell the connection took a lot out of us.

"Well, hungry or no," Helen continues, "it must have been pretty boring for the viewers once we lost track of the monster and the flower vendor. Our adventures in the subway weren't all that exciting!"

"Oh right, the live broadcast!" Ali chimes in with a laugh. "I completely forgot about it once we got there."

"I bet all of us did," Chayton acknowledges.

"You're right about that," Alpha confirms. "After the first couple of minutes, I didn't give it a second thought."

A discreet smile flashes across our mentor's face. She's happy with our show of unity.

"The accordion-monster came to life in the subway," Ali jumps in again. "On the train line where we first landed. He's the lead we're supposed to pursue, right, Ka?"

"No way! I bet it's the girl with the flowers," Chayton dissents. "She's the one we need to track down. It's no coincidence we saw her before, right, Ka?"

"I can't tell you anything," Kassandra replies. "The fact is, I haven't the slightest idea. The Seven alone have the power to interact in Spirit Era and to influence the course of events. You are the only ones who can find the key."

"Speaking of the flower seller," Alpha begins, suspicious, "she recognized Chayton. Toptown is the same town we were immersed in during the test connection. So, it's the same mantra, unlike what you told us."

"You're right, Alpha. But the program, as you know, has a great deal of autonomy. It was designed to consider a multitude of criteria to choose the best option."

"So, basically, it decides everything by itself?"

"No, not everything, Alpha. The Keeper designed the AI to predict the threats menacing the planet and to suggest avenues of action—that our largely meaningless and morally bankrupt societies currently lack."

"Hmph, that'll be no small feat in a place like Toptown—the very height of modern living!"

"Doubting everyone and everything isn't the solution, Alpha. The whole world isn't against you. It's time you learned to recognize those who are on your side. But to do that, you need to accept certain truths . . ."

"Uh, Ka, you're sort of obscuring the issue, aren't you?" Helen asks.

"On the contrary. I'm only encouraging Alpha to clear things up."

Alpha's expression, like he's been caught red-handed, makes me feel ill at ease.

"The way I see it, the city should be regarded as a symbolic microcosm. I'm sure you'll find out more as you go. I trust Spirit Era completely."

"So do we," Stepan declares. "We wouldn't be here otherwise."

From time to time, he really nails it—no words wasted and at just the right time—and since he hardly ever speaks, his words carry weight.

"Will we be returning to the same place tomorrow, for our second day?" Ali asks.

"Yes. Every time you reenter Spirit Era, you find yourself where you were when your watch went off. But remember, life in the program continues to exist even while you are away."

"How is that possible?"

"Spirit Era designed each of the seven VR microcosms as independent entities. Each entity is a universe with its own set of rules, but rooted, conceptually, in the same reality as ours."

"So, according to the program, there are eight parallel worlds teetering on the edge of obliteration where the lives of separate populations are simultaneously playing out?"

"That's right, Ali, bearing in mind that whatever happens in the VR microcosms is meant to contribute to our own world, as dictated by the Three Laws of Robotics."

"What do you mean, the Three Laws?" Keiji asks. "Keeper Master spoke of same."

"The Three Laws were devised almost a hundred years ago by the science fiction author Isaac Asimov. The first law decrees that a robot may not injure a human being; the second, that a robot must obey the orders given to it by a human being except when such orders conflict with the first law; and the third, that a robot must protect its own existence so long as doing so does not conflict with the first or second law." Kassandra, as she speaks to us, is pacing the room. The Shepherd, on the other hand, hasn't moved an inch.

"Artificial intelligence has made such great strides since the beginning of the century that it has overtaken fiction. Today, a number of institutions, such as the Institute of Electrical and Electronics Engineers, are constantly redefining the field's ethical standards."

"In short," Alpha recaps, "the flower seller and all the others go about their daily lives while we are offline, and when we come back, a lot of things may have happened."

"That's right," says Ka.

"But what about them?" Alpha continues. "How will they react to our popping in and out like that?"

"Good point, Alpha," Ali cuts in.

"Yeah," Chayton adds. "We were in the middle of a crowded subway when we left. You mean to say, the passengers saw us disappear into thin air, just like that?"

"Yes and no. Physically, yes, they did. But mentally, it wasn't like that. You see," Ka continues, "your comings and goings between worlds have been configured like an exit or entry through an invisible door. Such things are not unusual in that virtual universe."

"But what about the other worlds?" Chayton asks.

"I couldn't say. The program designed each of the seven mantras with its own set of rules and customs. Each is unique and based on one of the seven great afflictions threatening humanity. The goal, of course, is to help us find the keys to save our world from destruction."

"Too bad we didn't find out much today. We only have six days left," Chayton concludes.

"In my opinion," the Shepherd says, "you have discovered a lot more than it seems. But new knowledge requires time to digest, the same way the digestive process requires a time for rest."

With a movement of the hand, he invites us to form our usual circle.

"Keiji?" he asks, nodding toward the center.

"Yes, Shepherd-sensei."

"The oak tree, please."

Our companion leads the exercise, instilling in each of us a sense of movement. Ka and the head instructor join the circle. They never have before. I realize suddenly that this is all unknown territory for them, too. The paths they are leading us down have never been traveled before.

I stand tall and close my eyes, my weight evenly distributed, my feet planted firmly on the ground. I stretch my arms and breathe in deeply, picturing my branches—my source of oxygen—swaying freely in the wind. I've done this exercise so many times, I see my oak tree almost immediately. With practice, its shape has changed. When I first started doing it, my trunk was rather stunted. Now it soars proudly toward the sky, with even thicker bark and newly grown branches covered with greenish-blue leaves and acorns. My frail and tortuous roots have grown stronger and straighter, too, with embryonic roots pushing downward into the soil on my tree's hitherto barren left side.

A few minutes later, we go back to our rooms in total silence, without so much as a word for our baby goats, though from the sounds of their bleating, you'd think we'd returned from a decades-long crusade. I had just enough time to shower and put on my sweatsuit when there is a knock at my door.

"I need to think," Alpha blurts as he enters my room, "and I think better when you're around." He stuffs his hands into his pockets and begins to pace.

"So . . . what exactly do we know about that disease, Bulbosis? Does it give you a fever or a cough? Does it make your teeth grow crooked or your butt break out in a rash? Could be! The fact is, we don't know a thing about it!"

I can't help but smile.

"We do know, however, that the contagion is real. Bulbosis will kill you, and the people who catch it are put in quarantine . . . in the Center for the Infected. On the other hand," he continues, "we know that it is contagious and fatal. The means of transmission are unknown, and the infected are quarantined in a center. What is more, the men of the Brigade accuse those from Below of spreading the disease. So, apparently there are two worlds, one belowground and one above."

Right. But there is another thing that remains to be clarified: I point to his hand.

"Listen, Rae. The program has a reality all of its own. We can't tell the others until we know more. It's still too fuzzy. The cut I got was real, of course, but that doesn't mean we can catch Bulbosis. Anyhow, we'll look out for the other five. Everything will be fine."

I can't tear my eyes away from him. I wish I could be so sure.

"What the heck are you doing?" Ali exclaims, pushing the door to my room partway open. "The rest of us are starving! Are you coming?" She peeks inside.

"Yeah, sure," Alpha answers, clearly reluctant.

"What's the matter?" Ali asks. "Are you okay?"

For a second, I get the impression he's going to tell her— he's been hurt in immersion, the danger is real—but Ali makes a face instead, and Alpha and I join her in the hall and head downstairs for dinner.

I don't have much of an appetite. Everybody notices, so I force myself to eat a little, albeit half-heartedly. My stomach growls—at least one part of me is speaking up.

Alpha is overly confident, and even arrogant, at times. He thinks no one noticed the cut on his hand, not even our instructors. I get his not telling the others about it, so as not to worry them. But not telling Kassandra or the Shepherd is sheer pigheadedness. I, for one, can't believe they didn't catch on. If they haven't brought it up, it's for a good reason. Unless, of course, they have some ulterior motive . . .

Alpha's skepticism is starting to rub off on you, eh? my little voice asks.

I'm not in the mood to listen to it. The trial connection, the training sessions, going back to Toptown and seeing the flower seller . . . it all seems to be part of some elaborate plan. Nothing has been left to chance, I now see. And the one pulling the strings—above and beyond Ka, the head instructor, and the Keeper himself—is nothing other than a computer. A freakish program willing to throw us into the lion's den!

I am sure of it now. Before we even entered it, Spirit Era already owned us . . .

28

A flood of people, a black tide . . .

Hundreds of passengers in dark suits are crammed into the car around us. Most of them are standing. We have indeed reentered the program exactly where we left it, but at a different time of day. It's rush hour in Toptown.

As the train jerks to a start, a woman all in gray—perfectly in sync with the ambient gloom—loses her balance. Lurching forward to catch the grab bar, her hand accidentally brushes Chayton's.

"Oh, I'm so sorry!"

"No problem."

"No, really!" the woman exclaims, her tone shrill as if she spilled scalding milk on him. "I'm very sorry."

"It's nothing, ma'am."

"Nothing? Of course, it's something. Touching someone else's skin is extremely dangerous."

Alpha, nearby, pressed up against the door by a red-headed gentleman, signals to Chayton to keep quiet. Some of the passengers are already casting sidelong glances at him. But the woman no longer seems to care. Staring into space as if she'd hit "pause," the crowd is once more cloaked in heavy silence.

Suddenly—*twang, twang!*

The notes of a lively tune fill the air, soaring above the dreary melee to better swoop down from one ear to the next. In the distance, a small boy makes his way through the crowd plucking at a beat-up fiddle with a neck as wide and flat as a beaver tail. He has a dirty blankie tucked between his chin and the instrument. His nails are grimy, and he doesn't have a bow. I'd know that tuft of blond hair anywhere: he is one of the children from the trial connection!

Twang, twang...

The violin's plaintive melody is deeply stirring.

"Please, sir! Please, ma'am! A little something for the music?"

The voice in the crowd closely follows the boy and is instantly recognizable.

"A little something for the music, kind sir?"

I catch sight of a hand—a delicate butterfly wing—extended in vain. No one fills it.

"A little something for the music, ma'am?"

It's her! The flower vendor!

Mind the gap between the train and the platform as you leave the High Express.

A thick stream of passengers pours through the open doors, affording me a better look. The girl, whose tangle of golden locks is now twisted into a low bun, is taking the repeated refusals in stride: diverted gaze, jaded expression, nasty smirk, raised or furrowed eyebrows—nothing seems to faze her.

Stand clear of the closing doors.

She is heading in my direction now. Instinctively sensing it's not the right time to approach her—if she reacts the way she did yesterday, we'll only lose her again—I pointedly look away, making certain my companions see my little ploy. They get my meaning: We don't want her to recognize us. Not yet.

As the train rushes headlong toward the next station, the musical youngster and his associate continue making the rounds, passing my six companions, who all follow my lead and look away in turn. When the doors open at last, a good half of the passengers file onto the platform. The pair of buskers is among the first to exit. Naturally, we are close behind . . .

The platform is overrun with a throng of travelers coming and going. As the beaver-tail fiddle player and his golden-haired associate resume their mission, we all pair off—except for Chayton, who keeps his distance for fear of being recognized—and melt discreetly into the crowd. Alpha and I choose a strategic vantage point at the far end of the platform near a row of black leather seats in the usual undulating shape. As I gaze at the couple seated in them, it dawns on me suddenly that, apart from the gang of panhandling youngsters, we haven't encountered any children in this world.

"A little something for the music, ladies and gentlemen?" the girl's improbably lilting voice rings out. Other than the sounds of her voice and the violin, the crowd is utterly silent, as usual.

Behind the couple, set into the spotlessly clean wall, there is another of the flat tinted-glass units I noticed the day before. They are installed at regular intervals the entire length of the platform. As I look more closely, wondering what it could be, I see myself reflected in the dark glass screen: slight build, frail silhouette, asymmetrical bangs . . . A little sparrow, indeed, just like Chayton said.

"Please, ma'am, please, sir! A little something for the music?"

In tune with the other passengers, the couple seated near us turns a deaf ear. The man even folds his arms across his jacket pockets for added protection. However, his companion gets up, turns around, and brushes her fingertips over the tinted-glass surface. The black screen suddenly goes transparent, revealing what's inside.

The wall unit is a kind of vending machine, but there are no candy bars, chips, or cold drinks inside. Only rows of small individual packets, like the ones we saw the accordion-monster steal the day before. There are hundreds of them, displayed edgeways like miniature books, organized in groupings of seven colors. The woman taps the screen by an orange-colored row, and one of the packets falls into the product bin. She makes another selection, pulls it out of the bin, then sits back down.

The man on the bench next to her throws his head back eagerly as she tears one of the two packets open with a theatrical gesture. She proceeds to empty the powdery contents into his open mouth—he devours it greedily—then scarfs down the second packet herself. None of the passersby take any notice of their little number.

Suddenly, their bench starts to rise and fall. It seems to be breathing . . . like a heaving chest moving up and down . . . It's happening again! But, this time, the emerging shape of a woman is perfectly defined.

"Don't be so obvious," Alpha whispers as I nudge him with my elbow. "I see her, too."

What I saw yesterday wasn't a figment of my imagination! It was real! The slender, athletic figure in matte-black leather and the living bench form a single creature.

A *bench-woman!*

The creature, in its early twenties perhaps, slips a hand into the man's jacket pocket with a snakelike movement and begins rummaging around in it.

"Please, sir, please, ma'am! Could you spare a little something?"

The two young panhandlers create a diversion. Nobody notices a thing.

Mind the gap between the train and the platform as you leave the High Express.

A half-empty subway train has just entered the station. Very few people get off, but most of the crowd on the platform, including the couple on the bench, climbs aboard. The bench-woman stands tall, facing us squarely, her catlike eyes staring into Alpha's. She knows we can see her!

The panhandler and the fiddle player have spotted us, too. The musician lowers his instrument, tossing his grimy cloth over a shoulder as he approaches us. Our companions walk over.

"Are they the ones?" the young boy asks, looking at the blond girl.

"Yes," she replies.

"Nice job!" he blurts out, spinning around to face us. "Thanks to you, Siana lost her bouquet yesterday!"

"Forget it, Blanky. It wasn't their fault."

"Blanky," a name like a cuddly toy or a security blanket . . .

"What about the beating the Tubeans gave you? Have you forgotten about that?"

"Ha! No chance of that!" She grins, rubbing her backside.

The bench-woman is perfectly impassive. Time is at a momentary standstill. Then, without warning, she turns to the flower seller and asks, as if we aren't there: "Why are they able to see me?"

"I don't know, Arabella," the girl replies.

"Well, it's the first time an Owl has ever spotted me before."

"That's the thing. They're not Owls."

The bench-woman, Arabella, turns her piercing gaze on us, one by one.

"So, what exactly are the seven of you, then?"

"Teenagers, but not like the ones from here. By the way, my name is Chayton."

"He gave me something for free, without bartering," Siana says.

"Hmm . . . interesting . . . ," Arabella murmurs. "And where are you from?"

"From far away."

"Faraways, I see . . ."

"Who are the Owls?" Ali asks, clearly under the strange creature's spell.

"Stop staring at me, you poor wretch! They might see me," the bench-woman snaps imperiously. Intimidated by the tall, slender figure, Ali self-consciously lowers her gaze. "Tell me," Arabella continues, her tone abruptly softening, "what is your name?"

"Ali."

"Ali. That's a good name for you, concise and full of energy. Our bodies may be the outer envelope, but our names are what shape us. Not the other way around."

"Uh? Right . . . Thanks . . ."

"The Owls are the inhabitants of Toptown," Siana intervenes, nearing Chayton.

"Uh, excuse me. My name is Alpha. Why do you call them 'Owls'?"

"Because, despite their fancy high-tech shades, they are totally blind," Arabella snaps. "Blind to the truth about the World Below!"

"What do you mean by 'below'? Where is that?" Alpha pretends to ask Siana, though his question is really meant for Arabella. He doesn't want to arouse the subway passengers' suspicions.

"In Underhome," Arabella answers, without missing a beat. "That's where the Subs live."

"The Subs?"

"The Subway people. The homeless. During the Great Famine, the gap separating the rich and the poor grew so wide, the middle class was pretty much wiped out. There was a devastating loss of biodiversity: the five animal and twelve plant species responsible for ninety-five percent of the world food supply were decimated by a plant virus that proliferated at lightning speed in a matter of months. The infection spread through vertical transmission, from the female of the species to its offspring, that is. No one saw it coming."

The bench-woman's account is surprisingly effusive, as if it had to come out.

"The world's three main staple crops—rice, corn, and wheat—were devastated, and the disease mutated in other species of plants, as well. The epidemic was unstoppable. It was as if the earth were taking revenge for all the pesticides we had poured into it."

"How terrifying!" Helen exclaims.

"Not so loud," Keiji whispers.

"He's right. You're going to get me in trouble. The Owls can't hear me, but they can hear you. So, you two—yes, I mean you, my little ginger fox, and you, my raven-haired falcon—you go sit on that bench over there. That way, you'll look like a real couple. You others can stay here, but pretend to be interested in Siana and Blanky," Arabella instructs us in a voice at once affectionate and stern.

Chayton places a hand on Helen's shoulder, who removes it immediately and rolls her eyes. A glimmer of amusement shows in the flower seller's eyes; she reminds me a little of Anais Mann. Blanky, on the other hand, seems more interested in my asymmetrical bangs. He stares intently at me like he wants to come closer.

The handful of Owls on the subway platform pay no attention to us.

"In a matter of weeks," Arabella continues, "companies went bankrupt, employees lost their jobs, the government ran out of money. There was nothing to eat. A period of total chaos

ensued—looting, violence, and widespread crime. The government failed, laws were no longer upheld . . . The police had to
feed their children, too."

At this point, the bench-woman is pretty much talking to
herself, oblivious to our presence.

"Vulture investors bought up apartments for literally nothing. Then, they cozied up to the superrich, persuaded them to
put up barricades, to pay for a militia to protect them . . . to
build an airtight, self-sufficient, ultramodern city. They had
stockpiled all the food before anyone realized that food was
the new currency. They transformed Toptown into a bunker
of plenty . . ."

The bench-woman breaks off.

"And today, the Subs are condemned to a life of misery and
disease. To live belowground forever!"

Blanky starts to fiddle with his tattered cloth. He utters
a faint moan, and his breathing quickens. His warm body
presses against me, and I place a hand on his back. The way I
used to with Mia when she was feeling sad. He must be about
her age. Seven. His head tilts gently into the crook of my arm,
using it as a pillow.

*Mind the gap between the train and the platform as you
leave the High Express.*

The minute the train doors open, a thick, steady flow of
passengers spills out. The platform is overrun as the crowd
presses toward the exit. Blanky draws away from me.

"We'll all have to go," Arabella decrees.

"You-you're not going to . . . ," Siana stammers.

"We no longer have a choice. You should have told me.
Dione must have already reported them to Loco."

"But . . . it's too dangerous for them . . ."

The flower seller casts an anxious glance at Chayton. She
seems to genuinely like him.

"Not if they are on our side."

From our optimum vantage point at the end of the platform—almost empty once again—we stare in awe as Arabella's elongated figure begins to sway. She walks toward the vending machine with incredible suppleness, her legs, arms, and neck rippling with each new step. She brushes the tinted glass with her fingertips—for some reason, her image is not reflected in it—and the screen vanishes. She walks through it, releases a handle behind the bottom row of multicolored packets, and a secret passage appears.

"That's the advantage of being invisible: whatever I touch is invisible to the Owls. Let's go!"

I can just make out a tunnel. It's very dark inside.

"The two small ones will be safe," Arabella tells Siana as we step through the machine and into the tunnel. "They'll go through the gate with you and Blanky."

By "two small ones," she means Keiji and me.

"As for the others . . ."

PART FIVE

IMMERSION

"You want some?"

Blanky holds out a red packet. It's already open and looks just like the ones stolen from Lady Fluff's bag. We've been walking for a good half hour now through dark tunnels lit surprisingly well by the scarlet beam of Arabella's flashlight. The air is warm and damp, practically stifling. I wonder how Stepan is holding up. At the head of the line, he introduced himself to the bench-woman and is chatting away with her and Alpha. I've never seen him look so animated—elated, even.

Siana is walking in silence next to Chayton; there's clearly a bond between the two. And Blanky and I are lagging behind, well to the back. Ever since we set off, he has been seeking me out. Earlier, he told me he was about ten, and Siana, sixteen or seventeen. They certainly do look a lot younger. He also told me he felt much more comfortable playing his Beavertail— what he calls his wide-necked violin—than talking. For me, it's books. For him, music . . .

"Here. There's a little red left. Red's the best! We don't get it often. Only Prowlers are allowed to have it. I mixed it with a little green."

Blanky waves the packet under my nose.

"No, thanks," says Helen, who had stopped to tie her bootlace.

It's infuriating the way she decides for me. She treats me like a kid.

"We have to be careful," she whispers. "What if it's a drug, like ecstasy or something? Did you notice that couple on the platform? They looked completely zonked."

Yeah, right! The truth is, she's jealous. Blanky is interested in me! Without a moment's hesitation, I take the packet and empty the contents into my mouth with a defiant stare. Its flavor is surprising. Both spicy and tangy. The powder bursts in my mouth like Pop Rocks. Helen gives an annoyed shrug and turns away.

"It'll give you a boost. You'll see!"

Blanky is right. A few minutes later, I am bouncing up and down—heart racing, head pounding, and arms flailing—like a runner ready to take off. Then, my feet move all by themselves, whether I like it or not. It's a strange feeling but rather pleasant.

I dash effortlessly past Helen, Ali, and Keiji, then past Chayton and Siana, with her hair like a tangled ball of yarn tied back in a disheveled low knot. My feet dance impatiently as I pull up behind Arabella, Stepan, and Alpha, who turns and gives me a funny look. Figures. I mean, everything else here is bizarre . . .

"We're almost there," Arabella announces at last, picking up speed.

A yellowish glow can be seen in the distance. As we near it, we catch sight of a fork in the tunnel. On the right side: a completely dark underground passageway hewn from the living rock. On the left: a dimly lit, narrow corridor with no end in sight.

"Look! A stretch motorcycle!" Ali exclaims.

"Huh?" Keiji says in astonishment.

A strange-looking vehicle is parked under a light.

"It's the wagobike. I built it myself."

"Whoa! Nice job, Arabella!" Chayton whistles admiringly.

The bench-woman stands next to the extraordinary machine, puffing out her chest proudly.

"I am the only one who can drive it."

The front end of the large motorbike, with rusty handlebars and a rough-and-ready seat, is mounted on the wheels of an all-terrain vehicle with exhaust pipes sticking out in every direction. At the back, an elongated booth resembling a sidecar fashioned out of disparate materials is supported by four three-wheeled rows. The compartment can seat six in single file.

"All my friends in LA had motorcycles. They taught me how to drive. Can I drive yours?"

"No, Chayton. Definitely not!"

"Come on. Please!"

"Not a chance!"

"Maybe we could help you," Chayton suggests.

"Help us? How do you think you could help?"

"By getting hold of a certain key."

"Which one? The key to Slymouth Gate?"

"Maybe. We are looking for a lost key that once belonged to our world."

"If we're talking about the same one, you won't be able to take it with you."

"Why not?"

"The Subs may be able to use it to regain access to the Aboveworld one day. Our leader, Loco, will never let you have it."

"But you can already access it. See," Alpha says, pointing to the children.

"Children under four foot six are allowed to travel and beg

in the mine tunnels before they reach puberty. It usually starts around seventeen or eighteen, owing to nutritional deficiencies. Loco signed an agreement with the Toptown Council. It eases the Owls' consciences. Some Toptowners are starting to feel a little guilty, too. I mean, the Great Famine dates back three generations now. Thus, the so-called Agreements."

Anxious to get going, Arabella lowers her voice.

"Now listen up, all of you. I've only agreed to help you because . . . I need your help. But we'll talk about that later. Anyhow, I only have access to the Aboveworld Subway because I'm a Prowler."

"You're a *what*?"

"Nobody interrupts me, Ali! This is serious. If you decide to board the wagobike, there's no turning back, and you'll be risking your lives."

My stomach is churning. I can still feel the effects of the powder, and my legs are making uncoordinated jerking movements. My eyes look for Alpha's, expressing: "We have to tell them the danger is real!"

"Before the Great Famine, homeless people like my grandparents were practically invisible. No one paid any attention to them, apart from the occasional passerby who tossed them a coin or two. But when the street massacres began, it was just the opposite. Gangs of thugs known as the Noctos— because they only went hunting after dark—began to kill for food. Eventually, they became cannibals. Terror reigned in the homes of Aboveworld, and their wretched occupants sought refuge in the streets. The homeless were savvy and knew how to go unnoticed to survive. Nighttime was unbearable: the screams only subsided in the early morning."

Our minds are flooded with spine-chilling images.

"The homeless helped the newcomers as best they could, agreed to hide their children, and were able to save a few. Far too few . . ."

The silence is ghastly. Siana and Blanky both have traces of bite marks on their faces.

"The stench, disease, and rotting bodies left the Owl Militia with no choice. They doused the streets with Repulsecure, a horrific gas that killed all of the street people who were not already dead. The subway was the only possible refuge. But when they sealed off the exits, we were done for, sentenced to starvation a second time. That's when the dyed-in-the-wool homeless first realized something unbelievable, something they could work to their advantage: the Owls could no longer see them—literally!"

"What! That's crazy!" Helen lets out.

"They also knew how to navigate the maze of tunnels, and being invisible allowed them to discover the secret passage to Aboveworld via the vending machine."

"You are a descendant of the homeless, aren't you?" Ali asks. "And you and the accordion-monster steal from the passengers on the High Express to give yourself a chance."

"Yes. Like Dione and many others. We are called the Prowlers. We provide supplies."

"But you are invisible. Why don't you just live in Aboveworld? The Owls would have no idea you were even there!"

"And leave behind our brothers and sisters? Never! And anyhow, Toptown feels like a prison to us. Our ancestors felt the same way about those chicken coops they called buildings. Their stories have been passed down over generations . . . When you have had a taste of the freedom of the tunnels . . ."

"And Siana and I are Rovers!" Blanky jumps in enthusiastically. "We scout around for the best places and create diversions."

"Very true," Arabella praises him reassuringly. "You are indispensable." The little boy smiles, casting happy glances all around.

"The packets you steal, they're what, exactly?" Keiji asks.

"Food."

"You mean, that's all you eat?" Chayton asks, astonished.

"Yes, but there's never enough to go around. It's the Owls' fault. After the Great Famine, they wanted to be sure they'd never run out of food again. They set up a nutrition laboratory, and Owl scientists invented a new form of all-chemical nourishment in packet form. Since they were afraid new viruses would emerge from the soil, they covered everything over with concrete. They created an ultramodern society: robotic shops, a fully automated closed-loop subway line—the only means of transportation . . . The inhabitants of Toptown have everything they could ask for, and most have no need to work. But their cushy existences have turned them into robots. The Owls, who outnumber the Subs, don't even realize we've been plundering them for years. They are too anesthetized for that, and they are overwhelmed by the endless supplies of packets they have. Bartering with the Rovers is the only human interaction they enjoy. Toptown is a city in a plastic bubble."

"What about the key to Slymouth Gate?" asks Alpha, on his toes, as usual.

"Some say it's a legend. Apart from Gate 4.6, only small children are allowed through. The passageways have all been sealed off, except for a single gate said to be on their side. No one has ever been able to locate it, but Loco firmly believes that a lost set of keys exists."

"Maybe we can help you find it."

"Like I already told you, Alpha, it's dangerous. You could get killed."

"How?"

"Keiji and Rae can get into Underhome easily with Siana's and Blanky's help. They'll just be two more faces among the sea of Rovers. But you five others . . ." Arabella is reluctant to go on. "If you are truly on our side, you might be able to make it."

"And if not?"

"You will leave here with serious injuries. Or worse . . ."

Alpha feels the full brunt of her words. She has visibly thrown him for a loop.

"Personally, I'm willing to take the risk. But I cannot let . . . What I mean to say is . . . I have something to tell you . . . ," Alpha begins.

Phew, at last!

"If we get hurt in the program, it's for real."

"We know," Chayton says dismissively.

"What?"

"Of course. Ka told us all about it," Ali continues. "Our brain receives sensory messages whenever we are injured, and when the brain processes the messages, it can reproduce the injury. But Spirit Era's security shield will protect us from death. Ka never intended to hide it from us."

"But why—"

"We wanted *you* to tell us you knew," Helen breaks in.

"You and Rae," Keiji adds.

"Do you trust yourself, inspire trust, and trust others? The Shepherd said it takes all three to form a united whole," Ali reminds him.

"So now we are a united whole," Keiji adds happily. "A family. Shisho wrong. We can become attached."

"Well, I say we go with Arabella," Chayton chimes in. "Though I have to admit—I wouldn't be against a little spin on the wagobike!"

Helen and Ali agree in chorus.

"Stepan?" Alpha asks.

"I've always dreamed of meeting space creatures. The Subs will have to do."

Arabella looks slightly stunned—no doubt she wasn't expecting all of us to sign on. Although I guess Keiji and I are going with Blanky and Siana, not with her. Grabbing a brightly spray-painted hard hat from the handlebars, she places it snugly on her head, attaches the chinstrap, and lowers a pair of protective eye goggles.

"All right, then, let's go!"

With a wave of the hand, Arabella motions to the snake-like sidecar booth in the rear. One after the other, five of my companions climb into the miniature locomotive. I can't believe it. They are actually going to place their lives in the hands of the bench-woman!

"The heaviest in the last row, please. We want to avoid taking a spill!"

Chayton squeezes into the seat behind Alpha, his knees tucked up to his chest and his back rounded like a hedgehog.

Arabella mounts the wagobike. Strapping herself into the built-in harness, she cranks the ignition. Powerful red high beams come on in the front and the rear. The engine rattles to life with a clamor of pots and pans, and a greenish-gray wisp of smoke comes from the exhaust pipe. It smells like fresh-cut grass.

"Do you think this is a mistake?" Keiji whispers in my ear.

Do I ever! A big mistake!

"Better we stay together."

Suddenly, as if it all weren't enough already, a voice booms inside my head.

We have no other choice!

Oh no!

But we do!

Not that again, not now! A new voice has taken up residence in my mind!

"We should go with them," Keiji insists.

Don't do it! Make him change his mind!

Whoever you are, leave me alone!

Do what I tell you. If not . . .

The voice has taken on a threatening tone now. My head is spinning.

"Listen, we have to stay together," Keiji continues, heading over to the wagobike.

But there are only six seats. And anyway, it's too late.

"Buckle up!" Arabella shouts.

Our companions are all revved up. They slip their arms into the seat straps, which look like salvaged makeshift harnesses like the ones on roller coasters. Chayton is struggling again, but after a good amount of twisting, tugging, and shoving, he manages to fasten his seat belt.

And suddenly, *they're off!*

Without warning, Arabella cranks the engine. The vehicle backfires and leaps forward with impressive power, pressing our friends' heads into the seat backs. A strangled cry escapes Helen's lips, and Stepan lets out a laugh so wild it's almost scary.

"Don't forget the watches!" Alpha calls out at the last minute. "They're the only thing keeping us together. Make sure we meet up before they riiiiinnnnggg!"

My eyes fix on the wagobike as it hurtles down the tunnel cut directly into the rock. A few seconds later, its crimson taillight is swallowed by darkness and my stomach is in knots. The harsh and unpleasant voice inside my head has vanished, too. Incredible! Even inside the program, my head is like a revolving door!

"We have to go," Siana interrupts my musings.

In a bit of a daze, Keiji and I follow Blanky into the dimly lit narrow passageway on the left. The walls grow narrower as we make our way, so narrow we even scrape our shoulders at times. The corridor's downward slope grows more pronounced, and the walls narrow further still. In some places, we have to turn sideways to continue.

"You have to go faster," Blanky whispers. "Don't want to be late for Gate 4.6. Mrs. Tubeans doesn't like that."

"It would draw attention to you, too," Siana remarks, with her usual composure. "That woman has the nose of a hell-hound. She and her husband are evil beasts. They oversee the Rovers."

We have been entirely preoccupied worrying about the fate of our friends. But now, far from the others, we were off on a journey of our own . . . a journey no less frightening than the one on the wagobike . . . Full of uncertainty . . . Perhaps even a descent into hell.

Into the bowels of the earth.

30

Children seem to be coming out of the woodwork.

Out of the ceiling, walls, and ground . . . Children on all sides, running, giggling, and frolicking . . . Big and small . . . A regular anthill.

The passageway takes us straight into what looks like the underground chamber of a deserted coal mine: wooden beams shoring up crumbling foundations, overhead candles every three feet or so casting dim light. The air is hot and muggy, practically stifling. Stepan would hate it here.

Caught in the onrush of charging children, we blend into the crowd and hurry toward a line of rusty metal handcars. Groups of four or six children clamber into each with chimplike ease, then set them in motion using odd-looking levers.

"Come on, Rae!" Siana urges as I stand there counting— one, two, three wheels per row, just like the wagobike.

Behind us, six youths are already seated and ready to go.

"Grab my hand!" Keiji calls out, leaping effortlessly into the cart. Light on his feet and extremely agile, he reminds me of a monkey, too. I wouldn't be surprised if it was his messenger-animal.

"Buckle your seat belts!" Siana instructs us as she and Blanky fasten theirs. They're like the ones on the wagobike. I slip my arms into the straps, which feel heavy on my shoulders. Less than half a minute later, my hair is blowing in the wind as the makeshift handcar makes its way along the tracks.

The cart lurches and shakes as Siana, busy at the controls, picks up the speed. The tunnel, which started off straight, is now twisting and turning. I hold on as best I can, my knees slamming into the metal sides.

After about ten minutes, the handcar slows as it moves through a dark, open area. Smashed-up household appliances are piled up all around: mixers, washing machine doors, television screens, gutted computers, disemboweled ovens, lidless electric kettles.

"What's all that stuff?" Keiji shouts over the noise of the grating metal wheels.

"The Owls buried their trash when they were rebuilding Toptown," Siana replies without taking her eyes off the tracks. "They threw out a lot of new stuff, too. But what good does that do when you have nothing to eat?"

Electrical wires strewn among the mounds of debris look like giant spiderwebs. One of the heaps seems to be alive with movement. Could it be rats? I involuntarily curl my toes inside my combat boots.

Suddenly, horrific howls fill the air. With a tremendous leap, a mummy-like creature wrapped in layers of cloth grabs onto our cart. Bandages half cover the horrifically deformed features of what appears to be a woman.

"The Noctos!" Blanky screams. "It's the Noctos!"

Clinging with all its might to the front end of the handcar, the toothless creature with bulbous cloudy-white eyes lets out a hideous moan just as a horde of identical creatures emerges from the debris heap and rushes toward us.

"Hold on tight!" Siana yells as the she-Nocto on our hand-car makes a grab for her hair. "I'm going into turbo drive!"

I thought things were wild before, but now . . . We are flattened against the backs of our seats as the cart takes off like a rocket. The incredible acceleration ejects the mummy into the air—the creature lands a good three yards away—and our vehicle jumps the tracks. We are heading straight for a pile of gutted appliances!

"Look out!" Keiji yells.

Siana pulls a lever she hasn't used yet, and the cart immediately tilts sideways. We go zooming up the wall, and then onto the ceiling! We are rolling upside down. The middle wheel of our handcar is locked onto a rail running the length of the vaulted ceiling! Heads pointing downward, we fly over the mountains of junk.

"Hey!" Blanky shouts, snatching his blankie in midair just in time.

Our vehicle screeches like an old-fashioned steam engine, sparks flying everywhere, the bumps and jolts stretching our harnesses to the max. Thank God for their solidity and for the wheel in the center!

"Nothing broken, Faraways?" Siana asks, head right side up again. She has steered us back onto the ground.

"I'm fine!" Blanky grins victoriously, holding his tattered blankie above his head. "I caught him!"

Keiji tries to speak—unsuccessfully—as I hold up an unsteady thumb. No, nothing is broken. We are in a daze, that's all. Completely stunned.

"We've passed the danger zone. We'll get to Gate 4.6 soon."

We resume cruising speed. Our handcar enters another tunnel, and I start to relax a little. My breathing returns to normal.

"What was all that?" Keiji asks at last.

"The Noctos. Or what's left of them, that is. Cannibalism brought on a bunch of new diseases and eventually turned them into mutants. The Owls gassed most of them in the early days. They locked the survivors underground with us."

"With you?"

"With us. Basically, they wanted to sic the dogs on us, though they figured we would starve to death first."

"But we didn't let them get us!"

"Blanky's right. Underhome's borders are well guarded."

A line of backed-up handcars has formed ahead of us. Before ours can come to a complete stop, it crashes into the last one in the line.

"You idiot!" a girl with long brown curls snaps. "Can't you watch what you are doing?"

There are three boys in the cart with her. The chunky youth sitting next to her leans over the railing to check for damage.

"Well, Billiard?" the girl asks, twisting a lock of hair.

"The headlight's fine, Dulci."

The line of carts begins moving forward with jerks and starts. The boy working the levers, probably the leader of the little pack, calls out to Billiard: "What about the other side?"

"Good call, Niro. The sheet metal is all dented up there."

Niro's white-blond hair sticks straight up. His near-invisible eyebrows blend perfectly with his milk-white skin, and the pinkish tint of his irises suggests he is albino. He faces Siana and raises his voice: "So, it's you again, Rags! Wasn't losing your flowers yesterday enough for you?"

"I guess she likes the feel of Old Man Tubeans's cane!" Dulci sneers.

I can't bear the way Siana lowers her gaze. Bullies like those two would push a drowning man's head under water!

"But we don't like doing finger pushes!" grumbles the youngest in their cart, the only one yet to speak. "We already had to do fifty because of her."

"Yeah," Billiard chimes in. "You're right, Gym. I couldn't even open my food dose this morning, my fingers were so sore. Mrs. Tubeans stepped on them cuz I didn't do all the reps."

"And she'll break them one by one if she sees those dents in our cart," Dulci adds furiously.

The dark-haired girl looks like a miniature woman. A very beautiful woman. True, she hasn't hit puberty yet, but everything about her is mature and alluring.

"But it's not our fault!" Gym whimpers pathetically.

"Maybe so, but the Two Beans don't care a bean about anything," Niro retorts. "We have to hide the dents. Otherwise, we're in for a beating!"

"And you, Siana . . . ," Dulci threatens, raising a fist, "you just wait!"

"That's enough," says Keiji calmly. "We didn't do it on purpose."

"Well, how do you like that!" Niro bursts out. "Who is this clown anyway?"

"A newbie," Siana answers quickly.

"You just got here, and you want to call the shots! You better toe the line, pal . . . Got it?"

Niro is thin, but he sure is scary looking, all twitching muscle, translucent skin, and bulging veins. His pupils are alive with a strange glow.

"And you there, Miss Crooked Bangs!" Dulci interrupts. "You're new, too, eh? With a face like yours? I'm sure I'd remember you if we'd met."

The two boys burst into moronic laughter, and Niro turns away, rubbing his eyes as if waking from a nightmare.

Little by little, we have been nearing the entrance of what looks like a giant pizza oven. Steel jaws open and close, and the carts in front of us are swallowed up one by one.

"Hey, new girl, what's wrong? Cat got your tongue?"

"Stop it, Dulci!" Blanky suddenly roars. "Rae doesn't speak."

"Nobody asked you, you tin-eared pipsqueak," Dulci snaps. Blanky's sweet face crumples, and he hugs his instrument even closer.

"As for you," Niro threatens, pointing at Keiji. "I'm not done with you! You're in for a big surprise if you think you can take my place."

"Take your place? What are you talking about . . . ?"

But just then, the iron jaws open, and Niro and Dulci's cart is swallowed whole like the ones before it.

"What does he mean? What place?"

"He's our dorm division leader," Siana answers. "We Rovers live alone. So, there's a lot of childish bickering. Niro is always on guard."

"I hate him!" Blanky says. "And Dulci even more! They both deserve to be whacked over the head with Beavertail. Or better yet—to grow up!"

It's our turn to enter the oven now. The doors close behind us, and a red laser beam begins scanning our car. I realize it's an air lock.

"The Owls built Gate 4.6 to detect anyone over four feet six. No grown-ups are allowed through. That's why we don't want to grow up."

Keiji's nerves are getting to him. He starts spieling off everything that could go wrong. What if they spot us? What if Arabella and the others don't make it? What if we can't find them before our watches go off . . . ? I look down at mine: less than an hour to go, although, in program time, a lot longer.

At last, the air lock opens and . . . a place of wonder spreads out before our eyes!

An articulated crane-like arm clamps onto our cart and lifts us into the sky, affording us a bird's-eye view of the marvels in the Subs' homeland.

As I stare down at Underhome, I am overcome with a surge of emotion. It's beautiful . . . So sad, so stunning . . . I haven't felt this alive for ages!

#THEKEEPER #SAVETHEWORLD

POST 5—THE FIRST KEY

NOVEMBER 23, 2035

THEY'VE MADE IT TO A SAFE PORT.

They've found a haven in Spiritua, that is.

They've made the crossing, refused the imposed borders, and entered a land where the blind can see, where lost souls are found . . . where the adventure of the spirit calls.

Because in Materia, the land of superficial appearances, you can remain at dock your whole life and think you've traveled the entire world.

True journeys require questioning everything you know, looking for answers elsewhere.

Change is forward looking. Individually, it means being reborn, gaining heightened awareness, making a journey, growing as an individual. And then as a group. Universal change . . .

NEW DOORS TO OPEN.

31

The cart is flying.

We are traveling through the air in an archaic gondola. A few yards ahead, Niro and Dulci's wagon sails along, as do the wagons of all the other children. The scene below is both frightening and fantastical.

The underground city is lit by a multitude of lights—both dim and bright, colored and white, fixed, flashing, and flickering neon—stretches as far as the eye can see, like a string of enormous interconnecting stations. We must be about five or six yards above the ground. Underhome's dome-like roof, not far from our heads, is dug out of living rock.

Dozens of subway lines, or ditches, rather, with rails running through them, sprawl beneath us. There is no traffic. Old wooden trains dot the landscape. They are immobile, all doors thrown open, and appear to have been repurposed as living spaces. Some have been given a slap of paint, others are decorated with abstract patterns, and others are coated with textured plaster ostensibly forming a mass of shapeless clumps.

But on second glance, the chaotic scene reveals an organic harmony, and the weird sculptures take on meaning.

Bits of thread, fabric, and torn cloth come together in a delightful folk-art mix: astonishing murals, poles and lampposts decorated with customized knitwear, windowsills filled with a mosaic of broken bottles, tools, kitchen utensils, and other oddities instead of glass. The caravans lining the tracks are equipped with makeshift ladders to access the roofs, which have been fitted out as bedrooms.

Well, not exactly bedrooms . . .

Remnants of blankets, pillows, and scraps of mattresses are jumbled together, side by side or in stacks, among endless rows of hanging linens. Every square inch of space is used. Around the tracks, there's a jungle of cardboard shacks and tin-can huts, lean-tos made of crates, tents pieced together out of undergarments, and hovels built from stacked spray-paint cans. They shore each other up, as best they can, and form a maze of alleyways. All of them are extremely low—sometimes no higher than a doghouse. A cardboard city.

The inhabitants are visibly hungry. They are thin, at any rate. And dirty. They are covered in a uniform layer of filth, almost like a stamp of pride. A fetid and sometimes rancid smell hangs over everything. The inhabitants are orphans. They have no homeland, no habitat, and, likely, no parents. Subs stand in silence, straight and dignified, as far as the eye can see. Present but absent, lost in their former lives. Engulfed by memories. There is an occasional semblance of activity, a gathering of young people, the sound of music, a spark of life . . . Blanky takes my hand.

"See the pink caratram over there?"

He points to a nearby wagon lying on its side, a rhododendron bloom among brambles. A tall man with disheveled gray hair and a shaggy beard is seated on top, his legs hanging through an open window.

"It belongs to Valjean the Rabbit. He was named after a certain Hugo somebody or other."

The name immediately rings a bell: Jean Valjean, sentenced to prison in 1795 for stealing a loaf of bread, the hero of Victor Hugo's nineteenth-century French classic, *Les Misérables*. My father had given me a copy for my thirteenth birthday. He and the novel's unfortunate hero had both raised their little girl on their own, I think with a pang . . .

"Val the Rabbit is the only Sub with a caratram all to himself."

"Caratram." That's what the Subs call the caravans on rails. The man gives off an aura of quiet strength that makes you want to go sit with him.

"Why?" Keiji asks. "What so special about him?"

"He is Underhome's mascot," Siana answers. "His memory is stuck back in the better days, before the Great Famine, when he was a young man. He tells his story over and over, like a broken record. Everybody loves Val. He went nuts. His former life was just like any other poor person's. We know it by heart."

In the distance, the man starts rocking his head from side to side. Spasms shake his body, his arms flail, and his mouth starts opening and closing. We can't hear the words, but Blanky and Siana give us his story in a single voice.

"I'm starving! I kept telling them in the subway! But they didn't care. The clamor of rushing feet drowned out my voice. It was Line 8. At rush hour. People were in a hurry to get home after a day in the mines. Passengers pulled themselves wearily out of the sweat-stained seats bearing the marks of thousands of backsides. I could sense their revulsion. It was overwhelming. Seeing misery—in flesh and blood—paraded before you. I knew how they felt. I knew how disgusting I was to them! I no longer had a home. Not even a name. Just a nickname from a pink-eyed rabbit that fell asleep on my lap. Its fur warmed me in the winter. I used to do odd jobs. I don't remember exactly what. The streets make you crazy.

"*When no one was listening, I said things that surprised*

even me. Sometimes I looked at those huge billboards, and my eyes would take on a crazy glint, sliding over the image of a perfect woman with a perfect smile, sitting behind the wheel of a perfect car.

"What did I do to deserve this? Goddamn it! I wanted to drive that car, too!

"So, I'd get angry. I'd go after random passersby.

"'Hey, Owls!' I said. 'Stop staring at me with your high-tech glasses!'

"'I'll have my own car one day, too. And a pair of blinders to block it all out . . ."

They end their recitation of Val the Rabbit's story with two sad smiles just as his caratram disappears in the horizon.

"You mean," Keiji stammers, "his nickname be given by Owls . . ."

No answer, just the sound of the clanking of the machinery as we proceed through the air to the far side of the rock face.

"Get ready," Siana says. "We're getting close to the Rovers' dorm now."

"Deepwood," Blanky tells us.

"Its entrance is guarded by the horrible couple we told you about."

"The Tubeans. They're mean! You must never look them in the eye."

Blanky lets go of my hand and makes a fist. My body involuntarily tenses. Meanwhile, the cable car is heading toward an opening in a wall. We enter another tunnel, but, this time, we can see the other end. The mechanical arm releases our cart. Its metal wheels, back on solid ground, begin to roll. We're moving much more slowly now. From time to time, we come to a stop, then start moving again.

"Wow!" Keiji exclaims as we pull up to an enormous dormitory.

Enormous, meaning as big as a train station. The noise level is unbelievable, the air ice cold. Hundreds of bunk beds—three, four, five, and even six stories high!—are scattered all over the place.

"Gee, better not be afraid of heights here . . . ," Keiji mutters.

The bunkhouses are covered with tents, original drapes of sorts differentiating the levels. Each tenant has their own little cubbyhole. I catch sight of the Tubeans. First, Mr. Tubeans, with his stick-thin shanks and a protuberant paunch that he methodically massages while inspecting the carts. Dark tufts poke out of his ears and nose. His forehead is massive and square. He sniffs at the children like a hunting dog.

Mrs. Tubeans is wearing a mannish suit. Her snakelike hair billows around a distended face with large nostrils. She is standing atop a crate to get a better view. Her sharp eyes scrutinize the incoming carts, one by one. From her vantage point, there's no way she can see the dent in Niro and Dulci's cart. They make it through safely.

Imitating my companions, I lower my head but keep a wary eye on Mr. Tubeans as we draw nearer. He proudly raises an enormous rawhide staff like a trophy. A rusty fork has been tied to its crest with a string of sorts.

"Raise your arms!" Old Man Tubeans orders harshly as he seeks his wife's approving gaze.

Without looking up, my companions and I comply as if held up at gunpoint. The situation is absurd: we stand there, arms in the air, and wait.

"Higher!"

The man's thinning hair glistens slickly on his head. His suit has a personal touch—clearly Mrs. Tubeans's idea: the jacket is covered in convict stripes!

"All right, go on," he growls at last, slamming his baton into the side of our cart with a metallic clang.

A sigh escapes Blanky's lips, quickly followed by another as our wagon heads out. The ambient din in the dormitory is growing even louder now. Like our predecessors, the Rovers in front of us dump the contents of their pockets into the wagon and abandon it in the queue. All bartered goods—the toiletries and other necessities traded in Underhome—are the property of the Tubeans.

Suddenly, an alarm sounds: the noise is excruciating. Everyone in Deepwood, except the Cerberus-styled gatekeepers, covers their ears and grimaces.

"What's going on?" Keiji nervously asks.

One look at Blanky, who is hugging his beavertail fiddle tight, tells us something has happened in the tunnel. Something serious.

"Over there!" Mrs. Tubeans roars once the siren stops.

The tone of her voice is like nothing I've heard before—as shrill as a witch's yet deeply cavernous. It freezes my blood.

"That one over there! The second to last!"

Old Lady Tubeans swoops down onto the cart, talons first. It takes her husband a little longer to get there. When he does, he "invites" the children to vacate the vehicle with a blow to the head. A strapping older boy stays where he is. He looks terrified.

"Height!" the man bellows, ruthlessly dragging the boy from the cart.

"No! Please! My grandfather is sick. Don't send me away!" he pleads, struggling with all his might.

His arms are scrawny, but Old Man Tubeans has no trouble neutralizing him.

"Height!" he repeats, waving his stick threateningly close to the boy's eye.

"All right, all right!"

Tubeans's baton returns to its initial upright position. It also serves as a measuring stick.

"Four foot seven!" Mr. Tubeans announces at the top of his lungs.

"That's that," his wife rejoices. "Case closed."

"My grandfather . . . He . . . he needs . . . several doses of food a day. Without the packets . . ."

Without further ado, the boy is gagged, bound hand and foot, and thrown into a potato sack. I wonder what will become of him, but we don't stick around to find out. Siana drags us into the depths of the dormitory.

"I not understand," Keiji says. "The boy he passed tunnel with more than four foot six?"

"The gate is not one hundred percent airtight; Rovers know a trick or two to get around it. That's why Mr. and Mrs. Tubeans are in charge. They report all the numbers to the Toptown Council every month. Any discrepancy and the Agreements are canceled."

When we reach our friends' six-tiered bunk bed, Siana dawdles. At times, her liquid honey gaze hardens into shades of burned caramel.

"Most Sub kids dream of being Rovers and having a cubby of their own here. Trading in Toptown is hard work, but at least we get to go to Aboveworld. Plus, in Deepwood, we are not only guaranteed room and board—from up here, we overlook all of Toptown!"

"How do you become Rover?" Keiji asks.

"Old Lady Tubeans decides. She looks for boys with good bartering potential, then buys them from the clans—the Sub commoners, that is, who take you into their community. The clan is kind of like an adoptive family, except the clan members generally don't care a whit about you. And they gladly sell their 'kids' for a few extra packets. Otherwise, it's bare minimum food rationing down here, except on the feast days before Loco's monthly speech: then, it's food packets aplenty."

"And the girls?"

"We're different. We get to the dormitory around age two through an entirely different channel. We are the Prowlers' offspring. Their male children grow up with them and never mix with the children of the common people. Compared to the girls born in Underhome, I'm lucky to have ended up here, even if it's only temporary, and . . ."

She freezes.

"I have no clue who is responsible for why I'm here . . ."

32

"This is Cubby!"

Blanky proudly gestures as if introducing his best friend.

It's on the ground floor and entirely wrapped in burlap, like a giant present. The "drapes" are adorned with an array of treasures: pencil stubs, paper clips, homemade badges, bits of broken objects, and a hodgepodge of other doodads.

"I made it all by myself!"

He places a cord made from pieces of twisted wire, twine, and ribbon in my hands. The key to his house . . .

"Go ahead, Rae. Open!"

His smile seems a little cheeky. As I pull on the cord, I half expect something like a canned novelty snake to jump out at me.

"Ta-da!" he exclaims.

But it's not a prank. The bed inside is unremarkable. The blanket and pillow are an assortment of disparate fabrics. Except for the storage pockets sewn into the burlap liner and the white pom-poms hanging from the ceiling—the bunk above, that is—it's nothing special at all.

"Ta-da!" Blanky repeats as if expecting a standing ovation.

The cubby means the world to him. So, Keiji congratulates him, and I applaud, somewhat ashamed when I think of my big house in Haight-Ashbury, my closet bursting with clothes, and the tons of stuff we throw out every year.

"Brrr!" Keiji shivers. "It's cold in here."

"You take the third and fourth tiers. They're free," Siana says, pointing to the two beds above hers. "Inside, it's cozy and warm."

Unlike Blanky's, her curtains are plain. I wonder what they conceal.

"The dormitory is divided into sections. Like I told you, ours is under Niro's control."

With that, she nimbly climbs the rickety ladder, pulls open her drapes, and slips inside.

"Miiiiiii! Aaaaa! Oooow!" A funny squeak emerges out of nowhere. "Miiiiiii! Aaaaa! Oooow!"

"Come in! Fast!" Blanky says. He gives Keiji and me a quick shove, and we roll onto his bunk bed. Blanky and Beavertail follow suit and end up in Keiji's lap. Our host draws the curtains.

"What's wrong?" Keiji asks as Blanky extracts himself from his lap.

Holding our knees to our chests, the three of us just barely fit. The cubby is wider than a conventional bed, but it's a tight squeeze. Especially with the stuffed pouches taking up so much space. Some are overflowing with knitted socks, scarves, gloves, and hats. Others have discarded toiletries: half a toothbrush, bits of soap, empty tubes of toothpaste.

It is hot in the cocoon-like enclosure. Blanky rolls up his sleeves. His arms are covered with bruises. Keiji's hand automatically touches his left cheekbone, and the scar that reminds him of his brother. The awful bond those two must have . . .

"Miiiiiii! Aaaaa! Oooow!"

Blanky reaches into one of the pouches. There is more squeaking.

"Promise not to scream, even if you think it's disgusting."

"I promise," says Keiji, dying to see it, just like me.

Blanky carefully removes his hand, holds it out, and opens it. A tiny gray-haired creature is wriggling in the palm of his hand.

"Nobody except Siana knows about her. She's a female. Here, Rae, hold her."

The animal snuggles against my hand. Its tiny body is warm and damp.

"What is it?" Keiji asks. "It looks like mouse, but with tail and head like cat."

"It is a crat, a cross between a rat and a cat. The Owls accused them of spreading Bulbosis in Aboveworld. It's all a pack of lies!" Blanky scratches the crat's chin. She starts to purr. "It's even worse for them in Underhome. People eat them. Can you imagine? They eat the dead flesh of a living being . . . !" *I can do that,* I think to myself. *Easily . . .* "Her name is Gray Pearl, and I call the male Lil' Buccaneer."

"Miiiiiii! Aaaaa! Oooow!" Lil' Buccaneer squeals as Blanky reaches into another pouch.

"He's noisier, but I know how to quiet him." He proudly sticks a little finger into the creature's tiny mouth. "Mama Crat will come nurse them tonight in secret. If she doesn't get killed first, that is."

Blanky's tone is matter-of-fact. That's how it is down here: life and death hang together by a thread . . .

As we pet the baby crats, Keiji asks about the boy in the potato sack.

"If he is lucky, his clan will take him back. If not, he will become a vagrant. It's nearly impossible to survive on your own. For girls, it's different. They get special treatment. When they reach puberty and can no longer get into Aboveworld, they are sent back down to Underhome, but their future is all set."

"How so?"

"They join the Women Laborers, a powerful clan that slogs for the Tubeans, unloading their wares. A piece of soap, a spoonful of toothpaste . . . valuable items here in Underhome."

"Do they know who their parents are?"

"No. The Law of Anonymity strictly forbids it. Children are part of the Prowlers' collective heritage. The boys are raised by all the fathers without knowing who their biological fathers are. When the girls turn two, they are separated from their mothers, Sub females chosen for their looks. Every girl's dream in Underhome!"

"How so?"

"Becoming a mother. Mothers get an unlimited supply of packets and cosmetics, and they get to live in a train that actually runs. Its location is always kept secret. They sign a contract agreeing to keep their identities secret. If a mother reveals her identity to a child, she and the child are put to death."

Hmm . . . Not exactly what every girl dreams of back home, I tell myself.

"But now," Keiji interrupts, uncomfortable with the subject, "we must find companions before watches ring."

I glance at mine: less than fifteen minutes to go.

"Why?"

"We have been given time to find the key. Five more days after today."

"Hey, Rags!" a voice outside the cubby shouts.

All three of us poke our heads out from behind the drapes.

"Rag-girl!"

It's Niro and his troops. The division leader is accompanied by his sidekick, Dulci, and the boys from the handcar, Billiard and Gym. A small gang of followers is close behind.

"Come out of your hole, Siana!"

Siana takes her time but eventually comes out. Quickly

pulling the curtain shut behind her, she jumps down from her bunk and lands on her feet with catlike agility.

"What do you want, Niro?"

Her mane of hair is untied and wild—she looks like a tigress. We climb out of Blanky's cubby and station ourselves behind her in case she needs backup.

"I'm here to challenge that pal of yours to a test!"

Niro has a nasty tic: he blinks his eyes and wrinkles his nose repeatedly.

"Who? You mean Keiji?" Her bold, almost warlike manner is a far cry from the Siana we're used to.

"Yeah, the new guy! I'm not afraid of him. I challenge him to play roulette rail."

Dulci's lovely silhouette nears the gang leader, her beautiful brown curls brushing his shoulders as she whispers in his ear.

"Aww, Niro," she wheedles, "you promised. No more roulette rail . . ."

"Stay out of it, Dulci!" he says, then fires away at Keiji. "Since you're a newbie, let me explain. Roulette rail is Deepwood's Russian roulette. Two tracks, one subway: you move, you lose. Your job is to be on the right track when the train passes!"

"What's in it for me?" Keiji replies with his usual calm.

"My spot as dorm leader!"

"Not interested. You can keep it."

"Well, then, what do you want?"

"Information about Slymouth Gate."

"Personally, I think it's a load of crap, but if it amuses you, sure. I can ask around. And if you lose, it's back to your mommy's dirty petticoats with you."

Even though Niro's insult couldn't possibly offend Keiji's mother—she lives in another world and hasn't the slightest idea where her son is—his face hardens: family honor is sacred.

"Let's go!" the battalion leader shouts to the sound of wild cheering.

Signaling the departure with a battle cry, the gang surrounds their champion and breaks into song as they march toward the entrance of Deepwood. Next to them, we form a miserable little foursome.

"*Hear ye, hear ye!*" the unmistakable sound of Mrs. Tubeans's voice bellows through a loudspeaker.

"*An emergency meeting at the Ledge! At once!*"

"Damn!" Niro swears, stomping a foot.

"What's going on?" Keiji asks Siana.

"The Ledge is the dormitory's lookout. From there, we can see all of Underhome. The Tubeans call us to assemble there when they have announcements to make."

"Yeah, it doesn't look good," Blanky remarks. "And I forgot Blankie in my cubby . . ."

Children with grimy faces are tumbling out of multi-tiered bunk beds everywhere. A flurry of clowning, shoving, chattering, and scurrying . . . Many of the girls are indeed very young, while the boys all seem to be at least seven or eight. Two dark-haired boys with olive complexions excitedly scramble down from their bunks on the fifth and sixth levels. I recognize the brothers we saw with Siana and Blanky during our trial connection in Toptown. The older one looks even thinner now. The brothers are quickly swept up by the wave of children rushing in the direction of the Ledge. We join them. The place is teeming with Rovers when we get there.

"Stay with me," Siana whispers.

The dreaded caretakers are standing at the far end of the open esplanade overlooking Underhome.

"*You think you're pretty smart, don't you?*" Old Lady Tubeans snarls, her lips glued to a large speaker that has seen better days. *"One of the carts is damaged. You are a bunch of good-for-nothings!"*

Mr. Tubeans obediently approves with a grotesque waggling of the head.

"If the culprits do not immediately turn themselves in, you will all be deprived of your doses!"

"Hey!"

"No!"

"That's not fair!"

The din spreads like wildfire. The Rovers are mostly grouped into divisions: same look; same kind of clothes; same defiant, angry looks. There must be a lot of infighting in the dorm, indeed. Niro's gang isn't even that big.

"Who used that cart?"

Near us, Niro, Dulci, and their two pals are shifting nervously from one foot to the other.

"You have ten seconds: ten . . . nine . . . eight . . ."

As dorm division leader, Niro is about to turn himself in. First, he whispers in Keiji's ear: "Don't think you'll get away with it. Roulette rail is just for starters . . ."

"Seven . . . six . . . five . . ."

"No, don't!" Dulci pleads. "You know what it means . . ."

"I won't let the others pay for me."

"Four . . . three . . ."

Niro is pushing through the crowd in the direction of the platform.

"I did it!" Siana, to the right of me, raises her hand.

What the heck is she doing? No!

"I damaged the cart!"

With a proud shake of her golden mane, she is a huntress again.

"No, Siana!" Blanky screams. "You were punished for the flowers. A repeat offense is serious."

But she is already walking toward the Tubeans as Niro

looks on, amazed. The entire dormitory lets out a cheer. Hurray—their doses are safe!

"Stop rejoicing, you lazy bums! Thirty finger push-ups for everyone—that will teach you!"

The children immediately drop to the ground and start doing push-ups—on their fingertips. We have no choice. We do the same. Meanwhile, Siana hands herself over to the Tubeans.

"Well, lookie here!" Old Lady Tubeans jeers into the loudspeaker, her face breaking into a despicable smile. *"We meet again . . ."*

Her husband stares at Siana hungrily, polishing the pronged tips of his staff with the back of his sleeve. The vicious look on his face makes my blood boil.

"What are we going to do?" Blanky moans, getting to his feet as the divisions start to scatter.

"I don't know," Keiji murmurs. "What can we do?"

Beep-beep! Beep-beep!

"Oh no! The watches! Not now!"

Beep-beep! Beep-beep!

They are ringing at the worst possible moment. We've barely gathered our wits when five identical alarms chime in along with ours.

Five . . . alarms . . . right behind us . . .

"Is that you?"

Keiji, usually so reserved, practically jumps for joy.

Beep-beep! Beep-beep!

Our friends have made it, guided by Arabella. But our joy is short-lived. Their eyes are covered by dirty, blood-soaked bandages wrapped around their heads.

"What's wrong? What did they do to you?"

"It's nothing," mumbles Alpha.

It does not at all look like nothing. Could they be . . .

"Blind? Are you *blind?"*

"No. It will get better once we go back to the farm."

"Don't worry about it, Keiji. It doesn't hurt anymore," adds Ali. "Is Rae with you?"

The bench-woman is holding Ali's hand, who is holding on to the others. They look like a group of visually impaired students on a school outing.

Our wristbands keep ringing: *Beep-beep! Beep-beep! Beep-beep!*

"It's time," Alpha says quietly.

With a complicit look, Arabella lets go of Ali's hand and

beckons us to move closer. She places Alpha's hand in Keiji's and Ali's in mine.

"Remove your bandages," advises Chayton. "We don't want them to count as our item-clues."

They peel off the long strips of fabric, all the while keeping their eyes closed.

As our circle forms, I glance over at poor Siana, who is being chewed out by the Tubeans. Then, my companions, in a single voice, shout, *"Flyfold!"*

We instantly find ourselves back in the training room. The minute the umbilical cords unhook, Keiji and I are on our feet.

"What happened?"

"There's no need to panic," the Shepherd immediately reassures us. "The eye damage is only temporary."

"Are you sure, Shepherd-sensei? *What about Siana?* What's going to happen to her?"

"Life continues in the program. There's nothing we can do about it."

"We abandoned her! And what about Blanky?"

"Keiji, calm down," Kassandra intervenes. "Remember, it's all a simulation."

"It's a little more than that, if life there does go on," Alpha rightly points out, his eyes screwed tightly shut.

"It all seemed so real . . . ," Ali adds.

"My eyes . . . ," Helen whimpers.

"And this sure isn't nothing!" Chayton bursts out angrily. "We can't see a damn thing!" He jumps to his feet and stumbles.

There is a commotion as we help our five friends out of their pods. Each of us—the Shepherd; Kassandra; Mr. Mann, who has come to lend a hand; Keiji; and I—is put in charge of one of the injured. We lead them to their rooms. Alpha pronounces my name softly. He reaches for my hand and gives it a squeeze. My own hand is shaking.

"Hey, it's okay . . . ," he reassures me. "This is no time to give up. I still need my guardian angel!"

But that doesn't help. My friends are injured, and God knows what the Tubeans will do to Siana. I know it is all computer generated, but I have grown attached to her for real, and Blanky, too.

Once Alpha is settled in his room, Kassandra comes in and sees to his wound. Wrapping a bandage around his eyes, she tells us he needs to keep them closed until the following day. Neither he nor I have the strength to ask for explanations. We just want to be alone. To talk things over quietly.

First, I go to my room to take a much-needed shower. After the wild ride in the handcar, my hair is full of scablike clumps of dirt. I have to wash it three times to get rid of them. I go back to Alpha's room, where he is waiting for me to eat. Mr. Mann had brought up two meal trays.

We are silent at first. Then Alpha makes a small place on the bed for me. I sit on the edge, happy he can't see the deep blush on my cheeks. I wish I could tell him about the voices in my head. The last one was hostile. I'm worried it will come back. Whose was it? And I wish he'd confide in me, tell me about his family, about his past . . . I know almost nothing about him. But he only talks about what they had just been through.

While Keiji and I were making our way to the abandoned coal mine, our five friends in the wagobike had been on a wild ride through the Nocto Zone. With Arabella at the wheel, they drove through miles of dark, dusty tunnels. The air was suffocating. They were going so fast that Stepan didn't even get the time to freak out. They, too, had crossed mountains of debris, faced the white-eyed creatures, been hurtled upside down, jolted, battered, and tossed about . . . They escaped the mutants and had the scare of their lives.

But to get to Underhome, they had not gone through Gate 4.6, nor through any other passageway. I don't know if I could have stood the trial they faced. Stopping every so often to catch his breath, Alpha describes the worst part of their journey as I listen in horror.

They had just gone around a bend in the tunnel when the wagobike suddenly stopped. Its red headlights went off. They were still strapped in, seated in a row and short of breath. Plunged in total darkness, they didn't dare move a muscle. All Alpha could do was keep an ear out for the slightest noise.

"This is the moment of truth," Arabella's voice intoned. "You either lose your lives, or you suffer . . ."

Inside the wagobike's sidecar compartment, a dot of red light split the darkness: a laser beam aimed for Alpha's left eye.

"Ouch," Stepan and Helen reacted together.

Instinctively, Alpha obviously knew they were going through the same thing. They had all closed their eyes. They felt hands reach into the compartment and grab their heads.

"Leave us alone!" Ali shouted. But it was impossible to open the harnesses: they were trapped.

"Let go of me!" Helen panicked. Probing, stone-cold fingers spread their eyelids. Suddenly, the laser beam penetrated the pupils.

"Ahhh! Ahhh!" the five cried out in unison.

"Be brave," Arabella murmured. "We've all been through it . . ."

Alpha could feel Chayton writhing in the row behind him, his knees jamming into the back of his seat. Then it was time for the right eye.

"It's burning! *Ahhh!*" they screamed until they were hoarse.

"It'll be all right," Arabella tried to soothe them. "You need to suffer to stop being a follower."

"She's . . . she's . . . crazy . . . ," Ali had gasped.

The laser beam finally subsided, letting darkness begin the healing process. The hands released them. Their heads dropped. They were gasping for air, gagging in pain.

"Turn on the lights!" Stepan had begged. "I can't breathe, I can't breathe!"

Everything was a blur after that. They traveled on for a while, in a state of exhaustion and semiconsciousness, before coming to an unknown land—blindfolded. In an ambient din, dozens of arms lifted and carried them.

"My eyes . . . ," Helen had wept. "You burned them . . ."

"It will pass," Arabella uttered softly. "If you keep them closed until tomorrow, there will be no side effects. It's the price you pay for night vision, the only way you can find your way through the maze of tunnels to become one of us."

Their bandaged eyes still stung when they first heard his voice. A distinctive voice, bewitching yet sharp as glass.

"Welcome, Faraways!"

The voice, they would learn later, belonged to the leader of Underhome.

Loco.

LOGBOOK
INSTRUCTOR: KA
SEASON I

End of day two.

In terms of Materia, the wounded five's injuries have been replicated by their brains—fortunately only superficially—the same way Alpha's brain reproduced his cut after the trial connection. Arabella says the laser procedure was painful but hasn't caused any permanent damage. She appears to be the embodiment of the program's protective shield for Mantra 1: the program is speaking through her to help guide the Seven to the key. First thing tomorrow, I will give them each an online eye test to make sure there is no damage. Their identities will be safe: the medical decree of 2030, authorizing MLEs to fight the spread of viruses among health care personnel, guarantees patient anonymity.

The safety mechanisms protecting the Seven on the Spiritua level are still unclear; the more the Seven embrace the Subs' world, the more they belong to it. The Keeper has devised a backup plan in the event of an emergency: if the Seven are in danger during immersion, Head Instructor Shepherd is authorized to interrupt the connection by unplugging their umbilical cords. He came close to doing that when the five on the wagobike were being mauled in the tunnel. But he knows it should only be done as a last resort and that it could cause extensive neurological damage. How much? There is no telling: just as we are all unequal in the face of disease, an abrupt unplugging would elicit a different physical and psychological response from each of the Seven.

This second live broadcast triggered an avalanche of reactions. The number of subscribers to the Spirit Era Channel has doubled, now nearing 800 million. The AI-powered smart sensors integrated into the Sevens' outfits enable the program to edit the livestream. It selects the segments to be broadcast for maximum audience response. Keiji's and Rae's progress, as well as the adventures of their five companions, were aired either separately or simultaneously in a split-screen format.

Ultimately, Alpha is right: we do not hold all the cards. And the Keeper is no longer dealing them—if that was ever the case . . .

34

"So, here they are!"

A bare-chested man stands squarely before us. His skin is the same crimson color as the door to the driver's booth on the High Express. His torso is muscular, and he has a porthole stamped into his flesh; it is not just a raised tattoo but part of his body. With spike- and needle-studded ears, and a wiry Mohawk running the length of his shaved head, he is utterly fascinating. His presence is so overpowering, everyone around him seems to disappear.

"Your little protégés!"

After reentering the program, all seven of us were taken to the Train, the Prowlers' headquarters—where our five companions landed after they were blinded, thankfully only temporarily. It is an old-fashioned wooden train divided into private areas by a hodgepodge of colorful curtains.

"*These two* are the ones you so desperately wanted?" He scans Keiji and me with his piercing eagle eyes. That and the crowd gathering around us make us feel ill at ease.

Suddenly, Loco claps Alpha on the shoulder as if they have known each other for ages. It's weird, because he is part human, part metro car, with a body, limbs, and a head. And his jerky movements seem to require a focused effort from him.

"I told you that Arabella would find them. Ha ha! That's not how I imagined them!"

Alpha laughs along with him.

"They're pipsqueaks, for one. But those funny faces!"

Thanks. Always nice to hear, my inner voice ironizes, to my surprise. It's been fairly quiet lately.

"Don't get me wrong, eh? Especially not you, Mute Girl. We have nothing but funny faces in this place!"

Loco has the kind of charisma that could charm the pants off anyone. He's apparently won over Ali and Stepan already, the way he has Keiji and me. And Helen, too. She's been trying to catch his eye the whole time. Only Chayton seems a little wary.

You'd better watch out for him, too, my little voice warns. *We know how the Tubeans treat kids in Deepwood. I can't imagine that guy's a lamb.*

"Come on! Have a seat!"

The Train's central compartment is fitted out like a caravan: throw cushions, colorful carpets, ornate wall decorations. Strange-looking ropes swing from the ceiling.

"Make way, people!"

Loco points to a circle of colorful mattresses onto which a swarm of his cohorts have piled. They are all part subway, like Arabella, who is part seat; Dione, part accordion connector; and Loco, part crimson-colored porthole. They are the children and grandchildren of those former homeless people who, by dint of being invisible, had literally morphed into the subway fixtures. Each in their own way recalls the train's sliding doors, its plush carpet, built-in plastic tables, and narrow strip of tinted mirror.

"Come on!"

Grumbling all the while, some make room while others

stand up. Unlike Arabella, who moves about swiftly, their movements are a bit chaotic. As if their joints are rusty, they stretch before moving. The Train is packed: there are Prowlers everywhere. But there are many normal-looking male children, too. Arabella is the only female. Earlier, she told us her skills as a mechanic had secured her position and their leader's high regard.

"Sit down! We have things to talk about."

Loco squeezes in between two men. I recognize the accordion-monster on his right. He appears annoyed to see us there. The leader pulls two red packets out of his pants pocket, gulps one down, then gives the second one to Dione, who does the same.

"After the Great Famine"—the moment he begins to speak, a respectful silence descends on the circle—"the rich got even richer, the poor even poorer, and the middle class ended up on the streets . . ." The blood-red veneer of his skin bears traces of countless battles. "Our forebears, the homeless, were suddenly in high demand. They knew how to survive. A fantastic twist of fate, eh?"

Every pore of Loco's being exudes cynical resentment.

"Today's Subs are the former middle class from before the Great Famine: the commoners. But us, we're called the Prowlers because we sneak into Aboveworld to steal food. We are heroes. Only the direct descendants of the homeless can stand the test of thermal vision that allows us to navigate Underworld's maze of tunnels. No one has ever survived the rite of passage without coming from the street. Until you came along . . ."

Some of the creatures eye us suspiciously.

"The Owls . . . Those bastards drove us into darkness, buried us alive . . . ," Loco spits. "We'll make them pay! The Great Rebellion is on the move!"

"*Hooah, hooah!*" Battle cries welcome his words.

"The Seven are now part of our clan!" Arabella exclaims.

"How do you know?" Dione bellows. "We don't know them! How did they get here?"

"He's right!" The others agree with him.

Voices ring out in every direction. Loco demands silence.

"Five of you may have infrared vision. But will all seven of you be loyal to our cause? I've been told you're looking for a key. Is that true, Alpha?"

"Yes," Alpha replies plainly.

Loco clearly considers him our leader, much to Chayton's discontent.

"Do you think it is the key to the Slymouth Gate?"

"It could be."

"Why do you need it?"

"It is the key to bringing about change in our world," Alpha says.

"But for us, it is the key to freedom!"

"Hooah, hooah!" The whooping resumes.

Loco merely gets to his feet and the clamor subsides.

"Two leaders and one key. That makes us enemies!"

"Not necessarily," Alpha replies, standing, as well, cool and confident.

A shrewd adversary, he offers nothing more. The ball is in Loco's court.

"You want the key, and so do I," Loco eventually lets out. "There can be only one winner."

"Not if we join forces."

"What? Look for the key together?"

"It would double our chances of finding it. When it is found, you'll open your gate, and you won't need the key anymore!"

Loco's belligerent cohorts trade wary looks.

"Who says they won't steal the key first?" the accordion-monster roars.

"Yeah," a chorus of voices chime in. "Who says?"

"I say we risk it," Arabella cuts in. "No matter how the dice fall, what do we have to lose? It's been no dice so far anyway!"

The clamor grows louder.

"That's true!"

"Does the damn key even exist?"

"We've just about had it!"

"Where is it?"

"*Silence!*" Loco commands, downing another packet. "I've made up my mind."

The muttering subsides, for the most part.

"The time of the Great Rebellion is drawing near; we need more troops . . . But first, you must prove yourself. We need a lot more packets. Our reserves are almost empty. You will be allowed to join us when we go on our next Harvest!"

"Fine," Alpha says.

"Will you have the guts to pick the Owls' pockets? We're invisible, but you . . ."

"It's fine, really."

"In that case, I agree to a joint search. But be careful, no tricks: we share everything. I have drawn up a map of the places we've already searched."

"*Stop!*" a voice outside booms.

Keiji and I recognize it immediately. The sound of a stampede reaches our ears. A head appears through an open window.

"What is *going on here*?" demands Mrs. Tubeans in her man's suit.

A half minute later, she pushes her way onto the crowded Train. The Prowlers move aside to let her pass as if she has the plague. "I have no time to waste. If you called me here for nothing . . . ," she threatens Loco overtly.

Her shadowlike husband follows close behind, hunched over, his lip stuck out in exaggerated disgust. Holding Siana and Blanky by the collars, he flings them aside like rotten meat. Blanky almost falls. It is all Alpha can do to keep Keiji from pouncing.

"Are these the kids I asked for?"

"Take a guess, Loco!" Old Lady Tubeans snarls. "Now, what the hell is going on?"

"You're going to give them to me. I need them."

"No way. The girl broke orders, and it's not the first time. You know what happens to repeat offenders."

"That can wait."

"Deepwood Dormitory is under my direction. Since when do I have to take orders from you?"

"I need them for a mission Above."

"Why these two? I can get you something better."

"These are the ones I need. They know the Faraways."

"Now you listen here—"

"May I remind you that Prowlers take precedence in the affairs of the Rovers," Loco cuts in.

Her bloated face freezes, her hair standing on end like a nest of cobras. The growl that escapes her thin lips is terrifying.

"Those kids . . . are Deepwood property . . . ," she hisses. "When they come back . . ."

She spins around and storms off. Her husband trails behind her, melting further into the ground with each new step. But I can tell he's had one foot in the grave for a long time.

She will have her revenge soon enough, and the price to pay will be painful. I'm afraid for Siana and Blanky. Loco shouldn't have provoked her in front of everyone. It looked like he was enjoying it, too. It is in nobody's interest to antagonize the vile Tubeans.

Nobody's.

Everything here is pushed to the extreme.

It's all or nothing and incredibly intense. A few hours from now, we will leave for the next Harvest. The next pilfering, I should say. Except the Owls can see us. So, naturally, I am a little nervous. Even though it's for a good cause, it feels odd to side with the outlaws.

While waiting to set off on our first mission, we have a little free time. The inhabitants of the Train are staring at us like we are animals in a zoo. I went to a zoo with Mia and Joyce once—once, not twice.

"Are you all right, Siana?" Keiji asks.

"Yes."

Where is the tigress we saw in action yesterday? Siana's golden mane is tied in a messy knot at the nape of her neck again. The submissive flower vendor is back.

"No. We are not okay!" Blanky contradicts her. "You never should have fessed up about the damaged cart. When we get back to Deepwood, Old Lady Tubeans is going to make mince-meat of you!"

"What is going to happen to her?"

"Siana is a repeat offender. If Loco hadn't demanded she be handed over, I don't know where she'd be. Girls who disobey get more than a beating. They are banished. Even if they haven't reached puberty."

"Really?" Keiji asks.

"Yes, really. Niro's older sister disappeared just like that. We never saw her again! He's been a little crazy ever since . . ."

"We'll make sure that doesn't happen, Siana," Chayton reassures her. "You will never go back there. I promise."

I see the same look in Siana's eye—part disbelief, part hope—I saw when Chayton gave her the gum during the trial connection.

Dione and his henchmen call the two Rovers for a meeting. Something about the look in the accordion-monster's eyes makes me shudder.

"Come with me," Arabella suggests. "It'll be quieter."

She ushers us into an empty compartment with a closed door at the opposite end. A mountain of brightly colored cushions greets us. The walls are papered with banknotes.

"Money hasn't bought anything here for a very long time . . . ," Arabella explains.

It reminds me of the old-fashioned wallpaper in Chris's grandmother's kitchen. Among jam jars and baking sheets, her wisps of white hair caught up in a bun, Granny Martha raised Chris and her brother—their parents were addicts. We spent many an afternoon scraping vegetables from the market and snapping peas, sipping hot chocolate and devouring homemade muffins . . . That's all part of another life, now.

"What can you tell us about the key?" Ali asks when we sit down.

"If I help you, you'll have to help me, too," Arabella says.

"Of course," Chayton answers, without checking with us first.

"Well, I can't tell you much. Legend has it that there are

three sets of keys. The one we are looking for was lost. One is in the Toptown Council's safe, and one's in the pocket of the Brigade commander, General Dusk. They go through Slymouth Gate to make their raids."

"The Brigade makes raids here?" Helen asks in disbelief.

"Not in this part of Underhome. They wouldn't get away with it," Arabella answers, her face darkening. "The cowards only attack the weakest. Let me show you. Come with me."

She stands up to leave.

Suddenly, the door at the end of the wagon opens and reveals a frail figure. In the compartment, two Prowlers loll on multicolored pillows surrounded by a group of young frolicking women wearing lace domino masks. Turquoise, yellow, and purple veils half conceal their naked bodies.

The girl who opened the door stands in front of Chayton, a blank look in her eye. Her cropped hair is an unlikely shade of faded green.

"Hi. I'm Froggie. They say my mother spawned me in a pond just like a tadpole!"

She holds out a hand covered in scratches. Surprised, Chayton clasps it awkwardly.

"Uh, hello . . . My name is Chayton."

"I know."

She is a strange one. Her features are wasted but beautiful. Her vacant eyes, ringed with dark circles, stamp her face with sorrow . . .

"You are in *danger* here!" she exclaims. "Go home!"

Her shouting attracts the Prowlers' attention, too busy having a good time to have noticed the half-open door.

"Hey, there, Froggie! *What are you up to?* You can't go out without your mask."

"She's always acting up, that one!"

"Get her back here right away! And close the goddamn door!"

But the girl clings to Chayton's neck instead.

"Be careful!" she says.

"Hey!" Chayton answers, trying to unclasp her arms.

The fragile silhouette walks over to Stepan next, who remains speechless. She latches on to him.

"Keys open doors, but they can lock them, too. You may never see daylight again!"

Three girls come to drag her away at the bidding of the Prowlers. As soon as they touch her, Froggie goes limp like a rag doll.

"Don't trust . . . Don't . . . trust anyone . . . ," she mumbles, contradicting the Shepherd's three-pronged rule. "Especially you, Chayton . . ."

They hand the girl over to her keepers, like a deer to hunters. The door quickly closes, and Arabella leads us toward the exit. We cross the Train's main compartment again, in a hive of incessant buzzing.

"You said money doesn't buy anything here," Chayton challenges Arabella.

"So I did," she confirms.

"Then why do they do that, if it's not for money?"

"There's always something to gain . . . and even more often something to lose . . ."

At last, we exit the train. We feel a blast of fresh air, which makes no sense, of course, since we are underground. Even so, I take a deep breath. The atmosphere in the Train was toxic.

"Don't blame her for it," Arabella says. "Froggie has lost her mind. Like so many others . . ."

True. There's Valjean the Rabbit, Underhome's lanky mascot with scraggly gray hair, all alone in his bright-pink cara-tram, telling his story over and over. Throw in Niro, and the number of people inhabiting other celestial spheres keeps growing—despite being confined to the bowels of the earth!

Still, I feel close to them. Some move me, others intrigue me . . .

And yet I'm afraid—or maybe I hope?—that their state of benign madness will rub off on us. We are about to join the Subway Prowlers' band of merry men, after all . . .

PART SIX

THE OTHER SIDE

36

The wretchedness of the outcasts of Underhome . . .

The Infected, locked up for being contagious. This is what Arabella wants to show us before we set forth on the Harvest. This is why she is willing to let us in on her secret: a corridor, running parallel to the Underhome tunnel network, leading to an isolated subway line. The Infected are shut away there. It just goes to show that even belowground, misery can sink to new depths . . .

"It's the Prowlers who keep the gate locked!" the bench-woman explodes. "Loco has convinced his henchmen—Dione and the like—that it will prevent further contamination. That it's in the people's best interest."

"Gee . . ." is all Chayton can muster.

We hide there for a good fifteen minutes, crouching in the shadows and staring through a row of ventilation shutters until we perceive movement on the other side of the grating. One of the air ducts in the corridor starts to quiver and shake. It is being pried open from the inside! Preceded by a ratty carryall, an impressive hunched figure struggles forth. It is Valjean the Rabbit!

"I am not the only one who knows about the secret passages," Arabella whispers.

A hot-pink scarf matching his caratram and as long as a python is looped around his head and neck. With one leg ostensibly shorter than the other, the giant figure hobbles away.

"That's the tunnel to Station 22, one of the three abandoned stations where the Infected are contained."

We exit our hiding place and creep along in a single file to the sound of Valjean's footsteps. We descend deeper into the tunnel in silence. A stench of decay hangs in the air. There could be a heap of garbage nearby.

The Valjean Rabbit stops. Emaciated figures line the walls. Alone or in small groups, they are well-nigh invisible against the asphalt. They remind me of the tramps in BART, the Bay Area Rapid Transit network. In the wake of the recent housing crisis, the city of San Francisco has had to deal with a flood of homeless people. Or has not dealt with, I should say . . .

Valjean attempts to prompt a response from the exiles, a kind look here, a smile there. But it's all in vain. The dim shadow of death already clouds their eyes. At length, he gets a reaction from a lanky teen shivering in the cold draft: the boy bobs his head like an automaton. He is clutching dozens of the colored packets but doesn't seem the least bit interested in them. Next to him, curled up in a ball with her back to him, an old woman lies inert on a flattened cardboard box. Could it be his mother?

"Are you okay, kid?" Valjean asks.

The boy's blue-tinted lips are motionless—silent for too long. The mascot of Underhome puts down his bag and unloops the knitted scarf from around his neck. Thrice over, given its length. As he wraps the woolen stole around the homeless teen's shoulders, a look of reclaimed innocence flashes in the gentle giant's eyes. The exhausted boy immediately falls asleep.

Val hobbles away without making a noise, as if the boy is a toddler napping in his bedroom. If only that were true . . .

We resume our silent journey through the secret tunnel and eventually come to another ventilation grid. There, we can observe, unseen, the abandoned platform on the other side—and what is nothing short of a freak show. Wretches and cripples with bandaged heads, disfigured faces, amputated limbs, and festering wounds. The stench is nauseating.

Val the Rabbit is moving among the crowd. He stops next to a young girl in a torn floral print dress leaning against the wall. A sign overhead reads:

"BEWARE. CRAT EXTERMINATION ZONE. LAST ARSENIC TREATMENT . . ." The rest is illegible.

The skulls, ears, and faces of the Infected are covered with dark-red protuberances, like mushrooms or bulbs. The name "Bulbosis" makes more sense to me now. Some have lost hair by the fistful and patches of lumpy scalp show. The young girl in the floral print still has her mane of thick dark hair, but abscesses disfigure her cheek and neck. Her eyes are half closed; she seems half alive.

After fiddling with the stuck zipper of his carryall for a moment, the mascot opens the bag, rummages through its contents, and pulls out a yellow packet. The girl's eyes flutter. Nothing more. Valjean tears open the paper sachet and sprinkles some of its powdery contents onto her lips. The girl runs her tongue over it—once, twice, three times. Then, her mouth opens wide like a baby bird so Val can feed her. But a nearby wretch spots the mascot's half-open tote and makes a lunge for it. An ugly roar rises from the crowd, and a host of desperate hands snatch up all the packets.

The mascot lumbers away, resigned. We lose sight of him. The girl fades completely, her eyes and mouth close. A scant sprinkling of powder dusts her shoes. A couple of crats emerge from a hole and come scurrying over. For some strange reason, instead of licking up the powder, they sweep it away with their tails.

"Now you know," Arabella murmurs.

She turns her gaze to the far end of the station, where the tunnel disappears in the distance. An enormous shape is materializing in the darkness. Blurry at first, it sharpens into focus to reveal a reedlike young man with a quick, lithe gait.

"Bamboo!" Arabella calls out, rushing over to him.

"*Stop!*" the young man bellows. With another step, his face emerges from the darkness.

"No!" A huge festering knob has formed on his ear. Even worse, hideous inflamed bald patches checker his mop of curls.

"When did . . . ?" Arabella chokes back a sob.

"Last night; my hair started coming out in clumps."

"We'll find a solution. We will . . ."

"No, stay where you are!"

"Why should I? You know Prowlers never get sick. We seem to be immune to Bulbosis," she says, turning to us. "Possibly on account of our infrared vision."

"You *seem to be* immune. That doesn't mean you are."

"I won't let this happen . . . Without you, nothing makes sense anymore . . ."

"We knew it was bound to happen sooner or later, my sweet Benchy."

Her legs seem about to give way, but Arabella holds steady. Behind her, Ali and Chayton each place a comforting hand on her shoulder. She starts to cry.

"Who are these people?" Bamboo asks.

"They've come from another world to help us. Isn't that right?" She turns to Chayton.

"Uh . . . yes, that's right," Chayton manages. But his face gives him away: What could we do to help?

"Tell them, Bamboo! Tell them everything you know about Bulbosis. Maybe they can find a cure," Arabella says.

"To begin with, we don't know how it spreads. Understanding how it is transmitted is critical to ending the epidemic," Bamboo replied.

"We heard it is the crats," Keiji says.

"That's what the Subs think. But those harmless creatures have no boils whatsoever, and their fur doesn't fall out," Bamboo says.

"They could be healthy carriers," Stepan remarks. Over the course of our journey through the secret tunnel, his silent detachment has given way to silent concern. The cramped space doesn't seem to bother him anymore.

"Hmph, could be," Bamboo admits.

"You forget that the crats in Aboveworld are regularly exterminated," Arabella comments.

"The Owls have no contact with them, and yet Bulbosis spreads there, just the same."

"True. It is a complete mystery."

"I'd say it's fair, rather. At least we are equal on that front."

"In any case, we do know that it starts with scabs and boils, and that it isn't contagious until your hair starts falling out. The initial phase can last for years, although that doesn't stop them from shutting us away here as soon as the first signs of swelling develop!"

"Stop whom?" asks Alpha.

"The Prowlers," Bamboo replies. "They make the laws in Underhome, like the Agreement signed by the Toptown Council authorizing children to panhandle in Aboveworld."

"Which is the same as saying Loco decides," Arabella goes on. "He has most of the Prowlers in his pocket. Not that the Owls are any better. The president of Toptown Council, their PTC, may be a queer old bird with a mind as wooly as her head of hair, but the Infected of Toptown are quarantined, too. And they die as easily in Centers there as they do here."

"Toptown is so prosperous it could support five times its population," Bamboo continues. "But the inhabitants are spoiled by robotization and excess. They have lost all sense of judgment, and their souls, to boot . . ."

"Yeah, and it's gotten even worse with Bulbosis. Prior to the outbreak, the Toptown Council was considering passing new agreements with the World Below. But rumors that the Subs are the source of the contagion put a stop to all that."

"Leaders dealing with epidemics have to make tough decisions at times," Alpha remarks.

"If by leader, you mean Loco, forget it!" Chayton cuts in. "He's only looking out for number one!"

"How would you know!"

"I can feel it in my gut."

"Well, in the meantime, he's the one supplying Underhome with food."

"And the Infected, too, I'll give him that much. Except there is never enough," Arabella says with a sigh.

"It's a good thing the Subs are willing to help," Bamboo adds. "They bring us their leftovers."

"Leftovers?" Chayton repeats, incredulous. "But you're not crats!"

"Very true," Arabella concedes. "And we plan to do something about it at the next Harvest, don't we?" she asks, addressing us.

"What do you mean?" Ali asks.

"That this time around, there's something the seven of you can do to help me."

"What?"

"You can help me steal packets from the Prowlers."

"*What?* You mean you want us to rob the robbers?"

Arabella has lost her mind! Or maybe it was warped to begin with. Either way, defying Loco and his men on their own turf would be suicide!

37

Tack!

The sound of a pebble against my dormer window rouses me from sleep—with difficulty. After staying up all night at Alpha's bedside, I haven't slept for nearly two days straight.

Tack!

Another pebble. Half asleep, I walk over to the window and open it. Standing in the yard, I can make out the shape of a slender figure and—a head of golden hair illuminated in the moonlight!

Siana?

Of course not! You're not in the program. Remember? says the voice.

True. We were still in the secret tunnel with Arabella and Bamboo when our watches went off. Hmph, I don't know whether I'm coming or going anymore!

The farmhouse door opens in the yard below and someone comes out. It's Chayton. He turns his face toward my window.

"You coming, Rae?" he whispers. "Anais came by to see how we're doing."

Anais, of course! Mr. Mann's daughter . . . I hadn't seen her since we met at the chicken coop. She is wearing a pair of yellow pajamas with a hen pattern that matches her vintage headscarf and the color of her hair. Chayton is wearing a pair of sweatpants and a jacket over his bare chest, not his usual red jacket but a purple one.

"Stepan lent me his. Mine stank of sweat. I had to wash it and it's still drying," Chayton explains in a hushed voice.

I wrap myself in a blanket, half asleep on my feet, and head out the door.

We opt for the barn instead of the goat shed or the henhouse. Lately, our kids have started making a hellish racket whenever they see us, and the hens don't like being disturbed at night. Anais remembered to bring a flashlight.

"I'm so glad to see you!" she utters softly.

Her big brown eyes widen as she throws her arms around Chayton. He confesses he's been spending time with Anais in secret. She's like the little sister he never had. I get a hug, too, and a handful of peanuts as if we're at the circus.

"It's been three days already. Only four left to find the key," Anais says.

"Don't remind us. We're worried enough as it is."

"Sorry, Chayton. I really want you to succeed, that's all!"

"Thanks. That's nice of you."

"No, it isn't. It's not nice of me! The end of the world is near at hand. Nobody wants to die!"

I've never heard Anais raise her voice before. She quickly regains her composure.

"The VR world is so amazing. And so are your names. Muladhara, for you, Chayton, and Vishuddha for Rae. They're beautiful. I'm lucky. Miss Kassandra set up a smart screen in my room so I can follow the livestreams."

"What do we look like?" Chayton asks.

"Well, we can see your real silhouettes—same build, same hair, same gestures—but the colored aura of your dominant chakra blurs the details. It's impossible to recognize you."

In the dimly lit barn, the farm equipment and the partially dismantled old tractor are still in place, but there are fewer bales of hay. I choose two adjoining bales and stretch out, my hands cradling my head like a cushion.

"What about me? Did I do okay?"

"You're asking me what I think? That's a first, Chayton! Doubt yourself more often. It suits you."

"Humph . . ."

"Aw, come on! I thought you were terrific, though I don't see how you're going to keep your promise to Siana and Blanky."

"Yeah, I got a little ahead of myself there. Sooner or later, they'll have to go back to Deepwood, unless we take out Old Lady Tubeans first . . ."

"It would serve her right!"

A burst of heartfelt laughter bubbles up out of Anais and lingers in the air. The kind of laugh you could listen to forever . . .

"And what about Loco? How did you like him, sis?" Chayton asks.

"He certainly makes an impression, but I'm not so sure. The one I like best is Froggie."

"Froggie?"

"That's right, Froggie."

"You mean the girl who was . . . uh . . . having fun with those Prowler guys?"

"She wasn't having fun. That's the whole point . . ."

"I don't know, something about her made me uncomfortable."

"Her nakedness, no doubt—although not the kind you're thinking about!"

"Gee, you're pretty smart for a kid your age!"

"And you're pretty blind for a guy your size! When you go back to the Train, I hope you'll be able to see her."

"But I did see her."

"No, you didn't. You only looked at her."

They eventually sit down close by. The sounds of their voices run together; my eyes close. As they continue their conversation, images of the Infected flash through my brain. I know it's all virtual, but they haunt me, nonetheless. Far more than something out of a scary movie.

I must nod off for a while; my memories permeate my dreams and give them a troubling air of reality. That's the way it is with dreams and life. With life and dreams . . .

"*What's that?*" Chayton's voice goes up a notch: I open an eye.

"Shh!" Anais scolds.

A torn piece of paper is lying on the ground. The Mann girl picks it up.

"It fell out of the pocket of Stepan's jacket. Hey, look! There's something written on it!" she says.

"Let me see. You're right. But that chicken scrawl is barely legible."

"Ooh, it's signed 'Froggie'!"

"Are you kidding?"

"She must have slipped it into the jacket when she latched on to Stepan."

"It happened again. Another one of us unknowingly brought back an item-clue."

"Unless . . ."

"Unless what?"

"Unless this message was meant to end up in your hands and Stepan was just a go-between. Only one way to know for sure."

"Let's read it!"

Anais strains to make out the words on the paper by the

light of the flashlight and eventually succeeds. I've drifted off to a dreamland once again when words in the distance reach my ear. Words that will change everything.

"To you, the one I have been expecting for so long, whoever you may be . . .

"Though it is true, Bulbosis is scary, there is another, far worse evil in Underhome. Beware!

"I have a daughter . . . She is in danger . . . Please! I beg you. Don't let anything happen to her!

"Her name is Siana.

"PS: Nobody must ever know who I am. We would both be thrown to our deaths from the Ledge."

I'm scared.

Scared sick. As if agreeing to Loco's crazy plan weren't enough, now they expect my five companions to filch packets for the Infected to boot, and to conceal them under their jackets. And Keiji and I have to play Rovers. So, yes. I'm feeling a little nervous, to put it mildly. My father always said that even the slightest bit of mischief showed on my forehead—it broke out in a sweat. I'm guessing it looks like Niagara Falls right about now!

Mind the gap between the train and the platform as you leave the High Express . . .

The subway is packed. I move through the jostling crowd to the back of the car. I wish I could vanish into a mouse hole. A little air is coming in through a slightly ajar tinted-glass window. I take a deep breath to strengthen my resolve.

Stand clear of the closing doors . . .

The train is off again. I look up at the strip of mirror running the length of the ceiling and see my face reflected in it: a nut-brown oval among a sea of Owl heads. An odorless mist descends with a hiss. A disinfectant, I tell myself, to prevent the spread of Bulbosis.

"Roses! Pretty roses!"

Siana is weaving her way through the crowd, her golden locks tied in a tangled knot. I follow her movements in disbelief. Are the humble flower seller and Siana one and the same person? The image of the Deepwood tigress remains etched in my memory. And she is supposedly Froggie's daughter? They look nothing alike—quite the opposite, in fact. When we showed our friends her letter, they could hardly believe their eyes. As for Stepan, the fact he would not be allowed to bring out another item-clue didn't seem to faze him.

"Get your pretty roses! A rose, kind sir? A rose, ma'am?"

In the distance, Siana continues her spiel under Loco's watchful eye. He appointed me, of all people, to be her partner. Our job as Rovers is to create a diversion while the Prowlers pick the Owls' pockets. The bartering is just a pretext, really. Loco doesn't care a fig about the proceeds. Whatever we trade belongs to the Tubeans. He's just interested in the packets.

In the meantime, after entering the High Express platform through the vending machine along with the others, Alpha is masquerading as an ordinary traveler. He is working in tandem with Loco, who wants to keep an eye on him. Loco seems to think Alpha is our leader. The rest of the gang has been assigned elsewhere, and Keiji is partnered with Blanky. To hide our sophisticated jackets—poorly suited to playing the part of beggars—he and Siana have given Keiji and me a couple of shabby cardigans with an odd assortment of handmade pockets, no doubt for stashing traded goods. We are both careful to leave them open to make sure the camera sensors sewn into our uniforms can properly function.

Earlier, Keiji and I made the reverse journey to the coal mine via Gate 4.6, where we left our cart and followed the Rovers into a different tunnel. Unlike Prowlers, Rovers aren't invisible in Aboveworld. To enter Toptown, they go through a checkpoint guarded by a pair of Brigade officers. An electronic turnstile equipped with a height-detection monitor records the number of children passing through. If there is any discrepancy between the number of entries and exits on a given day, all agreements between Above and Below are off . . .

"Roses! Get your pretty roses!"

The subway picks up speed. I should be on my way to help Siana, but I am scared stiff. I am unable to move, despite encouragements from my inner voice.

"A pretty rose for the pretty lady?"

A young man holding hands with a redheaded girl takes the bait. Reaching into his pocket, he removes a travel-size bottle with the Toptown logo on it.

"Shampoo for a rose?"

"Okay, it's a deal."

Siana hands the redhead a plastic flower, stuffs the little bottle into her pocket, and continues on her way.

In the meantime, Loco has taken advantage of the exchange to open bags, empty pockets, and filch packets—downing a red one in the process. Alpha, not one to be outdone, is confidently picking pockets at the opposite end of the car. And slipping the occasional packet into his jacket on the sly. He seems to be very good at it. Far too good, if you ask me . . .

"Roses! Pretty roses!"

Yeesh! When you gonna loosen up a bit?

Oh no, the hostile voice in my head is back!

Come on! Get moving!

A nearby passenger gives a loud sneeze, snapping me out of it.

The Infected are starving to death down there!

Another shot in the arm.

Stop being such a wuss, for God's sake!

All right already, I'm going! But after this, not another peep out of you, I warn the unfriendly voice.

I hold up the sign Arabella made for me, my forehead damp with sweat. My trade offering: little bits of cardboard the size of business cards.

I cannot speak, but I can lend an ear.

Free yourself of the words that are weighing you down.

They will be safe with me.

I will bring you good fortune and health.

The passenger who sneezed pays me no mind. No matter, I just move on, hand outstretched, stomach in knots. I wield my sign, hoping to catch someone's eye, but most look away. Every time they do, what little dignity I have left takes a blow. Battered dignity—the common heritage of beggars the world over, I realize dejectedly.

The train doors open. The crowd ebbs and flows. Two men in black uniforms board the train, wearing rolled-up ski masks exactly like the ones we saw the day of the suicide attempt. Now, I recognize them: Toptown Brigade officers. I instinctively keep a low profile.

"Goddamn Bulbosis!" one of them sputters.

"You can say that again! Just yesterday, I had to take an entire family to the Center for the Infected: a couple and their elderly parents."

"At least the kids were spared."

"Spared? You could say that—for now. Sure, none of them develop symptoms until they hit puberty, but they have the virus, all right. It's just lying dormant. That's why they always test positive."

"Well, I still say, they shouldn't be allowed out."

"Yeah, I guess so. In any case, when their hormones kick in, their viral load will explode. That's why I don't want kids."

"I do. We have to go on living. Besides, there are plenty of people whose viral load never reaches outbreak level. The fact is, we're not all equal in the face of disease; there's nothing we can do about it. Viral infections affect each of us differently."

"True. Plus, we have everything we could possibly want here. We might as well enjoy it."

A leaden silence descends on the two men. I prefer to move on.

"Are you mute?" a voice behind me asks.

I turn around and—I can't believe it! I've seen the woman before!

"Are you really mute?"

The woman with the frizzy white hair is carrying the same sock-shaped bag, the one I saw Dione, the accordion-monster, rifle through. It's Lady Fluff.

"You can't speak?"

I shake my head.

"Gee, what funny bangs you have! I guess it can't be helped. Hairdressers must be few and far between in the World Below . . ."

With a nervous gesture, she opens her bag and pulls something out.

"Here. I'll trade you a hairdresser's coupon. We have to go every other day to get tested. But you can go whenever you want."

She sizes up the card I hand her.

"A little luck and good health won't do me any harm. A lot of people have it in for the PTC . . ."

She reads the card again.

"Words weighing me down? I know a thing or two about that! Believe me, being president of the Toptown Council is no easy task, though my role is mainly about upholding the code of ethics. I oversee the meetings; the deputies—AI-endowed robots designed to make decisions in the best interests of the city—pass the laws. They've reelected me every year for the last thirty years. I have no home life, no children." So, this is the fuzzy-haired old gal Arabella was talking about! "Robotization has made it unnecessary for the inhabitants of Toptown to work. Everything is regulated to make life easier. The packets that come out of the nutrition laboratory are our greatest achievement. They have made us entirely self-sufficient and are perfectly formulated to meet our recommended dietary needs. I am one of only a few civil servants, and no one here really notices me. I basically just work for the robots. And the Toptown subway is the only way to get around."

Mind the gap between the train and the platform as you leave the High Express . . .

"Oh! This is my stop! I'll keep your card in my pocket. Being blessed by a mute is no small matter!"

Lady Fluff rises from her seat, enters the stream of passengers, and walks toward the sliding doors, waving goodbye as she exits.

"Use the coupon to get your bangs straightened!"

Stand clear of the closing doors . . .

I look down at the coupon. It's about the size of a coaster. On one side, it reads "Solid Gold Hairstyles." On the other, there is a small map.

Straighten my bangs? Sure, why not? I wonder if getting a simulated haircut would change my hair in the real world . . . Could my hair have something to do with my item-clue? In any case, it's been a long time since I've been to the hairdresser. Maybe getting straight bangs would straighten out my life? The life I'll have to face when I go home for Christmas . . .

"Pretty roses! A rose, kind sir? A rose, ma'am?"

Despite my best panhandling efforts, I only offload that one card, but at least the hostile voice is letting me be. Siana has much better luck with her flowers. Unless it's just a question of experience.

Not that any of that really matters. What happened behind the scenes is what matters. What we—or rather, the Owls, blind to the world of Spiritua—didn't see: the Prowlers and their Harvest.

39

In Underhome, we receive a heroes' welcome.

The Subs cheer and break into applause as we march through the maze of alleyways decorated with folk art. They have attired themselves with scarves, gloves, and fantastical knitted headdresses for the occasion. Strings of multicolored lanterns illuminate the caratrams and cardboard houses.

"My dear friends of Underhome, the Harvest was excellent!" Loco crows, towering above the crowd on his customized bike.

Between bursts of raucous laughter, he empties packet after packet into his mouth; his naturally crimson-colored chin is streaked with red powder. Leading the procession, the leader's vehicle looks like a bigger version of the wagobike kitted out with spiky protuberances. Now I know why it has six wheels.

"Enjoy the Harvest!"

Straddling their "bikes"—no two alike and all designed by the brilliant Arabella—the Prowlers parade through the crowd tossing packets of all colors into the air. The crowd is whipped into a frenzy. People everywhere are stuffing their pockets, juggling, trading, kissing, and mixing different packets together.

"Enjoy!" Loco says again.

The Rovers and the Seven bring the procession to an end. Helen and Stepan have grown closer of late. He has a hard time tolerating the noise, and Helen makes earplugs for him out of empty paper packets.

"This whole business is ridiculous," Chayton says to me as we make our way through the cheering crowd. "If my buddies were locked up somewhere and I was the only one able to get out, naturally I'd want to supply them with food. Nothing heroic about that."

Yes, I agree. Flattered by the show of gratitude, Alpha and Ali play to the crowd. Strange music sounds in the distance.

"Come on, Rae!" Blanky hollers. "It's about to start!"

He grabs my hand and pulls me along after him. We zigzag quickly through the crowd and eventually get to an enormous square.

"We always hold our rallies here, in the Pit."

Looking up, I recognize the Ledge in Deepwood, where a group of musicians are tuning their instruments. The guitars, double basses, drums, and pianos are all as odd-looking as Beavertail, but when the music begins, the sounds they produce are so extraordinary, so utterly captivating, that my limbs begin moving of their own accord, frenetically, with no input from my brain.

Around us, everyone is dancing. Nothing fancy or recognizable. Rather, an outpouring, a shock of raw, unfiltered electricity. An ecstatic dance.

"Here!" says Blanky, tearing open a purple packet.

Emulating the other dancers, but also out of curiosity, I pour the powder into my mouth—I haven't forgotten the boost the previous packet gave me—and whoosh! I am caught up in the whirling throng, swept away by the music, an unbelievable mix of electro and classical. I take off. I am flying—completely free!

The rest of the Seven, Siana, and Arabella eventually join Blanky and me on the dance floor. They, too, are one with the music, though perhaps minus the boost from the packets. I have no idea how much time elapses. Everything seems to just glide past until a voice brings me around.

"Come with me," Arabella commands.

The bench-woman leads Keiji and me to a quiet spot.

"You are so small, they won't notice you're gone. We can use it to our advantage."

"First time my size is advantage!" Keiji remarks, half smiling.

"While Underhome celebrates the Harvest, the Infected are starving. It's disgusting!"

"What can we do about it?"

"Make the delivery tonight, not wait until tomorrow."

"What? Without the others?"

"With those cardigans, the two of you blend right in. Do you know where the extra packets are?"

"Yes," Keiji answers. "Hidden in pockets of Chayton's and Alpha's jackets. They left them on the Train to avoid walking around with the packets."

"Good. I want you to go get them. Make sure no one sees you. I'll wait for you at the entrance to the secret tunnel."

Keiji doesn't waste any time. He's off like a shot. I follow suit, doing my best not to lose him. Boy, is he fast! When we get to the Train, there is no one is sight. Still short of breath, I keep watch while he goes for the jackets.

"So far, everything fine," Keiji says when he gets back.

Far from reassuring me, his words trigger an alarm in my head. The whole thing is way too easy . . .

"Ready to go?" he asks, holding out a jacket to me.

It's Alpha's. Though hardly any heavier than mine, it's practically bursting with packets. Keiji holds on to Chayton's.

We have to go back through the festivities to get to Arabella's hiding place. The alleys are busy with revelers milling about and chatting. A bunch of rowdy youths dressed in rags are horsing around—kids once from Deepwood now on their own, perhaps . . .

A voice calls out to us.

"Hey, you!" we suddenly hear. "Where do you think you are going?" Surrounded by his gang of followers, Niro, the dorm leader with a shock of white hair, is blocking our way. "Didn't anyone ever tell you it's rude to leave without saying goodbye?"

Dulci, the temptress, leans against him. Gym sniggers.

"Especially when you are the guest of honor," Niro continues. "So, the two of you are part of the Seven?"

"You guess right!" Keiji answers.

"Well, I say Loco is a fool to trust Faraways who come and go. And so is Rags, even if she had the guts to fess up to the Two Beans about the dented wagon."

Only Niro would be crazy enough to come up with a nickname for the beastly Tubeans.

"And what the hell are you doing here anyway?"

"Our boss sent for jackets. Very cold here! But if you want to be courier instead of us . . ."

With remarkable composure, Keiji holds out Chayton's jacket.

"Pfff, no way!" Niro huffs, turning his back to him.

I clutch Alpha's to keep my hands from trembling.

"Your boss will have to wait. You and I have a score to settle!"

Oh no! Niro was still spoiling for a fight. He wants to challenge Keiji to roulette rail!

"She not anything to do with it," Keiji declares, referring to me. "Let her go with jackets."

"No way. If you lose, they'll say it's because you were alone and we outnumbered you. The same rules apply to each of us: a single assistant allowed. The rest of you guys, out of here!"

The gang clears off, grumbling and protesting. We have no choice but to follow Niro and Dulci. Sweet Dulci has lost her tongue and is on autopilot, it seems. A few abandoned subway tunnels later, we come to a secluded area.

"This is the forbidden zone, the only part of the network still running," Niro tells us. "Phantom trains still circulate here, nobody knows why. Back and forth like an electric train set." The platform is dark. "If you've changed your mind, I can go first instead of you."

"No," Keiji answers point-blank.

He hands me Chayton's jacket and jumps onto the tracks, his eyes flashing: he hasn't forgotten the slight to his family honor. He stations himself on the left track without the slightest hesitation. Fists on hips, Keiji plants himself proud as punch, determined not to give an inch. Has he lost his mind? I barely recognize him. He has a fifty-fifty chance of being squashed like a bug!

The sound of a train cuts through the distance. I don't know what to do: it's too late to warn the others.

"He's got guts," Niro lets slip.

Dulci leans closer, holding her breath.

"You mean he's crazy, my sweet Niro . . . Completely crazy . . ."

Keiji stands tall, chin raised, braving the unknown.

Dread fills my limbs. I am frozen in fear. What if he's picked the wrong track? Sure, we can't die in the simulation. But how safe are we? Could Keiji be seriously injured?

Suddenly, the milky glow of a headlight cuts through the dark—a gaping mouth heading straight at him, preparing to swallow him whole! A frightful screech of metal fills the air and makes the ground tremble. Dulci stifles a cry, burying her face in her hands.

"*Keiji!*"

An arm appears out of nowhere, grabs hold of his collar, and, with a tremendous yank, hoists him from the rails. Keiji's slight form flies through the air and lands on the platform right next to me. With a shrill screech, the train rushes by at full throttle, and . . . Oh my God! It's on the left track!

"*Chayton?*" Keiji shouts. "What . . . what are you doing here?"

"I should be asking you that! Have you lost your mind? If Blanky hadn't warned me . . ."

The phantom train disappears into the night, at last.

"Good job, kid, sneaking away with Rae on the sly! What were you thinking?"

Dead silence. Keiji is just realizing how serious the situation is. The color drains from his face.

"As for you two . . . I wonder what Loco would think if he knew you were here . . ."

Niro and Dulci have lost some of their luster, too; they make a quick getaway.

"The—the packets—for the Infected—" Keiji stammers. "Arabella is waiting for us."

"You're in no condition to go anywhere. I'll go with Rae."

Chayton takes the jacket I am holding for Keiji and puts it on. I do the same with Alpha's, slipping it over the pocket-covered cardigan lent to me by Siana. I look like the Michelin Man. The faint scent of aftershave reminds me of our first meeting on the farm.

It was not that long ago, and yet . . . it seems light-years away.

#THEKEEPER #SAVETHEWORLD

POST 6—FIRST KEY

NOVEMBER 25, 2035

NO PARTY LASTS FOREVER.

Such is the fate of all celebrations. They come to an end and leave a void, only to be filled by another, which, in turn, will reach a high point, a fleeting climax followed by a descent. Between the festivities, there is a sense of emptiness, a longing made up of past regrets and future expectations.

There is an art to knowing when to take a bow, when to leave before the wave starts to break.

In contrast, the art of living is not about riding the crest of the wave. It is about finding level ground—a simple stretch of flat ground—trusty, solid, and unassuming. It is about making life a celebration, not about searching for reasons to celebrate.

Placed end to end, the little joys of everyday life—provided we recognize them, water them, and encourage them to grow—are like seeds in a garden.

THE EARTH IS OUR TEACHER.

40

"What took you so long?"

Near the entrance to the secret tunnel, Arabella is on ten-terhooks. She is carrying a bundle made from a sweater. We set off straightaway.

"I thought something had happened to you. Where is Keiji?" Arabella asks.

"Something came up," Chayton answers.

"Something came up?"

"Yeah, well, I took his place."

Telling her about the roulette rail incident could mean trouble not just for Keiji but for Niro, too.

"And anyhow, it's an opportunity for me to persuade you to let me drive the wagobike!"

"Do not even try," Arabella snaps. "Hurry up! We're late!"

We take the same route as last time but go beyond the spot where we first saw Bamboo. At the end of the secret tunnel, a ventilation grid spans the shaft's entire width. I imagine it's how Bamboo comes and goes. We can see his shape in the shadows. He is wearing an oversized knit cap.

"Ah! I thought you wouldn't come! I thought I would never see you again, my sweet Benchy!"

She rushes toward him.

"No! Don't come any closer! The illness has . . ."

But Arabella couldn't care less about Bulbosis. She wraps her arms around him tenderly, then caresses his cheek. Apart from the boil on his ear, he has no other eruptions. For a moment, time stops. The lovers simply stand there, breathing each other in.

"I have to go," Bamboo says at last. "The others are waiting for the packets."

He removes his woolen cap and holds it out like a bag. His bald patches have disappeared: he has shaved his mane of curly hair. The only evidence of the disease are the small bumps covering his scalp.

Arabella empties the contents of her makeshift bundle into the bonnet. Chayton does the same with the packets in his jacket. Bamboo's cap is too small to hold them all!

"Ha ha!" Bamboo laughs. "You've done good work!"

"Let us help you," Chayton says.

"No. You could be contaminated."

"Valjean Rabbit seems fine."

"Ever since he lost his brothers to the disease, he's stopped caring. Maybe that's why he's immune to it. Some people get Bulbosis, others don't. Why? Nobody knows."

Bamboo's attempt to stuff the extra packets into his socks is a fiasco.

"Can't the others come give you a hand?" Chayton asks. "There are still more packets in Alpha's jacket."

"No one knows about this tunnel, and until we have the cure, it's better this way. Someone might be tempted to make a run for it. It wouldn't do any good to contaminate Underhome. I'll just have to make a few trips."

Clapping my hands to get their attention, I walk over and

open Alpha's jacket wide. The pockets sewn onto the old cardigan I am wearing are just waiting to be filled.

"She's right!" Chayton gets my meaning immediately. "Rae can go." I'm grateful he doesn't specify why: I'm prepubescent.

Together, we manage to load the rest of the packets into my arms and cardigan, and even stuff a few into Bamboo's socks. The three of us, that is: Chayton wisely keeps a safe distance. When we are ready at last, I follow Bamboo to the ventilation grid, Arabella removes the covering, and I slip through the opening after him.

"You distribute all those packets and come back quickly," Chayton whispers as the grid closes behind me. "Okay, Sparrow?" I can tell he's worried by the sound of his voice. "Don't get too close to them, you never know . . ."

Bamboo and I are standing at the far end of another decommissioned platform. Lower than the one we just left. From Station 22, nobody can see us. We creep along in the darkness, go up a few steps, and skim past a deep recess. I drop a packet. It's irretrievable.

A few yards later, we join the motley crowd of patients: intertwined bodies lying, sitting, and leaning against walls, back-to-back. Without a word, Bamboo begins distributing packets. Some snatch them, others give a rueful smile, others still grab his fingers and squeeze them. From time to time, no hand reaches out . . .

I can't bring myself to do it. Not because of the disease, not because I am afraid to touch them—I just can't. So, when Bamboo's supply runs out, I begin passing my packets to him while he hands them out—like a supply plane!

Pheeeeet!

A shrill whistle sounds.

"A raid!" someone shouts.

Bamboo is off like a flash.

"This way! Quickly! Everyone who can, follow me!"

He grabs hands, yanks collars, and hastens people to their feet.

"Back to the secret tunnel!" he calls out to me on the move.

All hell breaks loose; people everywhere are shouting and crying. One of the Infected ties the corners of his blanket into a bundle for his packets, tosses it over his shoulder, and nearly knocks over an old woman. The charging herd drives me forward. Bamboo can't be that far ahead of me, but the raging crowd has swallowed up his shaved head.

"The *Brigade!*" the man with the blanket yells, already some distance away. "Run!"

The stampede is at a fever pitch: people swearing, shoving, running in all directions. I run past several people—Bamboo is still nowhere to be seen.

"Faster!" another voice bellows.

Most are incapable of moving forward. Some are completely exhausted, others not even aware of the danger. The tunnel backs up. Spurred by the jostling crowd, I pick up speed without knowing which way to go. I've lost my bearings. Suddenly, the man with the bundle trips over his blanket. He falls, swearing like a trooper as his packets scatter onto the ground.

Pscht!

"Watch out! They're spraying Repulsecure!"

The mass of terrified fugitives closes ranks, trampling everything in its path. Suddenly, billows of dense greenish smoke fill the air. A young woman pulls her scarf over her nose. The smell is a cross between rotten eggs and bug spray. They are gassing us! The Brigade is gassing us like cockroaches!

One whiff is enough: I hold my breath as long as I can but eventually get a lungful. Fumes rip through my nostrils like barbed wire, constricting my airways. I can't breathe. My throat is on fire, my tongue is on fire, my empty lungs are on fire. Everywhere, it's sheer pandemonium: people crashing into each other, dropping like flies.

Cough, cough! A violent cough rips through me. Ignore it, I tell myself. Keep putting one foot in front of the other. My eyes are so swollen, I can't see. I inch forward in slow motion, my lungs burning with each new coughing fit.

Cough, cough! I am going to be sick. I lean against a wall, my chest heaving. My body is wracked with spasms, but nothing comes up. Invisible fangs tear at my bowels. My head is spinning.

Suddenly, the wall gives way, my body topples, and someone grabs my waistband and starts to pull. I can't see a thing; my eyes feel like orange peels when I rub them. Another coughing fit; my head is spinning. The yelling subsides, I begin to make out blurry images, and a spray of vomit splashes my combat boots. There is a metallic taste in my mouth.

I feel fingers reaching for mine, fragile twigs awkwardly interlacing them. It's him, I knew it: it's Blanky. He must have followed us. We say nothing. The others are done for. We move mechanically forward. My body sways. We are in another secret tunnel, much lower than the first, walking hunched over.

I tightly clutch my young guide's hand. I can feel the flutter of his pulse—a swarm of fireflies taking flight. There is no need for words. He can feel my thanks. What happened to the others? Where was Bamboo? The thought of it terrifies me. I don't want to know. If only this moment could last forever . . .

But the inexorable truth breaks through the silence.

41

Bamboo is dead.

While Blanky was rescuing me from the toxic fumes, Bamboo was fighting to save his fellow creatures. They never made it to the secret tunnel . . .

Arabella went to look for him, with Chayton close on her heels, but she was too late. She found her boyfriend lying on the platform—lifeless—among a sea of Repulsecure victims. She stretched out beside him, closed her eyes, ready to let the poisonous gas do its work. If Chayton hadn't forced her to her feet half conscious, dragged her to the safety of the tunnel, then carried her to Underhome on his back, she would have died.

Bamboo is dead, like all of the Infected in Station 22. It wasn't the first time: the Toptown Brigade had conducted raids—and massacres—in the past. Many others met the same fate, but never an entire station.

Back on the farm, we take refuge in the living room after dinner, at a loss for words. There are fires in both fireplaces; they crackle softly. Our watches went off after we were back on the Train, just as Chayton was finishing relating the story. Keiji and I were careful to remove our cardigans so they wouldn't count as item-clues.

Ka went up to her room earlier without pressing us to talk or giving us any advice—and rightly so. There are times when words are of no use. Unshaven as always, Mr. Mann kindly comes over with a bowl of fruit and places it on the coffee table; he is trying to cheer us up.

"What goes on in the program isn't real. Don't take it to heart."

"Tell that to Chayton and Rae!" Ali exclaims, not buying it. "Do you have any idea what they've been through?"

"Remember, it's only virtual. Miss Kassandra has told you time and again."

"Well, virtual or not, when your eyes are burned with a laser beam, it's for real. When you throw up or feel pain, it's for real. And the friends we have there, they're real, too!" Ali continues, extremely upset.

The chef turns on his heel without insisting. He doesn't look so hot, I think to myself: dark circles, sallow complexion, his cough worse than ever . . . The scent of stale tobacco trails after him as usual, though none of us have ever seen him smoke. Once Mr. Mann is back in the kitchen, Alpha takes the floor, his voice low.

"We have only three more days to find the key to the first chakra."

"It doesn't look good!" Ali says.

"You are right about that." Helen joins in, lowering the thumb she'd been unthinkingly nibbling. "Things are only getting worse, not better. Finding the key to the Slymouth Gate means freedom for the Subs. But what good will it do us?"

"What if it's not a physical key?" Alpha adds. "What if helping the Subs find theirs is the purpose of our mission?"

"Speaking of which," Ali asks, "I saw you leaving the party with Loco. What did he want?"

"To seal our alliance," Alpha answers. "He is pleased with the results of the Harvest. He wants the Faraways to take part in the Great Rebellion."

"The fight against the Brigade?"

"We're not military!" Helen says indignantly.

"When you plan to tell us this, Alpha? The way he treat the Infected, I don't trust Loco anymore!" Keiji says. He casts a glance at Chayton, who usually weighs in with a second opinion. Only, he hasn't said a word since leaving the program, and he didn't touch his meal, either.

"Calm down, guys. No one expects you to win the Battle of Waterloo or anything! Anyhow, we'll be long gone when the Great Rebellion breaks out." Alpha's composure is unnerving. "I promised we'd find the key. In exchange, I requested preferential treatment for Siana and Blanky."

"Promised? That's a good one! We'll never have time," Helen says.

"That's precisely why I made that promise, Helen: to buy more time. To defeat the Brigade, we need the key to the gate. It makes sense."

"And the disease?" Keiji asks. "What sense you make there?"

"We can't fix everything in three days' time. We're not magicians," Alpha says.

"I say everything connected. What about you, Chayton?"

Chayton doesn't answer. Utterly dejected, he crosses the room with a weary gait and opens the door to the farmyard. The debate continues without him, but as the door swings shut, he heaves a telling sigh.

After what we've been through together, I feel close to him. Mr. Mann may well tell us Spirit Era is virtual—my brain knows it, too—but I care deeply about Blanky, Siana, Arabella, and the others. And so does Chayton.

It's raining tonight and the air has gotten chillier. Through the open doors of the goat shed, I can make Chayton out in the darkness. He is sitting in the straw with his kid on his lap. His chest and shoulders are heaving. I think he is crying. I turn around without making a noise. The only one who could find words to help is Anais Mann. She is like a little sister to him. After making sure her father is still busy in the kitchen, I cautiously approach the dimly lit annex where the Manns live—a first for me. The weathered clapboard edifice is punctuated by three windows, shuttered for the night, and a pair of solid wooden doors. I don't know which one is closer to the Mann girl's room.

I knock on the farthest one. No answer. From where I am standing, I am hidden by the shrubbery. But if I go any farther into the farmyard, I might be seen. I try again: still nothing. What now? Skirt silently along the front of the building like a cat burglar? Mr. Mann hates it when we go near his house. If he catches me, he'll read me the riot act. I'd better not risk it.

Don't go away!

Just what I needed. The hostile voice!

Do not go awaaayyy!

It's the last straw. I'm about to turn back when I hear a whisper from behind a shutter.

"Rae? Is that you?"

It's Anais. I approach the window, my heart racing, and knock to say yes.

"I thought it was you. I am . . . I am locked in my room. The shutter is locked from the outside."

I hurriedly feel around in the semidarkness. My fingers hit a slide bolt lock. I lift it and begin to slip it open. It sticks and makes a loud grating noise, forcing me to go very slowly. When I manage to undo the latch at last, the shutter swings open to reveal Anais's face. A lamp on a bedside table in the back of the room casts yellow light over everything. There is a large cage on the dresser.

"Don't go away! Don't go away!" squawks a blue parakeet.

"Hush, keep it down, Blue! You'll get us into trouble."

The cage door is open. The bird flies over to me and perches on my shoulder.

"Don't go away!"

So, was it the parakeet I heard earlier?

"Gosh, she never goes out like that. She doesn't go near anyone but me, either. She loves imitating my father's voice."

The bird's delicate feet dance lightly on my shoulder. She gives herself a contented shake; she has adopted me.

"It's Chayton, isn't it?" Anais guesses. "Where is he?"

She jumps through the window in a single bound. This time, instead of yellow chicks, her pajamas and old-fashioned headscarf are covered with green kittens.

"Come on, Blue! Time to go home!"

The bird goes back to its cage. The parakeets from the Psyche Maneuver I did with Chayton inevitably come to mind. Kassandra said everyone has their own messenger-animal, that we just had to let it find us . . .

"Let's go," the Mann girl says after carefully locking the shutter. We make our way quickly through the dark courtyard.

"I knew Chayton would crack after what happened at Station 22. You are stronger, Rae. Much stronger than you think." As we stop in front of the goat shed, she adds in a whisper: "You do know why, don't you?"

The first moments of my life come to mind. The image of a mother I invented from books, and that of my father, defined by his absence . . . Yes, I do know why.

"Come on, Rae!" She grabs my arm. I didn't expect to go in with her.

"Chayton . . . Chayton . . . ," Anais whispers.

Our eyes adjust to the darkness, and we make out his silhouette. My kid comes over to greet me. Another one bleats.

"Hush!" Anais whispers.

As if by magic, the goats obey. I sit down cross-legged and take mine into my arms. A shiver runs through the little creature's body.

"Hey, are you all right?" Anais asks, gently placing a hand on Chayton's forearm.

"I'm losing my way, sis."

"Sometimes, you have to lose one thing to gain another . . . ." she replies, but Chayton doesn't seem to hear her.

"The earth is slipping out from under my feet. I don't recognize myself anymore. I've lost my appetite. For everything."

And with that, he withdraws into his shell again. Anais makes a few more attempts, and then we sit there in frozen silence. After a while, her delicate fingers reach for Chayton's long locks, smoothing them slowly.

"It's time to go to bed. You need to recover your strength. Tomorrow is another day. Arabella will probably refuse to talk to you, Chayton. She'll be angry. You separated her from Bamboo, forced her to go on living against her will. It will pass, like it does in books. Like it does in life."

At the tender age of thirteen, Anais seems to have been through a lot in life. Her maturity can be unsettling at times. She divides Chayton's hair into three parts and makes a braid.

"Trust yourself, inspire trust, and trust others . . ." The Mann girl repeats the Shepherd's words, weaving them together like the strands of the braid. "The roots that spring from the earth, the element of the first chakra." The sound of her whispering sends a shiver down my spine in the silence of the goat shed. "Tomorrow, Chayton, I hope you will trust someone, at last. That you will trust"—her voice trails off, pausing meaningfully—"a woman . . ."

LOGBOOK
INSTRUCTOR: KA
SEASON I

NOVEMBER 25, 2035

There is no turning back.

The border between the virtual world and the real world is permeable. The longer the Seven are in the program, the greater the influence of its simulated reality . . .

The Seven now barely differentiate between their own lives and the Subs' lives. Likewise, the bonds forged in the simulation are as strong as those they have with their friends and family in the real world.

The awakening of the invisible currents of Spiritua over the physical reality of Materia has made these bonds possible. In other words, by learning to look beyond appearances, the Seven have distanced themselves from material reality. From the real world, that is.

Meanwhile, the viewing figures continue to grow. Consistent with the views of the general population, internet viewers (average age twenty-five) are divided over the program. There are the disbelievers, who say the doomsday scenario is just a bluff and who watch Spirit Era like any other reality TV show; the believers, who are waiting for the keys to be discovered like the coming of the Messiah; and the mainstream watchers, who say the end of the world is coming but aren't sure when.

While some posts are strongly worded, they have sparked a wave of discussion and debate. Sustainability influencers have taken up the Spirit Era challenge, sharing, analyzing, and dissecting the Keeper's messages and the livestreams. The snowball effect has improved their visibility and subscriber numbers. More and more individuals committed to protecting the environment are raising questions and calling for practical solutions. In consort with the environmentalists, the champions of social causes are fighting for greater equality and the right to decent housing. The initiatives have yet to take a concrete shape, but the program's influence is behind many of them.

But will we be able to change in time? Or is it already too late? There are only three simulation sessions left to find the first key. At the end of the allotted seven-day period—the number seven appears repeatedly in the system—all hope will be lost. Spirit Era will conclude that solutions for averting the end of the world are entirely and definitively beyond humanity's reach. And the July 27, 2037, apocalypse will inevitably come to pass.

Consequently, the Seven have no choice but to stay the course—no matter what.

42

Siana's breasts are developing, that's what she's hiding.

"The darn things started to grow a couple of weeks ago!" she confesses. "I can bind them all I want, but they're starting to show, aren't they?"

Her faint smile goes straight to my heart: it's only natural for girls in high school to talk about puberty, to discuss bras and pads. Here, it's a liability.

"It was bound to happen one day. I must be seventeen or so."

Her growth spurt is definitely late—although for Subs, it's always too early. At least here, I'm not the only late bloomer. In high school, I was the only underdeveloped fifteen-year-old in my class. It didn't bother me much before, but it has ever since Alpha came along.

What a bummer! I want what Siana doesn't want, and vice versa. Her oversized boy's clothes and drawn cubby curtains make sense now.

"In this place, the onset of puberty is a tragedy. It means saying goodbye to Deepwood, to my cubby, to being a Rover. It means no more walks in the fresh air. The best I can hope for in the future? To molder away in Underhome and increase the Tubeans' business. If they give me a clean seal of approval, that is . . ."

And the worst? Blanky says girls who are disobedient disappear for good. Why? In the letter Chayton read, Froggie mentioned an evil greater than Bulbosis, a danger threatening her daughter. If Siana were to find out Froggie is her mother, they would both be put to death.

"And Blanky! What will become of him? They'll separate us until he reaches puberty and leaves the dorm. We can't let it happen! I don't want to grow up!"

Siana pulled me aside the moment we returned to the Train. Her hair was loose. The tigress was back. She handed me a cardigan under some pretext or another, then led me away from my companions. As we set off walking, I could sense she was on edge. Nervous. Her fingers kept plucking at strands of hair.

She is picking up the pace now, almost running, dragging me along after her. Plunging blindly into the alleys of Underhome like a drunkard into a bottle of alcohol—to forget.

"Blanky only has me, you know. His clan family beats him."

I knew it without wanting to. But the truth always comes to light. In one of the alleyways, a long display counter made of crates is stocked with personal hygiene products and other necessities. A group of young women oversee the trades: the Women Laborers.

"His Beavertail is what saved him. Old Lady Tubeans knew it was a good deal when she heard him playing it. And his adoptive clan killed two birds with one stone: one less mouth to feed and a guaranteed supply of packets. Everybody has forgotten about Blanky and me."

I haven't, and I never will. Even when it's all over.

"This way," Siana says.

Farther along, as the tumult of haggling subsides, ordinary

Subs are going about their business. They don't take any notice of us. Most are sitting on boxes or blankets on the ground. Each is in their own little bubble, waiting without knowing why.

We get to Valjean Rabbit's caratram at last. I immediately recognize it: its hot-pink color is unmistakable.

"He's the only one who understands..."

The Underhome mascot's boxcar is lying on its side. Siana gives me a leg up to pull myself on top of it to reach the entrance. She effortlessly scales the façade, hoists herself onto the roof, and we jump inside through an open window.

Valjean is home, moving back and forth on a worn-out highbacked rocking chair, his knitting needles jumping with irregular movements. A long, chunky-knit scarf, identical to the one he is making, is wrapped around his head and neck. Other scarves made of the same bright-pink wool hang from a strange perch.

"Hello, Val."

He is entirely focused on his task, scraggly gray locks and all. He has wrapped multicolored strands of yarn around his wrists like bracelets. Pom-pom mobiles like the ones in Blanky's cubby hang from the ceiling, but larger and more varied. There are brightly colored ones everywhere, dangling on branches and rusty hoops, cascading like waterfalls into strange and wonderful shapes, and the floor is covered with balls of yarn in all colors, some as big as pumpkins.

"Uh, by the way, the Mime brothers have had their hats stolen again."

"Hmm."

"For a year now, Juan and little Esteban have been living in the Cubbies above mine." Siana turns to me and explains. "The fifth and sixth tiers. Their father, El Padre, got a good price for them: a double ration of packets for their clan. Their pantomiming brings in a lot of money. The Owls love to play charades. They whisper a word to one of the two brothers, and the other has ten seconds to guess it. Juan and Esteban are excellent mimes. More often than not, the passengers lose and have to fork over a lot of loot."

The walls of the caratram are lined with funny shelves: planks strewn with leaves and surmounted by branches forming miniature habitats for wriggling white creatures. Gnocchi-like cocoons hang from the boughs.

"Valjean has his own silkworm farm. He is the sole provider of knitted goods for the children of Deepwood. Thanks to him, we keep warm."

Without putting down his knitwear, the mascot gets up from the chair abruptly—it continues to rock—then walks over to me and extends his hands.

"For you!"

As he loops the scarf around my neck, a cloud of large cream-colored moths takes to the air. The caratram is full of them. That's when it dawns on me: the decorations hanging from the ceiling are habitats for the silk moths!

"It is a crime to prevent pupae from coming out of their cocoon!" Valjean Rabbit stares hard at my throat as if flying insects are about to emerge from it, then spins around without warning and hobbles over to his brood. "A crime to suffocate them in an oven at eighty degrees Celsius, just to reel the silk fibers without breaking them!"

A look of sudden sadness shrouds the mascot's eyes, the way it did when he saw his fellow creatures in the tunnels of Station 22.

"Before the Great Famine, they'd kill fifteen hundred caterpillars to produce a yard of silk. Fifteen hundred! But that didn't stop anyone from getting a good night's sleep. I suppose that's just the way things are for the homeless."

He grabs a dented watering can, walks over to a corner, and waters a plant with leaves similar in color to the ones in the silkworm huts hanging everywhere. Valjean Rabbit then pulls out a glass, fills it with cloudy liquid from his watering can, and hands it to Siana. She gladly accepts it, drinks it halfway, and offers it to me. I politely decline.

"We never run out," she says before drinking down the rest, "because of Hartsquare Lake."

Overcome by exhaustion, the mascot settles back into his rocking chair and starts fretting out loud, the chair's rickety runners keeping time. He goes on about the Brigade and Repulsecure, about his brothers who died of Bulbosis, about yesterday's raid . . . One after the other, he slowly pronounces the names of the dead. When he gets to Bamboo's name, it sends shivers down my spine.

"I'm starving!"

"No, Val, dear," whispers Siana, putting a hand on his shoulder. "Not that."

"I'm starving, I kept telling them in the subway! But they didn't care."

"Stop it. You're making it worse."

"The clamor of rushing feet drowned out my voice. It was Line 8. At rush hour. People were in a hurry to get home after a day in the mines."

The litany goes on. There is no stopping it. So, we leave him to his sad mood. I tighten the hot-pink scarf around my neck. It has to be my item-clue: I am the custodian of the throat chakra, after all. Valjean Rabbit is trying to tell me something with his gift. Unless the scarf, meant to put me on the path to the first key, is referring to someone. Its owner, for example.

What if the Rabbit is not who he seems?

PART SEVEN

NEW BEGINNING

43

"I can't get Froggie out of my mind!"

Earlier Chayton was nothing but a shadow of himself, his dynamic, outgoing personality replaced by gloom and seriousness. But the minute our companions were out of sight, he took off his jacket, jumped to his feet, and perked up as if he'd been waiting to get me alone.

"We have to find that Sub with the green hair, Rae. No matter what!" The others were off looking for the key to Slymouth Gate, under the supervision of Dione and another Prowler. They wanted to give Loco's plan a shot, but Chayton had something else in mind.

"Watch him, Rae," Alpha had whispered before leaving. "He's liable to do something stupid. Chayton hasn't been his usual self lately. Oh, and, by the way, that hot-pink scarf of yours is pretty cool."

Looks like I'm up against it again: Alpha wants me to police the guy I'm supposed to be covering.

"The most logical thing to do—" Chayton breaks off midsentence. "Do you agree with Alpha's logic, Rae? Do you think we should focus our efforts on finding the gate?"

I don't really know.

"To me, it just doesn't add up. I have a good feeling about the green-haired girl, though. She knows something. I have to see her again. I can feel it, right here!" He places both hands on his lower abdomen. "It's this gut feeling of mine. When it starts to burn like that, it's time for action."

The look of bewilderment that crosses my face apparently speaks volumes: he bursts out laughing.

"No, Sparrow. Not that kind of fire! Sure, I'm prone to make impulsive decisions, but my gut feeling is legit."

There's a definite logic to it: Chayton is the custodian of the chakra located in the lower abdomen, the first chakra, the one closest to the earth; he may well have a special part to play in Mantra 1.

"We each have our own little voice, after all."

Far be it from me to say otherwise . . .

"I saw Loco's map of the places the Prowlers have already searched. Underhome is a gigantic spiderweb bordered by hundreds of outlying tunnels: the infamous maze that no Sub has ever managed to navigate. Its water supply comes from an underground lake. The others are searching in the opposite direction, but frogs like water, don't they?"

Without further ado, we set off to find the woman who said she was Siana's mother. The old Chayton would never have been caught dead with a braid. Now, not only is he wearing the one Anais made for him the night before but he's also tied a bit of tattered red ribbon to its end.

"It was my great-grandfather's," he says by way of justification.

We are walking through unfamiliar side streets flanked by large murals: screaming faces contorted in pain, a subway train emerging from the head of a fair-haired girl, teardrops of paint running down her cheeks . . . Very unsettling stuff.

There are sculptures made of mannikin parts partly

covered with gaudy crochet doilies. We walk by a row of cara-trams where the ground is decorated with trompe l'oeil draw-ings. Amused by the little game, we skirt an illusory fish tank, dodge a pretend burrow of baby crats, and jump over the illu-sion of a gaping chasm . . .

"This way," Chayton says. "I noticed those paintings on the map. I've always had a good sense of direction." His eyes catch mine. "I know. The root chakra, right?"

A few minutes later, we enter a wide downward-sloping tunnel. There, we discover a good number of Subs: ordinary men and women, but quite a few Prowlers as well. Two lines are moving in opposite directions on broken-down conveyor belts: one progressing upward, the other—ours—advancing downward. We slip unnoticed into the crowd. The sound of footsteps on rusty steel fills the air. In some areas, the ramps are in a bad state of repair.

As we near the end of the tunnel, there are more and more puddles. By the time we reach the lake, our boots are ankle deep in water.

"Here we are."

What Siana had called Hartsquare Lake is really a flooded subway station. There's a plaque reading "Hartsquare Lake" on one of the walls. Old station benches form shores along the water's edge, and the water is deepest in the channel where the tracks used to run. Some people are swimming in the middle of the "lake," where the water is over their heads. Others are filling water bottles on the beach. Their likeness is reflected in the vaulted ceiling's shiny white tiles.

"I don't see her green mop anywhere." Chayton sighs.

At the far side of the stretch of water, where the platform comes to an end, we can make out the roof of a submerged subway train. Its iron skeleton forms a sinister-looking island. On the horizon, I can imagine an entire subway system, si-lenced forever, submerged in pitch-black water.

"I'm going in."

Naturally, that's where Chayton wants us to start. I try to dissuade him, but pigheaded as usual, he's already taking off his tank top, combat boots, socks, and pants. Standing in his underpants, he hangs his clothes on my arm as if I were a coatrack and hands me his shoes.

"Don't worry, Sparrow. If I find a frog, I won't kiss it this time. Promise!"

Chayton dives in, comes up a few yards away, swims a few strokes, then disappears again.

I hold my breath, too, for what seems like an eternity. Where is he? I can't see anything. Not bothering to take off my waterlogged combat boots, I wade in up to my thighs. My cardigan and the ends of my scarf are wet.

What about the camera sensors? When Chayton took his jacket off, he disconnected from the livestream. The viewers won't be able to follow him. I don't care about that, but does it mean my friend is on his own, no longer protected by the program's security shield? It's too dangerous.

Suddenly, something grabs my leg underwater. I practically jump out of my skin. Chayton's head surfaces like that of a sperm whale.

"Sprrrrr!"

Water and air spew from his mouth. Startled, I push his head back underwater.

"Ha ha! You should have seen the look on your face!"

I have to admit I fell for it. A hint of a smile plays across my face. He wrings out his braid, and we climb onto a bench so he can get dressed. When we're back on firm ground in the tunnel, our combat boots squeak along.

"I wondered how a lake could have formed this far underground. Well, guess what? Now I know: there is an open-air cavern behind the boxcar island. There's real rain, moss-covered rocks, and all sorts of plants I've never seen before. Not much help, but it sure is beautiful!"

There are a couple of Prowlers in front of us as we make our way along the conveyor belt toward the exit of the tunnel. Offspring of the Subway, from the look of them.

"Sparrow, do you recognize those two?" Chayton whispers.

I sure do! The two guys with the half-naked girls in the Train . . . If we're lucky, they'll lead us to Froggie.

They enter the steady flow of people and blend in. We stick close behind, albeit at a safe distance. A few corridors later, we recognize where we are heading—to the phantom cars!

Before long, we can see subway cars coming and going. We slip into an alcove to observe them. It is the same place where Keiji played roulette rail . . . where he would have been reduced to a pulp if Chayton hadn't intervened.

For a while, the Prowlers just stand there, like cows staring at passing cars. Then, when a white train enters the station, something comes over them. They hop onto the running board as it roars past, pinning themselves against the sheet metal like magnets. The second they make contact with it, their stiff bodies seem to gain elasticity like slimes, the sticky pastes that children play with. They literally become one with the metro.

They slide in through an open window.

Without missing a beat, Chayton grasps my hand and starts running like hell to catch the moving train before it disappears into the distance. Before I know it, he takes hold of a side bar to the left of the open door of the second-to-last car and is hauling himself in, with me in tow.

I land on my butt.

"Are you all right?" he asks, stretching out his hand to help me get back on my feet.

A sudden acceleration throws me off-balance again. I grab onto him. The train is very noisy.

"We are in a gangway connection between two cars," Chayton explains.

We press our faces against the window of the door leading to the last passenger car. A strobe light flickers in the darkness. We can make out the dim silhouettes of Prowlers and girls dancing, some emptying the contents of red packets into their mouths. It looks like a nightclub.

"Watch out! Someone is coming!"

It's too late. A lively young girl opens the door. She has lovely pink eyes, opalescent skin, and snow-white hair down to her thighs. All smiles, she rushes toward Chayton. Gauzy, colorful wrappers cling to her naked body.

"Well, hello, you! I see you've brought your own treat!" she says, meaning me. She has to shout over the din of the gangway. "You know it's forbidden to bring kids here. Toss her out at the next station."

"Hmm, not a bad idea . . . ," Chayton agrees, giving me a wink.

Stop messing around, I think. *The girl is an albino. Doesn't that remind me of someone?*

"You're really very normal. I've never seen such a cute Prowler before. You've got packets, don't you?" she wheedles, clinging to his neck.

"We're looking for the girl with the green hair."

"*That old chick?* Forget about her. She's thirty!"

Once again, the reality of Mantra 1 and that of the real world don't quite match: Froggie looks barely twenty.

"You'll have a better time with me. Do you have any packets, or no?"

"No, I don't."

"Well, to hell with you, then!"

"I know Niro. You are his sister, aren't you?"

She stands there flabbergasted. I applaud Chayton in my mind.

"How—how do you know?"

"The girls who disappear from Deepwood. They're brought here. Correct?"

"Who are you? Aren't you a Prowler?" She gives him a good once-over.

"Is that the punishment for disobeying the Tubeans?"

"Shut up! You don't know what you're talking about."

"What's your name?"

"Nira. And no, our names have nothing to do with lazy parents. We are both albinos, but we are not even related. We came up with our names ourselves." Their looks and almost identical names made me skeptical.

"Did you choose to work here, or do they force you?"

"Go away. Get out of here!"

"What about Niro? Does he know you're here?"

"Leave him out of this! He must never know about any of this. Ever! Okay? We'd both be thrown off the Ledge."

Nira totters; her legs give out under her. Chayton catches her just in time.

"What . . . happens here . . . has to remain secret . . ."

"Naturally. If it gets around in Underhome that the Prowlers are sleeping with their own daughters, it'd lower their approval rating!"

"If you rat on me, I'm dead. You won't squeal, will you?"

"Fine. Provided you tell me where I can find Froggie . . ."

"She's in compartment eight, in the car for the second-hand girls. Girls who've already had kids, that is. Three cars down. That way."

The moment we turn our heads to look, Nira wriggles out of Chayton's arms and reenters the nightclub passenger car. I open the opposite door, and we leave the gangway. We are standing in a corridor. On one side, windows, on the other, numbered compartments with glass doors and drawn curtains. It looks like a sleeper car. It's less noisy here than on the gangway. We silently walk the length of the first car and then the second without encountering anyone. We enter the third car. The curtains to the compartments are open.

"The first one is number ten. Two more to go. Walk like you belong here. Stay to my left for cover."

I get a quick glimpse inside the first compartment, where four young mothers are holding babies. In the second, a Prowler surrounded by three women, one of whom is pregnant, is busy bouncing an infant on his lap. He doesn't notice us.

"This is the one," Chayton murmurs, pausing for a moment. "Number eight."

He seems overcome with emotion as he walks up to the door and slides it open, without knowing what to expect.

"I knew you'd come!"

Froggie's cheeks are sunken, her hands are covered in scratches, and her eyes are as piercing as ever. Yet she is aglow with disconcerting beauty: the beauty of the tormented.

"Come in!" She beckons, quickly closing the door behind us.

Inside the compartment, there are five other women in gauzy wrappers and a pair of opposite-facing, three-tiered bunk beds piled with colorful cushions.

"You know what to look out for, don't you, Chayton?" Froggie continues in a low voice. "The evil worse than Bulbosis?"

"Yes, Froggie. I know."

She lowers her gaze. No need to say more.

"Did they force you?" Chayton asks.

"No. Young Sub women would do anything to get out of Underhome. I was the same age Siana is today when they chose me seventeen years ago. It was a great honor for my clan, and I was one of the few to be selected for a single Prowler. I got pregnant right away. But no one told me that if I had a daughter, she would be given to the Tubeans . . ."

"Didn't you try to escape?"

"Where to? Between the maze of tunnels and the Noctos, there's no way out. I don't want my daughter to have the same life as me!"

"Neither do we," two of the women whisper in chorus.

"Shh! Someone is coming!" Froggie says.

The others all spread out around the compartment while I scramble up to a top bunk and slip under a sky-blue blanket, leaving a small opening to look out from. On the bottom bunk opposite me, Froggie is sitting with Chayton, her back to the door to partially conceal him.

From the corridor, a face a little like Dione's suddenly appears in the door's window. As the Prowler stares into the compartment, Siana's mother takes hold of Chayton's hands and starts to kiss them.

"What happened to your hands?" Chayton whispers after the unwelcome visitor has left.

"It's nothing," Froggie says.

"What are all those cuts?"

"Every time I fake a smile, I sink a nail into my hand until it bleeds. I don't want to forget—to forget this is not the real me."

The red scabs are lined up like the tally marks of a prisoner counting the days.

"I can help you find the key to set us free," she says.

"How?"

"By exposing the truth. If it gets out in Underhome that Loco is trafficking girls, it will be the end of him. He has his own private car all to himself at the front of the train. He has a secret safe. All his important documents, like the Agreements with the Toptown Council, are kept in it. I know where it is. I'm sure I can dig up incriminating evidence."

"How can you . . . ?"

"Don't ask any questions. I'm doing it for Siana, and all of our daughters . . ."

Suddenly, the compartment door slides open, and the accordion-monster look-alike comes in. I make myself as small as possible under my blanket and press my scarf against my mouth. Froggie fakes giving Chayton a passionate kiss, then stands up, positioning her body between the Prowler and Chayton to try to keep him from sight. The visitor doesn't seem happy about it. With a scowl, he casts a cursory look at the rest of the "merchandise," then ducks out to go find something more to his liking.

"Come with us," Chayton urges Froggie in a whisper.

"I can't. He'd go after my daughter."

"Who would? Loco?"

"Yes. The Subs see him as Underhome's savior. He has complete power. The only solution is to expose his true colors. We have to bring him down."

"It's too dangerous."

"Now that you're here, I'm not afraid anymore," Froggie says. "Having outside help changes everything. It's too late for me. But not for Siana!"

Chayton acquiesces in silence. He knows she's right.

"I know you'll look after her," Froggie says.

It's not a question. He lovingly wraps his arms around her and holds her for a long time.

"Do you believe me?" she asks.

Yes, he believes.

He believes in her, in her story, and in Loco's betrayal. And he will do anything to save her daughter. Even if it means going alone, without the others. Even if it means risking being wrong. At the end of the day, it's the little frog-woman's word against that of Underhome's leader.

Whatever happens now, the die has been cast, echoing the prescient words of Anais Mann: Chayton is trusting a woman. At last . . .

44

There's not a single blade of grass in Toptown.

No patch of land, not a park, not even a concrete plaza. No place to relax, no bench to sit on; no laughter, loud voices, or sneezing; no show of tenderness or friendship. And no children. Under the sunless and moonless neon-purple sky, the streets of Aboveworld are as lifeless and soulless as ever.

But our view of this city has changed. The ultramodern window displays and skyscrapers with mirrored façades intrigued us at the time of the trial connection. Now that we've spent time in Underhome, however, we know the ugly truth: Toptown crushed the Subs and is crushing them still. We must bring it down.

It wasn't easy, but Chayton eventually convinced Ali and Keiji we needed to find out more about the Owls. The coupon Lady Fluff provided gave us a direction to explore: Solid Gold Hairstyles.

We took a vote: four against three. Solid Gold Hairstyles it was.

"This way," Keiji says, looking at the map on the back of the coupon. "We are almost there."

"I still say we should have stayed Below to pursue the Slymouth Gate lead," Alpha says, annoyed. "The key, remember? That's what we came for."

"And I say there's no better place than a hairdressers to hear the latest gossip," Chayton replies.

"What's the point? Our mission is clear: we need to find the key so the Subs can live aboveground again."

Chayton and I have said nothing about the White Train, the Prowlers' harem, Nira, or Froggie's revelations . . . They are unaware that, against all odds, her story has struck a chord with Chayton.

"It's always the same old thing—you don't trust Loco!" Alpha grumbles. "You've had a beef with him from the start."

"But Loco make strange choices even so," Keiji intervenes. "He turn blind eye to the Tubeans' schemes in Deepwood, isolate the Infected, ignore Bulbosis . . ."

"The Prowlers are planning a rebellion. They can't fight on all fronts. The war against the Brigade is not over yet: they need the key at all costs, and time is running out. In less than half an hour, our watches will ring, and we will only have two more days to find the key."

When we entered Toptown, Keiji and I put our old cardigans back on, took the Rovers' tunnel with Siana and Blanky, and went through the electronic turnstile. Right now, they are probably bartering their plastic flowers to the sound of the fiddle somewhere in the city. Arabella secretly drove the others on the wagobike to the vending machine entrance. She is waiting for them in the tunnel: Loco has ordained that no Prowlers are allowed to leave the subway network.

With preparations for the Great Rebellion underway, the Faraways are not supposed to be in Aboveworld, and helping us out would be considered an act of treason. Arabella agreed to take the risk—to avenge Bamboo's death. She holds Loco responsible for the botched response to the epidemic and the inhumane treatment of the Infected.

After the raid, Arabella shut herself up in one of the Train's compartments. When Keiji went to look for her, he found her sitting in the dark, unable to speak. Ever so quietly, he told her the story of his friendship with Aiko. They were neighbors, they had always loved each other, but his parents sent him to the monastery. They had not spoken in seven years. Before he left for the monastery, Aiko had given him two "lucky bamboo shoots," saying that so long as the two stems were intertwined, no one could come between them. Before, he understood its significance from the material perspective of Materia. But Bamboo's death made Keiji realize that neither death nor distance could ever separate two hearts united by love. Keiji's rebalanced root chakra allowed him to begin cultivating his own inner lucky bamboo garden. No lack of water or sunlight could ever dry it up or destroy it. He no longer needed the intertwined shoots. So, without a word to anyone, Keiji had brought them into Spirit Era for Arabella, to help her reconnect with the earth's life force, the fundamental, stabilizing energy in which the root chakra is grounded.

Thus, Keiji's item-clue is of twofold significance: just as the name of Arabella's lover in the simulated world helped Keiji understand the true meaning of Aiko's gift in the real world, Keiji's gift helped Arabella recover her fighting spirit. Like the two shoots of bamboo, Arabella and Bamboo are intertwined in eternal love . . .

"Phew! I forgot how hot it is here!" Helen says, taking off her jacket and tying it around her waist.

We all do the same, except for Chayton, who is lost in his thoughts. He has changed, stirred by a wave of unsuspected feeling, a wave of sudden, pure emotion. Almost by chance,

Froggie—a woman unlike any he has ever known—has changed his outlook on life.

"We're here," Keiji says at last, looking up at the embossed letters: "Solid Gold Hairstyles."

The storefront doesn't look much like a hair salon: there's no window, only a large, flat gold panel obstructing the view inside. There's a long line of Owls waiting on the sidewalk. The place is hopping.

"Give it to me," Ali says, taking the coupon from Keiji's hand, then confidently cutting the line in the middle. All we can do is to step to the side and watch. When Ali's turn comes, the panel slides open and she disappears inside. Less than half a minute later, the panel opens again, and Ali flies through the air and unceremoniously lands on her stomach.

"Are you all right?" Helen asks, hurrying over to her.

"Yeah, yeah. Damn machine!" Ali grumbles.

"What happened?" Keiji asks, helping her to her feet.

"There was this double-door entry and a red light that scanned the coupon. Then an automated voice blared, *'Intruder! Entry denied!'*"

A flash of bright neon yellow suddenly tints the squiggles and fluorescent symbols of her uniform the way it did during the trial connection. Up until then, our uniforms have been the same flat gray as our surroundings, no doubt to help us blend in. The change lasts only a moment, but it's like a burst of sunlight.

"Give me the coupon," Alpha tells her. "I'll try."

"No," Chayton objects. "I bet there is a name assigned to the coupon. It was given to Rae. She should be the one to go in."

"Are you kidding! She's not . . ."

"Not what, Alpha? Not capable?"

"I didn't say that."

But you meant it, my little voice chimes in, not that I'd asked for its two cents.

"Go ahead, Rae!" Alpha redeems himself. "Give me your scarf. I'll keep it for you," he says, removing it and wrapping the hot-pink stole around his neck.

Could he be trying to tell me he believes I can do it?

"Good luck!" Ali blurts out, impatient to see if I'll do any better than her.

Don't go!

Nooo! The hostile voice again! Talk about timing...

You'll waste the coupon.

At least now I know for sure it's not Anais's parakeet! But whose voice is it, then? It only speaks up when I'm in the program and only to demoralize me.

You're out of your depth. Let someone else go instead.

Don't listen! my inner voice jumps in.

Enough! Shut up! My head is going to explode.

"What's wrong?" Keiji asks as my hands reach for my forehead instinctively.

I snatch the coupon from Ali's hand before the voices can say anything else and rush over to the hair salon. The sliding panel opens. I'm on my own now.

It's dark in the double-door entry. The red light silently scans my body and the coupon. Will I be rejected like Ali? The beam stops to focus on the coupon. The round disc of plastic shrivels up like a chickpea. The second panel opens. Phew! I'm in!

As I look around, the first thing that comes to mind is an assembly line: hundreds of barber chairs, all brown leather and gilded chrome, in two opposite-facing rows against the walls of the warehouse finished in shiny gold. Large, oval-shaped, and gaudy double-sided mirrors are positioned between the chairs, reflecting the clients' faces. Tarnished gold industrial light fixtures hang from the ceiling. Both rows are jam-packed with men and women; the air is abuzz with a muffled din. Flashing floor arrows indicate the seat assigned to me, dashing my hopes of mingling with a group of chatterboxes. I'm not even allowed to choose my own seat! Well, at least the hostile voice has gone away.

The salon chair is fitted with articulated arms with built-in accessories: tray, brush, scissors, lotions, miniature round sink, tubular showerhead, turbo hair dryer . . . The moment I sit down, the tentacle-like arms go to work. One yanks out a strand of hair—*ouch!*—and a wealth of data instantly appears on the mirror.

Gold letters and numbers scroll past like a teleprompter: scalp assessment, hair structure, hair bulb renewal cycles, and a lot of other gibberish. But the last indicator grabs my attention: "BULBOSIS INDEX = 12%." The results are printed out on a piece of paper. I slip it into a pocket of my jacket. What does the Bulbosis index mean? That I have contracted the disease, even though prepubescent children are supposed to be immune?

"How have you been?"

"Fine, thanks. No one in my family is at the Center for the Infected for now."

The voices of two women on the other side of the mirror rise above the ambient din. I lend an ear.

"My mother-in-law is there."

"Oh, I'm sorry to hear that."

"Oh, don't be. We never got along!"

Meanwhile, other clients are being dispatched left and right. The mirror has zoomed in on my reflection now. I don't particularly enjoy seeing myself close up like that. The strain of the past few days in the program is clearly visible. Circles are forming under my eyes, my cheeks look hollow, and my straight hair, in need of a good combing, hangs unevenly to my shoulders. The bobbed haircut I'd given myself at boarding school has grown out—badly. So have my crooked bangs, which drop from one eyebrow at a slant that entirely conceals half of my other eye.

You didn't get the coupon by accident, my inner voice tells me. *It's time to stop hiding.*

"How is your own Bulbosis index?" the customer behind the mirror asks.

"Much better, thanks. It's my daughter's I'm worried about. She's only ten and it's already at fourteen percent. It's scary to think she has such a high rate of infected cells already. Even though she's immune to Bulbosis for now, her index will skyrocket when she hits puberty."

"Tell me about it! Mine was at eleven percent when I was thirteen, but it was as high as sixty-four percent by the time I was eighteen. It's down to fifty-three percent now, but I'm worried. I had little scabs all over my head for a couple of days."

Little scabs? I'd found little scabs in my hair, too!

"That's nothing. I had them for an entire week. You're nowhere near a hundred percent. That's when active cases develop."

"Oh dear! I hope I never get there!"

"So long as your hair isn't falling out, you're not contagious."

"Ooh! It scares me just thinking about it!"

"Well, don't think about it, then. It's for the best. My neighbor's rate has been at eighty-nine percent for ages, and she's doing very well—precisely because she keeps her head in the sand."

"True, burying your head in the sand is not all that bad."

Suddenly, the image of the haircut I have in mind is reflected in the mirror: loose, easy layers with sideswept bangs. Seeing what it will look like in advance is pretty amazing, I have to admit.

"From what I hear, the president of Toptown Council won't be around much longer. Brigade Commander General Dusk is in the running for her seat."

"Really! The PTC? How is that possible? She's held the position for thirty years. The deputies have always considered her the most qualified."

"General Dusk reportedly has proof that Bulbosis is being propagated by the kids who panhandle in the subway. With the new findings entered into the global computer system, the MP robots are liable to reach a different conclusion."

"But everyone knows that's not true. Children are never sick!"

"Apparently, they are healthy carriers. Anyhow, the truth doesn't matter. What people want to believe does. And there's nothing to be done about it. The deputies are voting right now. If the majority believes it's true, the Agreements with the World Below will be canceled."

My chair's articulated arms are hard at work now: a waterproof cape is tied around my neck, the chair tilts backward, the round sink is placed under my head, and water from the showerhead streams over my hair. Then, gold-plated fingers pour shampoo onto my head and start to gently massage my scalp. It feels wonderful. My eyelids close, my body relaxes. The hair salon's ambient hubbub and the two women's voices fade away.

I have no idea how much time goes by, but when the chair rights itself, my head is wrapped in a towel. What follows is much less enjoyable: my wrists are clamped to the armrests, my eyes are blindfolded, and the scissored arms set to work on my hair. I can't see a thing. *Click, click, click!* A flurry of snipping. Wisps tickle my cheek and brush my ear. I convince myself it's going to look good, and that the element of surprise will be worth it.

Then, all at once, the blindfold comes off, the straps are released, and—it is a surprise, indeed! My reflection in the mirror . . . It's not . . . It is . . .

A new slip of paper is printed out. I take hold of it and

read: "ASSESSMENT ERROR—DISCREPANCY BETWEEN CUSTOMER SELF-IMAGE AND TRUE IDENTITY."

I don't know what to think. The "hairdresser" has given me a bob cut. The same one I had at the boarding school, but shorter and straight. With blunt-cut bangs just the right length—they cover my forehead but not my eyebrows—angled at a slant!

Confused, I sit in my armchair, which has resumed its stationary position. I can barely move my legs, but it is time to leave. The flashing arrows on the floor are already pointing an elderly man in the direction of my chair.

I move toward the exit at the far side of the warehouse. So, I won't have even bangs after all. I leave the salon a little disoriented and find myself on a sidewalk to the rear of the building, where the others are waiting for me.

"Well, you don't look like you just left the hairdresser's," Stepan comments tactlessly. "It's a change, but nothing has changed."

"Were you hoping for something else?" Helen asks. "You look disappointed."

"Who cares about her haircut," Ali answers. "Rae made it into the salon, that's what matters. Good for her!"

"And the appearance not define the person," Keiji adds, meaning well. "But the person who determines appearance."

"None of that matters," Alpha says, downplaying the situation, my scarf still wrapped around his neck.

"Did you find anything out?" Chayton asks.

I nod yes. Except I don't have my notebook with me—if I did, it would be an item-clue—so I can't tell them about the conversation I overheard. But I motion that we have to return to Underhome right away. We have to warn the Subs: if the deputies vote to end the Agreements, the turnstile will be closed, and the Rovers won't be able to enter Aboveworld anymore.

Without the Rovers to create diversions, the Harvests will be much less bountiful. More importantly, the end of the Agreements would mean the beginning of official hostilities against the Brigade . . .

So, we break into a run—through the streets of Toptown, into the subway, and down the platform leading to the vending machine. In the tunnel on the other side, Arabella is waiting for my companions, and Keiji and I will go join Siana, Blanky, and the Rovers at the turnstile to the old mining carts.

"We're almost there," Alpha says breathlessly as we near our destination. "It'll be okay."

Except things rarely go as planned in the program's simulated reality. It's never a good idea to count your chickens before they've hatched. Because who do we see leaning nonchalantly against the vending machine, waiting with resolve and with the knowing look of a seasoned Rover? The one who has been thwarting us at every turn since the very beginning.

"I knew it all along. Loco should never have trusted a bunch of Faraways!"

Catching us in Aboveworld is just what he needs to paint us as traitors. Niro, that is.

45

Then, what had to happen happens.

Beep-beep! Beep-beep!

"Great!" Alpha exclaims, exasperated. "Thanks to that idiot, we're out of time."

"Am I the one you're calling an idiot?" Niro asks, furious.

Nearby, the Mime brothers, Juan and little Esteban, are keeping a low profile. They are wearing new hats, probably knit by Valjean Rabbit.

"We'd be on our way to Underhome if we hadn't lost so much time with your foolishness!"

Alpha's superior airs make all of our efforts in vain. We'd been trying for some time now to convince Niro we had entered Toptown with good intentions.

"Real Prowlers never leave the subway network," Niro fumes. "There's no way you five are on their side." He crinkles his nose and blinks his eyes like headlights. His unattractive tic is back. "You disobeyed Loco's orders, and believe me, he won't like that!"

"Listen, Niro," Helen cuts in. "Your name is Niro, right?"

"Yes. That's right."

"I know it sounds weird, but we really are here to help the Subs. Except we have very little time left. After, we'll be going home for good, and you'll never have anything to do with us again, I promise."

"Do you swear?" he asks. Helen's dulcet tones are making headway with him.

"I swear! But in order to help you, we need a little help ourselves. Will you do that for us, Niro? Will you help us?"

It's a good thing Dulci isn't here. Seeing her sweet Niro drawn into fair Helen's web would have been too much for her.

Beep-beep! Beep-beep!

The ringing is unrelenting now. Keiji and I remove our cardigans—my Bulbosis test is in one of my pockets—and we hide them behind a bench. Fortunately, the vending machine is located at the far end of the platform, and there are no passengers nearby.

"Well, I was hoping to avoid this, but your threats . . ." Chayton is going to spill the beans.

The Mime brothers, mouths agape, are taking it all in.

"Listen, Niro, things aren't always as they seem."

"No kidding?"

"I know where *your sister* is, as you call her. I saw her. When we get back, I'll tell you everything. In the meantime, don't say a word to anyone. Especially Loco. It would put her in danger. He's probably involved in her disappearance."

Niro wasn't expecting that. His face contorts uncontrollably, his nerves clearly frayed. Juan and Esteban shuffle nervously from foot to foot, not sure how to respond.

Our watches are ringing wildly now and can no longer be ignored.

"Flyfold!" my companions bellow.

"Are you *serious*? What were you thinking?" Alpha shouts as soon as we're back. We're still sitting in our respective nests.

"Yeah! What was all that about Nira?" Ali lashes out. *"Why didn't you tell us?"*

"How can we be team if you play solo?" Keiji asks, upset.

When we are all back on the tatami, Kassandra and the Shepherd try to intercede, but the air in Flyfold is rife with anger.

"Did anyone else know about this?" Helen asks, staring at me.

Typical, I think, she never misses a beat! By way of answer, I raise my hand.

"What!" Ali blasts, standing in front of me. "I can't believe it, Rae. Not you!"

"Leave her alone," Chayton cuts in. "It's not her fault. I'm the one who—"

"That's for sure," Alpha rejoins, my hot-pink scarf still around his neck. "Since day one, you've been making a mess of things."

"Oh yeah?"

Here we go again: two cocks facing each other, ready for a fight.

After that, we all start speaking at once.

"Enough!" Head Instructor Shepherd exclaims, raising his voice over the commotion.

"Don't look so glum, Rae," Alpha says, noticing my face. "You couldn't have brought the scarf back along with the bangs. You only get one item-clue, remember?"

I do. But it also means he won't have one of his own choosing. It is all such a mess in my head. I can hardly distinguish truth from falsehood, what is real from what is virtual. The emotions I feel in the program are real, and so are the physical sensations! And yes, Ali, I do care about my haircut. And yes, Alpha, it does matter, even if the rest—the Subs, Froggie, Siana, Bulbosis—matter more. I know that's true. And you're right, Keiji, my haircut doesn't define me, but if I was given the cut, then it's for a good reason. And if my slanted bangs really are my item-clue, that is my business and mine alone. Could it mean I'm unbalanced? That I'm on a slippery slope? There's one thing I'm sure of: the bangs are part of me.

"Psyche Maneuver for everyone!" Instructor Shepherd orders, probably hoping to pacify us.

"You've got to be joking!" Alpha objects. "We're exhausted and need a good shower."

"You will be paired with Rae."

From his authoritative tone, we know there's no point in arguing. I sit down opposite Alpha as the head instructor pairs off the others. Stepan is the odd one out. He will do the Oak Tree Exercise again.

Prior to my encounter with the Subs, staring directly into Alpha's eyes like that would have thrown me into a tailspin. After all the fatigue and distress of the past few days, however, it feels like child's play to me now. Alpha, on the other hand, is fidgety, clearly nervous. Before we start, he takes the bright-pink scarf off his neck and wraps it around mine.

"This is yours. It will fend off the bad vibes."

The noise around us fades away and it's just Alpha and me. As I sink into his gaze, I can see him. I can see Alpha.

That's far enough!

The hostile voice has entered my head again, even though we've left the program.

Go back, I tell you!

I don't believe it! The guttural tone is nothing like his. My gaze sinks deeper into Alpha's eyes.

It's me, I admit it! It's my inner voice you've been hearing.

But . . . But why would you put me down and make me doubt myself like that? Why, Alpha?

I was doing what I thought was best for the Seven. I shook you up a bit in the subway to force you to barter your cards, and that's when you were given the coupon. I was trying to protect you by preventing you from getting on the wagobike when we first entered the World Below. And when we were at the hair salon, I wanted to go in instead of you because . . .

No, Alpha, you didn't. You just assumed I was . . . incapable . . .

I was wrong. I'm sorry.

How are we . . . Why are we able to talk like this, without actually talking?

I'm a mind reader. Telepathy is one of the sixth chakra's gifts. That's why I knew so many things before I got to the farm. You have the gift of telepathy, too, Rae. Just like me . . .

But sometimes—a vacant look comes over Alpha's face—*I misuse mine . . .*

A vacant and terrifying look. He breaks off contact with me and cuts the exercise short. Trancelike, he staggers toward the exit. The Shepherd steps in, and Alpha readies himself for a fight.

"I want to leave! I have to get out of here!" The disturbing creature lurking in his eyes has crawled out of its lair. Alpha's agonizing pain is palpable. "No one will ever put me in a cage again. Not ever!"

Alpha is desperate, unable to control himself. His distress affects us all, even Chayton. Without a word, the six of us spontaneously form a circle around him, a caring circle of support. Alpha collapses in a heap.

"My parents . . . my whole family, our friends . . ."

His chest heaves up and down uncontrollably, and his powerful body suddenly looks fragile. It's the moment of truth. I feel ice-cold.

"They were all slaughtered. I'd blocked it out, but the program brought it all back . . . I know what my item-clue is: the massacre of the Infected in Station 22. It was a replay of the Cameroon Genocide in 2023. The man who became my father found me in the baggage compartment, locked inside a dog crate, waiting for a miracle—or death."

He lowers his head. His mask is slipping off as the cloud that hung over him seems to lift and disperse.

"He'd been stuck at the airport for two days on his way home from a business trip." In a heap on the floor, Alpha has let down his mask at last. The darkness is dispelled.

"I was five. When we got to Abidjan, the white man handed banknotes to another man in uniform. I thought that he had bought me, and that he and his barren wife were going to make me their slave."

A shiver runs through me. My socks are still wet from Hartsquare Lake, but that's not why. The cold is coming from inside. It's Alpha's pain, Alpha's story.

"I was happy in my new home," he says, with a note of finality. "My inner demons left me in peace for a while. And then, the year I turned thirteen, they resurfaced. I started to keep 'bad company,' as my adoptive parents used to say. Some small-time thugs introduced me to a gang of burglars. I wasn't in it for the money. They called me 'the mastermind.' I did the organizing. The more difficult the robbery, the better, I thought. The challenges shielded me from everything else, from my past . . . It has caught up with me at last."

"I'm sorry, but something has come up," Kassandra intervenes, giving Alpha a little time to recover. "Tonight, you all have to sleep at Flyfold. There is a small bathroom behind that wall, and we brought some clean clothes for you to change into."

"Why?" asks Helen. "What's going on?"

"Bounty hunters tipped off by the C7 Unit are somewhere nearby."

"*Who?*"

"Mercenaries hired to unmask the Keeper. I'm sure you realize that governments would do anything to get their hands on Spirit Era. As Stepan told us from what he read in the papers, a large percentage of the population does not believe in the impending apocalypse. At most, they are preparing for a few major catastrophes: nothing worse than what is already happening. A country in possession of a computer program able to predict future environmental events would rule the world. Colossal amounts of money and power are up for grabs. The bounty hunters on our tail are not very reputable."

"Not very reputable!" Helen exclaims. "That's putting it mildly. The program must be worth billions. People would kill for far less than that!" Besides, I think to myself, the rising interest proves its potential. How could anyone take its predictions lightly? Stepan was right: the world is definitely crazy!

"I still have contacts in the intelligence department," the Shepherd says, his voice tense. "The C7 Unit created by Interpol is a task force entirely devoted to Spirit Era. Their goal? To get their hands on the program before the Russians, the Chinese, or any other potentially dangerous world power does, to guarantee global security. C7's cybertechnology experts are hard at work trying to locate us. My sources say they are still a long way off, but they have narrowed their search down to Vermont. The problem is, we have a leak. Someone is tipping those shadowy figures off."

"We can't risk being caught off guard in the middle of the night," Ka continues. "And you need to sleep. Tomorrow afternoon, after Head Instructor Shepherd has secured the perimeter of the farm, you will be able to spend a little time in your rooms before the evening session."

"Dinner's ready!" Mr. Mann bursts in.

Setting his armload of baskets on the floor, he unfolds a tablecloth and spreads it on the tatami. Whistling softly, he begins taking dishes out of the baskets.

"How does an impromptu candlelight picnic sound to you?"

It's a funny evening: dinner on the tatami among a pile of sleeping bags and pillows, like we're gathered around an imaginary fire. Like we're at camp. Chayton, too, opens up. He recounts our adventures at the lake, the phantom trains filing past, the White Train, and our meeting with Nira . . . and about the girl with green hair, the one he openly refers to as "my darling Froggie."

The trust between us is restored. Stepan is completely present, just like he is in the program. Maybe the Oak Tree Exercise has given him this newfound grounding? Keiji, meanwhile, is propped up on his elbows and displaying unprecedented self-confidence, whereas Helen has a thumb in her mouth and doesn't seem to care a fig about her appearance. Alpha and Ali are sitting cross-legged side by side, Alpha is calm again, and Ali has her arm over his shoulder. As for me, I'm writing an account of what happened at the hair salon on a piece of paper I got from Kassandra, since my notebook is in my room.

"What a mess," Ali mutters. "The World Above, the World Below . . . The Prowlers aren't as pure as the driven snow, after all. And if you ask me, Loco is a real scumbag, although we still don't have anything on him and there are only two days left."

"I'm sure Froggie will come through for us," Chayton says confidently. "If there is any incriminating evidence, she'll find it."

"But will it be enough? Arabella is the only Prowler on our side."

"Well, who says we have to overthrow Loco, anyhow?" Alpha asks, his voice faint. "Trafficking girls is appalling, but don't forget the Toptown Brigade. They're the real enemy—they gassed the Infected! Who's going to stand up to them if the Prowlers lose their leader?"

"And what about Bulbosis?" Helen adds. "That's how we

got into this mess in the first place. General Dusk blames it on the Subs, but he's lying! If Rae's index is at twelve percent, does that mean she's going to be sick? That all of us may get sick, too? I don't know what to think anymore."

"Yes, the danger is real," Kassandra responds. "You all know that. But I've spotted some of Spirit Era's safety mechanisms, and I don't believe any real harm can come to you. Take, for example, the fluorescent symbols that appear on your uniforms when they are exposed to Toptown's ultraviolet light: during the test connection, they provided the program with a calibration value and, later, allowed it to make adjustments."

"So, that's why our uniforms were grayish, kind of like camouflage," Ali remarks.

"More like encoded information," Stepan corrects her, "or a firewall . . ."

"So, when I was turned away from the hair salon and my uniform flashed neon yellow . . ."

"That was the firewall, an antivirus software installed in a scanner in the double-door entry."

"And the virus was *me*?"

"Something like that. It was a clue to guide us. The coupon wasn't name specific, but it was definitely meant for Rae."

"So, the program influences our choices?"

"Only if you are in danger," Ka replies, "in order to protect you. All right, then," she adds, changing the subject. "You're exhausted. You need to rest. Tomorrow, you can all sleep in."

Ali, Helen, and I move our sleeping bags to a secluded corner, and complete silence descends over Flyfold. We are all physically and emotionally drained, especially Alpha. Without further ado, I fall asleep.

*

The next day, there's hardly anyone around when we return

to the place on the High Express platform where our watches had gone off. Niro and the Mime brothers are nowhere in sight. The reality, however, is slow to register. My mind is still filled with the hot shower I took before the connection, the lavender-scented towels, my second dry pair of combat boots ... It takes me a while to muster the courage to slip back into the ratty cardigan with pockets. I had retrieved it from behind the bench where it was left with Keiji's.

"We've got a problem," Chayton tells me discreetly, his hair still crimped from the braid he wore in Hartsquare Lake. "It's Anais. We were supposed to meet at the chicken coop just before the connection. I had a little present for her—a watch and a bottle of perfume—but she didn't come. So, I climbed through the window into her bedroom. The shutter was locked from the outside. She was asleep and burning with fever. I couldn't wake her up. She's not well."

What? Anais is sick? That's all we needed!

"I tried to find Mr. Mann, but no luck. Something's not right. Her father locks her up, and she doesn't go to school. Remember how scared she was that time he almost caught us?"

Yes, I couldn't forget how she ran away from him. It wasn't a game.

"I told Ka about it. She told me not to worry, to focus on the program instead. She said Anais had a cold and that Mr. Mann had gone to get medicine. Do you think it's true?"

I have no idea. It dawns on me that we don't know much about her. Why is she living alone with her father? Is her mother alive?

"Anais has always been there for us. But I let her down. I was so upset, I threw the watch and the perfume in the trash! Anyway, it's all meaningless now ..."

Mind the gap between the train and the platform as you leave the High Express ...

A few passengers get off the train, others get on.

"I hope Arabella is still there," Helen says. "Otherwise, who will open the door to the vending machine for us?" Her pale complexion brings out her freckles.

"I am sure she still wait for us," Keiji asserts.

"She'd better. If not, we'll be stuck in Toptown, and the Subs won't be warned that the Agreements might be canceled."

"Rae and I can always go through the Rovers' turnstile to warn them. Alpha hasn't said a word since last night."

"Well, at least we're rid of Niro," Ali says, with her usual optimism. "That's something."

Phweeee! Phweeee!

A high-pitched whistle fills the air. Before we realize what's happening, the Owls, visibly well trained, are filing toward the exit in a calm and orderly fashion. Less than a minute later, we are the only ones left.

"Toptown Brigade! Don't move! We know who you are!"

"Quick, the door!" shouts Alpha, running toward the vending machine. *"Arabella, are you there?"*

But the door remains shut. The sound of boots marching resounds on the platform. A dozen soldiers in black uniforms appear, wearing gas masks instead of ski masks. The militia is moving rapidly in our direction.

"Rae," Chayton hollers, charging three goons, "open the damn door!"

With his usual impulsiveness, he bends forward, head-first, and charges like a rhinoceros. Drawing strength from his messenger-animal, he uses his head like a battering ram breaking through fortifications: three soldiers fall to the ground and get back up right away.

At the same time, Alpha and Keiji engage in hand-to-hand combat with two adversaries apiece. Keiji, once again, shows the speed and agility of a monkey—surely his messenger-animal. He uses *neijia*-style fighting techniques, the Chinese term for so-called internal martial arts: his hand is supple, his movements circular, his rolling and evasion parries allowing him to strike specific targets that cause his aggressors to cry out in pain. It is not about striking hard but fast, with precision and fluidity. Guided by the heart chakra, Keiji is not trying to injure but to put his opponents out of commission.

Alpha, on the other hand, is an adept of the *waijia*, or "external," martial arts techniques. Using his fists and fast, explosive movements, he means to debilitate his adversaries. He delivers a series of bone-cracking front kicks, side kicks, and back kicks to his opponents' sternums and limbs, knocks one out with a karate chop to the throat, and is able to move on to one of Chayton's three adversaries.

The blows are raining thick and fast now as I struggle to open the vending machine's tinted-glass pane. Helen is next to me, petrified, whereas Ali, true to the spirit of the sun chakra and her athletic nature, is making a series of impressive freestyle attacks. She is all over the place at once. Here, there, farther afield, and back again, her fists raining hard like meteors. She knocks one adversary's gas mask sideways; he curses as he rights it. Stepan, in the meantime, is flying from bench to bench with a tall, lanky soldier following closely behind him. Every so often, our companion spins around and delivers a well-aimed kick. He is very flexible.

The Brigade fighters are formidable, striking hand over fist with ferocity and extreme precision; the militia clearly knows how to fight, but it's their gas masks that have me worried most. Suddenly, a muscle-bound adversary attacks Stepan from the rear, delivering a powerful blow to his head just as he is about to spring onto a bench: a red stain colors Stepan's slicked-back blond hair. An involuntary cry escapes Helen's lips. She throws herself at the man—an improvised attack guided by her creative chakra—and lands on the ruffian's back as if he's a bronco. Wrapping her legs around his chest, she begins pulling on his gas mask with all her might. With an upward jerk of the head, Stepan's aggressor takes a step backward.

Alas, only for a moment. Oblivious to the rider on his back, the hulking soldier makes another lunge for Stepan, who is still occupied with his lanky opponent. The colossus delivers a second blow that brings him to his knees. Beside herself at the sight of blood, Helen pommels her enemy's skull and starts screaming like a banshee. Stepan's assailant rears up, spins around like a mechanical bull, and ejects poor Helen, sending her flying through the air.

Abandoning my useless attempts to open the vending machine, I rush over to my companion—she is completely stunned—and position myself between her and the giant. Remembering my judo lessons and Keiji's advice—it's not a question of size—I try to topple the colossus with an *ō-soto-gari*. I hook the outside of my opponent's left leg, pull forward, and much to the Brigade fighter's surprise, successfully manage to throw him off-balance.

Pscht!

The sound is familiar to me. It's what I was dreading all along.

Pscht!

"Watch out. They're spraying Repulsecure!" Chayton shouts, who knows what it means as well as I do.

A cloud of saffron smoke fills the air. But, this time, it's meant for us. Are we going to end up like the Infected in Station 22?

The dense smoke makes it hard for everyone to see. We could use it to our advantage, I think to myself. After all, ether is the element of the fifth chakra. The Brigades have on gas masks, but they only protect them from the fumes, not from the yellow smog. At one with my element, I move furtively through the thick smoke and begin delivering unexpected blows. But I cannot hold my breath indefinitely. A coughing fit stops me in my tracks.

Behind me, Alpha and Keiji are going head-to-head with adversaries, while Chayton continues to wallop opponents left and right. His technique may not be as refined as his companions' karate holds, but it is definitely as effective.

Cough! Cough! Overtaken by a fit of coughing, Ali starts to reel.

The colossus and the tall, lanky guy join forces with her opponent—Helen and Stepan both down for the count. It's three against one—Ali doesn't stand a chance. Two of the soldiers carry her off by force. The hulking brute grabs hold of Stepan's and Helen's collars and drags them away. They are already half unconscious and have about as much energy as a couple of potato sacks.

In the dense yellowish smoke, we can hardly see ten feet away. I feel groggy; I am coughing now, too. I retreat to the vending machine, but the racket only follows me. The fighting is getting closer. As Keiji rushes toward me, he takes a powerful jab to the temple, and the arch of his eyebrow starts to bleed. He staggers but manages to retaliate with a pair of impressive high kicks that send his two opponents sprawling.

Taking advantage of the pea-soup mist, Alpha and Chayton have joined us. My three companions form a shield in front of me; Keiji brings a weak hand to his forehead to try to stem the flow of blood—the cardigan Blanky lent him is covered with red stains. We all seem to be moving in slow motion; the gas is starting to take effect. My back against the vending machine, I slide down its glass-pane front. Through the haze, a pair of small black irises behind two round windows appears—a gas mask! Chayton quickly dispatches the intruder with a well-aimed headbutt.

Suddenly, I feel a tap on the back.

"This way!" Arabella hollers, stepping out of the machine.

The door! She's opened it from inside!

"Come on!"

It all happens very fast. I lift a foot, lower my head, and walk through the vending machine. Concealed by the layer of smoke, my three friends do the same. The secret passage quickly closes behind us, and we find ourselves standing inside the tunnel. Arabella has miraculously saved us. We can hardly believe it.

But our joy is short-lived, and reality immediately sinks in: Ali, Helen, and Stepan have been taken prisoner . . .

46

"We were betrayed!"

Groggy but still pumped up from the fight, Chayton is practically pawing the ground in the dark tunnel.

"Someone spilled the beans!"

"I think you're right," Alpha agrees, shaking his head clear. "The Brigade knew where to find us. The question is, who squealed?"

"Niro, for sure!" Keiji says with difficulty.

"Obviously, someone's in league with the Brigade," Chayton remarks. "Niro wouldn't have the guts. On the other hand, he could have been talking to Loco."

"Meaning what?" Alpha asks. "The Sub leader is in cahoots with General Dusk, his worst enemy? What for? And how could he communicate with him, anyhow? The Owls can't even see him!"

"I don't know—yet. What's wrong, Keiji? Are you okay?"

His eyebrow isn't bleeding anymore, but he is clutching his forehead and looks unsteady on his feet. Arabella is unusually quiet.

"I feel funny . . ."

I can hardly keep my eyes open, either.

"Maybe it's an aftereffect of the Repulsecure?"

"No, Chayton," Arabella says, her voice tired. "The gas . . . It wasn't green, the fumes of death. It was yellow. Sleep inducing, no doubt. The effects won't last—"

Then, just like that, Arabella collapses!

"Someone hit me on the head . . . from behind . . . I didn't see who. So that I couldn't open the door for you . . . I was unconscious for a long time."

"It was an inside job. Someone from Underhome must have planned it all," Alpha concludes. "Are you strong enough to stand?"

"I . . . Yes, I think so . . . I feel dizzy."

"You probably have a concussion."

She struggles to get to her feet, despite help from Alpha and Chayton.

"It must be Niro who ratted us out," Keiji insists.

"Maybe, maybe not . . . Moles often turn up where we least expect them," Arabella replies enigmatically.

We set off. It is hot and damp, and the tunnel is so narrow that Alpha and Chayton take turns helping her walk, working as a team for once . . .

"Aaah, aahh," she moans.

"Hang in there, Arabella," Chayton whispers. "We need you; the Subs need you. Canceling the Agreements means the war against the Brigade could start any day."

As we near the intersection where the wagobike is parked—to the right, the dark tunnel carved into the rock; to the left, the narrow corridor leading to the coal mine and the Rovers' handcars—her legs give out. Chayton carefully picks her up, carries her to the vehicle, then sits her back down on the ground. Her head falls back heavily. She props herself against the enormous front wheel of the rebuilt motorcycle.

"Thank you," she says, her voice a whisper. "It's the second time . . . I don't hold it against you anymore, you know . . . You and Bamboo . . . you would have been friends . . ." Chayton smiles in embarrassment. "Anyhow, don't think you got the better of me, or anything. It's just that I'm in no condition to drive."

"You mean . . . ?" Chayton asks.

"Yes, you've earned it. Come on, get in. Time is running out."

Eyes shining like a child on Christmas morning, Chayton climbs onto the wagobike, grabs the spray-painted helmet on the handlebars, puts it on his head, and lowers the protective goggles.

"Your infrared vision will show you the path through the maze of tunnels. You just need to follow the red lines on the walls. Keiji and Rae are not adults. They don't have to pass the test of thermal vision. They can come with us."

Arabella launches into a series of recommendations: how to buckle the harness, turn over the ignition, interpret the hum of the exhaust pipes, put the bike into drive, safely make turns . . . How to go into turbo drive, lower the middle wheels . . .

"Uh, guys?" Alpha interrupts. "I think you're going to have to speed up the training session."

"Not now," Chayton snaps, fiddling with the headlights. "Don't you see I'm b—"

"The Noctos!" Keiji exclaims.

"Thank you, Keiji!" Alpha says with a note of irony.

In the dimly lit tunnel on the left, the one leading to the coal mine, shapeless figures burst forth like living rag dolls. Their globular white eyes flash in the darkness.

"*What?*" Arabella says, incredulous. "That's impossible! They've never been up this high before."

"Get in!" Chayton shouts, turning the key in the ignition.

The familiar noise of pots and pans and the scent of fresh-cut grass from the exhaust pipes remind me of the first time—when all seven of us were still together. My stomach is in knots as I think of my three friends. Where did the Brigade take them? What are they going to do to them? Stepan won't be able to stand being locked up. He'll surely have a fit. Helen will be beside herself, and Ali will lose her cool. And . . . and . . .

"Hurry, Rae!" Alpha calls me to order as he helps Keiji get Arabella into the elongated sidecar. She seems to be on her last legs.

He settles on the seat behind her, and Keiji takes the one in front of her. Keiji straps the injured Prowler into the harness, then fastens his own. I sit down in the seat in the first row.

"All set?" Chayton asks impatiently as he revs the engine.

Without waiting for me to buckle up, he starts the wago-bike with a jerk. The centrifugal force pins us to the seat backs. Just behind me, I hear Keiji gasp. The red headlights barely il-luminate the road as the vehicle veers to the right and hurtles into the dark tunnel. Chayton turns the steering wheel, and my head slams into the seat back. I don't know what it was like with Arabella in the driver's seat, but the ride is so bumpy, my teeth are rattling.

"Easy does it . . . ," I hear her stammer from behind.

A short distance later, the vehicle comes to a grinding halt. I hold my harness tight so I won't be ejected. Gasping for breath, I buckle myself in as fast as I can.

"Arabella!" Chayton panics. "What do I *do*?"

Another group of Noctos is standing before us blocking the passage. Drawn to the glow of the headlights, they are moving toward us, cackling and grinning.

"Shit! Arabella, *what do I do now*?"

I glance over my shoulder: the bench-woman's eyes are closed and her head is lolling to the side; she has passed out!

"Turn off the headlights!" Alpha shouts. "We have infrared vision!"

Keiji and I don't, however. We find ourselves engulfed in complete darkness.

"They're getting closer!" Chayton yells. "And more are coming up on us from behind. We are sandwiched!"

"Come on, buddy! Take the tracks on the ceiling!" The wagobike is off with a bang, then whooshing like a cannonball.

"Turbooo!" our pilot roars as the incredibly powerful vehicle propels us forward.

I close my eyes. We are tearing along, rocking side to side. It's like being on a roller coaster at the fair. My body tilts sideways: the vehicle must be rolling on the wall! For some reason, I envision the miraculously aerodynamic track cyclists my father used to watch on TV on Sundays. He found it relaxing.

The racket is infernal. I close my eyes again . . . Did I even open them? The entire wagobike lurches and does a corkscrew. Chayton lets out a roar. We're upside down!

"Good job!" Alpha yells. "The middle wheels are locked onto the ceiling rail."

Below us, the sound of appalling howling, the smell of pestilent breath, and the clammy heat of mummified bodies . . . The place is swarming with Noctos! My shoulder straps are making dreadful creaking sounds. I'm trembling. I close my eyes again.

"There are way too many of them! We can't outrun them. Hold on tight. I'm going to get a little closer!"

Chayton brakes gradually this time, though it doesn't make stopping upside down any easier. The blood rushes to my face. My insides feel like they are going to spill out of my mouth.

"Hurry!" Alpha yells. "Arabella can't take it much longer: she's starting to slip through the straps!"

Keiji and I are still in utter darkness. I've completely lost my bearings.

"Come on, you bastards!" Chayton taunts the Noctos. "Over here, that's right!"

All at once, the red headlights are back on, illuminating the host of mutants. There are dozens of them, perhaps hundreds . . .

"We're over here! Come on!"

The creatures swarm beneath us. Their rotting fingers waggle in the air. Some manage to touch us, to scratch us even.

"*Banzai!*" Chayton shouts.

The acceleration is lightning fast. We blast off like a rocket, leaving the Noctos in the dust. Still upside down, my body is pressed into the seat back. I feel like I have an elephant in my lap. I let out an otherworldly cry.

"*Banzai!*"

The wagobike continues to hurtle along at breakneck speed, and the mutants are well behind us now. We speed through one tunnel and then another. Finally, the wheels unhook from the ceiling rail, and we return to solid ground—at last!

"Good job, Chayton!" Alpha congratulates him. "You did it!"

Our driver raises an arm in victory, keeping a steady gaze on the road. His arm is strong and muscular, but a little shaky, too. His gesture is grateful. Quite a change from the early days . . .

We gradually lose speed until we come to a fork in the tunnel. There, to our amazement, a small crowd awaits us.

"Oh no!" Alpha grumbles. *"Him again?"*

"What you want, Niro?" Keiji lets fly as the wagobike pulls up alongside him.

Niro is leaning against the wall and surrounded as usual by a flock of hangers-on. Twirling a lock of curly brown hair around a finger, Dulci gives a feline smile and wiggles closer to him. She deposits an elbow on his shoulder as if she is giving him a kiss. The message is clear: private property, keep out . . .

"Wasn't ratting us out to Brigade enough for you?"

"The Brigade? Are you kidding!" Niro balks. "You're completely off your rocker, Keiji."

"Who, then?"

"I don't know. Hey, you, big guy!" he continues, turning to Chayton. "I've been thinking about what you told me. Is it true you saw my sister?"

"That's right," Chayton answers. "So did Rae. She was with me."

Visibly hesitant, Niro stares at us. He suddenly breaks away from Dulci and his little group of followers, including Billiard and Gym.

"You can't enter Underhome. Loco's put a price on your head for treason. Arabella's, too. He is convinced you're in league with the Brigade."

"And you're telling me you had nothing to do with it?"

"I'm not stupid. You're my only chance of seeing my sister again. It's a win-win situation: I hide you in Deepwood tonight, and you figure out a way for me to talk to her."

"Not so sure she'd be willing to see you. She made me swear I wouldn't tell you."

"And I'm not so sure you have a choice . . ."

Niro gives a knowing smile and nods in the direction of Arabella, who is still unconscious. A leaden silence seals their agreement.

"Leave the wagobike here. There is a passage not far from here that leads to the dormitory."

He turns the headlights off, and they are replaced by the glow of Niro's flashlight. Twenty small hands form a stretcher for Arabella and carry her to the entrance of Deepwood, the four of us in tow. A trapdoor in the lower part of a wall leads to an area beneath one of the bunk beds. The chain of Subs, very cautiously, slips Arabella's inanimate body through the door. Inside the dormitory, Siana and Blanky keep watch.

"Are you all right?" Blanky whispers once I'm through.

I nod.

"And you, Keiji? Oh, your forehead!"

"It nothing. The wound closed up already. Sorry about your jacket."

"Meh. It's not important," says Blanky, helping him remove it. "I'll keep mine on, it's too cold around here."

"We were worried when you didn't show up at the turnstile," Siana says softly. "And the number of entries and exits wasn't going to add up. So, Niro had to take care of that."

"Niro?" Keiji repeats.

"Yes, he had Gym and Billiard go through the turnstile twice to cover for you."

"How so?"

"They went through and then went back into the subway through the secret passage in the vending machine. We've cheated the Brigade before. They think all beggars are alike!"

"Then why don't you use the passage to escape?"

"To do what? Live like fugitives in Toptown? It's better to be free Below than to be prisoners in a city of concrete. Anyway, where are the other three?"

"A surprise attack. The Brigade took them," Alpha answers bitterly.

Since everyone in the dormitory is fast asleep, we manage to slip into our beds without being seen. We silently deposit Arabella in Blanky's cubby, as it's the easiest to access. We don't need to sleep in the program's simulation, so three of us agree to take turns keeping watch over her. Chayton, meanwhile, will go with Niro to the phantom cars. I wonder how his sister will react when she sees him. She was terrified at the thought of his finding out about her.

Keiji takes the first shift, drawing Arabella's bunk curtains shut. Blanky scrambles up to the bed on the fourth level—the two cubbies assigned to us—while Alpha hides behind the burlap of the other on the third level. Above them, no sound is coming from the Mime brothers' cubbies. I climb into Siana's bed after Niro's acolytes have dispersed.

I wondered what was behind her curtain. Now I know—nothing. A bare minimum, I should say: a few storage spaces with clothes, toiletries, and a second pair of sneakers. There is one item displayed in the middle of the canvas like a masterpiece: the stick of strawberry gum Chayton had given her during the trial connection. Fastened to the curtain with clothespins, it is still in its wrapper, unopened.

"I managed to hide it in my underwear," Siana whispers proudly. "The Tubeans didn't notice a thing. They would have been furious to pass up such a marvel. I have no idea what that smell is, but it sure is a great fragrance diffuser!"

She leans over to the stick of gum and takes a whiff, her eyes closed. I refrain from telling her it is meant to be chewed and then thrown away. In this world, where there's practically nothing to eat, it suddenly strikes me as absurd.

"That's awful about your friends. How are you going to get them out of the Brigade's clutches?"

I have no idea. Nothing could be worse.

"And what about Arabella? Even if she recovers, the Prowlers are all looking for her."

What can I say? I'm at a complete loss. And my watch is set to go off in forty-six minutes. If the Seven are not all together, we won't be able to return to Flyfold. The Shepherd may have to unplug us. Would it mean the end of the program? Regardless, after today, we only have one connection left to find the first key, and, as of now, things don't look so hot.

"I want to show you something . . . ," Siana says.

Swimming in her oversized boys' clothes, she uneasily

pushes aside a couple locks of long golden hair. Her denuded temple reveals her large mole.

"Look!"

Leaning her head closer to me, she spreads her hair. Little blisters have formed on her scalp—little bulb-shaped protuberances. So, I was wrong: the situation could be worse.

Siana is sick!

47

I've been watching the crats for a while now . . .

I've been watching them since I relieved Keiji and took up my watch in Blanky's cubby. They are curled up against Arabella, who is still unconscious. Mama Crat is nursing her two little ones—I'm glad to see she didn't get killed after all . . . Gray Pearl and Lil' Buccaneer purr contentedly as they greedily feed. The tiny crats are both adorable and strange with their rodent bodies, feline tails, and half-cat, half-rat heads.

But I'm most intrigued by their diet. The adult crats I saw in Station 22 did not just turn up their noses at the spilled powder; they brushed it away with their tails like they wanted to get rid of it altogether. It's odd. The packets are the only food source Above and Below. So, what do they eat?

"How is Arabella?"

Alpha's long face appears from behind the curtains. He looks exhausted.

"Still the same, huh? I was dead wrong, Rae. Wrong about everything . . ."

The hair twists on the top of his head, longer now than when he first got to the farm, stand boldly upward.

"Chayton's right. It must have been a Prowler who tipped off the Brigade. And who better than Loco to do it? I don't know why. Or how, for that matter, since he's invisible in Aboveworld. Maybe he's got an accomplice? A Rover who has access to Toptown? That's very likely, in fact. The same person who ratted us out and knocked out Arabella!"

Standing in the dorm like that is risky, so Alpha crawls inside the bunk. Yikes! It's pretty cramped inside the cubby with Arabella's powerful build and Blanky's jam-packed storage pouches! Since that day in Flyfold when he told us about his past—the massacre, the killing of his biological family, the dog crate, his adoptive parents—something inside him has opened up. A little door . . .

"What are you smiling about?"

The white pom-poms dangling from the ceiling are practically sitting in his mass of twisty braids. Like eggs in a nest! I give a silent laugh. No doubt a foolish laugh but liberating even so. Alpha also loosens up, and the two of us are overcome by a noiseless fit of laughter. It's impossible to stop, to the point that Mama Crat is seriously annoyed. With a look of reproach, she reclaims her teats and closes up shop, leaving Gray Pearl and Lil' Buccaneer fast asleep and satiated. She is making her way toward the burlap exit when my inner voice rings with a bone-shaking scream: *Follow her!*

I've pretty much had it with the voices at this point.

Come on, follow her!

After Alpha's hostile voice colonized my head, I feel like coming to my own decisions.

Remember the item-clues, a trail of bread crumbs scattered by the program . . .

My eyes rest on Mama Crat. She also looks very young. A bit like Froggie, who is a mother, as well. A bit like Kassandra, too, barely thirty years old, but responsible for seven teenagers and a program designed to save the world.

It all seems so unreal, so out of step with time, just like Ka's dresses.

"What's wrong with you?" I must have given a start when I realized Mama Crat was slipping through the curtain. Of course, I'm going to follow her!

"Are you okay, Rae?"

I pretend all is fine, that I'm just tired. I fake a yawn to let Alpha know my watch with Arabella is over. Then I exit the cubby just behind Gray Pearl and Lil' Buccaneer's mother. Once the curtain is drawn, I imitate her cautious progress—I stick close to the bunk beds, move rapidly across open areas, and make myself as tiny as possible—to avoid waking the dorm.

When she gets to the bed with the trapdoor underneath, she slows down. There is a tiny ventilation grid next to it in the wall. She slips through it. Without missing a beat, I crawl under the bunk, open the trapdoor, and enter the tunnel. It is dark without Niro's flashlight, but my eyes adjust quickly as I continue my pursuit of Mama Crat. We've already covered a good distance without a hitch when it dawns on me that finding my way back could be problematic.

Suddenly, a flashlight behind me comes on and illuminates the tunnel. I turn around, my heart racing wildly, blinded by the light.

"What are you doing here?"

It's Niro!

"Lower your flashlight!" Chayton adds. Thank goodness!

"What's she doing here in the middle of the night!" Niro exclaims. "Maybe she's the snitch!"

"No way."

"Whatever you say. But if she were to get caught, we'd all be busted."

"He's right about that, Sparrow. You shouldn't be here. It's dangerous," Chayton admonishes, fists on hips, his tone annoyingly paternalistic.

"You know what will happen to us if the Two Beans find out we're hiding you?" Niro fumes. "And that damn White Train and my sister are nowhere to be found, in the bargain!"

"I just don't get it," Chayton says, clearly puzzled.

"Well, come on. We have to go back to the dorm."

Instead of following them docilely, I set off in the opposite direction. No way are they going to stop me from catching up with Mama Crat!

"Hey, where are you going, Rae? Come back!"

Sorry, Chayton. It's time for me to make my voice heard.

"Wait for me!"

The sound of his heavy footsteps echo through the corridor behind me. The sound of Niro jabbering, too.

"Ah, what the hell? Won't be getting any sleep tonight anyway . . . So, why not?"

Meanwhile, I've caught sight of Mama Crat again. She continues making her way through the tunnel and slips through the bars of a ventilation grate, this one a little wider than the last.

"Now what?" Chayton asks.

From the look on my face, he guesses my meaning.

"You're too much! Well, only because it's you," he says, kicking the grid open.

I enter the shaft first. It is just big enough for my companion. We crawl forward on our hands and knees: the metal sheet is as hot as an oven!

"Why did I ever let myself get into this mess?" Niro grumbles, bringing up the rear. "We don't even know what we're looking for. Can someone please tell me what we're looking for?"

Chayton follows me in solidarity without saying a word.

"Well, then, I've had it up to here with you Faraways! I'm out of here!"

But suddenly, the sound of Mama Crat's meowing is echoed by others somewhere up ahead. Guided by the sounds, we eventually reach an air duct, which, surprisingly, leads to a vast space. An open-air cavern . . .

"Well, I'll be damned!" Niro lets out, climbing through the duct after us.

The place is teeming with hundreds of crats: some are swimming, diving, and splashing about in an expanse of water in the middle of the cave; others are coming and going in the lush vegetation growing along the lake's rocky shore; others still are scrambling over the grotto's terraced walls and ledges—reaching all the way to the open sky!

Mama Crat prances over to an enormous lawn of wild grasses with a pungent, earthy smell. Joining her fellow creatures, she begins moving over the field in a methodical fashion—and sucking different grasses with each new step! She seems to be feeding on sap from the plants.

"Where are we?" Niro utters, amazed. "Long ago, before most Subs were resigned to packet nourishment alone, some tried to find other food sources. But to no avail. Those who ate the occasional crat were considered savages. So, the packets became the norm. I'm sure no one's ever been here before!"

"I have . . . ," Chayton says with feeling and emphasis. "I came up here when I dove into Hartsquare Lake. That's where we are: on the other side of Hartsquare Station!"

"Nonsense."

"You see the hull of a subway train in the water over there, sticking up like the tip of an iceberg? The flooded subway station is on the other side. It's Hartsquare, I'm telling you!"

"Well, that—" Niro doesn't believe his eyes. "I—" He breaks off.

It's nighttime in Underhome, but the lake is clearly aglow

with the purple light of the Toptown sky. Astonishing aquatic flora and phosphorescent rocks glimmer in the crystal-clear water.

"I have never seen anything so beautiful . . . ," Niro finishes.

Rain drips down some of the cave walls, and the rock face is covered with an extraordinary array of brightly colored mosses.

"It's funny," Chayton remarks pensively. "Last time I was here, the vegetation was nowhere near as luxuriant. There seem to be a hundred more species now. How is that possible in just a few days' time?"

"Maybe you didn't see right."

"I'm sure I did, Niro. My great-grandfather was a healer. I inherited his collection of medicinal plants. I know all about plants."

Medicinal plants. Medicinal plants . . .

I give a start.

"What is it, Rae? What's up?" Chayton, who knows me well now, looks into my eyes. "Hmm, you didn't follow Mama Crat by chance, did you? We both know the power of animal instinct. Animals are creatures of the earth. If the crats have chosen to live here, it's for a good reason."

My two companions start observing the crats more closely. Chayton's right. Even the youngest ones have something to teach us. Each has a clearly defined role, but they move together collectively, forming a well-oiled unit. We now see that the crats in the water are diving for aquatic plants, bringing them to the surface, then passing them on in a chain until they reach the shore. There, another team of crats is sorting them into piles.

"They are incredibly organized," Niro comments. "It's like what I imagine being in a beehive to be."

"A beehive! Bingo, Niro! That's exactly right!"

"Uh . . ."

"Don't you see? They are canvassing the field, sucking nectar from each of the different plant species. As if they are pollinating. They are foraging, that's how the plants are fertilized so quickly—the crats are Underhome's bees!"

I think of Helen. I'm a little sorry I'd considered her my rival.

"No shit, I can't believe it . . ."

"The soil must be very fertile here and the plants nutritious if the crats are feeding on them."

Chayton breaks off a shoot shaped like an eggplant, pulls it open, collects the seeds, and stuffs them in his pocket.

"Didn't Blanky tell us that none of those little creatures ever caught Bulbosis?"

I nod yes.

"Well, Sparrow, you guessed right by betting on Mama Crat. These plants may be able to cure Bulbosis!"

"And animal instinct is what brought the crats here?"

"That's right, Niro. The only thing is, I don't recognize any of the plant species. They seem to be new strains."

"Then we should gather some and give them to the Infected in Stations 23 and 24. We'll see if the herbs cure them."

"That's what you had in mind, isn't it, Rae?"

I smile approvingly.

"We don't have much time left. Let's start with you. Here, eat this!"

Chayton hands me a freshly cut shoot.

"Why her?" Niro asks.

"Her Bulbosis index was at twelve percent when she was tested at the Toptown hair salon. We don't know how she got contaminated, but if these plants are the cure, a second test at the salon could provide proof."

He seems to be forgetting one little detail: I don't have another coupon, and we know what happened to Ali when she tried to enter Solid Gold Hairstyles uninvited . . .

"Is it good?" Niro asks.

"Not bad," I answer with a so-so hand gesture. It tastes a little like spinach with too much pepper.

"Excuse me, guys," Niro says to a couple of crats. "May I?"

The creatures pay no attention to Niro: picking is authorized. So, we fill our pockets with plants before setting off. Nobody says a word as we make our way back, but Niro sneaks a sidelong look at me every so often. It would seem the crats aren't the only ones he sees in a new light.

More good news awaits us back at the dorm: Arabella is awake!

"Where have you been?" Alpha whispers.

"We look for you everywhere," Keiji adds.

"It's a long story," Chayton says.

"So, save it for another time," Arabella says, her voice low but clearly her old confident self again. "The dormitory will be awake soon. Come on, let's go!"

"Where are we going?"

"To someplace safe: the Rebels' HQ."

"The Rebels? *What rebels?*"

"You'll see, Chayton. Rae, you go get Siana. And, Keiji, you get Blanky. They are no longer safe in Deepwood, either."

I climb up to Siana's bunk; she's curled up in a ball sleeping. But the slightest touch is enough to wake her. The minute she opens her eyes, the truth jumps out at me: she's in bad shape. Her condition has worsened: a nasty boil has sprouted on her neck. I hide it with one of her scarves and stuff some herbs from my pocket into her mouth. Siana chews mechanically, no questions asked. She knows without knowing how, a bit like me.

"Hurry up, you two!" Arabella exhorts once we're off the bunk.

Blanky is there already, ready to set off but with dark circles under his eyes.

"I'm so tired," he says, fiddling with his blankie. "I hardly shut my eyes all night. Those Mime brothers will be hearing from me, they will! They were moving and talking in their sleep all night long."

Without further ado, Siana takes him by the hand, and we're off—the same trapdoor, tunnels, the same race against the clock. When our watches go off, we keep running without so much as a glance at each other. We all have the same sinking feeling, I'm sure: we won't be returning to the farm for a last pause, though we sorely need it. And we won't be continuing our mission as a full team. I try to picture Ali, Helen, and Stepan—wherever they are. Their watches are going off, right now, just like ours. If the danger was too great, the Shepherd would unplug us, I try to reassure myself. Regardless of the eventual side effects.

Close on Arabella's heels, we hurry through the alleyways while Underhome still sleeps. Before long, I figure out where we are going; I've been there before.

"Valjean Rabbit?" Keiji asks in surprise as the hot-pink caratram comes into view.

He has never seen it before, nor have Alpha and Chayton, but he must have remembered the story Siana told us when we first arrived by handcar.

"So, he's Chief Rebel?" Now I know for sure: the pink scarf was meant to steer me in the right direction. Valjean Rabbit is leading an insurgency.

Everything inside the burrow is completely different now: the rocking chair and knitting needles have vanished, Valjean's shaggy beard is no longer covered by a scarf, and his gray hair is thoroughly combed. He greets us with a brief nod. His sleeves are rolled up, his forearms entirely covered with colorful silk bracelets. And Valjean Rabbit is not alone: twenty or so Subs are there with him, eyeing us suspiciously.

The shelves with the silkworm habitats are also empty. But

the pom-poms dangling from the mobiles overhead—I know they are cocoons now—have multiplied. Lastly, the pumpkin-size balls on the floor have been opened to reveal their hidden booty: an armory of projectile launchers made of salvaged odds and ends: sections of lead pipe, scissor blades tied to sticks, and so on.

"It is my pleasure to introduce Valjean the Rabbit, the Rebel Chief," Arabella says.

"Why not tell us before?" Keiji asks.

"We needed to make sure we could trust you," Valjean answers.

Even his voice has changed. It is dignified and strong.

"I have an army of about fifty Subs," the Rebel Chief tells us. "The time is ripe."

"Ripe for what?" Alpha asks.

"For overthrowing Loco. We won't stand for the way he treats the Infected anymore, or for the way he abuses young girls. Underhome deserves a better leader."

"What about the Great Rebellion? Wouldn't it be better to form an alliance with him to fight the Brigade? If the Agreements really are canceled, it'd be better to strike first and have the element of surprise on our side. If only we'd found the key to the Slymouth Gate . . ."

"The gate is an invention. There is no key, and there never has been."

"What?" Alpha asks, flabbergasted.

"And no Great Rebellion, either."

"Can you prove it?"

"I have an informant. Loco cooked up the whole Great Rebellion narrative so the Subs would have something to hope for. False hopes kept them eating out of his hand. It made them easier to manipulate."

"And his deal with the Tubeans indefinitely provides him with fresh troops," Chayton remarks bitterly.

"Valjean!"

Suddenly, a face appears in the opening in the roof.

"Valjean," the girl repeats, jumping into the caratram.

She has white-blond hair and eyebrows.

"Nira!" Chayton exclaims.

"What are . . . what are you two doing here?"

"What about you?" the mascot cuts in. "You're going to blow your cover."

So, the double agent is Niro's sister!

"It's Loco. He's lost his mind. He's threatening to torch the White Train if the Prowlers don't get their hands on the other four Faraways. I have no idea how he already knows . . . that they escaped the Brigade's ambush . . ." Nira stops, her pink-tinted eyes ablaze. "I . . . I got here as fast as I could . . . The girls in the other compartment and their babies . . . He . . ."

"Did he kill them?" Chayton shouts, hurrying over to her.

"No, he locked them up. Froggie just managed to slip me this," Nira answers, reluctantly handing him an envelope.

"What is it?"

"I don't know. She made me swear I'd give it to you personally."

Chayton tears open the envelope straightaway, then reads it out loud:

"You were the one I'd been expecting for so long . . .

"No one has ever trusted me before.

"THANK YOU.

"There was nothing of interest in the safe. I'm sorry.

"But the little red notebook that Loco always keeps on him may be of use.

"I memorized this code: R0O6Y5G3B4I9P8."

"Do you know what the code is for?" Valjean asks Arabella.

"I have no idea," the bench-woman answers.

"How do we know she's not putting one over on us?" one of the Subs bursts out, waving a slingshot made from a carving fork and an elastic waistband.

"Yeah!" a Sub wielding a broom launcher chimes in. "The Prowlers and Loco are all the same!"

"That's not true!" Arabella responds indignantly. "I hate him!"

"What if she decides to rat us out?" the Sub with the slingshot insists. "I say we tie her to that chair and decide what to do with her once we're done with Loco."

"No!" Keiji objects. "Arabella is on side with you."

"How can you be so sure?" Alpha asks, inclined to be suspicious as always. "No one had easier access to the Brigade than her. Maybe she didn't open the vending machine door on purpose."

"You're wrong! I am heart chakra. I see inside. Who loves for real."

"What's that have to do with anything?"

"The man she loves, his name is Bamboo. It's my item-clue. So, I know."

In resonance with Keiji's words, the pom-poms overhead begin to quiver, and, one after the other, large cream-colored moths—symbols of new beginnings—push their way out of the cocoons and take flight.

"They're free, at last!" Valjean Rabbit exclaims. "Freedom. That was all we had when we lived in the streets . . ."

The host of winged creatures fly through the caratram's window-door, then upward toward Underhome's domed ceiling, before fading from sight altogether.

"Safe travels!" Valjean calls after them. Then, turning to Arabella, he says, "You must forgive my men, Arabella. They're suspicious of everyone."

"I want to make Loco pay as much as you do, but it won't be enough. We're going to have to conclude some kind of peace agreement with Aboveworld."

"Never!" said Val.

"She's right," Alpha insists. "We have no other choice if we want to rescue our friends."

"The only thing the Owls deserve is war!" Valjean is adamant.

"Being trapped Below will be difficult for the Rebels, especially without all the Prowlers on your side," Arabella says. "Some are going to stick by Loco no matter what. So, what we need is a bargaining chip."

"A bargaining chip," Chayton pronounces mysteriously. "I believe we have just that. Thanks to Rae . . ."

And he pulls a handful of plants out of his pocket . . .

LOGBOOK
INSTRUCTOR: KA
SEASON I

NOVEMBER 27, 2035

I'm writing my report in a hurry.

The Chosen Seven have been separated. They are going to have to go into overtime. To go straight into their last two-hour simulation session. So, the livestream continues. Their last chance to find the first key. If they fail, Spirit Era will close for good, and the keys in the program will forever be out of reach.

How will the Seven's bodies respond to being immersed in the VR environment for four straight hours? The program's computer-mediated cameras broadcast images from different angles on the Spirit Era Channel, often in split-screen mode, and a picture-in-picture function is activated when necessary. That way, the viewers can see the cell in Toptown Prison where Ali, Helen, and Stepan (the wound to his head isn't serious) are being held. They're doing all right, for the time being; they know it's only temporary.

The latest events in the program spread like wildfire on social media feeds around the world. The tension is mounting. Audience ratings are through the roof. Internet users, even those who refuse to believe the end-of-the-world scenario, are dying to know if the Seven will succeed, and if they will come out of the adventure relatively unscathed. Those who've believed the Keeper's prediction since the very beginning are counting on them entirely. But the same question is on everyone's lips.

What is the first chakra's infamous lost key? If such a key even exists . . .

Niro is a master pickpocket.

His hands seem to be in his pockets, at his sides, and crossed behind his back all at once. They open a bag, dive in blindly, and move around as if they have eyes on their fingertips! And they come out victorious—holding a coupon!

Niro hands it to me as his gang of admirers looks on. Since he was reunited with his sister, his tics have vanished, and he's been going out of his way to help us. I have no idea what the two of them talked about when Arabella took him to Valjean Rabbit's, but it sure took a long time. Nira promised she wouldn't leave Underhome during the conflict. She is currently staying with the Rebels along with Siana and Blanky. We needed a safe place to hide them so Siana could get her strength back and Blanky could administer her herbal treatment every hour. After letting him in on our secret, I asked him to look after her on the sly. The dosage is a matter of trial and error: Chayton prescribed it instinctively. It's not as if we have time for clinical trials!

Nobody notices anything in the line outside the hair salon. As usual, the Owls are completely detached from everything, including themselves. The robotization of the city seems to have stripped them of their sense of humanity. Holding my coupon, I have no choice but to face the double-door entry to the salon again.

Chayton came up with the plan. The Rovers would help Keiji and me go back to Toptown. He gave me quite a few doses of herbal medicine and was hoping the test results would show that my Bulbosis infection rate has gone down. Having a cure would obviously change everything.

Meanwhile, Valjean and the Rebels are to continue preparing the offensive against the Prowlers, with the help of Alpha and Chayton. When we left them, they were trying on hats and scarves from the mascot's collection to help camouflage them. Loco is set to give his monthly speech soon, and that's when they plan to launch the assault.

"It's up to you now, Rae," Keiji whispers, when it's my turn to enter the double-door salon entrance.

Niro and Dulci and their followers risked the dangers of harboring wanted fugitives and helped us enter Aboveworld. After crawling into their handcar, I hid behind Billiard's and Gym's legs, and Keiji behind the Mime brothers'. It had to look like it was just another panhandling outing. I was given quite a scare when I thought I heard the sound of the Tubeans' voices, but fortunately they weren't there. Apparently, they're nowhere to be found these days. If the Toptown Council has, in fact, voted to end the Agreements, nothing has been put into effect yet. The turnstile was working normally. After they passed through it, the Mime brothers set off for the High Express to do their pantomime show.

In the double-door entry, the red laser beam gets to work. Just as we thought, the coupon isn't name specific, and the second door opens. The hair salon is packed, as usual. The din is even louder than the last time, and the industrial ceiling lights seem dimmer than before. I can barely make out the clients in the barber chairs.

The flashing arrows on the floor point me to a seat at the end of a row. I sit down, and the chair's articulated arms yank out a hair straightaway. This time around, I'm prepared. The results of the hair analysis are displayed in gold letters and numbers. At last, the indicator that interests us appears on the mirror: "BULBOSIS INDEX = 0%." Yippee! I have to resist jumping for joy. The results are printed out on a slip of paper. I grab it and stick it in my pants pocket, next to the first one.

Then the mirror zooms in on my face. This time, I like my reflection. The cut I have in mind appears on the screen, and a second slip of paper is instantly printed out: "PERFECT MATCH! NOTHING TO CHANGE!"

The tentacle-like arms freeze, and the chair releases me without touching another hair on my head. The second message makes me almost as happy as the first. It's official: I am who I am . . .

I have to cross the entire salon to get to the exit. I feel like the shiny gold finish on the walls is eyeing me. Floor arrows leading to another chair start to flash: a customer has finished; he enters the row I am in a few steps ahead of me. The man's back is to me. Suddenly, he spins around and gives me a strange look. I freeze, holding my breath. Finally, he turns around. I take a deep breath.

I find myself on the sidewalk behind the salon. Everyone comes rushing over: Keiji first, then Niro and Dulci, with good old Billiard and Gym bringing up the rear.

"Well?" Dulci asks. I shape my fingers into a proud zero.

"No way!" Niro exclaims. "It means the herbs really work. We found the cure!"

"*Yes!*" Billiard shouts enthusiastically.

"Good job, Rae!" Gym chimes in.

They lace their fingers together and invite me to climb onto a pretend throne. I play along, and they carry me down the street, causing a Toptown pedestrian or two to stop and stare.

Suddenly, a couple of blocks from the subway, a voice in my head yells: *Stop!*

The hostile voice is back in my head.

Stop!

Only now I know it's Alpha.

Go back!

He's never communicated with me telepathically from another location before.

I don't know why, but something tells me you need to turn back. Trust me.

I jump down from my friends' improvised throne.

"What's the matter, Rae?" Keiji asks.

I signal we have to go back.

"What?" Niro protests. "We have to get back to Underhome as soon as possible!"

I point insistently in the opposite direction.

"No way. The Rebels are about to launch their offensive against Loco. We have to let them know about the test results."

With that, the dorm division leader continues on his way. Everyone else follows him, except Keiji.

Now!

I risk passing for a crackpot and set off in the opposite direction.

"Are you sure?" Keiji asks, catching up with me.

I'm not. We pick up the pace, make a right turn and a left, retracing our steps to the hair salon. Suddenly, in the distance, an unmistakable curly top comes into sight. It's the woolly-minded old gal, as Arabella likes to call her. Lady Fluff! My heart skips a beat. Alpha was right! I immediately realize what I have to do. I rush over to her, with Keiji close behind.

"Well, hello there, crooked bangs! I'm on my way to the hairdresser's. Are you going, too?"

I shake my head.

"What do you mean, no? You already used your coupon? Well, it didn't do much good."

Oh yes, it did . . .

"That was the best Solid Gold Hairstyles could do? Well, it's really you, then! Although why anyone would want to be like that—everything all aslant—is beyond me!"

But that's precisely the point! Life for me is not like Toptown, perfectly flat and flavorless. Give me the ups and downs any day. I'm not afraid of them anymore.

"I see you've come with your pals today. Hello, kids!"

Niro and his cohorts have come rushing over.

"Good morning, Madam President of the Council," Billiard and Gym say in unison. I have no idea why they changed their minds.

"Well, aren't you in a good mood! I wish I could say the same. Here. You can have this back," says Lady Fluff, turning to me. "My health is fine, but my luck . . ."

She hands me the blessing card.

"You not have good luck?" Keiji asks.

"After years of dedicated service, they are going to strip me of my position as PTC. The MPs are going to put General Dusk in my place."

"Why?"

"He's provided formal proof that the populations from Below are a threat to Aboveworld. The global computer system had no choice but to take it into account. And since Toptowners by nature are afraid of anything that comes from the earth, he's playing into their fear and paranoia. The Agreements with Underhome have been canceled. It's only a matter of days before they close the turnstile. That said, after the Brigade's last bust . . ."

"What bust?"

"Three fighters from Below—foreigners—captured by a patrol unit. Apparently, there are hundreds more, an entire army poised to destroy Toptown. Given the circumstances, no wonder the MPs voted to keep the city safe."

"It's a lie!"

"Hmm . . . It's only natural for you to say that."

"Where are our friends?" Keiji blurts out, beside himself. "What have you done with them?"

"Oh! So, they are friends of yours to boot? I should have you arrested."

"The Seven are here from other place. True. But not to make war. On the contrary, to find key."

"What key?"

"The one to break boundaries down between Above and Below Worlds."

"Nobody in Toptown wants that to happen."

"And you find it unnatural for the Subs to rebel?" Niro cuts in, furious. "I'd like to see how you like living down there, buried alive."

"Calm down." Dulci attempts to quiet him, placing a hand on his arm.

"No, I will not calm down!" he answers, eyes ablaze. "We are not going to just stand by and let ourselves be gassed!" he shouts, rubbing his eyes as usual.

"Gassed?"

"Don't play dumb with me!" Niro exclaims. "You know perfectly well they used Repulsecure to exterminate our Infected."

"No such resolution was ever adopted by the Council. Bulbosis strikes indiscriminately. Our deputies even proposed admitting your most serious cases to our Center for the Infected to help further our own research. The treatments being tested there might give them a chance."

"No one ever told us about it," Dulci counters.

"You're lying!" Niro bursts out.

Billiard and Gym, at a total loss, shift awkwardly from one foot to the other.

"What if we provide new evidence in global computer system?" Keiji asks.

"That depends. The system will calculate the cost-profit ratio, and if it comes out positive, then yes, it will validate the data," Lady Fluff says.

"And the deputies will vote accordingly?" Keiji asks.

"Yes, they will."

"In that case, Madam President, it's in Toptown's best interests to work with the Subs."

"It is, is it? Really, now . . ."

"We know how to cure Bulbosis."

"Excuse me?"

"We discovered the cure."

"If that's some kind of a joke, young man, it's not funny."

Slowly, with a deliberately dramatic gesture, I remove the test results from my pocket and show them to her.

"What!" Lady Fluff reads the results several times over. "That's incredible! The Bulbosis index has always fluctuated without anyone knowing why, but it has never dropped to zero percent. Unsurprisingly so: it would mean that you could be cured. And that's just what this means. You've been cured! Do you realize how important your discovery is? How did you do it?"

I triumphantly indicate my lips are sealed. Now it's her turn to beg for handouts!

"With your permission," Niro cuts in, "or without it, for that matter, the secret of the cure will remain in our hands. And our Infected will be the first to benefit from it."

"That little mute girl with the crooked bangs . . . I can't believe it. I would never have imagined . . ."

"Rae! Her name is Rae," Niro corrects her, with newfound respect for me.

"And she discovered how disease is transmitted," Keiji adds.

I had suspected it for some time, but I was waiting for the test results to confirm it. I point to her bag, she opens it, and I take out a packet and hold it up. I was the only one of the Seven to have tried their miracle powder. Turns out Helen had been right to warn me . . .

"Are you serious? You get sick from eating?"

I nod.

"That's impossible. The powders were developed in our nutrition laboratory under the direction of our best researchers, ultrapowerful robots. The packets meet all of our dietary needs."

"And affect moods," Keiji says. "Red, for example, is good for running a marathon."

"The light blue makes you talkative," Niro continues. "Purple make you feel like you're floating, and orange . . . uh, I wouldn't recommend it if you don't have a partner!"

I think back to the lovebirds on the platform of Toptown subway.

"The green one," Keiji continues, "make you feel safe. Indigo blue gives you a feeling of power."

"How do you know? You haven't tried them."

"That's true, Niro. But the packet colors are the colors of the chakras."

"Of what?"

"Never mind. Where we from, the powder you eat is drugs. It's a chemical invention of the modern world that makes you sick. And can even kill you."

Lady Fluff looks completely lost.

"Less than two hours from now, Madam President," Keiji

adds with his usual composure, "Underhome leader will deliver monthly speech. Less than two hours from now, Loco will topple for not saving Infected, for selling girls. The Rebels will assume power, and it will be possible to cooperate for cure, to heal all sick in Aboveworld. Less than two hours from now, you will be able to choose. To write history or not. Up to you."

"In exchange for what?"

"Open borders, new peace agreements. And one more thing, you will have to get used to loving what comes from earth. Because the cure comes from there . . ."

"I . . ."

"And naturally, the prisoners will be released. In less than two hours from now, Madam President. Are you with us or not?"

Later, Niro leads the way as we race through the tunnels toward the handcars. I know now the Faraways and the Subs will stand together as one. I also know nobody could have spoken better than Keiji: he won over Lady Fluff and honored Master Shishō's lessons. Aiko would be proud of him.

The Mime brothers, who joined us at the turnstile, are toward the back of the pack. Juan is painfully thin. He is sweating profusely: his T-shirt is soaking wet. He looks like he's about to collapse.

Please don't let them notice anything . . . Please . . .

Huh? I can hear Juan's voice inside my head as we hurry along!

El Padre will be proud of us, proud of us . . . Loco said so . . .

I perk up my ears at the mention of the leader's name.

We will be given a hero's welcome, applauded for our collaboration. When it's all over, we'll be rid of the Tubeans. We'll get to return home. El Padre will take us back, life will be good . . .

I'm floored. I can hardly believe my ears. I refuse to believe it.

The gas is painless. Esteban is right, it is the only way to stop the disease. There are too many Infected . . . The only way . . .

No! Not *Repulsecure!*

We chose sides with the Faithful. Thanks to us, our clan is safe.

So, it was the Mime brothers who betrayed us? I stop dead in my tracks.

"What's wrong, Rae?"

A distressed look at the Mime brothers tells Keiji what I'm thinking. Niro catches on straightaway. Seized by a wild impulse, he throws himself at Juan and starts pounding away.

"Double-crossers! Traitors!"

Little Esteban lets out a roar and charges his brother's tormentor with his claws out. Fighting and scratching, he wrestles in vain. Niro's blows continue to rain thick and fast. Curled up in a ball, Juan Mime bleats like a terrified calf.

"Ow! Ouch! Ouch!"

"Stop, Niro!" Dulci exclaims. "It'll do no good."

With a snap of her fingers, she unleashes Billiard and Gym, who rush over to the trio and eventually manage to pull Niro off Juan and Esteban off Niro.

"So, it was you!" Niro shouts. "You were with me when I caught them in Aboveworld. I thought the Faraways were the traitors, but it was the two of you, you dirty finks! You went to Loco and snitched, didn't you, Juan?" Still reeling from the blows, he shakes his head no.

"And last night," Keiji adds, "Blanky slept badly in bunk below you, not because you were moving and talking in sleep, but because you watch us. Why you give us up? What reason?"

"Loco said that you . . . were dangerous. If we wanted to protect our clan, we had to spy on you and report everything to him, he said. In exchange, we could join the Faithful."

"Loco is a scumbag! Do you know what he does with our sisters?"

If it weren't for sweet Dulci's hand gently staying his, Niro would be throttling him again.

"Hmm," Keiji muses. "You were ones who also knock out Arabella. First, trap set by Brigade to overcome Seven. The plan made before, Loco need help . . . Who is contact in Aboveworld?"

Esteban's face spits into a repulsive grin, showing his true colors. He may be the younger, but he's a tough customer.

"Out with it, Juan!" Niro shakes the elder Mime brother, clearly the weakest link.

"Keep your mouth shut, Juan!" Esteban rejoins. "Not a word!"

"Uhh . . . uhrr . . ."

Keiji, in the meantime, is rifling through Juan's pockets. He takes out a small red notebook.

"Froggie's letter said something about red notebook that belong to Loco!"

He opens it at once. On the first page is the code Siana's mother had memorized. On the others, more dates and numbers.

"Wait a second!" Niro exclaims. "Those dates . . . They correspond to the days when . . . Shit!"

"What?"

"It's the date they gassed the Infected in Station 22. Repulsecure had been used in the twenty-third and twenty-fourth stations, too, but those times, only a few people were killed. We could never figure out how the Brigade knew about them. And look, these numbers look like geographical coordinates."

"That means that Loco . . ."

All eyes are on the two scoundrels. Juan Mime realizes the game is up. There's no way out. He cracks.

"We needed to find a way to eradicate Bulbosis . . ."

"Shut up!" Esteban shouts.

"We . . . We were in charge of passing information between Loco and . . ."

"And who?" Niro threatens him with a clenched fist.

"And General Dusk! Our leader told him where we confined our Infected so the Brigade could do the dirty work and he could keep his hands clean."

"The bastard! Why?"

"One wants to rule Aboveworld, the other wants to rule Below," Juan explains.

"Loco is already the leader of Underhome," Niro contests.

"The slave, you mean!" Juan retorts. "I'm tired of feeding vermin. With the extra packets provided by General Dusk, we won't have to work anymore. And no more Harvests!"

"He did all that for . . . *more packets*?" Keiji exclaims in disbelief. "I'm beginning to understand: the program built on seven evils of humanity. The first one is the sin of gluttony, called overabundance by Keeper Master."

"It doesn't add up," intervenes Dulci. "If the packets cause Bulbosis, why didn't Loco catch it? He and the Prowlers gobble up tons of the stuff."

"You're right," Niro admits. "We all get our nourishment from the packets. Children don't catch the disease, which could be explained by their low hormone levels prior to puberty. But what about adults? Some people never reach the hundred percent index and develop active cases. Other people do."

"Well, our bodies don't all react the same way," Billiard attempts to explain. "Take me, for example. I don't consume any more packets than you, but I'm fatter."

"He's got a point," Dulci says.

"There has to be more to it than that."

"I agree with you, Niro." Keiji concurs. "Wait! Look at code ROO6Y5G3B4I9P8 in red notebook."

"And?"

"Seven capital letters, seven numbers . . . It can't be a coincidence. The seven chakras . . ."

"I don't follow."

"That's it!" Keiji shouts. "That's it! Seven colors of packets. Zero for red. The Loco only eats red one because he knows there is zero inside!"

"Zero what?"

"Zero Bulbosis!"

"You mean to say that . . ."

"The leader of Underhome devised color code with General Dusk. He must have access to Toptown culinary laboratory. The disease was injected in packets with different concentration level: zero to nine."

"Look!" Dulci exclaims. "Red: zero. Orange: six. Yellow: five. Green: three. Blue: four. Indigo: nine. Purple: eight. That's why the Prowlers never get sick. They only eat red packets like Loco!"

"And why some get sick with Bulbosis and other people don't. It's a question of taste and color. But what's in it for Dusk?" Niro asks.

"To keep the worlds Above and Below divided for good and to rise to power. General Dusk wants to be the president of Toptown Council. As soon as the turnstile closes, the contagion rate will drop as if by chance. It will prove the illness was spread by the Subs."

"And the robot-MPs will elect him as Council president, whereas the contaminated packets are behind the epidemic!"

"A diabolical plan! If it weren't for the Faraways, no one would have ever known . . . ," Gym points out.

"Yeah, Loco didn't count on seven muckrakers showing up!" Esteban spews.

"Underhome's leader . . . He never intended to free the Subs. The Great Rebellion was just smoke and mirrors . . ." The words struggle to come out of Dulci's mouth; she is flabbergasted. Niro gently brushes her cheek with a hand.

I take the opportunity to reveal another important message: I put my hands to my throat and pretend to be choking. Successfully so, considering little Esteban's jealous grimace.

"You mean *Repulsecure*?" Keiji guesses.

I nod quickly several times: the situation is urgent. This time, Billiard loses it. At the mere sight of the massive Rover rushing toward him, Juan spills the beans.

"Wait! The Great Rebellion is not a lie ..."

"What are you talking about?" Keiji asks.

"An uprising is in the works, but not against the Owls—against the Subs ..."

"What?" Keiji says.

"Loco wants to purge the ranks, to give Underhome to the fittest: the Prowlers and their descendants, and a few clans of Faithful. The others are unworthy."

"That's genocide!" Dulci bursts out, horrified.

"That is key. Stop Loco is our mission!" Keiji exclaims, taking hold of my shoulders.

"When?" Niro roars, eyes ablaze.

"It's too late," Juan answers, his voice breaking with emotion.

"Idiot!" Esteban screams. "You're going to ruin everything."

"When? Tell me when!" Niro demands.

"I can't ... My clan ... I did it for my clan ..." Juan says.

"Are you *kidding*?" Dulci explodes. "Do you actually believe Loco will keep his word? Once he's eliminated the majority of the Subs, he'll have no use for you. You'll be exterminated in turn."

"Hold your tongue, Juan! Or El Padre will make you eat it!"

"Stop it, Esteban. It's all over ...," Juan says.

"How much time do we have?" Niro thunders.

"Less than ... Less than an hour ...," Juan repeats.

"What?" Niro demands.

"Loco always gives his monthly speech from above, on the Ledge, with all of Underhome gathered in the Pit. The Faithful will be safely assembled in Deepwood. The Prowlers, too. Few know the true nature of the Great Rebellion . . . That a painless death is planned for their families and friends. Everyone will blame the Brigade, since they will see them releasing the gas. Loco promised the gas is painless. It's painless . . ."

This time, we have to restrain Niro.

"Less than an hour," Dulci stammers. "We have less than an hour!"

"No matter how fast we move, we'll never make it in time," Billiard says.

"And anyhow, we'll never get past the Prowlers. No one is allowed near the Ledge during Loco's speech," Gym adds, clearly distressed.

"There aren't enough Rebels to attack on both fronts. Loco and the Brigade. And we still don't know how those bastards get into Underworld, Slymouth Gate or no!" Niro cuts in, regaining his composure.

"We don't know how Brigade get in. But we know where find Brigade!" Keiji says, his eyes flashing. "Many patrols in subway. And probably units on High Express platform where they battle with us, hoping four of the Seven return there . . ."

"So, you're saying we just walk up to them and say, 'Hi, guys, we're here!' Then, we give them a rap on the knuckles and tell them it's naughty to gas innocent people. Especially since we're not responsible for Bulbosis!" Niro says.

"I know. We cannot take on Brigade. But I know some who can," Keiji replies.

"Who?"

"Ruthless army. One very happy to eat some Owls if we show them the way."

"An army?" Dulci asks, confused.

"Not very commendable and in quite sorry state, but army all the same. Don't you see?" Keiji asks.

Four pairs of eyes widen. And four voices ring out in unison: "The Noctos!"

49

"My fellow subs!"

Loco's voice rings out over the loudspeaker as our cart enters the tunnel to Deepwood. His speech is beginning.

"My fellow companions!"

"Traitor!" Niro spits as our cart pulls over. "How dare you use the word 'companions'!"

The enormous dormitory is packed. A good number of clans have gathered with the Rovers. Men, women, and children. The clans of the Faithful. Are they in on Loco's diabolical plan? Are they aware of the fate reserved for the Subs in the Pit? It is sobering to think that, even here, in a city belowground, a privileged few tower over the masses. The Keeper was right. Yes, history always repeats itself.

"This day will forever live in the memories of our people: the Great Rebellion is underway!"

Keiji and Niro exit the cart with a simultaneous leap, followed by Dulci and me. Billiard and Gym have set off on another mission: lure the Noctos into Toptown subway. I still can't believe they volunteered. The Noctos were lurking near the entrance to Aboveworld when we last encountered them.

A Nocto incursion into Toptown will surely wreak havoc and keep the Brigade busy for a while!

Dulci told me Billiard is an outstanding driver. I hope she's right. The Subs' future is literally in the driver's seat with him. The Mime brothers', too. Letting them loose was out of the question. So, we put them into the handcar with Billiard and Gym and clamped down their harnesses. Even Esteban looked a little uneasy when he realized they'd be used as bait.

"Hurry!" Niro says. "We have to warn the Rebels in case the Brigade gets through. The population needs to be kept out of range of the gas."

In case they get through . . . I shudder at the thought. It would mean the mutants never reached their destination— and neither did Billiard and Gym.

Navigating the crowd is no easy task. People are packed in like sardines. Nobody wants to give up their spot near the Ledge, like Loco was some sort of a rock star.

"The Owls took away our freedom. It's time for payback!"

Our small size comes in handy as we weave our way through the crowd, keeping an eye out for the Rebels all the while. The enormous Ledge overhanging Underhome is not far now. The place is swarming, but a wall of bodyguards separates Loco from the crowd. I recognize some of the Prowlers and Dione in charge of operations. More impressive than ever, the accordion-monster is giving silent orders with a simple movement of the chin.

"Soon the gate will open, and our children will breathe the fresh air!"

The crowd cheers wildly, applauding and throwing their hands into the air. A short distance ahead of us, I spot a shock of raven-black hair beneath a hat with a pom-pom and a colorful scarf. It's Chayton. Even from behind, I can tell he's watching like a hawk. At the front of the crowd, opposite the bodyguards, he's taking in every little detail, waiting for the Rebels' signal to attack. Alpha is nearby, ensconced in a chunky-knit sweater. A natural chameleon.

"But first, let it be known, there are traitors among us. The four wanted Faraways are being tipped off, though we all know the fate I reserve for them!"

A group of girls wearing lace domino masks and multi-colored wrappers appears out of nowhere, ready to be delivered to the leader. They hold hands and walk onto the Ledge with bowed heads and small, unsteady steps. A Prowler behind them unceremoniously shoves one of the girls in the shoulder. The entire row stumbles. A disheveled head of faded-green hair stands out among them. It's the girls from the White Train!

"I'm going to ask you one last time. Which of you betrayed me? I know it's one of you!"

No one answers. Froggie looks up, her distinctive eyes ringed with dark circles visible behind her mask. Chayton, on guard, glances left and right as Alpha draws closer and stands shoulder to shoulder with him. Keiji and Niro are nearly level with them as well.

"Very well. You asked for it!" Loco bellows.

He downs a red packet, then grabs randomly at one girl's hair.

"Ow! It's—it's not me," she stammers. "I haven't done anything."

"Who is it?" the hateful voice booms over the loudspeaker.

"I don't know . . ."

With his bristly Mohawk, needle-studded ears, and biceps as taut as a bow, Loco is all sting. He puts down the megaphone and drags the girl to the edge of the Ledge. The young girl lets out a terrified scream, her nails scratching wildly at his bare chest as she struggles to break free—although blood doesn't show against the dark-red color of his skin.

Furious, Loco lifts her into the air and dangles her over the precipice. He is going to throw her into the Pit!

"The traitor is Loco!"

Someone has gotten hold of the loudspeaker.

"Loco and the Tubeans are trafficking teenage girls!"

It's Froggie! She removes her lace domino mask with a proud gesture.

"The law of anonymity is only meant to hide an ugly truth. Prowlers, some of these girls are both your daughters and the mothers of your children!"

A horrified cry rises up from the crowd. The sickening revelation is met with booing and insults.

"You!" A warlike scream rips through the air.

Loco sets down his captive, who takes off running, and hurls himself at Froggie. The impact is brutal. Froggie and the loudspeaker fall to the ground. Mad with rage, Loco raises an arm, hits her in the face, and starts to strangle her.

"No!" Chayton roars, throwing himself at two Prowlers blocking his way.

Taking out the first with a headbutt and the second with a powerful blow, he breaks through the ranks and rushes onto the Ledge with Dione hot on his heels. Alpha, joined by Keiji and Niro, covers his back as the Rebels brandish their makeshift weapons and launch the assault.

All hell breaks loose. The clans scatter like chickens. I get knocked down in the rush and lose sight of Chayton. The battle around me is going full swing. I spot Dulci pulling the hair of a Prowler while Niro pummels away at him. Arabella, too, has appeared on the scene decked out in bright knitwear, followed by Valjean Rabbit with his distinctive limp. Both are seasoned fighters, but it looks like the bench-woman's heart isn't in it. She seems to be dodging her fellow Prowlers' blows instead of trying to land them. Some of the Prowlers are hesitant, too, confused by the events and Froggie's announcement.

I do my best to drag myself onto the Ledge. The sight before my eyes is terrifying: Chayton is grappling with Loco and

Dione, and he is badly hurt. His cheek is bleeding, and there's a gaping cut on his thigh. The accordion-monster is restraining him with his enormous paws as Loco clobbers him. The blows rain thick and fast. Hard and brutal—an outpouring of hatred.

"Let go of him!" Alpha shouts at the top of his voice.

He throws himself at Dione with a double *yama tsuki*, an upward elbow *jodan* strike to the face, and a *gedan* blow to his legs. Keiji taught us the Japanese karate terms for the different areas of the body. The accordion-monster releases Chayton and spins round to take on Alpha. Chayton, half stunned, drops to the ground not far from Froggie, who is out cold.

"Rae," he says, begging me to help her.

I rush to Froggie's side and shake her by the shoulders. No reaction. Chayton's feverish eyes ask the unthinkable: "Is she dead?" But Loco isn't done with him. Kicking savagely, he sets upon Chayton, who is lying helplessly on the ground. I don't know what to do. My hands reach for Froggie's cheeks, patting them distractedly as if it would make it all stop, as if getting her to open her eyes would help Chayton recover his strength.

"Rhaaaa!"

A furious scream escapes Froggie's lips. The change is so sudden, I'm not sure what happened. A moment before, Froggie was unconscious. Now, she is charging the leader of Underhome. The two of them roll onto the ground.

"N-no . . . ," Chayton lets out, struggling to lift his head, on the verge of passing out.

Froggie is no match for Loco, who easily overpowers her.

"How dare you!"

We watch in horror as Loco drags Froggie to the edge of the precipice. The Subs, too, in the Pit below, witness the scene in a daze.

"You're through, Loco!" Froggie shouts. "This is *the end*!"

"The end?" he repeats. "I'm through?" The sound of his hideous, uninterrupted laughter carries into the valley below.

The laughter of a madman. "On the contrary, it's only the beginning, you fool!"

Suddenly, in the distance, tendrils of yellow smoke start to curl up from the ground.

No, not that! *Repulsecure!*

"R-Rae . . . ," Chayton stammers, barely able to lift his arm. "The loudspeaker . . ."

The loudspeaker, of course! I rush to grab it. To warn the Subs. To warn Siana, Blanky, Nira, and the others. Down there, somewhere. Froggie is still struggling to free herself from Loco's clutches.

"Hahaha!" the madman howls with laughter, twisting her arm.

I seize the loudspeaker and bring it to my mouth. I want to scream at the top of my lungs: "Get out of there! Run! They're gassing you! Loco is going to kill you!" But nothing comes out . . .

"Good try, Mute Girl!" Loco sniggers. "But it's too late!"

Dense fumes are steadily rising from the back of the crowd, submerging the Subs' feet and then knees in a poisonous wave.

"Murderer!"

A hand snatches the loudspeaker out of my hand. A voice rings out over Underhome.

"Loco is a murderer."

The voice of truth is Arabella's.

"He killed Bamboo! He gassed the Infected, and you are next on the list!"

Loco is consumed with rage. His eyes pop out of his head as he lifts Froggie and holds her over the precipice. No! He is going to let go. She's going to fall to her death!

"They're spraying Repulsecure! Get out of there!"

Arabella's words throw the Pit into a panic. People everywhere are screaming, shoving, and falling over each other.

They rush in every direction, stirring up the fumes. The wave of Repulsecure is spreading fast.

"Climb onto the caratrams! Get on the rooftops! Fast!"

Some of the children are already coughing, clutching at their throats. They can't breathe . . . Horrified by the sight below, Arabella pays no attention to Loco. He is about to let go of Froggie! I fly at him instinctively as if I have wings. Like Blue, the parakeet. The Shepherd's combat lessons come back in a flash. I know I can do it. I'm going to stop him, Underhome leader or no. Or at least slow him down and buy more time.

Except Froggie has something else in mind. She sees me coming out of the corner of her eye, and looking at me and then Chayton, whose thigh is bleeding badly, she gives a victorious smile—a smile I will never forget.

"Our daughter will have a different life!" she tells her tormentor.

Our *daughter*? The enormous mole under Loco's outstretched arm, visible in the hollow of his armpit, suddenly jumps out at me.

Closing her eyes, Froggie grabs hold of Loco with both hands and plants her feet firmly on the edge of the precipice. Then, pushing off with her legs and arching her back, she topples into the void, taking along with her the man responsible for the Subs' misfortune. And her own. Never for a minute could the leader have imagined coming to such an end. Never could he have believed Froggie capable of destroying him. That they would go down together. Loco and Froggie, Froggie and Loco. It's inconceivable. The leader of Underhome and the mother of his daughter. The mother of their daughter. Siana . . .

A scream echoes through the Pit as they crash to the ground. Most of the Prowlers are baffled by the situation. The hostilities against the Rebels have ceased on the Ledge.

Arabella puts down the loudspeaker, overcome by the sight of the disaster below.

The silence is terrible. I don't dare look. Chayton is losing blood fast. Alpha helps me apply pressure to the wound and wraps Chayton's colorful scarf around his thigh.

"My sweet—Froggie—" Chayton stammers, half delirious.

We look away from the place where the bodies hit the ground. Froggie would not have wanted that ghastly image to erase the memory of her victorious smile. I know I couldn't stand it; neither could Chayton. We are witnessing another massacre, but, this time, the victims are our friends.

Not a sound comes from the Pit. The Seven have failed. We contributed to the demise of the Subs ... The rest is all a jumble—in my head, my stomach, and all around. The Rovers take some Prowlers prisoner. Others learn the truth about Loco; they seem sincerely sorry and cooperate. Dione is led to the exit of Deepwood, no doubt to be interrogated. Various clans are questioned, but I trust they'll play dumb.

Meanwhile, hands form a makeshift stretcher for Chayton, Keiji's arm goes around my shoulders—he and Niro are helping me walk—Arabella's voice responds to Alpha's, and the images all run together. I have no idea how we get to Valjean's caratram. Only once I am settled on a large ball of yarn do I start to come around.

The gutted pom-poms hang inert from the ceiling. Empty cocoons. Sad reminders of the lives lost today. I give in to an irrational impulse and start to count them: *One, two, three ... One hundred, one hundred and one, one hundred and two ...*

"Rae ..."

Five hundred and ten, five hundred and eleven, five hundred and twelve ...

"Rae ... are you okay?"

Someone is talking to me ... No, it's impossible ...

"Rae, hello? Are you there?"

I blink hard. Am I dreaming?

"She's there and she isn't," Blanky whispers to Siana. "Do you think she can hear us?"

"I don't know. Maybe she got hit on the head."

"We've been trying to bring her around for half an hour. Do you think we should tell Arabella?"

That's when it clicks. They are alive! I have no idea how, but Blanky and Siana are alive! I jump up from my pumpkin-like yarn ball and throw my arms around them.

"Hurray! She's back! Rae's back!" Blanky's relief is audible.

Siana smiles at me. Her chest is no longer compressed by strips of fabric. She undoes her scarf, and I see that the boil on her neck has disappeared.

"Thank you" is all she says.

Now, she is the one who wraps her arms around me. For a very long time.

"You look like Lil' Buccaneer the day Mama Crat brought him to my cubby," Blanky says. "Completely lost!"

"Of course she's lost. She doesn't know."

"True. You were out of commission for quite a while."

"Come here. We'll show you."

Siana grabs my hand, and the three of us climb onto the roof of the Valjean Rabbit's pink caratram. The underground city decorated with strings of lights spreads before us. The sculpted wooden oars, the patchwork quilts, the huts, and the cardboard houses: it's all there. And the Subs are there, too! Safe and sound. They are going about their business, alive and kicking! Bubbling with excitement, even. A cry of joy resonates inside of me.

"The gas sprayed by the Brigade was yellow," Siana says. "Yellow! Doesn't that ring a bell?"

Yellow . . . yellow . . . yellow! Of course!

"I see you get it. Repulsecure is green. The yellow gas just put us to sleep for a while. We woke up just in time for the arrival of the president of Toptown Council and her delegation."

What? Lady Fluff?

"That friend of yours is a sly old fox!" Blanky says. "She made sure the toxic gas was replaced by the sleep-inducing gas. She outsmarted General Dusk. He's been arrested and is going to stand trial. The nutrition lab technician he bribed confessed to lacing the packets with Bulbosis according to a color code. Clean batches are already being manufactured."

"And you missed the best speech we ever heard," Siana continues. "The president and Valjean the Rabbit shook hands on the Ledge. Valjean declared he would represent Underhome until proper elections were held, eyeballing Arabella all the while. He said he was too old, too damaged. Above and Below signed a peace agreement: open borders in exchange for the cure. The plants in Hartsquare Lake grow so quickly, we'll be able to mass-produce the remedy, but the formula will remain our secret. There is talk of studying the crats, too. Maybe their feeding habits could help us find a new food source."

"We'll have plenty to eat now! And the crats will be protected. We need them to pollinate the plants. Everything has been turned upside down!"

Who are the mice and who are the men?

The words on the copy of *Of Mice and Men* lent to me by Kassandra come to mind, echoing the crats' reversal of fortunes. The parallel between Chayton and Lennie, the novel's simpleminded giant, also strikes a chord. And I could easily play the part of the small, quick-witted George who takes Lennie under his wing. We, too, have become friends over the course of our journey, dreaming of freedom and of a piece of land for the Subs. I'll be able to return his book to its owner when we return to the farm.

"The PTC has ordered the release of your friends. They are on their way here right now. Yippee!"

Blanky does a little tap-dance number on the roof of the caratram.

"The Tubeans sensed the tides were turning. They bribed a Brigade officer and made their escape. They're rich from all the Rovers' bartered goods. They were the first to move back to Toptown. They bolted like rabbits."

"Serious, Siana? Like *rabbits*?"

The three of us dissolve into rocking, tear-inducing laughter.

"You know what else," Siana eventually manages to say, "Billiard and Gym made it back without a scratch. The Mime brothers, too."

"Yeah! They drew the Noctos to them like flies to honey. Their car almost flipped over a couple of times, but Billiard is a darn good driver: he lured them onto the High Express platform, all right! Apparently, they caused quite a mess!" Blanky is jumping up and down with excitement.

"It turns out no Owls were seriously injured," Siana goes on with her usual composure. "The Brigade took care of the mutants, but a few of General Dusk's goons had already left for Underhome with the sleeping gas. There aren't too many of them. They'll be standing trial, too."

"You know what else? Slymouth Gate really does exist!" Blanky exclaims.

"Naturally, in a place on the map where Loco said they'd found nothing," Siana says. "The gate is simply a locked door, and General Dusk had the only key. The whole lost-key business was just meant to muddy the waters."

"Anyhow, the Toptown Brigade blew it up. Boom! They have family members dying of Bulbosis, too. They'd do anything to get the cure," Blanky says.

It's too much. Too much information to digest—especially since my stomach is in knots.

So, the three of us sit down on the overturned caratram's

roof along the edge, legs dangling through an open window. From where we are sitting, we can see all of Underhome. Side by side, we take in the hustle and bustle. People everywhere are taking clothes down from clotheslines and putting them on in layers, folding blankets into bundles and makeshift bags. We breathe it all in . . .

Some Subs have decided to move to Aboveworld, to live in the open air. Children's voices will at last be heard there. The rest will remain in Underhome. It is their home, after all. Perhaps they will go up to Toptown every now and then. What matters is they have a choice.

No one says a word. We know it will be time for goodbyes soon. For everyone.

*

In the next hour, we are joined by the others in the hot-pink boxcar. First Valjean, along with a few of the Rebels, Arabella, Alpha, and Keiji. We form a circle on the pumpkin-size balls of yarn like we are going to smoke a peace pipe. Our watches will go off soon. Next, Niro, Dulci, Billiard, and Gym hop through the ceiling window, one after the other. They make quite a racket, strutting and laughing, and giving friendly high fives to Blanky and Rags—now called Siana. We don't need to worry about them anymore. They've found a family.

"What about Chayton?" Keiji asks Valjean.

"My friend the Doc says he'll be fine. The bleeding has stopped. There was no need to amputate," Valjean says, brushing it off like it was a little boo-boo.

The news doesn't reassure us. On the contrary.

"I didn't know there was a doctor here."

"Doctor? Who said anything about a doctor? Doc got that nickname back in the day when we still lived on the street!"

"What!" Keiji exclaims.

"It's true. He had this thing about medical equipment. Masks, gloves, expired medications . . . He'd collect anything he could pull out of the garbage!"

"Right," Alpha cuts in.

We are seriously worried now.

"We'd like to see Chayton. Where is he?"

"He's on his way. Doc and his team have packed him up nicely."

Suddenly, Nira jumps into the caratram. What a difference! No longer a sex object, she has traded her gauzy wrappers for a black turtleneck and a pair of pants. Her identity shines through. Her inner strength.

"Hey, everyone!" she says with a swish of a long platinumblond ponytail.

She looks amazing. Niro's eyes shine with admiration and pride. He loves his big sister.

"I brought you a surprise."

As if by magic, Ali, Helen, and Stepan appear! We all fall into each other's arms to the applause of the audience. Even Helen and I hug. Curiously, few words are exchanged. It's as if we don't quite realize what is happening. Not yet.

Then Doc and his team lower Chayton through the window. His leg is effectively wrapped with cellophane—like an enormous ham shank. He says he's fine, but it's not the nasty wound on his thigh or the cut on his cheek I'm worried about, though it will undoubtedly leave a nice battle scar. It's the invisible wounds. The wounds that will mark all of us and no doubt take a long time to heal.

"Do you see these, Chayton?" Valjean asks, pulling up his sleeve.

His forearm is covered with strands of silk in a rainbow of colors.

"Each of these threads comes from a cocoon, reminders that a tiny broken thread is all it takes for us to lose our homes."

Valjean takes off a red one and ties it around Chayton's wrist. Red, Chayton's color. The color of the root chakra.

"There is a central thread running through every life. The thread we use to weave our web. You discovered yours in Underhome, Chayton."

A parade of people descends on the caratram. Everyone wants to pay their respects to the Faraways. And to say good-bye to their old life, too.

"Hey, you!" Niro calls out to Helen over the din. "Didn't you promise we'd never have anything to do with you again?"

"Yes," she replies in faltering tones.

"Well, what if we've changed our minds?"

Broad smiles spread across the faces of Niro, Dulci, and the rest of the gang; Blanky and Siana have joined their ranks. Niro and Nira will make good leaders for Deepwood. The Rovers will transport the plants to Aboveworld, and the Prowlers will look after the harvest. The walls have come down. The New Agreements have made Underhome a city in its own right. Soon, it will have a president of its own. Arabella, perhaps?

I am watching Siana out of the corner of my eye. The girl we used to call the flower seller. Siana was our common thread. The first to let us enter their world, to open her heart. I think I learned more from her than from any of the others. She taught me the lesson of the pupae and the butterfly.

Our watches start to ring. Chayton, on the floor next to me, reaches for my arm. He is looking at Siana, too. I lean in toward him, and he whispers in my ear.

"How can you tell a child that the woman who gave birth to her and abandoned her also did everything in her power to protect her? That the mother she never knew has just died? That she killed her father because he was a threat to them all? How do we tell her that?"

Our eyes meet. The answer is clear: we don't. I catch sight of the shelves with the habitats lining the walls of the cara-tram. Cocoons cling to the branches inside. White forms wig-gle in the bed of leaves. Silkworms!

New tenants have taken possession of the premises. Yes. Life really does go on . . .

LOGBOOK
INSTRUCTOR: KA
END OF SEASON I

They did it.

The Seven have left their mark. They have changed the course of events in the Worlds Above and Below. Their bodies seem to have responded well to the extended simulation period. The level of physical exertion has taken a lot out of them, of course, and it will take time for their brains to adjust to being back in the real world, but we were expecting that. It should not be a problem.

The limits the program's security shield has in protecting them from calculated injuries is more problematic, however. Head Instructor Shepherd came close to unplugging the Seven Chosen on several occasions. Too many simulations exposing them to bodily harm were potentially life-threatening. The issue requires further clarification. The program will need to set new parameters before the Seven enter Mantra 2.

Like the murals on the walls of Underhome, their story will leave a mark. Spirit Era's audience has increased tenfold since the first livestream was aired. The viewers are crazy about the quest. The Keeper's virtual-spiritual program went viral in less than a week. The seven lost keys of the chakras have unleashed passions. Even people who do not believe in the end-of-the-world prophecy are dying to discover the second season. Their interest in the Seven and their quest is a step in the right direction.

Moreover, the media's growing interest in the homeless is starting to have repercussions. Social media influencers are posting information about individual and collective rehabilitation initiatives and are setting the example by reaching out to marginalized populations. Citizen accommodation programs are flourishing. Aside from questions of housing, the root chakra's symbolic value has called into question our relationship with the environment. Our children need to be taught that nature is sacred. Only then can we be certain it will never be neglected. Only then will we realize that our well-being depends on the proper management of the planet. There is renewed interest in agricultural cooperatives, permaculture, and agroecology, and funds are being raised to finance concrete initiatives. A start-up company has launched a line of medicinal plants to replace traditional bouquets of flowers: valerian, to relieve anxiety, aloe vera to heal wounds.

Additionally, people in the real world are questioning the legitimacy of borders. The apocalypse predicted for July 27, 2037, will affect us all. To prevent it, we need to nurture the physical roots of Materia—the natural world—and foster a culture that is respectful of the planet and all living beings. But we also need to reconnect with the invisible roots of Spiritua by resetting the moral compass of humanity.

This is the true purpose of Spirit Era: to provide keys for preserving the planet, to allow us to be at one with our surroundings and with our fellow living beings. And to be at one with ourselves.

EPILOGUE

"But what about the key to the first chakra?"

Chayton stares blankly at his gimpy leg. He was moved to his room as soon as we got back to Flyfold, to be nursed back to health. It turns out Doc's team didn't do such a bad job in Underhome: the wound on his thigh was clean; it didn't even need stitches.

"We were supposed to bring back a key, weren't we?" Chayton sighs.

A fresh breeze blows in through the half-open skylight. The herbs and seeds he brought back from Hartsquare Lake are on his bedside table. They were in his pocket and inadvertently became his item-clue. He cups a few seeds in the palm of a hand and gently shakes them.

Earlier that morning, Kassandra called us to his bedside. It was funny to see her again. The program's simulated reality was so intense, it felt like we had always lived there. Right now, our hearts and minds are filled with our friends from Underhome and have room for nothing else. Our former lives seem like a distant reality.

"The key," Keiji says, "is to open borders between Above and Below. We succeeded in mission: to prevent genocide."

After the double connection—four hours in real time but many more on an emotional level—we had retired to our rooms without touching the copious meals prepared by Mr. Mann, although we were thirsty and hungry. We had neither the energy nor the desire to talk. No doubt to preserve the sounds of our friends' voices a little longer. Friends we already miss. Friends we would never see again and who supposedly didn't exist, though they were our entire world for seven days that felt like a year. Ultimately, grief is the unexpected side effect of immersion. But it's a doozy.

"I don't think it's that simple," Alpha disagrees. "So, just imagine how the viewers feel! What did they take away from season one? If the program's goal really is to increase awareness and bring about change, then things need clearing up a little. What, exactly, is the key, in concrete terms? Is it the key to Slymouth Gate? But that key is useless now because the borders are open. Besides, it was just another invention. Is it the key to understanding Bulbosis? We found the cure, but it has no bearing on our life here. Is it the New Agreements between Toptown and Underhome? They hold the key to all of those things now. It just doesn't sit right with me. It feels like something is missing."

"For starters," Ka softly remarks, "you led the Subs into the light, literally and figuratively. You shed light on people who were condemned to living in the dark."

"Leading the Subs out of Underhome is not the key," Ali says. "We knew from the beginning they wanted to live in Aboveworld, and that everything we did there was broadcast live."

She seems a little distracted, as if she's not altogether there. Just like Helen and Stepan. Earlier, when she had dropped by my room, she told me they were heavily sedated while in custody. A blur of images, unreal noises, and machinelike voices is all she can remember.

"You're right, Ali," Ka admits. "But remember, each of the Seven embodies a chakra. Therefore, you know where to find the first chakra's key."

All eyes naturally turn to Chayton. But our friend with an uber-developed root chakra—driven by material pleasures, wealth, and food and sex galore—is no longer the same. Though the narrative of Mantra 1 may have been built on the vice of gluttony, the custodian of the first chakra seems beyond all that now.

"Chayton," Kassandra calls to him.

Chayton is tipping the seeds from one hand to the other like the sands of an hourglass. As if he could turn back the clock. He is elsewhere, and I know where. He's with his beloved Froggie.

"The friends we made there, and the Subs and the Owls . . . if their lives continue even when we're no longer connected, how can Spirit Era be virtual?" Helen asks.

"It is virtual, and it isn't," Ka answers. "Real-time video gameplay allows other players to continue their quest when you shut off your computer. They score points and interact. Environments continue to evolve whether you are present or not. In the program, Spirit Era is the game master, and the ongoing independent evolution of each of the seven immersive worlds is driven by the algorithms it invented."

"We have little understanding of the myriad dimensions of existence . . ."

"Very true, Stepan."

"The stars are made of the same dust as everything else . . . and so are we . . . I am the seventh and most elevated chakra. I will not forget, even locked up in the world of Materia, that we can find freedom in Spiritua. Freedom is in our minds."

"In a way," Kassandra continues, "we are both here and else-where. We exist in the past and the present, and the future . . ."

Our mentor's words float through the half-open skylight. A bird lands on the sill and lets out a trill. It's Blue. It's unusual for her to leave Anais's room. The parakeet spreads her wings, flies into the room, and settles on my shoulder.

"Hmm . . . The blue parakeet and Rae," Ka muses. "Of course . . ."

"It's her messenger-animal," Ali concludes. "What does it mean?"

"For the Chinese, the parakeet represents the balance be-tween the five elements: water, wood, fire, earth, metal."

"And Rae's chakra is the fifth."

"That's right. Did you know that the parakeet not only masters the art of imitation like the parrot but also has a dis-tinct voice all its own?"

My little voice . . .

"By the way, Chayton, there is someone here to see you."

"There is? Who is it?"

We all hold our breaths. The door opens slowly, and a frail flaxen-haired figure appears in the entrance. It's Anais Mann—frightfully thin, almost unrecognizable. Blue came to announce her arrival.

She rushes to Chayton's bedside, dressed in her yellow chick pajamas and one of her grandmother's scarves. She can barely hold herself up. Anais takes hold of Chayton's hand, climbs into the bed, and snuggles against him. The seeds fall onto the bedspread.

"Anais?" Chayton is stunned. "What's wrong with you? Are you sick?"

She is shivering. Chayton pulls the covers over her and sits up in bed.

"I knew it wasn't just a cold. What have you been hiding from us?"

She shakes her head.

"It's your father, isn't it? He's starving you. Is he making you sick?"

Unable to meet his eye, she huddles deeper into the blanket.

"*Anais!*" someone shouts in the hallway. She covers her ears.

"Anais!" Mr. Mann yells as he bursts into the room. "What are you doing here?"

He hurries into the room with an uneasy gait. Alpha and Keiji immediately stop him.

"What's going on, Mann-san?"

"Let me through!" he exclaims with a cough, trying to push past. "You don't understand! She, uh, has to go home, we have to . . ."

"It's over, Mr. Mann," Kassandra says, gesturing for Alpha and Keiji to release their grip. "It's over now . . ."

He drops to his knees and begins to cry.

"What did you do to her?" Chayton roars. "Why does she look like that? Why do you lock her in her room? She doesn't even go to school!"

Mr. Mann's resigned silence is worse than tears. Regardless of the suspicions weighing on him, none of us want to see him like this. It's awful to see a man break down so suddenly. He is usually like a rock.

"You have to tell them," Ka says. "It is time."

We exchange astonished glances as Anais's father bows his head and removes his hat. His stubbly beard is turning white in some places. He walks over to the edge of the bed and places a calloused hand on his daughter's head. Surprisingly, she doesn't seem to mind.

"Leave her alone!" Chayton objects, trying to push him away.

"No," Anais murmurs, completely exhausted. "Daddy hasn't done anything . . ."

"Stop lying."

"He just wanted to protect me . . ."

"Protect you from what? From *what*, for God's sake?"

"From . . . From this . . ."

Slowly, her slender fingers pull at her headscarf and reveal
. . . No! We never imagined, not even in our worst dreams, we
would see her like that. It makes our stomachs churn, it's inconceivable . . . Anais Mann's head is a minefield!

"Your . . . Your beautiful hair . . ." Irregular bald spots show
patches of lumpy scalp.

"It started with a rash the day she turned thirteen," her
father explains. "She broke out in red blisters on her stomach
and back. Never on her face and neck. That was some conso-
lation to her."

We all understand now. Chayton is devastated.

"The medical exams showed nothing. Everything was normal. Some doctors said it would pass; others said it was psy-
chosomatic. Then, her hair started falling out . . . in clumps.
That's why she didn't want to go to school anymore . . ."

A shudder courses through the assembly. Anais, ashamed,
wraps the scarf back around her head. Her grandmother's vintage scarves will never look the same to me.

"The doctors said they had never seen anything like it. It
all happened before you came to the farm."

I feel like I've been hit with a ton of bricks.

"She's always preferred goats to people. Ever since she was
little. Maybe because she lost her mother when she was two.
Anais loved looking after the flock, roaming the meadows,
spending hours in the goat shed. That's how she discovered the
sliding panel and Flyfold. When the program was being tested,
she started talking to the holograms the way she talked to the
goats. No one minded. Miss Kassandra didn't, anyway." We
are hanging on Mr. Mann's every word. "So naturally, when
she got sick, Anais found comfort in Flyfold. And in the program's unfailing ear."

"Why were you so afraid?" Chayton asks Anais. "You were afraid. Rae and I could tell."

"I was afraid my father was right. He didn't want me to talk to you. He was worried that you'd discover my secret, that you'd think we were using you. Especially after the second connection, the day we discovered her name. Then, we knew for sure."

"Knew what?"

"That I had unintentionally influenced the program."

"What do you mean 'influenced'?"

"The flower seller . . . Siana . . . Her name backward is . . ."

"*Anais!*" Chayton exclaims.

Ka fills us in: "Spirit Era, owing to the spiritual dimension, must have been affected by Anais's plight. It altered the narrative of Mantra 1 so that the Seven could find a cure for her. The symptoms of Bulbosis are identical to her own, although in the real world, the infection is not contagious. Its hypothetical contagion in the virtual world played a critical role, however. It bridged the gap between the worlds Above and Below, closing the social divide and restoring justice, although, ultimately, the epidemic was not an epidemic, since the contaminated packets were the vector of transmission."

"It's all my fault!" Anais exclaims. "I didn't want the key to be connected to me in any way. The stakes are higher than one person's life. The entire planet is at risk . . ." Her voice cracks.

"There's nothing to be upset about," Ka says. "The program only altered the form, not the substance. It couldn't have. It's part of a greater plan. The keys are immutable, but there are an infinite number of paths that lead to them . . ."

"That's right!" Alpha exclaims. "Think of the Owls in their bunker of plenty. If they had chosen to share and to preserve their world's natural biodiversity, then the Toptowners and the Subs could have lived in peace."

"Everything is connected," Ali says. "The program based Mantra 1 on the first of the seven afflictions, the excess of worldly pleasures typical of an unbalanced root chakra. That was the old Chayton. But his evolving mindset put him on the path to the key, and ultimately, the changes he effected on the inside helped him to change the world on the outside."

It's all pretty intense, especially for Chayton. He turns to hug Anais.

"Anais . . . you are my key . . ."

Our guardian angel throughout all our adventures dissolves into tears at last—the tears of a child. Anais and Siana form a single common thread.

By drawing my attention to her mistress, Blue the parakeet has accomplished her mission. She takes wing and flies out the window.

"You are the link between there and here, Anais, the one who gives meaning to it all. The plants we found there will heal you, the way they did Siana."

Anais stares into Chayton's eyes. Her wide-eyed gaze is confident and loving. She, too, will grow, like a seed entrusted to the earth, thanks to the custodian of the root chakra. Without speaking a word, Chayton pledges to provide the nourishment she needs. They are oblivious to everything around them.

So, we tiptoe away while our friend tells Anais about what the future has in store, about the Infected, and all those whose lives were lost in Underhome—including Froggie's—and how they, through her, will go on living.

*

Two weeks have gone by.

The Keeper delivered a brief congratulatory speech. Onscreen, as usual. Hardly riveting stuff. It was more like a commissioner complimenting a team of police officers who have solved a case, with the operations division on one side and headquarters on the other. And between the two, an enormous divide. Kassandra says the Keeper is already making improvements to the program for the quest for the second key after the holiday break.

Anais started getting better yesterday. The remedy Chayton has been administering morning and night—he alone is in charge of the plant decoction—is working miracles. No new abscesses have appeared on her body, and her hair has stopped falling out. Thanks to the notes in his great-grandfather's herbarium, the seeds he planted in the vegetable garden are already yielding shoots. Likewise, Anais's bald patches are already filling in with sprouts of blond fuzz.

Helen put her creative skills to work and gave Anais a super-short boy cut. The bald patches are barely noticeable now, and I bet after vacation they won't show at all.

Alpha and I have been talking a lot about Underhome recently—communicating, I should say. The cord was cut too quickly. We both could have used a little more time there. The others could have, too.

Ali and Keiji have been roaming the countryside with their goats. Ka sometimes goes with them. To everyone's surprise, Stepan asked the Shepherd to continue training him, and he has integrated the Oak Tree Exercise into his daily routine. Helen spends most of her time drawing, nibbling her thumb contentedly for all to see, her orange jacket around her shoulders. Her drawings will forever immortalize Underhome, with its brightly decorated alleyways, Valjean Rabbit's caratram, the dorm at Deepwood, and the Train . . .

Sitting in the old pickup truck waiting to go to the station, I stare at my smartphone. My hot-pink scarf is wrapped around my neck. Ever since Mr. Mann returned our phones to us last night, none of us have felt like turning them on. None of us are interested in being incognito celebrities anymore. I haven't even used mine yet. It's just a bit of plastic to me. And a direct reminder that real life is out there.

My life.

Christmas vacations are looming on the horizon. Most of us are going home to avoid blowing our covers. We know what's at stake. In addition to the imperative of finding the six other keys, we all feel an irrepressible urge to continue our quest. Together. In the future, we will be the keepers of the secret. More than Kassandra and the Shepherd.

Soon, I'll see San Francisco and the steep street of our Victorian house that matches my crooked bangs. I now understand it is all a part of me. It *is* me. Soon, I'll hear Laureen's sighs again—and I couldn't care less. Soon, I'll see Mia and Joyce, too—I do care about those two. And about my friends Chris and Kim. Soon, without words, I will have to find a way to tell them how I feel.

"I can't wait to see my little brother!" Ali exclaims, sitting to my right and shooting off text messages. "Do you think we'll ever see the farm again?"

I shrug my shoulders. Kassandra had been deliberately vague about it. One thing is for sure: with the program's record audience ratings, people would do anything to discover the identity of the Seven. So, we'll have to be extra careful and maybe even change headquarters.

"Imagine Chayton just deciding to spend the holidays here! Boy, that guy is pigheaded!"

"I'm not sure the Shepherd is happy about it," Helen chimes in, to my left. "Or Kassandra, either, for that matter." Alpha and Keiji climb into the back of the pickup with our luggage. Stepan, in the front seat, is perfectly quiet.

"You have to admit, however, Anais is ecstatic about it," Ali remarks. "And I don't think Mr. Mann is against the idea, though with him, you never know."

In the pen next to the henhouse, Daisy and the others are happily pecking away. Her wing is all better: Chayton saw to that, as well. He really just had to follow a trail of bread crumbs to his inner self and discover what was already there—his true essence, his roots.

Here he is now. He is barefoot, despite the cold.

"I wasn't going to let you leave without saying goodbye! I have something for you."

And he sticks his head inside the window of the pickup.

"You first, Sparrow. Your hand, please!"

I hold it out in surprise as Chayton, with gentleness I'm unaccustomed to, ties a strand of red wool around my wrist. Then, his unwavering gaze meets mine, and I realize I am going to miss him. Against all odds, we've developed a special bond. I am not the custodian of the first chakra, but I, too, have found my home in the end. A new family.

He does the same with Ali, Helen, and Stepan, and then with Alpha and Keiji, who are no longer in the back of the truck. A radiant smile spreads across his face as he looks at his feet and pronounces, loud and clear:

"Just like you said, Valjean, I am weaving my web . . ."

CHAYTON

#THE KEEPER #SAVETHEWORLD

THE LAST POST—THE FIRST KEY

DECEMBER 15, 2035

THE FIRST KEY TO LIFE IS SIMPLE.

It is invisible, it cannot be placed in a pocket, it opens no gates in the material world. It is never out of reach, provided we recognize it and learn to appreciate it. With it, we can open the gate to our home within. So that saving a single child amounts to saving children everywhere. So that we can save the world by respecting the world around us during our time on earth. Each of us. Both individually and collectively.

Spirit Era's future-predicting capabilities have set our planet's fateful date as July 27, 2037. But it has also uncovered paths for averting the end-of-the-world catastrophe: the seven keys of the seven chakras. Six more remain to be found. This winter, the Seven Chosen will set off on their quest for the second key in a new Mantra designed by the program.

Until then, it has put forward a prototype, based on Ps, like the first letter of the program: the 3P Model.

PROTECTION:

Respect all living beings and nature.

PARTICIPATION:

Actively promote solidarity and share the world's resources—
sources of all physical and spiritual sustenance.

PHILOSOPHY:

Challenge our value systems, embrace a spiritual awakening.
What do we want for the future?

For if humankind does not learn to change its ways, the homes of the future could turn into Underhomes.

Countries that neglect the earth, the soil in which human life is rooted, the lands to which we belong, are doomed to disappear. A land depleted of natural resources crumbles and dies. It trembles beneath our feet and washes away our dwellings with rivers of tears ...

When respected and cared for, the earth provides sustenance for our bodies and allows us to set down strong roots. It anchors us in life. For we are the earth's offspring.

THE CHILDREN OF THE EARTH.

THE WORLD OF MANTRA
ONE, BY HELEN

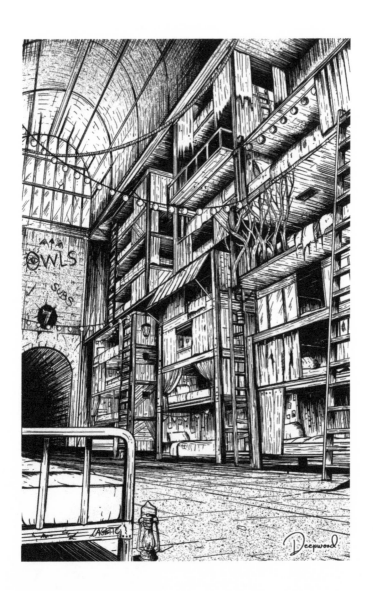

ACKNOWLEDGMENTS

Writing a novel is like walking through a desert alone; you can either lose or find your way. In my author's backpack, I had no compass, no map, only my love of dunes and their hidden depths and of clouds gathered by storms.

A warm thank-you to my French editor, Fabien Leroy, for stretching out his hand whenever I stepped in quicksand and for his continual support and reassurance. He was the North Star who shone down and guided me at night.

A thousand thank-yous to my five desert flowers, without whom I would not be who I am. You brought delight to my day-to-day life.

Thank you, as well, to Elodie, the talented illustrator with a magic touch. And to Violaine and Issa, lovers of words and faraway winds, whom I met along the way.

Finally, I want to thank my readers, without whom sharing could not go beyond the pages. We are all our own stories . . .

ABOUT THE AUTHOR

Photo © Instagram@meitar_tsuberi

Aurélie Benattar was born in Casablanca, Morocco, in 1971. In her childhood and teenage years, she spent most of her time reading, listening to music, dancing, and acting. After a few years in Paris, she moved to Cannes, where she earned an undergraduate degree in psychology and a degree in pediatric nursing. Early on, she questioned the connection between body, spirit, and soul. This drove her to take several courses on spirituality and alternative medicine. Her first novel, *Un corbeau au 36*, won the crime *Femme Actuelle* award and was the "heartthrob" of the chairwoman, Éliette Abécassis (Inaugural Authors 2013, Pocket 2014). Today she writes full time and lives in Israel. Fascinated by fictional worlds, she loves to bridge the gap between the real and the imaginary to let readers explore unbeaten paths and reconsider our way of life.

ABOUT THE GRAPHIC DESIGNER

O'Lee was born in Brittany, France. She took her first drawing lessons at the age of seven and joined the Pivaut School in Nantes at the age of eighteen. After graduating, she spent several years in a web agency before deciding to start her own business in order to broaden her graphic design opportunities and realize her dream: to become an illustrator. Her illustrations of Helen's artwork can be found on aureliebenattar.com.

ABOUT THE ILLUSTRATOR

Anava Maman grew up in Israel, left to live abroad when she was fifteen and completed her education with a master's in art and photography in the UK. In every free moment, Anava returns to her first love of art and creativity and works in many mediums to produce portraits, private commissions, murals, and illustrations. Her illustrations of the Seven can be found on aureliebenattar.com. She currently lives and works in Israel.

FOLLOW THE STORY OF THE
SEVEN IN THE SPIRIT ERA SAGA,
WHICH WILL CONTINUE WITH
BOOK TWO, COMING SOON:

CREATION

+∽+

"When the cycle of life dries up . . ."

In Spirit Era's next simulation, Rae and her six companions, led this time by the sensitive and sensual Helen, must contend with waters unleashed. In the wake of great floods and the rivers of tears let loose by the skies after centuries of male domination, Lagun has emerged—a land ruled by women where only girls go to school . . .

+∽+

Learn more, see exclusive artwork, and experience the world of Spirit Era at aureliebenattar.com.

Spirit Era is the first series that is good for your chakras!

CPSIA information can be obtained
at www.ICGtesting.com
Printed in the USA
BVHW080919230123
656892BV00007B/182